Praise for the novels of *USA TODAY* bestselling author Delores Fossen

"An entertaining and satisfying read…that I can highly recommend."　—*Books & Spoons* on *Wild Nights in Texas*

"The plot delivers just the right amount of emotional punch and happily ever after."
—*Publishers Weekly* on *Lone Star Christmas*

"Delores Fossen takes you on a wild Texas ride with a hot cowboy."
—*New York Times* bestselling author B.J. Daniels

"Clear off space on your keeper shelf, Fossen has arrived."
—*New York Times* bestselling author Lori Wilde

"This is classic Delores Fossen and a great read."
—*Harlequin Junkie* on *His Brand of Justice*

"This book is a great start to the series. Looks like there's plenty of good reading ahead."
—*Harlequin Junkie* on *Tangled Up in Texas*

"An amazing, breathtaking and vastly entertaining family saga, filled with twists and unexpected turns. Cowboy fiction at its best."　—*Books & Spoons* on *The Last Rodeo*

DELORES FOSSEN

SUMMER AT STALLION RIDGE

HQN

ISBN-13: 978-1-335-94931-8

Summer at Stallion Ridge

HQN
22 Adelaide St. West, 41st Floor
Toronto, Ontario M5H 4E3, Canada
www.Harlequin.com

Printed and bound in Barcelona, Spain by CPI Black Print

CONTENTS

SUMMER AT STALLION RIDGE

CHAPTER ONE

LAST RIDE, TEXAS, just wasn't a good place for an adrenaline junkie. Or apparently for brides. Sheriff Matt Corbin now had proof of both.

Matt knew the adrenaline-junkie part firsthand because in the past three days, he'd gone from being an Amarillo SWAT team supervisor to being sheriff in this small Texas town. Along with being a ranching community, Last Ride was also his former hometown where the latest reported incident involved two escaped macaws named Dorothy and Toto flying through the door of the local bakery and chowing down on some fresh bear claws.

The part about Last Ride not being a good place for brides, well, the proof of that was standing in the center of Main Street. Literally, in the center.

Right in front of the Last Ride Police Department.

Dressed in full bride gear, the curvy blonde was sobbing and cursing a blue streak while onlookers on the sidewalks, well, looked on in both shock and likely in anticipation of hearing some really juicy gossip. The bulk of the bride's profanity seemed to be aimed at somebody named Cilla, who in the bride's opinion was a fiancé-stealing skank.

The bride wasn't alone in her verbal bashing. Nope. There were a half dozen people in the street with her. The least vocal of the bunch was a middle-aged couple dressed to the nines, and they were quietly urging her to move. The bride's parents, judging from the resemblance.

Four women in shiny guacamole-colored dresses—bridesmaids, no doubt—were tugging and pulling at the bride, trying to get her out of the street. Two were saying soothing "there, there" kind of stuff and offering unlimited tequila shots and ice cream, temptations that clearly weren't working. The other two women were vowing to kick the cheating ass of somebody named Keaton.

Even though Matt had been born and raised in Last Ride, he'd left at eighteen and hadn't lived here for sixteen years. That meant he didn't know or recognize the names of some of the people in the crowd or the parties involved here. That included the bride, the fiancé stealer and the ass-kicking target, but it didn't require any of the cop skills that he'd honed for the past fourteen years to deduce some things.

Obvious things.

First, Keaton and Cilla had either screwed around with each other, perhaps had even run off together, and second, the cursing bride wasn't at all happy about it. She'd likely exited the Methodist church just a half block up and then decided to vent her feelings where she stood.

"Ah, hell," the woman behind Matt grumbled. It was Deputy Azzie Parkman, and she came swaggering out the door of the police station. Hitching up her hip holster, she stepped up next to him. "Want me to turn the hose on them to get them moving out of the street? Or I can grab the bull-horn and yell loud enough to make them all deaf?"

Even though Matt had held the sheriff's office for only three days, he'd already come to some conclusions about the seven deputies he'd inherited. Especially Azzie. She was seventy-one, had been a deputy for fifty years and she had no intention of retiring. She was also the size of a Mack truck, and despite her senior-citizen status, she could probably kick the asses of anyone who needed such a kicking. Ditto for being able to deafen them.

"No hoses or bullhorns," Matt muttered. "You know the bride?"

"Sure do," Azzie snarled. Then again, everything she said was a snarl. "She's Tiffany Parkman. A distant cousin of mine which, of course, can be said of about a third of the town."

Azzie was right about that. The Parkmans were *the* prominent family in Last Ride, and they had also taken that whole "go forth and multiply" deal and run with it. They owned the bulk of the businesses and occupied positions on every governing and social group, but that obviously didn't make them immune to premarital spats.

"She's supposed to be marrying Keaton Dayton right about now," Azzie added after she checked her watch. "He's Darrell Dayton's kid."

Darrell Dayton's name rang some bells for Matt. More old money and prominence.

Unlike Matt's own family.

His mother had been the polar opposite of money and prominence, and she'd been the reason Matt left Last Ride. The reason he hadn't returned until now. And it was his sincerest wish in life that no one would ever associate his name with the piece of shit his mother, Candy Lynn Corbin, had been.

Gathering a deep breath, Matt stepped off the sidewalk and went to the wedding party. His first challenge was dodging an elbow that one of the bridesmaids slung at his gut. Inadvertently slung. The redhead was still tugging and pulling, trying to get the bride to budge, but Tiffany had apparently locked her heels onto the pavement and wasn't budging.

"Folks," Matt said, raising his voice just enough to be heard. "I need you to get out of the street. You're backing up traffic."

That was the God's honest truth, even though *traffic* was a bit of an exaggeration in Last Ride. Still, three cars were either trying to get by, or else the drivers were sitting there and gawking right along with the bystanders.

"If you want, you can all come in my office, and we can talk about this," Matt added.

The bride stopped cursing, and she snapped toward Matt. She wasn't crying now, but there were plenty of telltale streaks of prior tears running through the thick makeup on her cheeks.

"Sheriff Corbin, I want you to arrest that cheating sack of cow dung." The bride flung fingers painted murderous red in the direction of the Methodist church. "What Keaton did is a breach of promise."

Probably, but Matt didn't want to spell out the bad news for Tiffany. That Texas didn't have what was called a heart balm law. That the offending parties couldn't be arrested, and that even though Tiffany could try to sue her fiancé in civil court to recoup wedding costs, she might never see a dime. What she also wouldn't be able to do was kick the cheater's ass or egg on any of her bridesmaid posse to do it for her.

Tiffany's demand did give Matt some insight though as to why she was right here in this very spot. She'd likely run out of the church and come in the hopes of getting that arrest.

"Why don't we go to my office?" Matt repeated, and he

glanced around at the quickly growing crowd. "And the rest of you need to clear the street."

Tiffany still didn't budge, but she did start crying again. And wailing. "Keaton had sex with that skank at his bachelor party," she sobbed. "There were pictures." She whipped out her phone from a side pocket of her poufy dress and showed him.

Yeah, that was a guy having sex all right. Clearly, Keaton was an idiot, but since the news of his idiocy seemed to be recently learned information for Tiffany, it wouldn't do to tell her that she was better off without him.

Just when Matt was ready to scoop up the bride and carry her out of the street and to his office, Tiffany stopped wailing, and her gaze zoomed to someone in the crowd. A tall blond woman. And much to Matt's shock, the bride started ripping at her own dress. She caught onto the heart-shaped neckline and gave it a fierce yank. Fabric and lace ripped and little pearls the size of pencil points went flying out like gnats.

"Emory," Tiffany called out. "I knew I should have had you make my dress. Things wouldn't have turned out like this."

The last part came out in another wail, but the renewed sobs didn't stop Tiffany from continuing to strip. The woman was darn good at it, too, considering she was also fighting off the bridesmaids and her parents who were trying to stop her.

Tearing off the rest of the top, Tiffany shucked the dress over her head, tossing it onto the street and stomping on it. That left her wearing just a white corset, white thigh-high stockings and "begging for a sprained ankle" high heels. With those heels pecking away on the asphalt, she made her way to a blond-haired woman who'd just arrived on scene.

"Emory," Tiffany sobbed again, and she flung herself into the woman's arms.

Matt didn't have to ask Azzie the identity of the newcomer. Nope. Even after all these years, he knew exactly who she was.

Emory Parkman.

Seeing her was a real blast from the past. A bad one. Because she'd been the reason he'd gotten some serious ass-kickings of his own.

Emory's rich thuggy brothers hadn't taken kindly to Matt sneaking a kiss from her when they'd been in middle school. Even though Matt hadn't attempted any other kisses, the ass-kickings had continued through high school and until Matt had filled out enough to kick them both right back.

Much ill will had ensued from that.

Matt supposed Emory's branch of the Parkman tree wasn't exactly the Hatfields and Matt wasn't exactly a McCoy, but there was enough bad blood to create a feud of sorts.

Emory's blue eyes locked onto his, and her gaze held. And Matt got another "Oh, hell, no" moment when he saw just a smidge of the old heat that had led to that ill-advised kiss. Heat that thankfully vanished when Tiffany yanked Emory even tighter against her, squishing Emory's face right into the bride's poufy hair.

"If you'd made the dress, this wouldn't be happening," Tiffany wailed. "Everybody knows your dresses are good luck." Sniffling, Tiffany pulled back. "Well, mostly good luck."

"Emory owns Flutters and Flounce, the wedding dress shop up the street," Azzie explained. The deputy didn't get into why the garments were considered *mostly* good luck, and Matt didn't especially want to know. He might be thirty-four now, but seeing Emory was giving him some déjà vu moments he'd rather not déjà or vu about.

"It's okay," Emory murmured to Tiffany. "Why don't we go inside the police station, and I'll help you get back into your dress? There's not much to the panties beneath the Merry Widow you're wearing, and you're probably exposing more than you want to expose."

That was the God's honest truth. The thong obviously left both of Tiffany's butt cheeks bare, and the front swatch of lace left zilch to the imagination.

Sobbing harder now, Tiffany nodded and thankfully started moving with Emory toward the front door of the police station, but she stopped when someone called out to her.

Matt spotted the black-haired pretty boy in a tux threading his way quickly through three trucks, two cars and perhaps every resident of Last Ride.

"Crap on a cracker, here comes trouble," Azzie grumbled. "That's Keaton."

Yeah, Matt had already figured that out because he'd seen the resemblance to Keaton's father. A father who was following in his wake. Matt figured the other tuxed guys behind him were the groomsmen.

"Tiff," the groom called out again.

Tiffany's eyes narrowed, and Matt could have sworn little razor-sharp lightning bolts zinged out from the slits. Growling—yes, growling—she curled up her fingers like claws and went after him.

Azzie stepped in front of the bride.

Matt did the same to the groom.

Since both Keaton and Tiffany kept moving, they all sort of collided. Worse, so did the bridesmaids and groomsmen who had obviously closed in to do whatever the hell they thought they could do. It resulted in more flying elbows, stomped-on feet and a whole lot of cussing. The bridesmaids started whacking the groomsmen and Keaton with their bouquets.

When Matt caught one of those elbows to the chin and was smacked in the eye with a bouquet, he knew enough was enough. This might be giving him a spattering of adrenaline, but more than that, it was just plain pissing him off.

"Stop it," Matt yelled, and he wasn't surprised when the wedding party/brawlers stopped. Azzie wasn't the only one here who had a cop's voice, and Matt was reasonably sure he'd coated his with a crapload of meanness.

Everyone froze. All cursing and shouting stopped. Bouquets and elbows inched down.

"You," Matt snarled, pointing at Keaton. "In there now." He hiked his thumb to the police station. "You, too," he added to Tiffany.

That order sent Tiffany into another downward spiral of sobs, but the woman made her way to the sidewalk. And she latched on to Emory who had somehow managed to pick up the discarded wedding gown.

"I'll help you get back into the dress," Emory assured her. "I have a mini sewing kit in my purse."

While Emory led Tiffany inside, Matt kept hold of Keaton. "If Tiffany doesn't want to talk to you, this ends now. You'll leave and won't cause any trouble."

"But she has to listen," Keaton insisted. "She has to let me tell her how sorry I am."

Matt looked him straight in the eyes and repeated every single word about this ending now if Tiffany didn't want to talk. "You see how much of her butt's bared?" he asked, motioning to an exiting Tiffany. "Well, that's how much of yours was bared in the photo she has of Cilla and you."

Keaton looked ready to defend himself about some portion of that observation, but he finally gave a resigned sigh. Then he added a nod before he started inside the police station with Matt.

"Make sure the rest of them leave," Matt told Azzie. "I want this street cleared."

Azzie didn't waste even a second shouting at the top of her apparently very healthy lungs. "Y'all get the hell out of here now. I mean it, go, or I'll arrest the whole whiny, nosy, sorry ass lot of you."

Matt made a mental note not to assign Azzie any tasks that required tact and diplomacy. Or an inside voice.

With his grip still on Keaton's arm, Matt and he stepped into the police station, and he welcomed the rush of cool air from the AC. It might be only the first of May and still officially spring, but it was still plenty hot, and the brawl had caused him to work up a sweat.

Matt glanced around and didn't see Emory or Tiffany, but he figured they were in the bathroom doing some literal CYA. Since Azzie and he were the only ones on duty, the place was empty except for Thelma Baker, who held the job title of dispatcher and receptionist.

Neither of which, Matt was learning, she did particularly well.

Right now, Thelma was playing Candy Crush on her phone while she blew a bubble with her wad of sugary-scented pink chewing gum. Gum that matched the color of her pants, top, sandals, jewelry, hair and toenails.

"Lots of excitement for your first week of work, Sheriff Corbin," Thelma remarked without so much as an ounce of inflection in her voice. "You arresting him?" She spared Keaton a glance.

"No," Matt assured her, and he led Keaton to his office. Such that it was.

Matt's predecessor, Waldo Lyle, had been sheriff for thirty-plus years and apparently was a fan of wood paneling, poorly painted Texas landscapes and horseshoes. The frames of the paintings, the rims around the chairbacks and the drawer pulls were made of horseshoes. Added to that, a line of them had been nailed above and around the door and window.

"Sit," Matt instructed Keaton, and he took out two bottles of water from the little fridge in the corner. And, yeah, it was also covered with horseshoe magnets.

The realization of his major screwup of screwing Cilla must have been sinking in because Keaton groaned and raked a hand through his thick mane of black hair. "I've really messed up."

"Yeah, you have." Opening his water, Matt dropped down in the chair behind his desk. "My advice is to give Tiffany some time to cool off and then you can try to apologize."

Keaton looked up, and he appeared to hang on Matt's words. "Thanks," he mumbled. He opened his water, had a long drink and then eyed Matt. "Hey, I remember you. I mean, I knew you were the new sheriff that everybody's talking about, but I didn't peg you until now. You used to live out there by Old Sawmill Road."

In Last Ride, that particular address was the not so subtle code for the bad side of town. And, yeah, Matt had lived there all right until he was fourteen, when his mother finally lost custody of him, and he'd gone to live on a ranch with his grandfather. The ranch had been a huge step up in Matt's world, but to a Parkman or a Dayton, it was still the wrong place to be. Hence, the reason Emory's brothers had tried to pound him into dust when he'd kissed her.

Azzie must have accomplished her "crowd clearing" duties darn fast because she came back in, moving to his doorway where she stood like a sentry. She also aimed some serious stink eye at Keaton.

"Old Sawmill Road," Keaton repeated. "Yeah, yeah, I definitely remember you." And this time, it wasn't a "lightbulb above the head" kind of remark. There was a hint of smirking. The kind of smirking some rich assholes wallowed in. "Your mother spent a lot of time here in jail."

As insults went, it was pretty puny. His mother, Candy Lynn, had indeed been jailed, repeatedly, but those arrests had been some of the least scandalous things she'd done. Her affair with Emory's highbrow father, Dr. Derrick Parkman, had certainly caused plenty of talk and trouble. Heck, even her death had been a gossip-spurring mess. Still, Matt had no intention of even addressing Keaton's remark.

Azzie clearly didn't feel the same about that.

She stepped in the office, moving to the side of Matt's desk so that her stony gaze could spear Keaton. "The sheriff mighta been born in a big pile of horse crap that his mama caused, but he didn't stay there. Might suit you to remember that. Because the way I see it, Keaton Darrell Dayton, cheating on your fiancée makes you the smelliest pile of horse crap around."

As usual, Azzie made that sound like a threat. But she'd pretty much hit the nail on the head.

"Don't worry," Azzie continued, shifting her attention to Matt. "People will soon forget your upbringing and your mama."

Not likely. Then again, Matt had had zero success in

personally pushing it aside. It was one of the big reasons he'd left Last Ride and stayed away. But he'd had a bigger reason to return. To move back to a place where no real adrenaline fix was anywhere on the horizon. Because there was no other place he could be.

Because of Jack.

His three-year-old son and the owner of his heart. Jack owned it enough for Matt to toss aside the life he'd made in Amarillo and follow them when Jack's mother/his ex, Natalie, got engaged to her old high school sweetheart. The engagement had come with a move to Last Ride three months earlier, and since Matt hadn't wanted five hundred miles of distance between him and his son, he'd made the move, too.

He heard the woodpecker-tapping sounds making their way to his office. Tiffany's heels, no doubt, and Matt got confirmation of that a moment later when Emory and she stepped into the doorway. Tiffany was wearing the wedding dress.

Sort of.

Emory had obviously gotten creative when it came to ensuring the garment would stay on her body. There were circles of white duct tape adhering the ripped fabric and strips of lace to Tiffany's generous curves.

Keaton practically jumped to his feet, and he reached out for Tiffany who batted his hands away. "No," she snarled. "You will not touch me. You will not speak to me." She rattled off those demands as if she'd rehearsed them, but she apparently faltered on what to add to that. "And you can go straight to the hottest corner of hell and take Cilla with you."

That seemed a reasonable stance for Tiffany to take, but

Matt needed to try to make sure there were no more tussles in the street or an escalation of what had already happened.

"You have a right to be angry," Matt told the woman. "But Keaton and you shouldn't be working this out on Main Street. You need to both cool off first."

"Oh, I'm cool," Tiffany insisted. "Ice cold and certain I never want to see or speak to this piece of dung again."

With that, Tiffany spun around, muttered a thank-you to Emory and headed for the front door. Keaton didn't go after her. Something Matt would have stopped had the man tried. Keaton just stood there, shaking his head and looking as if he'd gotten a mule kick to the balls.

"Don't worry," Keaton muttered. "I'll give her some time."

Despite his dejected look, there still seemed to be some hope in Keaton's voice. Hope that he could win back his bride. And, hell, maybe he could do just that.

"I need some time, too," Keaton added a moment later. "So, maybe we can delay the chat you wanted to have with us. I'll just go home and won't cause any more trouble." He waited for Matt's nod to confirm the chat delay before the man headed out.

"I'll make sure everybody stays out of the street," Azzie volunteered, and she was right on Keaton's heels.

Leaving Matt alone with Emory.

He expected her to leave, but she didn't. She gave her enormous purse an adjustment so she could fit through the door with it, and she came into his office.

"You had duct tape in your purse?" Matt had to ask.

Emory nodded. "And lace. They're fast fixes for malfunctioning foundation garments and hems. Safety pins are, too, but I didn't have enough of those in my sewing kit to do the job." She came closer and sat in the chair that Keaton had just vacated. "We need to talk."

Well, hell. This couldn't be good.

"Are your brothers, Ryder and Ruston, planning on trying to beat me up because I kissed you when we were thirteen?" Matt came out and asked.

"No. Probably not," she amended, adding a sigh. "I'd like to think they've forgotten all about it, but people in this town have long memories and hold grudges well past normal expiration dates."

They did indeed, and Matt had already heard plenty of gossip about the town council offering the sheriff job to Candy Lynn Corbin's son. Of course, there'd been no other candidates for the job so they hadn't had much of a choice when Sheriff Lyle had retired. Now, Matt had to make sure he did the best job possible and didn't give anyone any reason to stir up memories of Candy Lynn.

"I take it you weren't a wedding guest," Matt commented, giving her jeans and red top a glance.

Emory shook her head. "Tiffany and I are distant cousins, but we aren't close." She paused. "Do you remember the Last Ride Society?"

Matt was reasonably sure of all the things he'd expected her to say, that wasn't one of them. He thumbed back through his memory and pulled up a vague recollection of some social club for the Parkmans. Then again, there were dozens of social events swirling around that particular family.

"Are you here for some charity donation?" he asked.

Emory's expression let him know it wasn't anything nearly as tame as that. "No." She took a deep breath as if preparing for a speech. "The founder of Last Ride, Hezzie Parkman, set up the Society so that future generations of

Parkmans would research the tombstones in the local area. That's the verbatim mission statement," she added. "Every quarter, a Parkman heir's name is drawn, and the heir in turn draws the name of a tombstone to research."

Matt started to say "okay" with a tone of "what the heck does this have to do with me," but he studied Emory's troubled eyes and expression that told him this had plenty to do with him.

"Bottom line this," Matt insisted.

She nodded, did more breath gathering. "I'm the Parkman heir for this quarter, and I have to thoroughly research the tombstone I drew. *Thoroughly*," she emphasized. "With personal accounts, photos and anything else I can dig up about the deceased. Lots of people get involved. There'll be gobs of buzz about it."

Well, hell.

Matt suddenly knew right where this runaway truck was heading, and it was about to smack right into his plans to keep a low profile of his shitty past.

CHAPTER TWO

EMORY TRIED TO keep a somber expression. It should have been easy since she was indeed somber and sorry to have brought this news to Matt's doorstep, but there was also some metaphorical drooling going on beneath the surface. Just one of the many side effects of being around a guy with the looks of a cowboy fallen angel.

A really naughty one with an amazing mouth.

The black hair and sizzler blue eyes weren't so bad, either. In fact, there was nothing about this lanky lawman that didn't add to the mental drooling that was going on.

"You drew Candy Lynn's name for this Last Ride Society deal," Matt spelled out, getting her mind off his looks.

Getting her mind off his looks for a blink anyway.

Still, she focused on the conversation since she knew this was going to cause him some grief. Considering she had already contributed much grief to Matt's life when they'd been in middle school, Emory hated to add more.

She nodded. "I drew her name," Emory confirmed, and she gave him a recap of what that meant. "I'll have to take that thorough research I do on her, compile it into a report, and it'll be filed in the Society's library where anyone can read it."

That amazing mouth of his muttered something she didn't catch, but she thought it might have been some profanity. "What happens if you refuse to do the research?" he asked.

Emory had anticipated this and didn't have good news in that particular arena. "It'll create a lot of gossip and put even more focus on it than it would if I just went ahead and did it."

Judging from the look Matt gave her, he wanted to challenge that logic. But couldn't. He might not have lived in Last Ride for the past sixteen years, four months and eleven days, but he no doubt knew the score. Gossips gossiped, and Last Ride was a hotbed for blabbermouths.

"Certainly, your parents won't want you to do this," Matt threw out there.

As reminders went, it was a whopper. No, her parents wouldn't approve. In fact, they would disapprove to the extreme. That's because Emory's father, Derrick, and Candy Lynn had had an affair shortly before Candy Lynn's death. When the affair had come to light, it'd been very ugly, messy and painful for Emory's family.

Especially her mother, Nancy.

Her mother hadn't been at the Last Ride Society drawing today, but she'd already texted and tried to call Emory six times. Emory hadn't responded, yet, because that conversation was going to require a whole bunch of soothing. First dibs on attempted soothing, though, went to Matt.

"I'll be as discreet as I can with the research," Emory assured him when he cleared his throat, no doubt to prompt her out of her silence. "And I can lace over some of the details."

His eyebrow winged up. "Lace over?"

"Sorry, it's my solution for concealing ugly fabric a bride might choose. Or for hiding body bulges, weight gains, weight losses and wardrobe malfunctions. Well-placed lace can cover a multitude of sins."

Now, it was the corner of his mouth—which was still amazing—that winged up a smidge. Not a ha-ha happy smile, though. Nope. This humor was as dry as West Texas dust.

"*Some* of Candy Lynn's sins," Emory amended.

She didn't spell out that the lacing over would be a huge pill to swallow. From everything Emory knew and had heard about the woman, she didn't deserve to have anything covered, concealed or laced. But Candy Lynn's sins wouldn't hurt the woman now. Nope. But they'd sting the heck out of Matt and her parents.

Emory stood, figuring that Matt might like some privacy while he cursed his mother's name. He'd probably curse Emory's, too, for dumping all this on him. Unfortunately, there was more dumping to come, but that could wait.

"I don't think I'm a candidate for lace," he grumbled.

Emory shrugged and nearly blurted out that he'd probably look good in any and everything. Or especially nothing at all. But Matt didn't need to be informed of her lust levels for him.

"Why'd Tiffany say your wedding dresses were mostly good luck?" Matt asked just as she was about to turn to the door. "*Mostly*," he emphasized. "Is that a code word like *lace*?"

She'd figured he'd already heard the gossip about that. Then again, most blabbers these days were more focused on Matt and his questionable roots. Her roots were just fine, what with her being a Parkman, but there were some blemishes on her reputation, both personally and professionally.

"Since I've been in business for the past eleven years, I've personally made one hundred and eighteen wedding dresses for residents of Last Ride," she explained. "One hundred and sixteen of those couples are still married to each other."

While that wasn't a world record or anything, it sure beat the averages. So much so that a San Antonio newspaper had done a story about it, calling her the Marriage Whisperer.

"And the two failures?" Matt asked.

Emory tapped her index finger to her chest. While she wasn't especially eager to share this with him, he'd hear it soon enough, and it was better for her to give him the sterilized version. It'd be minus the "bless her heart", "poor little thing" and "she's obviously a turd magnet" comments that others would dole out.

"My first marriage ended in divorce after he cheated on me with my then best friend and former business partner. As for the second one, it turned out he wasn't actually my husband after all since he was already married to someone else." That one had ended in an annulment.

Since Matt was divorced, he probably didn't think it was a big deal for her own marriage to have ended. Still, coupled with the annulment, it wasn't a smashing endorsement for a wedding dressmaker. She definitely hadn't had any successful "whisperings" when it'd come to her own particular I dos.

Emory turned again to leave but nearly ran into Azzie. Many people in her gene pool were rich snobs but not Azzie. The woman was a cop all the way to her sensibly soled shoes.

"Just saw the delivery truck drive by," Azzie told Matt. "It's headed in the direction of Stallion Ridge."

That caused Matt to check his watch and get to his feet. "They're early."

"Yep," Azzie verified. "But not to worry. I'll hold down

the fort until change of shift. Go ahead," she prompted. "You don't want them unloading your furniture when you're not there. God knows where they'll end up putting it if Zeke and Zella are running the show."

Emory knew that Zeke and Zella Hawkins was the couple who looked after Stallion Ridge, the ranch that once belonged to Matt's grandfather. And now to Matt. However, she hadn't known that Matt would be moving back there so soon. She'd heard from multiple sources that he'd been staying at the inn just a block from the police station. Those multiple sources had mentioned that Matt hadn't spent much time looking over Stallion Ridge, that instead he'd just dived straight into the job along with hanging out with his son.

She opened her mouth to "mention" something about Stallion Ridge, but Matt was already heading for his office door. He did stop, though, and for a couple of seconds his gaze connected with hers.

"I don't want to know anything about the research on Candy Lynn," he insisted, and walked out.

"Stirring up crap," Azzie muttered. "That's what'll happen. You can't dabble around Candy Lynn without stirring up crap."

Truer words. But it was also truer words that the stirring had already started. Nothing Emory could do about that other than try her hardest for the low-key approach. It was wrong to hope that gossip of Tiffany's wedding disaster might overshadow anything about Candy Lynn, but for Matt's sake, Emory hoped that it would for at least a day or two.

Emory said goodbye to Azzie, got a grunt of acknowledgment from Thelma and she left, heading up the street toward Flutters and Flounce. Other than a scattering of rose petals, sprigs of baby's breath and seed pearls, there was no sign of the wedding party. Some signs of gawkers, though. There were still a few folks pointing at the debris in the street and murmuring about it.

"Hey," one of those folks called out to her. It was Monte Klein, a shop assistant at the antique shop, Once Upon a Time. "I just heard about the drawing," he said from the other side of the street. "How'd the sheriff take the news?"

So, apparently Tiffany's wedding hadn't overshadowed Candy Lynn, after all. Using gestures that in no way answered Monte's question, Emory just shrugged, smiled, waved and kept on walking. She had to repeat the evasive process two more times when she got similar queries from others she passed on the sidewalk.

She ducked into Flutters and Flounce and immediately felt the cool rush of the air from the AC. As usual, the place smelled of silk and freesias, Emory's favorite flowers. The afternoon sun was hitting the crystal tiaras in the display window at just the right angle to send rainbow prisms dancing over the room.

This was her shop. Her happy place. Well, most days, anyway. And Emory figured here was where she'd get a reprieve from chatter about Candy Lynn and have a moment to recover from her encounter with Matt.

But she was wrong.

The shop was packed. This despite there being no appointments and on a day when most folks should have been out enjoying the spring weather. Emory had purposely kept her calendar clear so she could take her grandmother to the drawing, and she'd left her seamstress assistant, Susie Quaid, to man the place.

There were four teenage girls oohing, ahhing and giggling over the trio of gowns that Emory kept on display.

Isabel Dickinson and her newly engaged twin daughters, Cara and Kelly, were seated at the desk in the corner and were browsing through the portfolios of design options. Bernice Parkman was in the other corner seated with the portfolios of "mother of the groom" dresses. She had both the "soon to be" bride and the mother of the groom with her.

And then there was the tall curvy brunette wearing pale blue scrubs.

Still wearing her nurse's ID badge, she was holding the hand of her three-year-old son, Jack, who'd made use of the toy plastic tiaras that Emory kept in a basket by the check-out/reception. Jack wasn't wearing them on his head but had maneuvered them onto his arms like superhero biceps cuffs and was making *pew-pew* sounds as if aiming rays at some enemy he was battling.

"Emory," the brunette said as soon as she saw her. "How'd Matt take the news of the drawing?" she asked in a whisper.

Of all the people in town who wanted to know the answer to that, the brunette actually had a personal stake in this. Because she was Natalie Corbin, Matt's ex-wife and the mother of the tiara-wearing preschooler, Jack. Like Matt, she had been born and raised here, and her folks also still lived in Last Ride.

"Matt's not happy," Emory answered in the same hushed tone, especially since she knew that Natalie and she now had the ears of the teens and the other customers. She was hoping Jack's nonstop *pew-pewing* would cover at least some of their conversation. "Stating the obvious here, but it's been a tough day, what with the drawing and Tiffany's wedding."

"Tiff should have asked you to make the dress," Susie interjected from across the room, letting Emory know that

Jack's *pews* weren't doing the job. She either needed to take her voice down to the practically mute level or else shift the subject.

Emory went with option two. "The furniture truck arrived so Matt went to Stallion Ridge," Emory added to Natalie.

Natalie released a quick breath that Emory was certain wasn't one of relief, and she glanced around at their audience. Heck, there were even some window-shoppers who were peering inside as if they were lip-readers in training.

"Could we go into your office for a minute?" Natalie asked, scooping up her son. "I know I don't have an appointment, but—"

"This way." Emory motioned for Natalie to follow her, and they threaded their way through the teens to her closet-sized office.

The shop was fairly big and had once been a Victorian cottage around the time Last Ride had been founded, but Emory had devoted the majority of the space to the sewing room and dressing area. If she had paperwork to do, she usually did it at her home office anyway since the shop was only open four days a week.

"Grrr," Jack said, holding out his tiara arms. "Pew, pew, pew. Bam, bam."

Emory had a nephew about Jack's age so she was semi-fluent in preschooler speak and figured the little boy was taking his superhero game to the next level.

"First, let me get this out of the way," Natalie said, and she took a small plastic bag from her purse. It contained about two dozen tiny amber stones. "These were on my great-grandmother's wedding gown. I found it in the attic of her old house. Time and moths got to the gown, but I salvaged these. I was hoping you could work them into the dress you're making for me."

Emory took the bag, studied them and nodded. They were high-quality faceted glass, and while Natalie had wanted a traditional ivory bridal gown, Emory was sure she could make use of them. Along with making use of the bits of handmade lace that Natalie wanted incorporated from her baptismal gown and the teardrop-sized white silk rosebuds the woman had found in an antique shop and fallen in love with.

"Maybe they can go around the cuffs of the lace sleeves," Emory suggested over Jack's fight noises.

Since Natalie's wedding was three months away, Emory had already started sewing the garment, but she was still a couple of weeks from doing such things as beading and trim work.

Natalie nodded and deftly dodged one of the tiaras that Jack was swishing through the air like a fan. "I know this is my second wedding, and I should probably just go with something less fussy, but I keep finding things I think will make it perfect."

"You're the bride," Emory assured her. "If fussy is what you want, it's what you'll get."

This time Natalie smiled with her nod. "I just want to have everything right this time around." Her smile faded. "Is Matt really okay?"

It took Emory a couple of seconds to shift gears from fussy bride to hot cowboy cop. Of course, the flag for indicating that conversational shift was right there in Natalie's *right this time around*. It no doubt referenced that things hadn't been right with Matt and her.

"I'm not sure," Emory said in answer to Natalie's question. "He's not happy about the drawing, but he obviously wants to be back here in Last Ride."

"No, he wants to be with Jack," Natalie corrected, and she sighed. "Last Ride doesn't hold a lot of good memories for Matt."

No, and Emory knew she was part of the reason for that. Maybe a small part compared to the junk Candy Lynn had put him through, but she wasn't innocent here in contributing to Matt's cruddy past. She should have figured out a way to rein in her older brothers way back then, and she'd sure as heck figure out a way to do it now, if necessary.

"I didn't insist that Matt move back here," Natalie went on. "And Vince and I tried to work it out so he could move closer to Amarillo, but his practice and family are here. My family, too," she added. "I wanted to come home so I could see my parents more often. Plus, Vince's folks are here, and they just love Jack to pieces."

Vince Parkman was Natalie's fiancé, and he did indeed have family here. Including Emory, since Vince and she were first cousins. Natalie had been right about the practice, too. Vince was only one of two pediatricians in Last Ride. Added to that, Vince and Natalie had been childhood sweethearts, homecoming king and queen and garnered pretty much every high school award and accolades that a couple could have.

Natalie and Vince's relationship ended when he was in medical school, and Natalie hooked up with and married Matt. Now, the homecoming queen was divorced and had reconnected with her king. A regular Cupid's arrow kind of rosy future.

Well, except for Matt, of course. Rosy didn't seem to fit him right now.

Because Jack was getting a little fidgety, Emory took

a tiny wedding favors bag of M&M's from her desk and waited for Natalie's nod of approval before she gave them to the boy.

"I'm worried about Matt being at Stallion Ridge, too," Natalie went on, opening the gold foil candy bag for Jack so he could gobble them up. "I think he feels guilty because he left his grandfather all those years ago. He wasn't there for him, even though his grandpa Will took him in when he was a teenager."

Emory had heard some talk about that, but she'd also known Matt's grandfather and didn't believe the man held any resentment toward his grandson's departure. Just the opposite. He'd wanted Matt to be happy, and not being in Last Ride was Matt's solution to happiness.

"Matt should be at Stallion Ridge with the movers by now if you want to check on him," Emory suggested.

But Natalie immediately shook her head. "Our divorce might have been amicable, but we're not in a place where he'd pour out his soul to me."

Natalie paused and stared at Emory in such a way to make her think that Natalie was hoping Matt would do some soul-pouring to her. Not likely.

"Matt and I talked about the drawing, but not much else," Emory explained.

"Oh." Natalie blinked, and obviously she clued right into what Emory was saying. "So, Matt doesn't know where you live?"

Emory shook her head. Drew in a long deep breath. "Nope. But he's about to find out."

CHAPTER THREE

MATT HAULED A box of books into his old bedroom and glanced around. It was like walking into a time capsule.

A large cluttered one.

In hindsight, he should have come to Stallion Ridge earlier and cleared out some of this old stuff to make room for the things he'd had moved from Amarillo. But when he'd taken a cursory glance around the place three days ago, he hadn't given it more than that—a glance. Then he'd decided to give himself a day or two to settle. It hadn't helped. He still wasn't settled, and now he had a bigger problem of settling while trying to maneuver around stuff that shouldn't be here.

He didn't do a mere glance today. Matt took a longer look around the room. At the sports posters still on the silver-blue walls. At the twin-sized bed, now piled high with clothes that'd been taken from the closet, no doubt so there'd be space for his current stuff. Unless he was planning on losing some of the muscle he'd worked hard to build, the old clothes weren't going to work.

"I cleared out the closet for you," he heard Zella say from behind him.

Wearing a loose cotton dress and her usual high-top sneakers, the woman stepped into the doorway. Like her husband, Zella was in her early seventies, and they'd helped manage Stallion Ridge for as long as he could remember.

They lived on the grounds in a guest cottage just a stone's throw from the main house. Matt's grandfather had left the cottage to the couple in his will, so Matt was hoping that meant they'd be there for the rest of their lives. He'd need all the help he could get managing the ranch, the house, his job and his life.

"I won't mention the girlie magazines I found at the back of the top shelf," Zella added.

Matt groaned under his breath. "Good."

"Won't mention the panties that were crammed in one of the pockets of your old jackets, either," the woman said with a humph. "I'm pretty sure they belonged to that Carlyle girl. I'm guessing she gave them to you as some kind of memento."

Nope. Jessie Carlyle had left them in his truck after they'd had a clumsy round of sex when they were teenagers. Matt had managed to spot the bright red panties on the floorboard a split second before his granddad had gotten in so that Matt could drive him into town. Matt had stuffed the panties in his pocket and obviously hadn't worn the jacket again.

"I won't mention the dirty picture I found in your old backpack, either," Zella added. "It was from that Riley girl, the one you dated your senior year."

He recalled that, too. That Riley girl, Rebecca, had loved using her grandmother's Polaroid camera, and Rebecca had favored being photographed wearing just a skimpy towel that she'd arranged to gap in very interesting places.

Matt set down the box of books and glanced in the closet to see how much would fit. Not all of the books, but he could use the guest room for overflow. Of course, it might be overflowing in there already since that's where he'd told the movers to put the furniture and boxes of kitchen stuff.

Soon, he'd have to go through the entire place and see what would stay and what would need to be given away.

"Your granddad's room and closet are a lot bigger," Zella pointed out.

Yeah, it was, and it had an en suite bath, but no way could Matt move in there. That was still Grandpa Will's space. Even though he now owned Stallion Ridge, the part of the ranch that felt most like his was this room.

"Thanks," Matt assured the woman. "This'll be fine."

He set the box of books on the hardwood floor by the desk that was jammed with football trophies, some high school textbooks and old CDs. In the sixteen years he'd been gone, he had come home to Stallion Ridge maybe a dozen times at most. On the visits before he'd been married to Natalie, he'd just slept in this bed and ignored the clutter. After their marriage, they'd used the guest room because it had a queen-sized bed.

"Brings back memories, huh," Zella commented.

That was another *yeah.* Good memories because being here meant he hadn't been with Candy Lynn in the falling-down shack on Old Sawmill Road. Bad memories because he hadn't been here when his grandfather had needed him most. William Matthew Donnelly had died alone while sitting on the front porch. That'd been nearly a year ago, but in some ways the grief of his death felt as fresh and raw as it did when it'd happened.

Matt drew in a long breath, hoping to ease the sudden pressure he felt in his lungs.

"It'll be okay, boy." Zella patted his arm.

"You didn't *mention* the Last Ride Society drawing," Matt commented when she started out of the room.

Zella paused, shrugged. "I try to mind my own beeswax. Well, unless it involves sexy stuff that I find in your closet."

With those boundaries clearly defined, Zella left him. Matt wasn't offended by the invasion of his privacy because nothing around here felt especially private. The same way it hadn't when he was in high school. Even those folks who had minded their own beeswax—whatever the heck that was—knew his mother.

Or at least knew of her.

Candy Lynn sure as hell hadn't kept any of her dirty little secrets tucked away on closet shelves or in the pockets of jeans. Nope. And by carrying on the way she had, she'd also made sure that plenty of Matt's life had been an open book, one that had no doubt been dished up daily as gossip.

Shoving all that aside and cursing himself for sliding into the past, again, he took one more look around before he headed out. He made his way down the hall that already had boxes stacked against the wall. Eventually, some of the contents would go into the office. Once he cleared out his grandfather's things. That was one of his grandfather's spaces that he would use in part because it was already set up with a desk, filing cabinets and bookshelves and also because it didn't feel as personal of an area as the master bedroom.

He crossed through the open living, dining and kitchen, his boots thudding on the restored hardwood floors. The kitchen had been recently remodeled, but the burgundy leather furniture centered in front of the massive fireplace was showing its age. His grandfather had had plenty of money, but he'd tended to put it into the ranch rather than the house itself.

One step outside and onto the back porch and Matt saw the proof of that money being put to use. Sporting the silver logo of a rearing stallion on the hayloft doors, the two white barns practically gleamed. Ditto for the acres of white fences, corrals and guest cottage with its cobalt blue shutters. Zella had added a rose garden since the last time he was here.

Matt shifted his attention beyond the outbuildings and spotted a half dozen palominos grazing. There'd be plenty others in the huge stretch of pasture behind the barns.

When Matt had inherited the place a year ago, he hadn't had the heart to sell the horses because they'd been his grandfather's pride and joy. Thankfully, Zeke and Zella had agreed to keep running things, and Matt had hired several ranch hands to help them stay on track. Even without his personal attention, Stallion Ridge continued to make money.

His grandfather had invested some cash into the porch, too. There were overhead fans, built-in corner heaters and not one but six fancy brass bug zappers. Grandpa Will had loved being out here, but he'd had a lifelong battle trying to keep away the bugs. That's why the porch also had white clay pots filled with all sorts of insect deterrent flowers and plants. He caught the soothing scents of what he thought were lavender and rosemary.

Checking the stonework on the exterior around the base of the back porch, Matt was about to go to the front where the delivery truck was parked, but then he spotted the man making his way toward him. A welcome sight because it was his good friend, Brody Harrell. Brody was carrying a six-pack of beer and sporting a grin.

"Welcome home," Brody greeted, and he gave Matt a quick one-arm hug before pushing the beer into his hands. "A housewarming gift."

"Thanks." Matt wouldn't mention that it'd take a lot more than beer to warm the house, though. Still, it was good to see his old friend. Once, they'd been as thick as thieves, and it was because of Brody that Matt had all those football trophies on his desk.

Brody hiked his thumb in the direction of the delivery truck. "I offered to help, but they said they're nearly finished."

The offer of help and the nearly being finished didn't surprise Matt. "I gave Natalie most of the furniture during the divorce, and I've been living in an apartment in Amarillo. I only had a couple of rooms of stuff." Matt set the beer on the porch, opened two bottles and handed Brody one.

"You doing okay with all of this?" Brody asked, tipping his head to the house and then the sheriff's badge.

Since this was Brody, Matt had no intention of giving him the "right as rain" pat answer he'd been giving everyone else. "It's an adjustment." One that he'd no doubt be tackling for a long time. "I'll be here because it's where Jack is."

Brody nodded, sipped his beer. "I remember your granddad saying that folks were either born with roots or wings and that you got the wings."

He had, indeed. Wings that'd needed a bigger place. One with those punches of adrenaline that he craved. He'd found that as SWAT team supervisor. Well, sometimes that had been the fix. Other times, even that hadn't been able to stave off the unsettled feeling that had a bad habit of tightening his gut.

"For Jack, I'll grow roots," Matt muttered. For Jack, he'd do whatever it took. That included shooing bear claw–eating macaws out of the bakery, defusing a possible wedding brawl.

And coming home.

"What about the Last Ride Society drawing?" Brody

asked as they strolled toward the front of the house. "Water off a duck's back or pain in your ass?"

"Ass pain for sure." Matt didn't dodge or hesitate. "There's enough talk without adding that."

Brody didn't dodge or hesitate, either. He made a fast sound of agreement. No doubt it was the sound of experience because just last year Brody had gotten caught up in the drawing when his girlfriend, Janessa Parkman, had been the researcher. It had turned out well enough for them, though, because Matt had already heard some buzz that Brody and Janessa would probably soon get engaged.

"And what about Emory? You'll be okay being around her?" Brody asked a moment later.

Matt shrugged. "It's a small town so I'll probably see Emory every now and then, but it won't be that hard to stay out of each other's way."

Brody stopped, his beer in mid-lift. Matt glanced at him and wondered what the heck his friend's puzzled expression was all about, but his wondering ground to a quick halt when the car pulled into the driveway. Matt had no trouble seeing Emory behind the wheel.

She waved at them as if it were perfectly normal for her to be at Stallion Ridge. Then she drove past them and turned into the small parking area next to the cottage. The spot right by the new rose garden.

"What's she doing here?" Matt asked.

At the same moment, Brody said, "You didn't know Emory lives here? Nobody told you?"

Even though Brody had only asked two short questions, the words got a little jumbled in Matt's head. Probably because they didn't make sense. Then again, it didn't make sense for Emory to unlock the front door of the cottage and set some groceries inside.

"Emory bought the place from Zeke and Zella about five months ago," Brody explained. "I figured one of them would have told you."

No. They hadn't, and this was definitely something he should have been informed about. This was his *beeswax*. Matt glanced around, looking for Zeke or Zella, but when he didn't see either of them, he turned back to Brody.

"Why the hell did they sell the cottage that Grandpa Will left them?" Matt demanded.

Brody lifted his shoulder and scowled in such a way that seemed to say *I'm just the messenger here*. "They decided they wanted to live in town since that's where most of their friends are. They bought the little house behind Once Upon a Time."

"Town is only a couple of miles away," Matt snarled.

And he was going to have a discussion about that with Zeke and Zella. For now, though, he was apparently going to have a chat about it with Emory because she'd finished putting the bags of groceries inside the cottage and was now making her way over to him.

"I'll give you two a minute," Brody mumbled, and he headed in the direction of the moving truck.

Matt wasn't sure if that was too much time or not enough. *Too much*, he decided on the spot when the breeze tugged at her turquoise colored cotton dress, molding it against her body in such a way for him to see, well, pretty much everything. She was tall and somehow managed to be willowy and curvy at the same time.

He felt the same punch of heat he'd felt for her way back when. And Matt cursed it. Something he should have done way back when instead of acting on it and kissing her. It wasn't necessarily fair to want to keep some distance between them, but he had enough on his plate without fanning flames that shouldn't be fanned. Her family hated him, and he needed to focus on his new old life here.

"I didn't tell you about the cottage," Emory said before she even reached him, "because I figured you already had enough to absorb with the drawing. Plus, I was hoping you'd hear it before it was time for me to come home. Judging from your expression, though, Brody just spilled it to you."

Home. That's the word that came through loud and clear. This was already home to Emory.

"I guess the gossips didn't get around to *spilling* it," he grumbled. "What with all the talk about Candy Lynn's son becoming sheriff."

She nodded and brushed away a wisp of her blond hair that the wind had blown onto her cheek. It was such a simple gesture so why had it caused his stomach to clench? Because his body was stupid, that's why.

"I wouldn't have bought the place if I'd known you would ever come back here to live," she explained. "You always said you'd get out and stay out, come hell or high water."

Yeah, he'd indeed said that all right. Now he was eating those words. "Anything else going on with you that I should know about?"

"I'm making Natalie's wedding dress," she readily admitted.

Maybe she thought she'd see some disapproval on his face over that. She wouldn't. Matt didn't necessarily buy into the bunk about Emory's dresses being *mostly lucky,* but he wanted Natalie to be happy. Because that in turn would improve Jack's chances of being happy. If Vince Parkman and Last Ride were what Natalie needed for that happiness, then Matt was willing to give the man, and the town, his blessing.

"Anything else?" he pressed. "I'd like not to get blindsided by something else for at least the next twenty-four hours."

Emory cocked her head to the side, studying him again. Then smiling. Not a big beaming smile but one with a sly edge to it. "You mean like nightly loud parties, nude gardening or weddings in the pasture?"

Of course, his brain, and another stupid part of him, latched right on to the nude gardening. The breeze didn't help, either, because it swirled her dress around again, this time lifting it up enough for him to get a glimpse of her thigh.

Her smile widened. "No loud parties, weddings in the pasture and I'll keep nude gardening to a minimum." She stuck out her hand. "Want to shake on that?"

Matt was sure he was frowning, but it had nothing to do with the truce she obviously wanted. It was because he was trying to figure out how the hell he was going to look out the kitchen window and not get a too clear image of Emory naked except for gardening gloves.

He shook his head, but because the stupid part of him was still playing into this, his gaze locked on her mouth. That mouth he suddenly wanted to taste.

"The last time I kissed you, your brothers saw it and beat me up. Repeatedly," he grumbled.

No way had he intended to say that aloud. It'd just popped out. Of course, no way had he wanted to have the urge to kiss Emory, either.

"It's not a good idea for us to be living so close to each other," Matt managed to add.

"Don't worry," she said, her voice a sexy siren's purr. "You'll never even notice I'm here." With a smile that was the perfect complement to that purr, she fluttered her fingers in a little wave, turned and walked toward the cottage.

Matt just stood there, knowing that what she'd said was a Texas-sized lie. Oh, yeah, he would notice all right.

CHAPTER FOUR

With a line of dressmaker pins pinched between her lips, Emory stood back and eyed the dress she'd just fixed onto the mannequin.

It definitely wasn't her most attractive creation. Then again, it was hard to stay anywhere in the "attractive" wheelhouse when the bride had insisted on a patchwork quilt design for her big day. Not shades of white silk patchwork with delicate appliques, either, but rather the full-blown country quilt theme with calicos, florals and geometrics in every color of a child's superdeluxe box of crayons.

Emory had decided to go ahead and do the dress just as requested, and then she'd cover the entire thing with fine ivory Irish lace from neck to hem. The patchwork squares would then just peek through the tatting and hopefully tone down the riot of colors. If the bride wasn't a fan, the lace could be removed, but Emory was betting she'd be able to convince her that the unmuted scheme was much more flattering on a queen-sized bed rather than a woman's body.

Using her forearm to push her hair from her face, Emory reached out to shut the patio doors. The morning had been cool enough that she'd wanted to enjoy the breeze while she worked in the second bedroom that she'd converted into a sewing studio. Now, though, the temps were climbing so she'd need to turn on the AC rather than risk sweating on the bridal gown.

Emory made the mistake of glancing out the doors before she closed them, and she froze. She nearly swallowed the dressmaker pins when she caught a glimpse of Matt. Good gravy. The man could stir all kinds of things inside her. Silky, needy things that she shouldn't be feeling for a man who was clearly trying to avoid her. That avoidance was likely why she hadn't seen him for the past three days since he'd learned she was his neighbor.

Cowboy dreamboat was by the side of the barn, and he had his shirt completely unbuttoned. All the way. She could see toned pecs and abs. Really nice tight abs that could have graced a page of one of those hot guy calendars. He was doing some hot guy stuff, too, just by standing there and drinking water from the hose. He was sweaty and drop-dead gorgeous.

She immediately made a mental note—no gawking at Matt while she had sharp, pointy objects in her mouth.

The saddled black stallion next to Matt was having his own drink from one of the water troughs, and she figured they'd just come back from a ride. One of the ranch hands, Arnie Carver, came out of the barn, and Emory was close enough to hear him offer to take care of the stallion, but Matt waved him off.

Then Matt looked in Emory's direction.

Their gazes arrowed together like potent magnets and held for a couple of moments. Muttering something that she was dead sure was profanity, he passed the stallion's reins to Arnie and swaggered his way toward her. Well, probably not an actual swagger, but Matt had the whole cowboy thing down pat. The walk. The look. The attitude. The amazing fit of those jeans he was wearing.

Emory kept her gaze pinned to him, wondering if he was going to admit that he didn't want to keep his distance. That maybe he wouldn't mind recreating their middle school kiss.

"Your shirt's unbuttoned," Matt said when he got closer.

Emory blinked, looked down. *Crud. Crud. Crud.* Her shirt had indeed come unbuttoned, exposing her comfortable but skimpy bra and the pushed up tops of her breasts. She definitely wasn't a candidate for one of those calendars, but she'd exposed a lot of skin.

She attempted to mutter some profanity of her own, and the pins fell out of her mouth and pinged onto the hardwood floor around her bare feet. Emory snapped the sides of her shirt together and started buttoning. She nearly pointed out that his chest was also exposed, but she didn't want to end the peep show he was giving her.

Matt stepped in, bent down and started picking up the pins. When he finished, his gaze skirted around the room as he stood. She suspected it was a look that cops did when they were taking in the place in one fell swoop. The swooping stopped in its tracks, though, when his attention landed on the mannequin and bodice.

"That's, uh…different," he said.

"That's the kind word for it."

"Well, I was going to say ugly, but I didn't want to insult you."

Emory shrugged. "No insult. It's not my design. I'm just sort of an innocent bystander when it comes to this particular bridal statement. It's *different* enough that even my assistant has opted out of anything to do with it. Want to learn to sew so you can help me?" she asked, going for some levity to soften up some of the tension between them.

"No. I'd rather castrate a thousand bull calves," he grumbled.

"Since I doubt that's an especially fun chore even for a rancher, that clarifies just how strong of a no that is." She paused and considered that enough of an attempt to ease the tension. "You've been dodging me."

"I have." There was no hesitation whatsoever. He propped his hands on his hips. "Easy to do since I've been busy."

The busy part wasn't BS. Emory had seen him leave for work before seven in the morning, get back after five o'clock and then put in some hours on the ranch. Matt was obviously unpacking as well since there was a stack of collapsed empty boxes on the back porch.

As usual, Zeke and Zella had been tight-lipped about what was going on in the house and with Matt himself. Emory respected them for that since that meant there were only a handful of people who didn't blabber about such things. Still, Emory had heard the gossip about Candy Lynn, Matt and his past that should have long since been put to rest.

"Look, I'm sorry if you're getting grief about the Last Ride research," she said. "I've been trying to be discreet. I haven't spoken to anyone about it. I've just been going through anything about her I could find on the internet."

Matt went all cop on her again and plastered on a big-time poker face. Their gazes met again, as if he were playing an eyeball version of chicken. Probably because he meant it as some kind of warning or dare for her not to give him these impromptu updates on his mother.

But the chicken gaze turned into something else.

The heat came. Stirred. Stayed. And made itself known in various parts of her body. Her breasts seemed especially pleased when his eyes lowered in that direction. Her own eyes went in the direction of his bare chest.

"You must have had a good reason for kissing me in middle school," she tossed out there. Emory was about to foolishly add that the reason was still there, but Matt spoke before she could say anything else.

"Yeah," he said with his gaze, now hot and needy, pinned to hers.

As confessions went, it wasn't wordy, but it was sure as heck thought-provoking. And effective. Emory didn't consider herself a wanton woman, but Matt could certainly bring out all sorts of wantonly thoughts.

She began to spin a fantasy about him stepping closer. Of him bringing in the scent of the saddle leather, the pasture. Of him sliding his hand around the back of her neck and drawing her closer and closer until his mouth pressed against hers.

"Yeah," he repeated, snapping her out of that fantasy, and when she focused, she thought that maybe he had an ESP thing going on because he seemed to know exactly what she was thinking.

"Gotta go," he added. "It's my day off, and I'll be picking up Jack soon."

"Have fun," she managed, but immediately got sucked into another fantasy when she watched him walk away. The man had a fine cowboy butt to go with the rest of all his fineness.

Emory probably would have just continued to stand there and daydream about it, but the sound of the car engine put a stop to that. Because this particular engine had come to a stop in front of the cottage. Shutting the patio doors, she made her way to the front of the house. Not a long journey at all since the cottage was only a thousand square feet.

She groaned when she looked out the bay window and saw her visitors. Nancy and Derrick. Her parents.

They stepped out of their Lexus and headed straight for her porch. Since they rarely visited her here at Stallion Ridge and never had together, this wouldn't be good. Of course, Emory didn't need a crystal ball to know why they'd come. Nope. Candy Lynn and Matt would be at the top of their discussion list.

Emory tried to put on a carefree expression when she opened the door to greet them. With her mother's excitable personality and low tolerance for stress, Emory had learned to wear masks around her. She'd also tried to develop amnesia about her father's affair with Candy Lynn. And her mother's reaction to it. She loved her parents, but walking on eggshells around them was a way of life.

"How nice," Emory said, smiling. "I was just about to take a break and fix myself a glass of iced tea. Come on in."

"Your shirt isn't buttoned right," her mother immediately said, and her gaze drifted toward Matt who was heading toward the barn.

Perhaps her folks had seen Matt walking away from the cottage. If so, they might think some hanky-panky had been going on. And there had been, sort of. If you counted sweaty leather fantasies.

"We went by the shop," her father added, trailing behind his wife as they came in the cottage. Apparently, he wasn't even going to touch on the subject of a possible reason for a misbuttoned shirt. "Susie said you were working from home today."

Emory nodded, went to the kitchen to pour three glasses of iced tea. "We've got four dresses going in the sewing room at the shop. Two of them are poofy and take up a lot of space so I decided to work here."

"And to see Matt." That came from her mother, and she'd spoken it through pinched lips.

This time, Emory nodded, shrugged and nearly spilled the iced tea. She bobbled the glasses, recovered and got the drinks into the adjoining living room where her parents had already taken a seat on the sofa.

Like the rest of the cottage, the sofa and chairs were light and cheerful with their gold and mint tones, but there was no such cheerfulness in her parents' expressions.

"Let me speculate about why you're here," Emory said, handing out the tea before she took a seat across from them. "You're worried about the Last Ride Society research I'm doing on Candy Lynn."

Her mother's fingers clamped around the glass. "So, you are doing the research, after all."

She'd made it seem as if Emory had left the task up in the air. She hadn't. "Yes. According to the guidelines I got, I'll need a photo of Candy Lynn's tombstone. That's the only part of the research that I'll be doing out of the house. Everything else will be done behind closed doors, and I won't be interviewing or talking to anyone about it."

Her father's blue eyes, which were a genetic copy of her own, narrowed. "But people will be able to read it once you turn in the report. You shouldn't be doing this, Emory. You shouldn't be dredging up the past."

She wanted to tell him that dredging wasn't required, that the past had a way of staying firmly in the present in Last Ride. That was the yin and the yang of living in a small town. People were usually there for you and had long memories of anything and everything that went on.

"That woman nearly ripped my family to pieces," her mother muttered.

Because Emory was part of that "nearly ripped to pieces"

family, she wasn't immune to the tremble in her mom's voice. Nope. And it didn't matter if the tremble happened way too often. When it came to Candy Lynn, Nancy Parkman had cause to unload a boatload of emotions. She'd been hurt, and it didn't matter that it was nearly two decades ago.

"Certainly, Matt doesn't want you to do this research," her father added.

"He doesn't," Emory readily admitted. "But as I told him, the talk will be there whether I do it or not. There's also a provision in the guidelines where the name will just be assigned to someone else." She'd discovered that the night before when she'd actually read through the paperwork she'd gotten from the Last Ride Society. "Trust me, I'll be a lot more discreet than someone else might be."

No way could her parents argue with that. There were some who'd treat this like a big meaty bone.

With his jaw muscles twitching, her father stood, set down his tea on the copper penny coffee table and went to the window. "I'm sorry for what happened between Candy Lynn and me, but I just keep paying and paying for what I did wrong. This will cost me patients. It'll cause more talk that will hurt your mother."

The last part was true. Nothing could be done about that. But Emory doubted her father would lose many patients if any at all. He was a family practitioner, and doctors were in short supply in Last Ride. The loss of patients would have come nineteen and a half years ago when news of his affair had come out. Correction—when Candy Lynn had blabbed about the affair to anyone who'd listen. Emory had been fourteen and plenty old enough to understand what was going on.

Plenty old enough to understand the gossip that'd followed.

Candy Lynn had died of a drug overdose, but she'd planted the notion in some of her friends' heads that Dr. Derrick Parkman might try to kill her to get back at her for ratting him out. Of course, the ratting out had happened after Emory's father had refused to pay Candy Lynn hush money. There'd been an investigation, but her father had been cleared of any wrongdoing and the townsfolk rushed in to comfort her mother. That hadn't completely quelled the gossip, though.

And never would.

Yin and yang in action.

"You should talk to Alma Parkman," her father added a moment later. "She's president of the Last Ride Society, and she can get the rule changed. No one should be digging into Candy Lynn Corbin's life."

Emory wanted to point out that it would stir up talk if she made such a request. Still, she'd try, and that's exactly what she told her parents.

"I'll drop by and see Alma on my way to the shop," Emory assured them.

Her father's jaw unclenched. Her mother's mouth steadied. "I'll talk to her as well," her mom said. "And what about Matt?" she pressed. "Will you start up with him again?"

There was nothing that Emory liked about that question. She was ready to rattle off the comeback that there was no *again* because the last time had been merely a kiss. There'd likely be no again because Matt didn't want to get tangled up with her. She was a sore reminder for him. Not as much as Candy Lynn, of course, but a lesser reminder could still take you places you'd rather not go.

Before Emory could say any of that to her parents, she

heard the sound of another car engine, and like her parents' Lexus, this one, too, pulled to a stop in front of her house.

"It's your cousin Millie," her father relayed since he was still at the window. "Your mom and I will be going."

Nancy didn't waste any time doing just that, maybe because she thought Millie Parkman was there to talk about the research and drawing. After all, Millie's name had been drawn just a year earlier. But Emory was pretty sure this visit had nothing whatsoever to do with that.

"Millie and Joe McCann got engaged last night," Emory explained. "Millie texted me and asked if she could come by sometime this morning and talk about wedding dresses."

Of course, that didn't mean the subject of the drawing wouldn't come up, but Emory suspected Millie had bride stuff on the brain right now.

Her parents went out just as Millie made it to the porch. There were hugs of greeting, but her father cast Emory a "fix this Candy Lynn mess" glance before they went to their car.

"I hope they aren't leaving because of me," Millie said. She shifted the huge leather purse she had hooked over her shoulder.

"No," Emory assured her, and she slipped her arm around Millie's waist to ease her inside. "So, let me see the ring."

Millie's smile was sun-bright when she thrust out her hand to show off the engagement ring. It wasn't traditional, but it was beautiful with sapphires flanking a large square-cut diamond.

"Very nice," Emory assured her, and she gave Millie another hug. "A huge congrats to both Joe and you."

"Thanks. I'm so happy I'm about to burst. Of course, I want you to do the dress."

"And I, of course, want to do it," Emory assured her.

Emory didn't make all the dresses sold in her shop. Susie did some, and Emory also bought a few from seamstress acquaintances of hers. But she'd personally make whatever Millie wanted. Her cousin was a widow and had had a tough road dealing with the grief so it was good to see her happy again.

"I'm, uh, about to burst in other areas, too," Millie said. She stopped, giggled and then pressed her hand to her stomach. "I am so knocked up."

The next hug she gave Millie was just as heartfelt as the others, but Emory still felt the little sucker punch. A baby. Something that Emory had always wanted. In fact, it was almost certainly why she'd jumped into her second marriage. She, too, had been pregnant, but she'd had a miscarriage only days after the wedding.

"By the way, I have to swear you to secrecy about me being knocked up," Millie went on. "And I have to beg and plead with you to do a rush job on the dress. Joe and I want to get married next month before I start showing."

Next month wouldn't give her much time, but Emory would make it work. "Any idea what kind of dress you want?"

"This…" Millie said, taking a plastic bag from her purse. She pulled out a cream-colored beaded dress. "It's from the 1920s. Very *Great Gatsby*."

Since Millie owned the town's antique store, Emory figured it wasn't much of a surprise that she'd want something vintage. It was a simple design. The polar opposite of the quilt dress in her sewing room.

"Obviously, this dress was meant for a tiny woman, which I'm not," Millie went on. "But I was hoping it could be a pattern of sorts."

Emory took the dress, studied it and nodded. "I could even use some of the beads and lace." She could already see it coming together.

"So, you can do it." Millie giggled with delight and pulled Emory into another giddy, giggly hug. "Thank you, thank you, thank you."

"You're welcome, you're welcome, you're welcome," Emory teased. "Just drop by the shop this afternoon, and I'll do your measurements and start the pattern."

"Great. Oh, and we're having an engagement party next week at the drive-in," Millie went on. "No gifts, please. Just bring yourself and a date if you want. The renovations are done so we want to show off the place."

Emory could definitely understand the desire to show it off. The drive-in had been abandoned for several decades until Millie had decided to buy it, and together, Joe and she had restored it. With its grand opening just a few weeks away, it was a welcome addition to Last Ride.

"Joe's loading the drive-in screen with photos of the town, the local ranches and such," Millie explained. "Of course, there'll be shots of Stallion Ridge…" The woman's words trailed off as her gaze went to the window. "Wow."

There was something in Millie's tone that made Emory believe her cousin wasn't wowing about the view. Nope. Matt walked past the cottage, heading toward his house. His shirt was still unbuttoned, and his natural swagger was still going on.

"Wow," Millie repeated, fanning herself. "He looks like one of those calendar pages."

"What I said," Emory muttered, and she stepped closer to admire the view. "FYI, you're engaged and marrying the man you love. A man who just happens to qualify for his own calendar."

"All very true," Millie acknowledged with a grin, "but I'm allowed to look at other *pages*." She turned to Emory. "There's no way you're not seriously attracted him. Please tell me you're thinking about dabbling back into the romance waters."

Oh, Emory had done more than think about it, and the *mmm* sound she made confirmed that. Probably not a confirmation she should have made, though, because Millie got a bright matchmaking look in her eyes.

"I'll invite him to the engagement party," Millie insisted. "Joe was probably going to do it anyway, but I'll stop by and tell him about it now. That way, the two of you could ride together."

In theory, since they were neighbors, it made sense. But Emory was betting Matt would come up with a reason for them to drive separately. Or not go at all. No way would he want anyone to think they were on a date. Still, Emory didn't burst Millie's matchmaking bubble. She just made another of those sounds and gave Millie a goodbye hug as she headed out of the cottage and toward the house.

Emory had barely gotten her door closed when her phone rang, and she winced after she saw the name on the screen. Alma Parkman, another cousin and president of the Last Ride Society. Emory was betting this wasn't a call about a possible wedding dress.

"Alma," Emory greeted. "I'm figuring you just got off the phone with my mom."

"I did." Alma's sigh was loud and long. "Nancy gave me an earful. You want the good news or the bad?"

"There's good news?" Emory asked.

"Good-ish," Alma qualified, "but there's nothing *ish* about the bad."

"All right." Emory's own sigh was even louder, even longer. "Let's start with the bad."

CHAPTER FIVE

"IF YOU LOOK up the word *stupid* in the dictionary, there'd be a picture of these two next to it," Deputy Azzie Parkman griped in a whisper to Matt. Well, as much of a whisper as Azzie could manage. "They're troublemakers, both of them. Seems to me they got exactly what they deserve."

Matt silently agreed with Azzie's first comment but not the second. He wasn't sure anyone deserved to have glitter superglued to one's dick and balls. That was exactly what had happened, though, in what was apparently a locker room squabble gone way wrong.

He eyed the two teenagers who were now standing across from each other in an examining room of the Last Ride Hospital. The fourteen-year-old boys, Ian Parkman and Theo Dayton, both had on paper gowns and every now and then glitter would drift from their crotch areas and flutter to the floor.

"I want Theo arrested," the woman behind Ian insisted.

She had introduced herself to Matt as Heather Parkman, Ian's mom, and her snarling was only slightly louder than the woman's on the other side of Azzie. That woman, Stacy Parkman, was Theo's mother, and both women had nearly gotten into a fistfight in the ER, which was the reason Matt had been called in. Since the EMTs had feared an all-out brawl once the boys' fathers arrived, Matt had brought Azzie with him in case things got out of hand.

"He started it." Theo flung an accusing finger at Ian. The movement caused more glitter to fall.

Since Ian had already said something similar, Matt figured it was going to take a couple of questions, followed by a couple of answers to get this all sorted out. He had some time since the attending ER nurse had said it'd be at least fifteen minutes before the doctor could examine them.

"You—" Matt snapped, pointing to Theo. "What happened? You—" he added pointing to Ian "—stand there and hush until he's done."

Even with the warning and what he was damn sure was his cop's hard eye, Matt still had to shush the mothers so he could hear Ian.

"I'd just finished a shower after PE and went back in the locker room to get dressed," Ian explained. "That's when Theo squirted me with the glue and tossed glitter on me. I got pissed off and did the same to him."

As explanations went, this one was clearly full of holes, but it was a good starting point. "You just happened to have glue and glitter with you in the high school locker room?" Matt asked Theo.

That silenced both teenagers, and the boys suddenly got very interested in looking at the floor. Matt figured they weren't counting flakes of glitter.

"Well?" Matt demanded.

"I brought the glue," Theo finally admitted in a very reluctant, very soft mumble. "Ian brought the glitter."

Behind him, there was the clamor of male voices that announced the fathers had likely arrived. Matt simply hitched his thumb at Azzie to indicate he wanted her to deal with them while he continued this interrogation.

"And who or what was the intended target of the glue and glitter?" Matt pressed when the boys clammed up again.

"Cameron Byers," the boys finally said in unison. It was Ian who picked up the explanation after another "slow as a drunk slug" moment. "Cam thinks he's hot sh…stuff," the boy amended after he glanced at his mother. "He's always bragging about how big his di…willy is. We thought we'd teach him a lesson."

Azzie appeared to have been right about Ian and Theo deserving this glittered mess. "So, this was premeditation with the intent to assault a fellow student because he was running his mouth?"

Matt figured the cop words of *premeditation*, *intent* and *assault* would make them want to crap their pants. If they'd had on any pants, that is. And it worked. Color drained from the boys' faces. The mothers started rattling off protests, but Matt silenced them, too, by starting to recite the Miranda warning.

"Ian Parkman and Theo Dayton, you have the right to remain silent…" Matt stopped and glared at both boys. "Should I keep going? Should I then wait until the glitter is scraped off your genitals to arrest you, put you in handcuffs and march you up Main Street to the police station where you'll be detained until you get a bond hearing that might not happen until tomorrow?"

That silenced even the moms, and Matt waited another heartbeat before he continued.

"Or should I assume you've both learned a very valuable lesson," Matt pressed, "and that you'll *never* do anything like this again?"

"They won't do it again." That insistence came from Heather, but Stacy wasn't that far behind in voicing something similar.

"We won't do it again," came first from Ian.

Then from Theo, "We swear. We won't get anywhere near Cam."

"Good." Matt held up his index finger in a warning. "And FYI, if you lapse and do something else stupid like this, I'll charge you for this incident and any subsequent one. That should be enough to land you both in juvie."

Unless these two already had a record, that likely wouldn't happen. Then again, Azzie had called them troublemakers so maybe they'd already seen the inside of the police station.

Matt waited another moment to make sure his threat had sunk it. He could tell from the boys' stark expressions that it had. For the time being, anyway. So he turned to leave and nearly smacked right into someone.

Emory.

If she hadn't staggered back a step, they would have landed body to body. As it was, his arm still brushed against her breast, and even through his clothes, he felt the contact.

He'd missed her, he realized. And he hadn't wanted to think about her, much less miss her. In fact, for the past three days since their "unbuttoned shirt" encounter, he'd tried, and failed, to put Emory out of his mind.

"Are the boys okay?" she asked. There was a concern and urgency in her voice.

Matt picked up on that urgency, and he didn't let her clothes distract him. Not much, anyway. Emory was wearing a denim skirt that hit well above her knees, a blue top that molded to her breasts. And she was feathery. Literally. There were tiny bits of white feathers on her face, hair and clothes.

"Are they okay?" she repeated, glancing back at the fathers who were still arguing with Azzie.

Matt glanced at them, too. And he groaned. Because

the men were very familiar. Emory's brothers, Ryder and Ruston. They'd changed some in the past sixteen years, but Matt still had no trouble recognizing them. There weren't many people in Last Ride who were bigger and beefier than Azzie, but these guys could match her size for size.

"Ian and Theo Parkman are your nephews," Matt stated.

She nodded. "They're two of them. I have three. I was working at the shop today, so Stacy called me and asked me to come right over. Are either of them hurt?"

"They're both fine." Matt stopped, regrouped. "Well, they do have glitter glued to their budding manhoods, but other than that, they're okay. A revenge prank gone wrong," he added when Emory gave him a blank stare.

She nodded, relaxed her stiff shoulders and peered in at the boys and their moms who'd moved into the lecture mode of "you're grounded for the rest of your life." The dads, with Azzie marching along right behind them, started toward their sons.

Ryder's attention landed on Matt, and the man muttered something under his breath. Probably some prime curse words. There were more mutterings when Ryder's gaze shifted to his sister. Even though there was plenty of distance between Matt and her, Ryder apparently didn't care much for them sharing the same breathing space.

Ruston barely spared Matt a glance, but he was sporting a "not again" expression for his son. Matt would give them a few minutes to see if they had any questions for him.

Any confrontations, too.

It'd been a few years since he'd had to fight Ryder and Ruston, and he hoped the men had gotten their tempers under control. He really didn't want to haul Emory's brothers in for assaulting a police officer.

"Has anyone told my dad about this?" Emory asked, drawing Matt's attention back to her.

"Probably. The nurse said a doctor would be in soon to examine them," Matt told Emory. It would probably be either Dr. Derrick Parkman or Natalie's fiancé, Vince. Natalie, too, worked in the hospital as a labor and delivery nurse, but he doubted she'd show up in the ER. "Then they'll get started on removing the glitter."

Speaking of removing, that's what Matt did. He reached up, plucked a small fuzzy bit of feather from her hair.

Emory groaned and gave her hair a shake while she brushed off her clothes. The wispy feathers flew through the air. "It's white turkey marabou down. One of the brides wants her entire veil coated in it. I was working on it when I got the call from Stacy."

"Well, I suspect your cleanup will be less painful than your nephews'." Though he couldn't imagine why any bride would want a feather veil.

Emory nodded, met his gaze. "You've been dodging me again."

"Yeah," he admitted.

And he'd managed it for the past three days. During that time, the heat obviously hadn't cooled down between them. Neither had the gossip about the drawing and Candy Lynn. That gossip was neck and neck with the speculation that Emory and he were having a hot, sweaty fling.

"You might have heard talk about the research," Emory threw out there, and then she took another deep breath. "My mom asked Alma to change the rules of the drawing so that I wouldn't have to do the research on Candy Lynn."

That got his attention. No, he hadn't heard about a possible rule change. "And?"

Emory shook her head. "Bad news. Alma said since the

specifics are actually spelled out in Hezzie Parkman's will, it would take a special meeting of the Last Ride Society and a vote with at least seventy-five percent of the members agreeing. According to her, there's no chance of getting that many Parkmans to agree on anything. Plus, all the bickering and discussion it'll cause will create even more gossip than the research itself."

Yeah, it would, and Matt was certain it would also prompt many, many people to ask for his opinion on the subject.

"Alma, however, agreed to either help with the research or delay putting it in the library," Emory went on. "I turned down the help because I'm not sure Alma would be very discreet with the research. She likes to gab," she added. "But I did tell her that I'd ask you about a delay to add the report to the library. Maybe if she can put it off long enough, people will lose interest in it."

And maybe teenage boys would stop doing stupid pranks that would land them in the ER, but Matt wasn't counting on it. In fact, such a delay would probably rev up the chatter.

Matt shook his head. "Don't delay the research. Just get it done so the firestorm about it will pass."

Of course, that was wishful thinking. The firestorm of the actual research might become old news, but Candy Lynn had left a nasty legacy behind that would cause tongues to wag forever.

Matt turned when he heard the approaching footsteps, and he had a déjà vu moment, whirling him all the way back to middle school when he saw the expression on Ryder's face. Emory's brother looked as if he was spoiling for a fight.

"Are you arresting my son?" Ryder demanded in a voice loud enough to have Azzie coming to Matt's side.

Matt had to tamp down his reaction to get into a pissing contest with Ryder. One that Matt was sure he'd win. But while such a contest might give him some payback, it didn't apply to the current situation.

"No, I'm not arresting him or Theo. Well, not unless they do something else stupid. For now, though, I think they've learned their lesson."

Azzie made a sound to indicate her skepticism about that. "They've got an entire tub of glitter glued to their peckers. Not sure somebody who does that is capable of lessons learned."

Ryder shot her a glare, but the glare eased up some when he turned back to Matt. "Thank you for cutting me a break."

Matt shook his head. "No cutting. What happened didn't warrant an arrest. Still, you should talk to Ian about bullying and retaliation since that seems to be what was going on."

Oh, Ryder didn't like that mini lecture, but Matt didn't care. He just hoped it got through because even some kid acting like an a-hole didn't deserve to have his genitals assaulted with glue and glitter.

Ryder glanced at the exam area when he heard his wife arguing with Ruston—Theo's dad. Cursing under his breath, Ryder went to them with Azzie right on his heels.

Matt turned back to Emory to pick up their conversation, but he immediately got another interruption. This time it was Dr. Vince Parkman, Natalie's fiancé. Matt liked the guy well enough, but he was sure they'd never be best buds. Not because Vince had replaced him. The man hadn't. Matt's marriage to Natalie had ended six months before she'd started seeing Vince. Still, Matt figured there'd always be some unease at being around his ex's new guy. Especially since the new guy was from the superstar gene pool in Last Ride.

"Vince," Matt greeted.

As usual, the doctor gave Matt a polite nod, and he shifted his attention to Emory. "Your dad got tied up with an appointment, so I drew the short straw. I understand there's glue and glitter involved?"

Emory nodded. "And stupidity."

Nodding and sighing, Vince went to the examination room, and once again Matt turned to Emory. Hell. He'd forgotten what he was going to say to her. Not good. Because he was letting her face, her body, *her* distract him.

"I need to warn you about Millie and Joe's engagement party," Emory said before he could get his mind back on track. "I assume you're going since Joe and you are friends."

They were indeed friends, and yes, Matt was going. "What warning?"

"My shop assistant's mom is catering it, and she got a look at the guest list. With the exception of Joe's teenager daughter, it'll be a couples deal. As in, you and I will be the only two unattached adults there."

Matt started to shrug that off, but he stopped in mid-shoulder lift. That's because he got a flash of how this could play out. Folks there would likely try to matchmake Emory and him.

"There'll be some talk about the Last Ride Society," Emory added. "About how the last two drawings have brought the couples together. First, Millie and Joe. Then, Brody and Janessa."

Oh, yes. There'd be some matchmaking attempts all right. This was yet another "knock upside the head" consequence from this stupid drawing.

"I could just go ahead and ask you to go with me," Emory threw out there. "It'd be like cutting them off at the pass."

Matt gave her a flat look. "More like giving them additional gossip fodder." He tipped his head to Ryder who was scowling and pacing outside the now closed exam room where Vince was no doubt with the teens. Ryder wasn't alone. The other three parents were also pacing, and Azzie was watching all of them as if they were a barrel of pissed off monkeys.

Emory followed Matt's tipped gaze, and she scowled, too. "My brothers don't rule my life."

"No," Matt answered without hesitation, "but they can stir up enough bile for it to get back to your folks."

That caused her to sigh, but then she shook her head. "Sooner or later, my parents are going to have to deal with the memories of Candy Lynn."

Matt was betting they'd want to go with the later rather than sooner on that, and it was extremely likely that they'd carry the mark of Candy Lynn to their graves. His expression must have conveyed that because Emory sighed again.

"Yes," she muttered in agreement. "The buzz of all of this brings the badness to the surface." She paused, glanced back at her brothers who were still pacing and glowering at the exam room. "I suppose it's doing the same to my brothers. After all, they had to live through the scandal of dad's affair, too."

So true. That affair and the investigation following Candy Lynn's death had scalded a lot of people. It was no doubt another reason for her brothers to loathe him.

"It's occurred to me that one day someone might draw my name and be researching my own tombstone," Emory went on. "Trust me, that's a little unsettling. Not because it makes me think about death, but I don't relish the idea of somebody hashing and rehashing my failed relationships and my seriously bad taste in men. Present company excluded."

For some reason—a stupid reason—that made him smile. He didn't want her to exclude him. "Oh, I'm just a different kind of bad," he assured her.

She nodded. Smiled, too. And then Emory did a stupid thing. She leaned in and brushed her mouth over his. The contact lasted barely a second, if that, and when she pulled back, her eyes widened.

"Sorry," she muttered, and she appeared to be gearing up for an even longer apology, but the sound of her brother's voice cut off whatever she'd been about to say.

"Emory?" Ryder called out, making a beeline toward them. "Have you lost your mind?"

She turned to face Ryder head-on, and yeah, he'd seen that quickie kiss all right. Emory went as stiff as a sturdy flagpole and maybe would have even moved in front of Matt had he not stopped her. No way was he letting Emory stand as his shield.

"No, I haven't lost my mind," she snarled in response to her brother. "But you have if you think you have any right to tell me who I can or can't kiss."

As if to prove her point, she leaned in and kissed Matt again. Well, it was mouth-to-mouth contact anyway, but her lips were so stiff in anger that it was more like having a rock pressed against him. Matt thought he'd better check for a chipped tooth once he dealt with Ryder.

Matt met Ryder's slitted angry gaze. "If you've got something to say, say it to me." He didn't bother to make that sound like less than a threat.

Ryder took one menacing step closer to Matt. "You'll stay away from my sister."

Oh, that was so the wrong thing to say. Matt respected his badge too much to get into a shouting, shoving match with this moron, but he didn't rein in his sudden petty streak.

"Emory, will you go to Millie's engagement party with me?" Matt asked, without taking his own narrowed gaze off Ryder.

"Of course. I'd be happy to go with you." Emory brushed a kiss on Matt's cheek before she took hold of her brother's arm. A hard mean hold. "Come on. Come on," she repeated when Ryder didn't budge. "You'll have enough gossip to deal with over your son's glittered balls without stirring up more."

Apparently, that logic got through to Ryder's mule-headed brain. That and the fact that the exam room door opened and Vince stepped out. Ryder gave Matt one last glare before he turned to leave. Emory gave Matt one last smile before she did the same.

Matt stood there, watching them walk toward the exam room. And that's when he realized exactly what he'd done.

He had a date with Emory Parkman.

CHAPTER SIX

EMORY GROANED WHEN her phone rang and she saw her mom's name on the screen. This would no doubt be round thirty-three in her mother's attempts to convince her not to go to the engagement party with Matt. Over the last five days, some of those attempts had been in person, both at home and at the shop, but the last two dozen had been phone calls.

She considered just letting the call go to voice mail, but the last four attempts at that had told her it was an ineffective ploy since her mother just continued to call. So Emory hit the answer button, putting the phone on Speaker so she could continue to work on one of the three dresses in her home sewing studio.

"Ian's testicles are inflamed," her mother said the moment she was on the line.

Well, that was a new greeting. All her others had started with a lecture on why Emory shouldn't be seen with Matt.

"Uh, is Ian okay?" Emory asked while she hoped, hoped, hoped that her mom hadn't insisted on getting visual confirmation of the teenager's inflamed balls.

"No, he's not," Nancy answered, not in a snap but more of a grandmotherly whine. "He's in a lot of pain, and some of the kids at school are making fun of him because he can't sit through his classes."

Emory wanted to point out that this might teach Ian

a lesson, but she felt for the boy. Teenagers did plenty of stupid things, and she didn't like that something like this could and would stay with her nephew. Not the inflammation. That would no doubt go away. But it was possible he'd be dubbed glitter nuts or some other cruel but sadly accurate label.

"Ryder and Heather are going to talk to the principal about Ian doing his classes online for a while," her mother added.

That'd be a temporary fix, but in the long run it could cause more harm. Because sooner or later Ian would have to go back and face anyone giving him grief.

Much like Matt had done with Ryder and Ruston back in middle school. Or more recently at the hospital. Matt certainly hadn't taken any of Ryder's BS, and in a roundabout way that'd led to her kissing Matt.

And to Matt asking her to the party.

Oh, what a tangled web could be woven in the name of spur-of-the-moment, unthought-out payback, and she was certain that Matt was having many regrets about that lapse. So was Emory, but the regrets were for Matt and for the discomfort she'd caused her parents.

"Anyway, I thought I'd throw a little dinner," her mother continued. "You know, to cheer Ian up. It'd be just us, immediate family. Of course, I want you there."

Emory sighed. "Let me guess. The family dinner is tomorrow night, the same time as Millie and Joe's engagement party?"

Her mother hesitated, probably figuring out how to say this. Then again, she'd likely already scripted and even rehearsed it. "Yes, but I know you'll want to put family first."

It was a big bucket of sloppy emotional blackmail, and Emory wasn't going to bite. Well, not fully. "I can drop by and see Ian tonight and explain to him that I've already accepted the invitation to go to the party. Or you can re-schedule the dinner for another time. One that is after Ian has healed enough to sit down and enjoy a meal and one that doesn't conflict with the only evening where I already have somewhere else to be."

"Emory." Her mother sighed, too. "Please rethink what you're doing. There's a lot of talk, and it has to be hurt-ing Matt."

That stung. Because it was probably true. Any time Matt's name was coupled with Derrick Parkman's daugh-ter, it would spur gossip about Candy Lynn. It was just one of those nasty little pairings that neither Matt nor she could fully avoid.

"Mom, I have to go," Emory said when she glanced out the window at the SUV that pulled just to a stop next to the cottage. "And, no, I'm not putting you off. I have a fitting, and the customer just arrived." Someone she'd expected a half hour ago.

She wouldn't mention that the customer was Natalie, since that might spur her mom to give a repeat lecture of how the gossip might be bothering both Matt's ex-wife and even their son. And speaking of their son, Jack was with Natalie when they got out of the SUV.

Emory was thankful to see them. The newsflash of the hospital kiss had almost certainly made its way to well, ev-eryone, and Emory had worried that it would upset Natalie. Not because the woman still loved Matt. If that were the case, then she wouldn't be marrying Vince. Still, Natalie might have objected to her son's father being the bull's-eye of so much gossip.

"Bye, Mom," Emory said, ending the call and knowing she'd have to phone her back later and try to soothe the feathers she'd just ruffled. She made it to the front door just as Natalie knocked.

"Sorry I'm late," Natalie immediately apologized. Like her earlier visits to the shop, she was wearing her scrubs. "The sitter canceled so I had to pick up Jack from pre-school. Vince's parents are out of town, and Vince is on shift at the hospital. My parents are in San Antonio, and Matt's tied up with a domestic dispute out on Old Sawmill Road so he couldn't do it."

That sent a spike of alarm through Emory. Even though Last Ride wasn't exactly a hotbed of crime, domestic disputes could turn ugly. Then she mentally cursed herself. This was his job, and she couldn't have worry spikes like that. Well, she could, but she shouldn't. The bottom line was that Matt wasn't hers to worry about. Even if it felt a little as if he were.

"Anyway, I'm sorry, but I'll have to reschedule my fitting," Natalie added. "I would have just called, but I wanted to drop off more of the glass beads I found. Plus, I had to bring Jack to Matt. He'll be here soon." She extracted a small plastic bag from her purse. "They're a close match to the ones from my great-grandmother's dress, and I thought you might need them to fill in any gaps or such."

So Natalie wasn't just blowing off this fitting. Or the dress itself.

Emory took the bag, thanked her. "No problem on re-scheduling. I'll be here in the morning, or you can drop by the shop on Monday."

Natalie's long breath seemed to be one of relief. Relief that vanished when she checked the time. "As soon as Matt gets here and takes Jack, I have to go back to the hospital. Elsa Dayton is in labor."

Emory knew Elsa and recalled that Natalie and Elsa had

been good friends in high school. Elsa was probably counting on Natalie being there.

"You can leave Jack with me," Emory suggested.

Natalie blinked, clearly surprised by the offer. "Oh, but—"

"I have three nephews," Emory reminded her. "I've had a lot of experience babysitting."

"But you're working," Natalie pointed out.

Emory shrugged. "Nothing pressing. I can watch Jack until Matt gets back." That way she could see for herself that he was all right. "Just text him and let him know Jack's with me."

"I wanta stay," Jack insisted.

The boy's attention was already roaming over the room, so he was clearly ready to explore. His gaze landed in the corner that was filled with toys, which Emory had set up for her youngest nephew, Greer. Since Greer and Jack were both three, the toys would be age-appropriate and had been personally approved by Greer's mom.

Natalie's forehead bunched up, and she was obviously having a debate with herself as to what to do. The debate ended, however, when the woman's phone dinged with a text. "It's the hospital," she relayed to Emory. "I really need to get back."

"Then go," Emory insisted, giving Natalie a nudge toward the door.

Even when Jack joined in on that nudging, Natalie still hesitated some more before she finally gave her son a goodbye kiss. "Mommy won't be long," she assured the boy before she looked at Emory again. "You've got my number, right? Of course, you do," she said, waving that off. "And you're sure you don't mind?"

"I don't mind." Obviously, neither did Jack because he was trying to close the door in his mother's face.

After another goodbye kiss and a wave, Natalie finally left, and Jack made a beeline for the toys. There were books, blocks and even a heavy plastic toy workbench, but the boy went for the two-foot-tall brightly colored rocket. It was basically a magnetized stacking toy, and it kept Jack occupied for under a minute before he moved on to the other toys. But none of the toys could hold a candle to the way his eyes lit up when he saw the horses by the pasture fence.

"Can we go ride 'em?" the boy asked.

Emory hated to put a damper on that enthusiasm, but she shook her head. "Sorry, buddy. We can have a closer look at them, though. Come on. We can go out the patio door."

Nodding, he got to his feet. "Did you kiss Daddy?" Jack asked just as she took his hand.

The question threw her so much that Emory nearly stumbled. She mentally stumbled, too, so she stopped to look down at him. "Uh, where did you hear that?"

He lifted his shoulder in a shrug that she thought was a whole lot like his dad. "Papa Vince and Mama said."

Little pitchers did have whopping big ears. So that confirmed that the gossip had indeed reached Natalie. Emory waited, hoping the boy would add more. Especially more about Natalie's opinion on the smooching matter, but he jiggled her hand to get her moving again.

Wondering if she could press the subject of the kiss talk, Emory led him into the sewing room and opened the patio doors. They didn't go outside, though, because Jack paused by the feather gown that was on the dress form. He eyed the huge basket of feathers on the floor beside it.

"A *biiig* chicken dress," he concluded.

A wise assessment indeed, except it was technically a

biiig turkey dress. "It's not your mom's," she assured him. "That's hers."

She pointed to the much more tasteful featherless gown on the dress dummy on the other side of the room. It was sleek but had interesting details, what with the addition of the antique lace and tiny beads that sparkled at the cuffs. Emory always tried to do her best with all her bridal designs, but some turned out better than others. Natalie's gown was shaping up to be one of her favorites.

"Will you marry my daddy?" Jack asked. "Mama kisses Papa Vince."

Oh, the logic of a three-year-old. And, oh, the lack of answers from the woman he was giving a seriously questioning stare.

"Uh, no. Your daddy and I aren't getting married," she settled for saying.

Just as Matt stepped through the patio doors.

Of course, he would have arrived at this exact moment, and he volleyed glances between Jack and her. Emory figured, though, that his cocked eyebrow was for her and her alone.

"Someone heard about us *k-i-s-s-i-n-g*," Emory explained.

Apparently, Matt was accustomed to three-year-old logic because he lowered that eyebrow in the same motion that he lifted his shoulder. She couldn't tell if that particular shrug was from resignation or if he simply didn't want to discuss this in front of his son.

She looked Matt over from head/cowboy hat to boots and didn't see any damage. However, there was some strain on his face, but that could be from the worry about the gossip.

"Did everything go okay with your domestic disturbance call?" Emory asked.

"Well enough," Matt assured her, and their gazes connected for a few seconds. Long enough for her to know that situations like that brought back his own memories of when he'd been a kid and at the center of some calls out to Old Sawmill Road.

"It's a *biiig* chicken dress," Jack volunteered, his voice cutting through her thoughts. The boy flung his pointing finger at the garment.

Matt scooped him up, kissed him on the top of the head. "Sure looks like it."

"Can I play with the feathers and see the horsies?" Jack asked, aiming that question at Emory.

She glanced down at the basket. It did look appealing in the aftermath of an exploding pillow kind of way. If the basket were bigger, she might find it fun to dive right into it.

"We have to go," Matt told the boy. "Emory has to work."

Emory opened her mouth to repeat what she'd told Natalie about her not having anything that was pressing, but this was probably time that Matt wanted to spend with his son.

"I can give you some feathers if your dad doesn't mind," Emory told the boy when he repeated his request to play with them. She waited until Matt gave her the nod before she crossed the room to get one of the cloth bags with her shop's logo.

"When you're making a dress, do you ever think—this will be the one that ruins my lucky streak?" Matt asked her as she scooped up handfuls of feathers.

"All the time." No lie there.

She considered it with each project, and while she didn't want any good marriage to end, Emory often wished that someone other than herself would break the cycle. Then she might not feel like so much of a failure when it came to I dos. That was probably a prime example of really bad logic, but the thought stuck with her plenty of times when she was faced with the possibility of a new relationship.

Like now, for instance.

She handed Jack the bag of feathers and waited for his hand to dive in before she spoke to Matt. "Look, I'm giving you an out on being my date for the engagement party." Which would in turn give him an out for anything else he had in mind. "I don't want you to catch any grief from my brothers or the gossips."

Jack flung some of the feathers in the air, and the little white tuffs drifted like snow to the floor. Matt's eyes, however, stayed fixed on her. "We're both going to the party. Might as well drive together."

Drive. That's the word that dug deep into her mind. Not date. So he was setting boundaries, after all. That was good, she assured herself. Or rather, she *lied* to herself. But she couldn't fault Matt for wanting the most peaceful road he could manage.

"You've got company," Matt pointed out when they heard the sound of an approaching car. His gaze held seconds longer, and with the feathers still fluttering between them, he took Jack out through the patio doors.

Sighing over the little crack he'd just put in her heart, Emory closed the doors and went to the front of the house. One glance out the window, though, and she frowned. This wasn't one of her customers, a friend or someone who was newly engaged, but she did recognize the reed-thin brunette who stepped from the sleek silver Audi.

Frannie Parkman.

Her husband, Verney, owned the town's hardware store and was also a member of the town council. She watched as Frannie hauled a box from the trunk of her car and then made her way to the porch. Emory went to the door and opened it for her.

"Oh," Frannie said, the apology in her voice. "I was just going to leave this for you."

When she set down the box, which was sealed up with yellowing tape, Emory saw the note on top. A note that simply said, "Here are some of Candy Lynn's things that I thought you might want to look through for your research."

Emory had to thumb back through her memory to recall that Frannie's name was linked to Candy Lynn's. In fact, they'd been friends.

"Thank you," Emory said, eyeing both the box and Frannie's wary expression. "Do you want to come in?"

Emory stepped back to clear the way, but Frannie hesitated and glanced around as if checking for anyone who might be looking. At the moment, no one was there. Zeke and Zella had the day off, and Matt had taken Jack in the direction of the pasture fence, probably so the boy could see the horses.

"Why don't you come in?" Emory invited again as she lifted the box. "I was about to take a break and have an iced tea. Would you like some?"

Frannie shook her head, but with her wariness going up a notch, she did follow Emory inside. Emory set the box on the island that divided the living room from the kitchen and got herself that glass of iced tea that she really didn't want. However, she did want to find out what this visit was all about.

"There's stuff in the box that'll help with my research?" Emory asked. She kept her tone as cool and neutral as she could manage. Hard to do, considering there was nothing neutral for her when it came to Candy Lynn. Because anything and everything about the woman could still hurt Matt.

"Possibly," Frannie said.

Nothing cool about that response. The woman's dust gray eyes darted around, and she scrubbed her hands along the sides of her perky yellow dress.

"At the time of her death, Candy Lynn was renting an apartment from my uncle," Frannie went on after a couple of dragging moments. "It was just one room over the liquor store," she added in a mumble, "but he asked me to go through it and collect her personal things. There wasn't much, but I boxed them up and then put it up in the attic once I married Verney and moved in with him. Truth is, I forgot about it until you drew her name at the Last Ride Society meeting."

Emory's hand tightened on her glass. "Did you tell Matt about this?"

"No." Frannie's answer was quick. "I, uh, thought it might bring back bad memories. It certainly would for me, and that's why I didn't go through it. I haven't opened that box since the day I packed up her things."

Oh, yes, it'd bring back bad memories for Matt. But Emory wasn't sure it was her right to keep this from him. She'd need to do some thinking about that.

"Candy Lynn and you were friends," Emory threw out there. She also poured a second glass of tea for Frannie and sat on one of the stools around the island, hoping that Frannie would do the same.

Frannie nodded, did more of that nervous glancing around, and then on a heavy sigh, she finally took the stool. "We were neighbors when we were kids. And friends. Best friends," she amended. She drank some of the iced tea like medicine. "Candy Lynn grew up hard."

Emory had heard dribs and drabs about that. Alcoholic parents who'd long since moved away from Last Ride. They hadn't left a good legacy behind them. Well, with the exception of Matt and now his son, they hadn't.

"Candy Lynn married young," Emory said to prompt the woman to continue talking.

Frannie gave another nod, followed by another long pause. "She was sixteen when she married Matt's father, Johnny. He got killed in a motorcycle wreck a few months later."

"When Candy Lynn was pregnant with Matt," Emory inserted. She'd determined that from the dates of the newspaper articles and old social media posts she'd read.

"Yes. That's why they got married. Candy Lynn was pregnant." Frannie gulped down more of the tea. "I don't know how much of this you want to hear…"

"As much as you can tell me. I'm hearing a lot of gossip about Candy Lynn, but most of that talk is coming from people who didn't truly know her. You knew her," Emory pointed out.

"I did." That cause Frannie to drag in a long breath. "Look, I'm not happy about the things I did in my past, and some of those things were with Candy Lynn. But it's in the past, and I just want to make sure all of this gets put behind me. That's why I'm asking you not to mention me in the research report. It could end up hurting Verney. It could end up hurting the business."

Emory doubted everyone in Last Ride had developed amnesia about Frannie being BFFs with Candy Lynn, but she nodded anyway. "I'll keep you out of this."

That seemed to make Frannie relax a little. "All right," she muttered, and she repeated it again before she continued. "After Johnny died, Candy Lynn turned to drugs and seemed to do whatever she could to punish not only herself but also everyone in Last Ride. She believed folks had badmouthed Johnny and hadn't given him a fair shake, and she thought that's why he had such…reckless ways."

It took Emory a moment to pick through all of that, but she latched on to one gasp-worthy nugget in all of that. "Candy Lynn used drugs when she was pregnant with Matt?"

"She did," Frannie verified. Her forehead bunched up. "I tried to stop her, but sometimes, well, sometimes I didn't try hard enough. All of that was before I married Verney," she added and paused. "I know she hit Matt. And she used to lock him in his room when she went out."

Emory felt her stomach twist in a hard knot. She'd heard about the abuse and figured it must have been bad for Candy Lynn to have lost custody when Matt was fourteen.

"Matt's grandfather tried to help," Frannie went on. "He was over there a lot, making sure Matt got fed and taken care of. He wanted Matt to live with him, but Candy Lynn refused. She said she was going to hang on to the only piece of Johnny she had left."

Again, Emory had to absorb that. And stop her hands from clenching over the abuse. "I read some old newspaper articles about CPS being called in because of Candy Lynn's abuse," Emory said.

"Yes. They'd come in, and she'd straighten up for a while, and then she'd go back to her wild ways." Frannie paused, met Emory's gaze again. "It was during one of those times that she had the affair with your father."

Emory had known this would come up. Hard to skirt around it. "You were still friends with Candy Lynn when that happened?"

"Not so much. I'd just started seeing Verney, and I…" She stopped, shook her head. "I just didn't want to be associated with Candy Lynn and her antics."

That was reasonable. Verney was from a good family. A fairly well off one. And while Emory had always found Verney a little stuffy and old-fashioned, he'd seemingly weathered the gossip of marrying a woman from the wrong side of town. Anytime Emory had ever seen Frannie and him together, they appeared to be a happy couple.

"Candy Lynn called me the day before she died," Frannie went on, her words barely a whisper now, "and I told her I never wanted to see her again."

Oh, there was guilt in that confession. Maybe because Frannie thought her words had contributed to Candy Lynn's overdose, but from everything Emory had heard, Candy Lynn hadn't needed any help on her path of self-destruction.

"Anyway," Frannie said, standing and dragging in another of those long breaths, "her things are in that box. There was an old computer, one of those big ones, at her apartment, but I didn't take it. I'm pretty sure my uncle tossed it. Candy Lynn used to keep a diary of sorts on it so it's probably for the best that it's no longer around."

That snagged Emory's attention, but after a couple of seconds of thought, she had to agree with Frannie. Emory only wanted the broad strokes for the research. Best to stay clear of the nitty-gritty if she wanted to get her stomach unclenched. Plus, it was entirely possible there'd be some things about the affair, and about her father, in such a diary.

Yes, it was good that the computer was long gone.

"Just please keep your word about not including my name in any of this. Thanks for the iced tea," Frannie added, setting down her glass. She got up and headed for the door.

Emory followed her and then stood there in the doorway to watch her leave. She considered calling out a thanks for dropping off Candy Lynn's things, but this didn't seem like a thank-you kind of situation. Obviously, the drawing had dredged up some bad memories for a lot of people, Frannie included.

She waited until she'd heard Frannie drive away before she went back inside, pulled off the tape from the box and opened it. The musky scent came up like a cloud, and Emory wondered if she should have done this outside. No. Not with the possibility of Matt and Jack seeing it.

She peered down into the box at the jumbled assortment, and one by one Emory took them out and set them on the island. A small X-rated figurine of a couple having doggy-style sex. A bookmark shaped like a penis. Six paperbacks, and with these, Candy Lynn had skipped the sex theme and gone with horror. A surprise, considering the woman had likely had enough of that in her childhood.

There was a silver framed photo of a young man standing next to a motorcycle, and there was enough resemblance for Emory to know this was Matt's father. She sighed because she'd need to tell him about this box after all, since she'd want to give the photo to him.

The next three photos were all of Candy Lynn in various poses and attire. Even with all the bad things Emory knew about her, she couldn't deny that the woman had been drop-dead gorgeous with her black hair and vivid blue eyes. She'd had the alluring sex appeal of a Marilyn Monroe or a young Liz Taylor and, like those women, Candy Lynn had had the lush body to go with those looks.

Emory put the photos aside and kept taking out things from the box. Pulpboard and foam coasters from various bars. Cigarette papers that the woman had likely used for rolling joints. Matches—back to the penis theme with those because the erect genitalia were prominently featured on the box.

She kept at it, removing more matches, more bookmarks and something else that Emory quickly set aside because she thought it might be a plastic cock ring. That gave her an ew-moment. So did finding the small box from a crematorium. According to the label, it contained Johnny's ashes. Great. She'd have to really open Matt's wounds when she handed that over to him.

She made it to the bottom of the box to a large plastic bag of drawing pencils and a thick sketch pad, one with a fancy metal front and back that had Candy Lynn's name engraved on it. Emory had to take a deep breath before she opened it to the pages. She definitely didn't want to see naked drawings of Candy Lynn with her father.

But no parental nudity here.

There were several dozen pages of sketches, each with Candy Lynn's signature at the bottom of every page. The first was filled with fairly realistic drawings of dreamy blue eyes. The next, realistic renditions of mouths. Then of hands void of any jewelry or fingernail polish. Finally, of bare butts. Well, one butt anyway. Judging from the curves, it was a female derriere. Probably Candy Lynn's.

So, body parts that Candy Lynn hadn't chosen to link together to form an entire person, though, it appeared she'd had the talent to do something like that.

There was probably some kind of metaphor in the woman's choice of art, but Emory didn't want to take the time to explore it. However, she would be able to add some of this to the research. It was positive and wouldn't elicit any gossip. She could even add that Candy Lynn had shown some interest in reading and collecting, though Emory wouldn't mention the doggy-sex figurine, penis stuff or the cock ring.

Emory stood back, eyeing the assortment, and her attention landed on one of the books. Specifically, at the slight gap in the center pages of one of them. She plucked it from the stack and saw that it was a Dean Koontz novel, but when she opened it to the gap, she spotted the disk.

It wasn't a shiny CD but a very old floppy disk tucked into a paper sleeve. Emory had never actually seen one other than in pictures, but according to the date penned on the sleeve, it was from twenty years ago, right around the time Candy Lynn had died. But that wasn't the only thing written on it. Below the date was something that put a knot right back in Emory's stomach.

Candy Lynn's Sweet, Sweet Secrets.

CHAPTER SEVEN

WHILE MATT PULLED on his cowboy boots, he debated just how big of a mistake he was about to make. *Damn big*, he decided. Because his plans were still on for going to the engagement party with Emory.

Of course, he'd made a point of reminding her that they'd just be driving together, but since he wasn't an idiot, he knew it could turn into a whole lot more than that. Emory and he would be seen as a couple, which would set tongues wagging. Then again, plenty of tongues were already in motion about them so this would likely just be a fresh angle on the already existing gossip.

And the existing silence.

The day before, he'd seen Frannie come out of Emory's house and he had plenty enough memories of his mother to remember they'd been friends. Or rather partying buddies. There'd been times when Matt had woken up to find both women crashed in the hovel where they'd lived back then.

Crashed and not always alone.

Matt had gotten a very early education about sex because neither Candy Lynn nor Frannie had been especially quiet or discreet about the men they'd brought back with them after a night of drinking and doing God knew what else.

Frannie had moved on from that kind of life. Way on. She'd married a man that many considered homely, but Verney seemingly made up for his lack of looks with his decency. Verney was the polar opposite of Candy Lynn, and he'd apparently carried Frannie many rungs up the ladder of respectability when she'd married him and settled down.

Matt wondered if Candy Lynn would have ever managed to do something like that. Hard to believe since he'd been on the receiving, and viewing, end of so much of her shitty behavior.

But that was just the tip of Matt's *wondering*.

At the top of that particular list was the notion of why Frannie would have visited Emory. Since he hadn't heard even a smidge about Frannie and Emory being friends or Frannie being part of a wedding that required Emory to make her a dress, it was probably connected to the Last Ride Society research. On the surface, that seemed reasonable, but it didn't mesh with the way Frannie had distanced herself from her past. Why jump right into the middle of that past by volunteering info for a report that plenty of folks could end up reading?

With that question still circling through his head, he headed out the back door of his house to go to the cottage. What he hadn't expected to see was Zeke and Zella having Cokes on the porch while kicked back in the rocking chairs. They'd turned on the trio of overhead fans, which probably helped keep the mosquitoes away, but it was still plenty warm.

And puzzling.

Since he'd returned to Last Ride, the couple had still done their usual duties, but they'd made a habit of calling it a day around six o'clock and going home. Since it was nearly seven in the evening, they likely had a reason for staying late. A reason that didn't have anything to do with enjoying a Coke or the evening.

"Is something wrong?" Matt asked.

"Bobby Ray Carson," Zeke said, getting to his feet.

The name rang huge clanging bells for Matt. "He was one of Candy Lynn's boyfriends. He moved from Last Ride before I came here to live with Grandpa Will." Matt didn't have fond memories of the man, and Bobby Ray had used his fists a couple of times on both Candy Lynn and Matt.

Nodding, Zella got to her feet. "Bobby Ray was seen in town earlier today. Alma Parkman called us a little bit ago to let us know, so we decided to stay and tell you about it. Didn't seem right to leave you a note or interrupt you since you were getting ready for your date with Emory."

Matt opened his mouth to correct them on the *date* part. But what would be the point? Conclusions had already been drawn in that particular department, and besides, it sure as hell felt like a date, anyway.

"Did Bobby Ray say what he wanted, why he was in town?" Matt asked.

"Alma told us when she spotted him, he asked her about the drawing. He said he'd heard something about Emory drawing Candy Lynn's name."

Matt silently cursed. As the sheriff, he didn't want a lowlife like Bobby Ray being on his turf, and he figured it was too much to hope for that the man had turned over a new leaf the way Frannie had.

"We figured you might want to check up on him," Zeke added. "There's probably not much he can stir up about Candy Lynn that hasn't already been stirred, but you never know."

Nope, you certainly didn't, and Matt seriously doubted it was a coincidence that the man would be showing up now. Maybe Bobby Ray thought there was something to be earned—or hidden—from the research.

"Spread the word to the hands," Matt told Zeke. "If they

spot Bobby Ray on the ranch, I want to know about it. I don't want him bugging Emory about any of this."

When Zeke nodded, Matt thanked them both, and while he walked to the cottage, he took out his phone. He texted Azzie and asked her to do a background run on Bobby Ray Carson first thing in the morning.

Will do, Azzie immediately texted back. Enjoy your date.

Groaning at that, Matt went to the cottage door, knocked and then groaned again when Emory answered. The groan was in part because his tongue practically landed on the porch. Emory had clearly dressed to get the attention of every part of his body.

Millie had said the party was casual, and like Matt, Emory was wearing jeans, but in her case, the jeans clung to her in all the right places. Ditto for the sleeveless red top that did its own clinging to her breasts.

Her hair was long and loose, tumbling and falling over her shoulders in such a way that made him want to reach out. To brush back those strands and drop a kiss on her bare flesh.

Hell.

Yeah, this sure felt like a date all right. One that his body was hoping would end with more than just the gawking and fantasizing he was doing.

"You look amazing," she said, sliding her gaze down him as he was sliding his gaze back up her.

Their eyes collided and, of course, he saw the heat there. He wasn't sure how cool blue eyes like hers could manage to have that much sizzling heat in them, but this was Emory. The woman could accomplish all sorts of things, and that included putting huge dents in his resolve to make sure this stayed a drive instead of a date.

"You look amazing," he repeated to her.

Rather just stand there and continue to stare and lust, he motioned for her to get moving toward his truck.

"Is everything okay with Zella and Zeke?" Emory asked the moment she slid onto the seat. "They don't usually stay this late."

He took a moment to try to shake off the effects of her jeans and to figure out how to best put this. Cops were generally worrywarts in a cop-like way, that is, but he didn't want to pass that worry on to Emory until he knew if there was a problem. However, he also didn't want to blow it off as nothing. Especially since Bobby Ray might come looking for Emory.

"One of Candy Lynn's old boyfriends was in town today," Matt explained.

"Bobby Ray Carson," she readily supplied. "Alma texted me."

Matt didn't know why he was surprised that Alma had apparently made this her particular mission. Funny, though, that the woman hadn't informed him. That might have fallen into the area of her not wanting to upset him with blasts from the past, but this was one blast Matt wanted to know about.

"Is there a problem with Bobby Ray?" Emory asked as Matt drove away from the ranch.

"No, but I just wanted to give you a heads-up in case he dropped by the shop to talk to you about the research."

He waited for the springboard comment to cause her to, well, spring into a conversation as to what she should do if that happened, but Emory merely made a sound of agreement.

And the silence crawled on.

As usual, the scenery was darn good in and around Last Ride, but Matt doubted Emory had become enthralled by the stretches of summer pasture, full trees and the occasional sprigs of color of what was left of the wildflowers. He also doubted it'd keep her attention for the entire ten-minute drive to the party.

"You're dodging me," he finally said, using the very words she'd often used with him.

"Sort of," she admitted. Then she paused. "I figured you wouldn't want to talk about Bobby Ray because it'd mean talking about the research and your mother."

"True." Matt couldn't argue with that logic, but Bobby Ray could now be a current problem and not merely an annoyance from the past. "Is that why you're also not mentioning Frannie visiting you?"

"Sort of," Emory repeated. Her gaze finally swung in his direction. "Frannie gave me a box of your mother's old things."

Oh. Matt let that sink in. Added another mental *oh.* By the time he did a third mental repeat it'd morphed into an *oh, shit.*

He definitely hadn't been expecting that, and it felt a little like a punch from a pissed off heavyweight. A reaction he detested. Then again, he detested pretty much everything about the memories of his mother and the effect they had on him. He had to take a moment to tamp down feelings, to process it. To silently curse. It was something he did a lot when the subject of his mother came up.

"There's a photo of your father that I thought you might want," Emory went on, her voice barely a notch above a muttering whisper. "And his ashes."

Matt did another mental, *Oh,* followed by a punch of a whole different kind.

Considering that the man married Candy Lynn, Johnny Corbin probably hadn't been squeaky clean. Then again, plenty of men had gotten involved with Candy Lynn so Matt was willing to give his father a break. Especially since he hadn't been the one who'd created so much hell in Matt's life. Johnny died before he'd had a chance to become an asshole to his son.

"I thought Jack might want to see the picture when he's older," Emory added a moment later. "I can keep it and the ashes in the cottage, or I can give them to you."

His first instinct, an incredibly strong one, was to tell her to keep them, but that wasn't fair. Emory was just the middle man in this, and it was obviously making her as uncomfortable as it was him.

"I'll get them tomorrow," Matt told her. "Was there anything else in the box?" he tacked onto that.

Emory looked at him again, sighed. "I can bring it over with the photo and ashes, and you can see for yourself."

Her tone and expression was more than enough to let him know he wasn't going to care much for the contents. "There's sex stuff?" he pressed.

"Some. A figurine of a couple having sex, a cock ring and some penis bookmarks."

Matt was sure he frowned. He hadn't especially wanted to know *that*, and he should have better explained his question. What he should have asked was if there'd been any notes, love letters or such between Candy Lynn and any of the men she'd had in her bed. Because that meant there was possibly something about her father.

"At least I think it was a cock ring," Emory added. "Either that or it belonged to someone with gigantic fingers."

Frowning even more and *so* wishing he now didn't have that image in his head, Matt turned onto the road, passing the sign announcing the place as the Firefly Drive-in. He got an instant distraction, one that he welcomed, when he saw the huge screen already scrolling with pictures. It wasn't pitch-dark yet, but he had no trouble seeing the photo of the town square as it'd looked about a hundred years ago.

Within a few seconds, the picture shifted to a live one, a video of Millie and Joe. Obviously, someone was filming the guests and the feed was being sent to the screen. Millie and Joe both smiled and waved when they saw themselves. Then the display shifted to yet another vintage photo, this time of the town's inn.

The guests had parked on the silvery cobblestones that had replaced the grass and inevitable weeds, and folks were now milling around the two concession stands and in the large pavilion that had seating. All three areas were sparkling with tiny white lights that looked like fireflies—no doubt a tribute to the drive-in's new name.

Matt hadn't driven out here since his return to Last Ride, and the last time he'd seen the place, it'd been a dump. Millie and Joe had obviously done a great job bringing it back to life.

"Wow, it looks amazing," Emory said, moving to the edge of her seat to better take in the place.

He made a sound of agreement and parked. Matt didn't budge, though. Like Emory, he just sat there, watching the photos scroll across the screen. He wasn't surprised to see one of Joe, Brody and him in their high school football uniforms. They were grinning and holding up a trophy that the team had won for the district playoffs. Good times. Old times.

Seventeen years ago was pretty much a lifetime for both Joe and him.

During those years, Joe and he had both married and had a child, and neither was still married to the mothers of their offspring. He'd gotten divorced and Joe had lost his wife in a car accident. Now Joe had moved on from that grief, and apparently from the lousy childhood he'd had. A childhood that could give Matt's own a run for the money in the crappy department.

Even though he was parked a good twenty yards from the partiers, Matt spotted Joe and Millie in the pavilion, and yeah, there was a cameraman nearby. Joe and Millie were chatting with Natalie and Vince. Jack wasn't with them, of course. Vince's parents were babysitting him, and Matt had forced himself to ignore the little tug that gave him. He sure as hell hadn't been able to give his son another set of grandparents in addition to Natalie's folks, and he refused to resent that Natalie's new husband could do something he couldn't.

"Brody and Janessa," Emory said, pointing to the couple who appeared on the screen. They were in front of the concession stand, and they smiled and waved. Apparently, drive-in food was the theme for the party because they were eating corn dogs.

Matt would definitely want to say hello to them before the night was over, but for now he just continued to sit there with Emory. She looked at him. Smiled a little. When their gazes stayed connected, he felt the heat start to rise. Since it was inevitable, he didn't bother cursing himself or his body. Matt just let it roll right through him.

He looked at her mouth, at those lips, and he figured he could up the mistake of being with her by kissing her. His body was all for that notion, and he realized the rest of him was getting on board with it as well.

"There were other things in the box," Emory murmured.

It took him a moment to pull himself out of the brewing lust, shift gears and realize she was talking about the box Frannie had given her. "What?"

"There were some sketches of body parts and a computer disk," she explained.

He paused, trying to figure out if those three things were related. Matt recalled his mother doing some drawing. Recalled, too, her spending a lot of time on her computer. Those had been the quiet days when she'd been in between boyfriends or recovering from a hangover.

On the drive-in screen, Matt saw the photo of his Grandpa Will standing next to the sign for Stallion Ridge. A happy picture that was in direct contrast to the unhappy feelings he was having right now.

"She labeled the computer disk as 'Candy Lynn's Sweet, Sweet Secrets,'" Emory added.

Everything inside him went still. "You've read the disk?"

She shook her head. "It's for one of those old computers. I figured I could get one from Herman Keller's repair shop since he has a lot of old stuff like that." She was talking fast now, her words running together. "I could get it, read the disk and give you a summary of what's on it."

That was sure as hell tempting. But he wouldn't crap out on something like this. Plus, he could see the worry in her eyes over what she could find in something called "Candy Lynn's Sweet, Sweet Secrets."

"You think there might be something on the disk about your father?" he came out and asked.

Emory nodded. "I'm not especially eager to read anything that involves him having sex with your mother."

Matt was right there with her, but he was almost positive Candy Lynn had documented at least some of her conquests. Since Dr. Derrick Parkman would have been one of the biggest conquests of all, Matt was betting the details were there. Maybe the details, too, of how she'd beaten and nearly starved her own son. Then again, that wouldn't have been nearly as titillating for Candy Lynn as the sex stuff.

"I don't want you to read the diary alone," Emory insisted.

"Ditto," he answered with just as much insistence. Because if there was indeed stuff about her dad on there, he wanted to be there with her. "Tomorrow night when I get home from work, we'll go through the diary together."

She sighed, the sound of frustration and resignation. Emory unhooked her seat belt and finally got out of the truck. Matt did, too, and he joined her so they could start walking toward the partygoers.

"Sorry about putting a damper on your mood," she muttered.

Her own mood didn't seem especially light, and Matt was sorry for that. Damn his mother for being able to dole out this kind of misery even now.

He stopped when they were still about twenty feet away from the pavilion, and Matt turned Emory toward him. He wanted to say something to smear away these dregs, but he didn't have time to speak before Emory moved in.

And she kissed him.

It took Matt less than a second to shift gears. Then again, the lust wasn't something he needed to recoup. It was always there whenever he was around Emory, but the lust soared mountains with the heat from the kiss.

Man, he needed this. Needed her. And despite the haze from the kiss, he knew that need wasn't a good thing. Still, it didn't stop him from taking what was likely meant to be a kiss of comfort and turning it into something much deeper. Literally. Their tongues met, fooled around a little, and he got the heady jolt of her taste.

Yeah, he needed that, too.

That need was the reason he kept kissing her, kept taking more and more while he hooked his arm around her. Matt drew her closer until they were pressed against each other like perfectly fitted puzzle pieces. He for damn sure would have slipped even deeper into the heat if he hadn't heard the hoots and catcalls.

Emory and he flew apart, and despite his hazy brain and vision, Matt spotted the man who had his camera pointed right at them. And there on the big screen were Emory and him. Even though they were no longer locked together, Matt knew their kiss had just gone public.

CHAPTER EIGHT

EMORY GOT OUT of her car and wrestled the bagged feather gown from the back seat. It was finished, thanks to the three hours she'd devoted to it that very morning. The additional feathers that the bride, Madison Dayton, had insisted on made it poufy enough that it was like wrapping her arms around a squishy tree trunk.

Stumbling and cursing, she wedged her way through the back entry of her shop and managed to do a Frankenstein-style walk across the room to deposit the gown on the table near the dress form she'd use to display it for the bride. Emory hoped the woman would be coming in soon for the final fitting and to take it home because all the feathers were making her eyes itch and water.

Emory gulped down a quick cup of coffee and went from the sewing room into the front of the shop. Sometimes silence was golden. But not in this particular case. Chatter among the customers and Susie came to an immediate halt, and all eyes turned toward her.

Of course, this silence was about the kiss.

No way would thirty-two guests have kept that quiet. Well, not quiet to anyone but her. So far, no one had actually confronted her about it, including members of her gene pool, but that was in part because Emory hadn't taken any calls or answered texts from them when she'd been at the

party or even after she'd gotten home. She had given Matt
a quick good-night kiss and gone straight to the cottage.

Alone.

Matt hadn't suggested going with her, and Emory certainly hadn't pushed it. It was hard to think about having a long dirty kissing session, what with "Candy Lynn's
Sweet, Sweet Secrets" hanging over them. Hard to think
of it but not impossible since Emory had done some dirty
thinking about having Matt in her bed. But the timing had
been way, way off. Best to get the disk read, deal with the
aftermath of emotions, and then they could decide if they
were going to be bedmates.

She figured Matt would have a definite no in the bed-
mate department. Or rather his logical mind would want
to say no. A whole lot of trouble could come out of it. But
lust often stomped on trouble just for the fun of it. On common sense, too.

"Uh, are you okay?" Susie ventured to ask.

That's when Emory realized she was just standing in
the doorway and probably had a blank stare on her face.
The four customers, all young women that Emory knew
by sight, had been browsing the stock, but they were now
obviously waiting to hear her answer to Susie's question.

"I'm fine," Emory assured them.

It wouldn't nix any gossip, no chance of that, and soon
it would be all over town that she was in a funny mood or
some other obvious observation. With her watery feather-
reddened eyes, the observers might think she'd been crying.

Emory fluttered her fingers toward the sewing room.
"I'll be in the back finishing up Millie's dress."

Emory turned to retreat, but the front door opened and
Tiffany Parkman rushed in. Either the woman had a very
rosy glow or the summer heat had gotten to her. Of course,

Tiffany looked a lot better than she had slightly less than a month ago when she found out about her cheating groom-to-be and had stripped to her underwear on Main Street.

"I'm getting married," Tiffany blurted out.

More silence, and Susie's and the customers' attention shifted from Emory to Tiffany.

"Congratulations," Emory said, and she hoped it hadn't sounded as if she'd added a question mark after that.

Tiffany thrust out her hand to show Emory the huge diamond. Emphasis on *huge*. The thing had to be at least four carats, and it sparkled enough to trigger eye twitches.

"Keaton and I worked things out," Tiffany gushed, "and he gave me this ring to make up for what he did."

Since the guy had cheated with his fiancée's friend, Emory hadn't thought a ring, any ring, would have made up for that, but it wasn't her place to judge. However, she did get a tingling feeling about this, and she doubted the ring's sparkles were responsible for it.

"I can't use that old dress," Tiffany went on. "So, I want you to make me a new one. Will you do it? Please, please, pretty please with a cherry on top, will you make it?" The woman was tiptoe bobbing and had her hands clasped in mock prayer.

Bingo. Emory had been right about the tingling. She seriously doubted that Keaton would mend his cheating ways enough to make this marriage last "until death do us part" stage. That meant this could be the end of Emory's "mostly good luck" streak for wedding gowns. It could also be the beginning of validation that Emory wasn't the Typhoid Mary of brides. That, in turn, might make her feel less guilty about starting up something with Matt. She didn't want to believe in bad karma and juju, but it was certainly a head-shaker that she couldn't create her own happily-ever-after when she'd done it, in part, for so many others.

"Of course I'll make the dress," Emory assured her. "We can schedule an appointment to sit down so you can tell me exactly what you want—"

"I want this." Tiffany whipped out a magazine from her purse and tapped the gown on the cover. A beaded one with elaborate cascading ruffles and tiny lights. Yes, lights. They twinkled through the yards of lace on the ruffles.

Emory studied the picture. "The dress might be too wide for you to walk down the aisle at the Methodist church," she pointed out.

"Oh, we're not getting married there. Everything will be different about this wedding. My dad's redoing the barn on my grandparents' ranch. It'll be polished and lavish. Out with the old, in with the new," Tiffany declared.

Emory wondered if that meant no bachelor party for Keaton, but she merely smiled and nodded at the other wedding details that Tiffany rattled off. The rattling continued even when Emory's phone rang. When she saw Matt's name on the screen, she knew it was a call she wanted to take.

"Excuse me a minute," Emory said, motioning for Susie to come over. "Go ahead and schedule Tiffany for an appointment for a fitting and consult so she can choose fabrics." She handed Susie the magazine. "I'll be right back."

While she hit the answer button on her phone, Emory hurried into the sewing room. Since a conversation could still be overheard from there, she went out the back door to a shady sitting area she'd set up for lunch breaks.

"Herman Keller only has parts for the old computers, not a complete one that's functioning," Matt said without a greeting. "There's an old computer with a power cord in the storage room here at the police station." He paused. "What size of disk was in the box?"

She had to bring up the image of it in her mind. "I'm guessing maybe about three or four inches."

He muttered what sounded like profanity. "The slot for this one is larger than that."

Too bad because Emory could definitely see the advantage of not having to go to anyone else to find the right system to read the disk. Anyone else they brought into this could start a new thread of gossip. Gossip that could get back to her parents.

"Do you happen to remember what kind of computer Candy Lynn had?" Emory asked. "Frannie said it got tossed, but if you remember the brand, we might be able to find one on eBay or some site like that. We wouldn't have it by tonight when we wanted to read Candy Lynn's diary, but we could possibly get it soon."

There was a short silence where Matt was obviously giving that some thought. "Sorry, but I just can't remember. She was pretty territorial about it and never let me use it."

"Probably because she didn't want you to read any portion of 'Candy Lynn's Sweet Secrets.'" She sighed. "Let me run home, measure the disk." She'd tucked it back in the book and left the stack of paperbacks on her desk. "Then I can do a search on the internet. One way or another, we'll find out what Candy Lynn wrote in that diary."

Though Emory still wasn't sure that was the right thing to do.

The diary felt a whole lot like Pandora's box. Once opened, there was no telling what might spill out of it. But it had also become a shiny, irresistible lure. And with reasoning, which might or might not be total crap, the disk might explain why the woman had led such a miserable life.

"Don't make a special trip home," Matt said after another pause. "We can come up with a solution tonight."

"Sounds good. I can fix us some dinner."

His next pause was a whole lot longer. "That sounds a little like a date."

"Yes, it does." And she left it at that.

"I'll see you tonight," he finally said, and he ended the call.

Smiling a little, Emory turned to go back inside, but she gasped when she saw the man watching her. And there was no doubt in her mind he'd been doing just that. No doubt, either, as to who this was.

Bobby Ray Carter.

Emory had some vivid memories of the man when he'd lived in Last Ride, and the years had been especially kind to Bobby Ray. He'd kept some of his "golden boy" looks. She estimated he was in his midfifties, but he could have passed for someone a decade younger.

He smiled and, tipping his cowboy hat in greeting, came closer. "Sorry, didn't mean to startle you."

Oh, he'd done more than merely startle her. He'd given her the tingles and not in a good way. Emory tried to replay the conversation with Matt, to figure out what she'd said that Bobby Ray might have overheard.

He could have heard plenty, she decided.

Then again, there was likely nothing in that diary that would be a surprise to him since he had been Candy Lynn's boyfriend.

"I'm glad I caught you out here," Bobby Ray added a moment later. He grinned in a nonthreatening "I'm a good ol' boy" kind of way. "I didn't like the notion of going into a wedding dress shop to see you."

"You wanted to see me?" Emory asked. Despite the bad

tingle, she made sure she met his gaze and kept her chin up. That was the advantage of having two hard-assed brothers. She knew how to stand up to men like Bobby Ray. Well, if standing up to him was actually needed, that is.

He nodded, kept a sliver of the smile in place. "I thought you'd want to interview me for the research you're doing about Candy Lynn."

"I do," she lied. "Maybe we can set up a phone conversation." Emory checked the time. "I can't interview you now because I have a bride coming in for a fitting." Part lie, part truth. A bride was coming in that afternoon, but she had plenty of time before that. She just didn't want to spend that time alone with Bobby Ray.

"All right," Bobby Ray agreed. "You want to key in my number, or would you rather give me yours?"

"I'll key yours in." She did that as he rattled it off. Later, Emory would decide if she'd actually call him or not.

"You know, Candy Lynn really messed over a lot of people," Bobby Ray said, causing her gaze to go back to him. "Me, included. I was in bad shape for a while because of her. Not that I'm holding grudges. I'm not. I'm a changed man, and I might not be where I am today if I hadn't had to wade through all of her muck."

Emory didn't know what kind of changes he meant, but it was obvious the man was well-off. Or at least was giving the appearance of that with his pricy alligator boots. The Stetson didn't appear to be a cheap knockoff, either.

"I figured you'd have to include my name in that research report," he went on, glancing down and muttering something under his breath that she didn't catch. "I just want to make sure you get the story straight."

She thought of Frannie, of the woman's insistence that her name not be included in the research. Bobby Ray wasn't asking for exclusion, but it was obvious he was concerned about what might come up.

"Well, I'll be going so you can get back to your work." Bobby Ray tipped his hat, turned and walked away. "Call me when you can manage that interview."

Emory had a quick debate with herself as to what to do about his visit before she texted Susie.

I need to run an errand. Can you handle the shop by yourself for the next half hour?

Susie was quick to reply. Can do.

Emory didn't head for her car. Nor did she intend on going home to get the disk size. Not yet, anyway. She walked around the shop, peering onto the sidewalks for Bobby Ray. Thankfully, there was no sign of him, so she started walking toward the police station.

When she passed by the grocery store, she heard some teenage boys make kissing sounds. She also got a few knowing smiles. Even a wink. Emory ignored them all and ducked inside the police station.

The receptionist, Thelma Baker, glanced up and went back to the game she was playing on her phone, but Emory didn't pay much attention to her, anyway. That's because her attention zoomed in on the woman in Matt's office. Kerry Watkins, the owner of the pet store, Fowl Feathered Friends.

The woman's pet macaws, Dorothy and Toto, were squawking and flapping their wings while they darted around the room. Kerry was dashing to round them up while Matt stood, hands on hips and shaking his head. Azzie was standing by, too, giving Kerry a baleful look as only Azzie could manage. A third deputy, Brian Warner, who was the youngest of the police force, was beside her.

Fowl Feathered was an apt description for the bird duo who were better suited to the names The Wicked Witch and Flying Monkey than Dorothy and Toto. They were constantly escaping, and then lying in wait to fly into other businesses when a door was open. Once inside, they created havoc in the form of bird droppings and broken merchandise. The wedding shop was one of the few places on Main Street that hadn't been hit, and Emory hoped it stayed that way. She'd met her quota of feathers for the year.

"They don't mean any harm," Kerry pled to Matt. "Honestly. They just don't like being cooped up."

"They have to stay cooped up," Matt answered in his flat cop's voice. "And you're going to have to pay for the damages done to the hardware store. Verney's not very happy with you right now, and he wants the mess they made cleaned up."

Kerry gave a mopey nod and managed to latch on to one of the birds. Matt snagged the other. He got bit in the process, and he cursed when he handed Toto, or maybe it was Dorothy, off to its owner.

"My advice," Azzie snarled, "go ahead and get them back to your shop before they cause any more damage."

Stepping closer, Emory saw some of the damage. Horseshoes had been knocked off the wall and were now on the floor. Of course, with the abundance of horseshoes in the office, it would have been hard for the birds to fly in any direction without knocking down some.

With a macaw in each arm, Kerry came out, giving Emory a cautioning look. "He's not in a very good mood."

Emory wasn't sure if she was talking about Matt or the

macaws because one of them gave her a squawk and, in Emory's opinion, the beady eye.

Matt looked up when he spotted Emory, and for an instant she saw the surprise flash over his face. Azzie did short volleying glances at both of them and promptly excused herself.

"I'll see if we've got anything in the supply cabinet to clean up bird crap," Azzie told him. "Watch where you step," she added to Emory as she and her fellow deputy exited the room.

Emory took that advice to heart when she went in Matt's office. She immediately saw three splats of poop and figured there were more.

"Trouble?" he asked.

As always, Emory had to get past the zinger of attraction for the hot cowboy cop. A zinger that even Dorothy's and Toto's poop hadn't managed to dampen. It wasn't especially comfortable, but whenever she was around Matt, her heart fluttered, her stomach flip-flopped and it took her a moment to remember to breathe.

The man was certainly potent.

She nudged his potency aside. Well, as aside as she could manage, considering he was right in front of her. "Bobby Ray overheard our conversation about your mother and the disk," she whispered.

Emory watched the stages of him process that. The surprise, the concern and finally the pissed off cop's response. "What the hell was he doing at your shop?"

"I was outside because I didn't want to be overheard." Like now. That's why Emory glanced over her shoulder to make sure no one was listening. The only person in the squad room was Thelma who was still hunkered over her phone.

"Did Bobby Joe threaten you or something?" Matt demanded.

"No," she quickly assured him. "He said he was there to offer me an interview for the research, that he was worried about how he'd be portrayed in the final report."

Matt's sigh might have been of relief, and watching where he stepped, he closed the door. "I had Azzie do a thorough background check on Bobby Joe. He has a sheet but nothing recent. His last arrest was fifteen years ago for drug possession, and he's been clean since then." He paused. "He's a clown."

Emory did a mental double take. "You mean like an actual clown?"

Matt nodded and glanced at the report he had on his desk. "He's Squeaky the Clown on a TV show."

Emory required another double take. Not because Squeaky didn't ring any bells. It did, *he* did, literally. He was a very annoying bell-ringing clown on a show called *Kiddie Palooza*. Ian and Theo had clamored to watch it when they were little, and Greer was still a fan.

"Well, no wonder he's worried about the research on your mother," Emory said, shaking her head. "Parents would balk if they knew their little kiddos were watching a convict. How'd he ever get a job like that with his police record?"

"I'm guessing the producers thought he'd cleaned up his act."

She cringed at that because she recalled an episode of Squeaky squirting strawberry jam at some other clowns in one of the skits. Ian, who'd been five or six at the time, had tried to reenact the scene with Theo. Emory had been babysitting them and had to hose them down in the yard.

"Apparently, the bad vibe I got about Bobby Ray was way off," she muttered.

"You got a bad vibe from him?" Matt had shifted to the cop mode again.

Emory waved it off. "It's been a strange day, what with the itchy eyes from the feathers and people making kissy noises." Matt didn't question that one bit, which made her smile. "You've been getting kissy noises, too?" she asked.

His mouth went flat. "Apparently, our big-screen debut is all over town. How much flak are you catching about it?"

She was about to say none at all, but the knock on the door stopped her. So did the voice she heard. "Sheriff Corbin?" her mother called out. "I need to speak to you."

Crud. So, apparently dodging her mother's texts and calls hadn't been a good ploy after all since the woman was here to see Matt.

Matt opened the door that he'd just closed moments earlier, and Emory turned, expecting her mom to be shocked or angry that she was there with Matt.

"Is it true?" her mother asked, her gaze sliding from Matt to Emory.

Well, at least her mom hadn't made mocking kissy noises. "Yes, Matt and I kissed at Millie and Joe's engagement party," Emory admitted.

While that didn't seem like news to her mother, and probably wasn't, her mom didn't jump into a lecture about why future lip-locks between Matt and her shouldn't happen again.

"Not that," her mother said, her tone more than a smidge scolding as she looked at Emory. "Though that is something I want to discuss with you." She shifted her attention back to Matt. "I was asking about Candy Lynn's diary. Is it true? Did she leave one behind?"

Emory was still trying to figure out how to answer that when Matt spoke up. "What makes you think she did?"

"This," her mother said, pulling a piece of paper from her purse. "Someone left this on the windshield of my car. I found it just a couple of minutes ago."

Matt took the paper, and Emory moved closer to read it for herself. "Bury the past by burning Candy Lynn's diary disk," the message said.

And it was signed Squéaky the Clown.

CHAPTER NINE

MATT GLANCED AT the clock. It was over two hours past when his shift should have ended, and while he didn't mind staying late, the truth was he didn't have any pressing work to do. He was putting off going home and dealing with "Candy Lynn's Sweet, Sweet Secrets."

AKA her pain in the ass diary.

It didn't please him that he was dodging, and he felt guilty that Emory was probably at the ranch, waiting for him. Especially since she'd let him know the exact size of the disk, and he'd texted her to tell her that he'd found an adapter for the old computer in the supply room. An adapter that should allow them to read the diary.

Emory had responded to that with a thumbs-up, but before that Emory and he had done a lot of actual talking and texting. Not with just emojis, either. In the past eight hours or so since her mother, Nancy, had dropped the Squeaky bombshell and then left the police station, Emory and he had talked plenty about why Bobby Ray would have done something like that.

Or if he'd actually done it.

It seemed stupid for the man to wave a red flag around like that, especially since Nancy hadn't even known about the diary. Well, she probably hadn't. Matt wasn't getting a good feeling about any of this, but he didn't have enough info to stretch that lack of a good feeling into something sinister.

Bobby Ray likely would want such a diary destroyed. Heck, so would Emory's father and any other man in town that Candy Lynn had slept around with. In fact, Matt was hard-pressed to think of someone who might want such a document to be read or preserved.

After Emory and he had chatted about all of that, she'd had to get back to the shop. But after she'd left, Matt had put in some time trying to track down Bobby Ray to find out if he had indeed sent that message to Nancy.

Matt had managed to get the clown's number from Emory, but all his calls had gone straight to voice mail. If Matt hadn't reached him by tomorrow, he'd have Emory give it a try. Bobby Ray might be doing his own dodging by not wanting to speak to a cop.

Forcing himself to move, Matt picked up the bulky computer that he'd tucked behind his desk and hauled it up. The timing was good because the receptionist was gone, and the two on-shift deputies, Hogan Dayton and Ollie Bellows, were out on a call; a resident had complained of an escaped cow trampling her garden. Only Azzie was in the squad room, and she'd volunteered to stay until the other deputies returned.

"I'm guessing you got something you want to read on that old computer," Azzie commented as he came out of his office. "Anything I can do to help?"

Matt considered just blowing that off, but it occurred to him that Azzie would have been a deputy at the time of his mother's death. Plus, the woman wasn't prone to gossip.

"When my mother died, do you remember anyone saying anything about her keeping a diary?" he asked.

Azzie thought about it a moment and shook her head. "I don't recall anything like that."

"Were you involved in the investigation?" he pressed.

"Sure. We all were. Not many suspicious deaths around here, so Sheriff Lyle had all of us working on it. That would have been me, Ollie and Ty," she said naming the current deputies who'd been around twenty years ago. "We had three more who've since retired." She named those off as well before she paused, eyed him. "Why, you think we missed something?"

"No," he assured her.

Though they had missed the disk during what should have been a thorough search of Candy Lynn's residence. Well, they had missed it if it'd been there at the time. Matt was getting that not so good feeling again.

He really didn't want to question Frannie about all of this, but it would probably be a smart thing to talk to her. It was possible the woman had concealed the disk and then included it in the box of things she'd given Emory. Unfortunately, Matt couldn't think of a smart reason for her to do that. If she'd been worried about what was in the diary, Frannie could have just destroyed it, and no one would have even known it existed.

"Any chance we still have the reports of that investigation?" Matt asked Azzie.

"Sure. Not here, though. About ten years ago, Sheriff Lyle had all the records moved to a big storage room in the courthouse. You want me to get the files for you?"

No, he didn't want that, but like the conversation he should have with Frannie, it needed to be done. Of course, there was no way to keep it quiet that he'd be taking a look at those files, which meant there'd soon be speculation that he was reopening the case. Heaven knew what kind of crap that would stir up, but he'd sworn to uphold the law. While there hadn't been a crime connected to his mother's death, that note left on Nancy's car was a clear sign that somebody wanted something to stay buried. Usually that pointed to something embarrassing or illegal.

"Get the files when you have a chance," Matt told Azzie as he headed out. "No hurry." That was because the diary might keep him busy for a while, and he didn't want to dig into what would be multiple wounds at the same time.

Matt hauled the computer to his truck, and he started the drive home. He immediately tried to shift from cop to rancher mode since he knew in the next couple of days he'd have to put in at least a couple of hours doing paperwork for Stallion Ridge. Added to that, he wanted to check on some new horses that'd been delivered the weekend before. If he had to take on double duty, he wanted to take the time to enjoy the good parts about being a ranch owner. The horses were the good part.

His phone rang, and he smiled when he saw Natalie's name pop up on his Bluetooth screen. Because he knew it wouldn't be Natalie but rather Jack. He got confirmation of that when he hit the answer button on his steering wheel and his son's voice poured through the truck.

"So," Jack started, as if they'd already been talking for a while, "can I have a pony?"

That only widened Matt's smile. Since he'd just been thinking about spending some time with the horses, he couldn't fault his son for wanting the same thing. But he had to tread carefully here. Natalie didn't want Jack riding until he was a little older. Added to that, this pony request wasn't a first. It came up nearly every conversation.

"A toy pony?" Matt asked, knowing it was going to cause his son to groan.

"No. A pony that poops."

Jack would zoom in on the pooping part. Matt had let the boy *help* muck out the stalls, and it hadn't deterred the boy one bit from wanting his own defecating animal.

"What'd Mom say about this?" Matt countered.

"No," Jack admitted on a heavy sigh. "Can I have a puppy?"

Natalie had nixed that, too, believing Jack wasn't old enough for that kind of responsibility. And he wasn't. But that didn't mean Matt couldn't help Jack learn those responsibilities, and Natalie probably wouldn't care as long as the dog stayed at Stallion Ridge. Matt made a mental note to put a trip to the county animal shelter on his list.

"Get five gold stars on your charts, and then we can see about the puppy," Matt suggested.

Natalie had a gold star chart thing for pretty much everything she wanted Jack to do, so it shouldn't be hard for the boy to get five.

Jack let out a whoop and then immediately said he had to go. Probably so he could get started on earning those stars. Matt worked in an "I love you, buddy," before Jack ended the call.

Feeling a whole heck of a lot better than he had just ten minutes earlier, Matt pulled into his driveway just as the sun was setting. He also set an alarm for forty-five minutes so he could call Jack to tell him good-night. It was one of their nighttime routines that Matt hoped his son would want to continue for years. He might not be there in his room to put Jack to bed, but he wanted to be part of that.

He half expected to see Emory on his porch waiting for him, but because there was no sign of her, he first went inside his house to grab a beer from the fridge. He ended up taking the entire six-pack and downed half of one of the bottles before he set the rest on her porch and went back to his truck to get the computer. Since that required both of his hands, he used the toe of his boot to knock.

"Come in," Emory called out.

"Can't. My hands are full."

He heard her footsteps, some mutters and what he thought was some rustling around. The kind of rustling when things were being hurriedly moved around. It occurred to him then that she might have someone inside with her. Maybe a man.

It also occurred to him that he felt an unwanted punch of jealousy.

Hell. That was what he got for kissing her, for lusting after her. For—that thought snapped down shut when she opened the door while wearing a wedding gown, and Matt had to repeat his mental *hell*.

"Come on in," she said, immediately turning away from him. "This won't take long."

Matt cautiously stepped in and surveyed the scene. Emory was wearing a wedding dress all right. A wide poufy one, and it was open in the back.

Wide open.

From nape to an ample amount of her butt cheeks. Matt was able to see plenty of skin, the back of her bra and discovered that she either had on no panties whatsoever or the pair she was wearing were supremely skimpy. His body was intrigued with both possibilities.

"This won't take long," she repeated, scooping up a fake flowered bouquet the size of a truck tire.

Once Emory had the bouquet clasped in front of her, she proceeded to walk between rows of lit candles of varying sizes. And scents. Matt picked up on fruit, flowers, coffee, wood and some kind of baked goods.

She'd arranged the candles in a walkway between her living room and kitchen. Not a long distance, but she didn't make it one step before the pouf gown bowled over the first two candles. The flames didn't go out, and in fact, some of it sparked onto the gown.

Cursing, Emory batted out the embers with the bouquet, tried another step and cursed some more when two more candles went down. She tossed the bouquet on the counter and groaned.

"This isn't going to work. Madison Dayton will have to come up with another idea for her walk down the aisle," she grumbled.

Ah, he got it, then. This was some sort of dress rehearsal. One that had obviously engrossed her and taken plenty of time to set up.

Hiking the dress up to well above the candles, and therefore up to her knees, Emory threaded her way out of the walk of flames and then turned around. She blinked as if just remembering he was there.

"Sorry," she muttered. "I didn't forget about the disk. Or that you were coming," she went to him. "Let me help you."

"I've got it," he insisted when she reached for the computer. "But grab the beer I left on the porch."

She went in that direction. Matt tried to talk himself out of looking. Tried and failed. He watched the fabric shift and shimmy as she walked and felt a huge mountain of lust when he still didn't see any panties.

Emory brought in the beer. "Thanks for this. I got busy so I had pizza delivered if you're hungry."

He was hungry all right but not for food. Man, he wanted her, and he supposed this level of heat was a major miracle, considering he'd come here to read Candy Lynn's tell-all.

"Put the computer on the desk in the corner of my sewing room," she instructed as she set down the beer next to a pizza box. "Let me get these candles blown out, and I'll be right in."

When she leaned down, she must have felt the breeze on her skin because she reached behind her, felt her lack of clothing and cursed again.

"You have to do this sort of thing often?" he asked, going toward the sewing room. The cottage was small so he had no doubt she'd be able to hear him during her candle blowing.

"Often," she verified. "Most of the churches in Last Ride were built over a hundred years ago. There's not a lot of aisle room. Especially not a lot of aisle room for a bride who wants to walk through tea lights on the floor. I'll have to recut the gown."

"Or you could go with flameless candles," he pointed out.

"That's a no-go. The bride wants actual fire to symbolize her relationship with her soon-to-be husband. Sort of a metaphor, I suppose. One that'll cause a nonmetaphorical five-alarm blaze if I don't convince the bride to go with a sheath. You're sure you don't want to learn to sew and help me redo an entire dress?"

"I'll pass. I've still got those calves to castrate. Maybe some deworming to do."

"Fun times ahead for both of us," she joked.

He set down the computer and turned as she came in. She had the pizza, beer, some paper plates and napkins. Her expression was a lot more focused, too.

"How much of my butt did you see?" she asked.

Matt should have said *enough* and left it at that, but the heat was still fueling his brain and made him say something stupid. "Much less than I wanted to see."

He grinned.

She didn't. Well, not at first anyway. Then she chuck-led. "Well, avert your eyes, or you'll be seeing more. Let me change out of this, and I'll be right back."

Because he was still firmly in the stupid mode, Matt had no intentions of averting anything that gave him a further glimpse of her backside, and he smiled as she sashayed out of the room. Of course, the lust encouraged him to go after her, but he didn't want to leap into sex with Emory.

Okay, he did.

He really wanted that. But the timing was way too bad for that. So Matt drank more beer and started setting up the computer. He'd plugged it in at the station, just to make sure it still worked before he hauled it all the way to the cottage. It'd booted up just fine and hadn't required a pass-word. It also wouldn't need to be connected to the Wi-Fi to read the disk, which was a good thing because the unit was too old to have a Wi-Fi card.

Once he had the computer on and ready, Matt glanced around the room. Like the other times he'd been in here, there were gowns on the headless mannequins. Other dresses, too, that he supposed were for mothers of the brides. But it was the pint-sized cowboy outfit that caught his attention. Jeans, leather chaps, a vest and even a cow-boy hat.

"It's for Jack," Emory said when she came back in.

She was wearing a summer cotton dress the color of a blueberry. Proving that stupidity didn't need naked butts to be interested, he felt another punch of lust. Until what she'd said sank in.

"For Jack?" he asked when her words got through his whirling thoughts about her.

Emory nodded, went to the small mannequin and gave

the chaps an adjustment. "He's the ring bearer for Natalie and Vince's wedding, and he wanted to dress like a cowboy. A heads-up," she continued, "during the fitting, he told me that he wanted to wear it when he rode his pony."

The boy was planning ahead, and Matt hoped he didn't change his mind and want to wear something else when he got a dog instead of a horse.

"Have some pizza," Emory insisted, taking them both out a slice. She took a big bite of hers while she kept her gaze on him. "This isn't a solid tit for tat, but I confess I saw you mostly naked."

He stopped midbite of his slice. "Excuse me?"

"Two mornings ago when you came running out of your house to shoo away the rooster on your back porch. You were wearing only your boxers, so I saw you mostly naked."

He did indeed recall some rooster-shooing because the darn thing wouldn't quit cock-a-doodle-dooing. Matt hadn't known, though, that Emory had witnessed all of that. He doubted it'd caused as much of a heat storm in her as it had when he'd seen her back and butt.

Or maybe it had.

Her little smile said there had definitely been some tit for tat going on. Whatever the heck that meant. He wanted to hang on to that smile. On to the heat and especially hang on to the memory of the peep show she'd given him. But the disk was like the mother of storm clouds hanging over their heads. She must have seen that, too, in his eyes because she sighed.

"All right. Let's eat, drink and not be merry." She pulled the disk from her purse that was on the desk and handed it to him. "If the disk is password-protected, let's agree to destroy it."

He shook his head. "Can't. Not because I'm hell-bent on

reading what's there," Matt quickly added. "But if there's anything that pertains to her death, I can't just ignore it."

That cooled the heat, and he saw the worry creep into all those shades of blue. "Because you think someone might have helped her into the grave."

Matt shook his head again. "No, I think it was an overdose, plain and simple, but I can't put on blinders."

Not even if that's exactly what he wanted to do in this case.

Sighing again, Emory washed down another bite of pizza with some beer and sank down into a second chair she dragged from the corner. Matt took the seat directly in front of the monitor and, after taking a deep breath, he slipped in the disk. After a few clicks and the whirring sound of the computer hard drive the file popped on the screen. As advertised, the document was titled "Candy Lynn's Sweet, Sweet Secrets."

"Holy Moly, it's nearly six hundred pages," Emory pointed out, tapping the page count at the bottom of the screen.

Apparently, Candy Lynn had had a lot to say. Perhaps even more than on this single disk because, according to the date above the first entry, she'd started this particular diary about thirteen months before her death. Matt would have been thirteen then, and it hadn't been a pleasant time to be under the same roof with Candy Lynn. Since that'd also been when he'd been beaten up by Ryder and Ruston, it hadn't been a pleasant time out from under her roof, either.

He scrolled past the date, not sure what he'd find, but the first entry started off in a much more normal way than he'd imagined.

"A new diary, a new day," his mother had written. "And a new man." She'd added six exclamation marks to that.

"Greg Betterton's picking me up soon. Got high hopes for this one, so that's why I'm starting this new diary."

Matt remembered Greg. He'd been one of the hands at Colts Creek, one of the biggest and richest ranches in the county. Since the man hadn't tried to punch or belittle Matt, he didn't have a lot of memories of him. The next entry, Matt saw why. A week later, Candy Lynn hadn't mentioned Greg but had instead talked about a date she was having with another man. *Date* in this case was no doubt a euphemism for sex and/or drugs.

He didn't bother to read the details of what Candy Lynn had been planning to wear for said date. And he skipped over the next rant over her losing her job at the diner. However, the skipping stopped when he got to an entry with his own name.

"That shit kid of mine needs to be taught a lesson, and I taught it all right," she'd written. "I smacked him upside the head with my purse and told him if he ever sassed me again, I'd kill his sorry ass. I should just go ahead and give him to his precious Grandpa Will. The bastard wants the brat, and that's why he's not going to get him."

Considering all the things Candy Lynn did to him over the years, getting smacked with a purse was tame. Still, it'd caused Emory to suck in her breath, and she slid her hand over his.

"I would say I'm sorry, but I don't think you'd appreciate that," she muttered.

No, he wouldn't. He could stomach gossip before he could pity. Matt eased her hand away so he could keep scrolling. It didn't take him long to get to the account of her scoring some drug or another. Other blatherings of hating her *bastard father*. She'd spliced that with almost perky details of another date, a new boyfriend or an outfit she'd bought.

"Why didn't Candy Lynn get along with your grandfather?" Emory asked.

Matt had had a few conversations about that with Grandpa Will, and while Candy Lynn had disputed some of the facts, she just hadn't been very credible.

"Apparently, she had a problem with teenage drinking and getting into trouble. He figured it was because she'd lost her mother when she was young, so he got her into counseling. Candy Lynn would ditch the sessions to get high with her friends." Matt had to pause. "I think they had a lot of clashes over the years. Plenty of them about me."

Emory made a sound of agreement, and she stopped him from scrolling by clamping her hand over his. "I'm torn between wanting you to destroy the disk or just to read all the hundreds of pages and getting it done. Like ripping off a bandage. Then you can put it aside and never think about it again."

Fat chance of that. It'd be an especially fat chance if there was something connected to her death. For instance, if Candy Lynn had given the name of the person who'd supplied her the drugs that'd ended up killing her. There be a lot of bad stuff before that, of course. And maybe not just bad for him. Matt wasn't forgetting that Emory's father might have made some star appearances in this diary.

"Here's what we can do," Matt suggested. "We'll do a word search for your father's name, and we can glance through those. Then I'll read the rest of it some other time."

She'd definitely caught on to him. "I'll read it," she insisted. "All of it. There's nothing in there that'll make me think less of you," she assured him.

Maybe, but there were probably things he didn't want

her to know about the abuse. Her leveled stare told him she was well aware of that, too.

"How about we just skip to the last few pages?" Emory suggested. "Then tomorrow night we can argue or discuss how to go about reading the rest of it."

Since the last pages would be the ones that could name her drug supplier, Matt could see the logic in that. Still, he intended to read every word of what Candy Lynn had written. He just didn't intend to do that with Emory around. For now, though, Matt did go to the last ten pages and began to scroll through those.

The entries had been written shortly after she'd lost custody of Matt, and there were lots of rantings about that. Those mostly cursed Grandpa Will. But there were also some lines about how much more fun she could have now without having to deal with a smart-mouthed kid.

Emory made another of those sounds of sympathy, but Matt could have told her that having his mother call him names didn't sting. A lot of the sting had been soothed over simply because he hadn't had to live with her any longer.

Matt kept scrolling through the rant until some words jumped out at him.

"The son of a bitch threatened to kill me," Candy Lynn had written. "The SOB said either my signature or my brains were going on the papers, but either way he was getting custody of the brat."

The SOB in this case was Grandpa Will, and Matt hadn't known about the threat. He'd only known that Candy Lynn had finally quit trying to get him back. Despite all the crap written in the diary, that made him smile a little. Yeah, Grandpa Will had done right by him. Of course, then that caused the smile to fade because Matt couldn't say the same. He definitely hadn't stuck around to return that doing right by the grandfather who'd saved him.

Emory moved his hand aside, scrolled to the last entry. There was no rant. Just a short entry about her going to a party. There was an almost manic description of what she'd be wearing and how she was pissed off at Frannie, who wasn't going so she could "suck up with the rich bitches." The following day, Candy Lynn was found dead from the overdose.

So, no smoking gun with the name. Of course, the supplier could be somewhere in the other five hundred plus pages.

"Let's save the rest for tomorrow," Emory insisted.

Matt didn't want to do that. He wanted to plow through it now. Alone. He'd just have to figure out a way to get Emory out of the picture.

"I'm not leaving," she said. Either she'd developed sudden ESP or he wasn't wearing his poker face tonight. "But let's play a game."

He was about to tell her that he wasn't in the mood for games, but then Emory shucked off her dress, leaving her in just her bra and panties. He'd been right about the skimpiness of the panties. Barely there. Barely. Ditto for the bra. The tops of her breasts rose high above the swatch of white fabric and lace.

Apparently, his body was interested in this particular game. Even if his brain shouldn't be.

"You should rethink this," he warned her. Not easily, but he managed to say the words, though, he wasn't the least bit sure he actually wanted her to do that.

"This isn't strip poker or sex." There was a *duh* in her tone. She went to the large garment bag that was bulging on the hanger rod, unzipped it and pulled out the feather dress he'd seen her working on. "The bride started sneezing like crazy when she tried on the dress so it has to be, well, plucked. No sewing involved, just plucking, so let's make a game of it."

Again, he was about to go with a repeat of rethink this, but she yanked out the feather garb and slipped it on. The bride clearly wasn't as busty as Emory because even unbuttoned, the bodice still clung to her. It was so distracting that he forgot all about a game. Hell, he forgot how to speak. But Emory filled him in on the rules.

"If you can pluck off at least three dozen feathers in the next five minutes, then we'll read more of the diary. If you fail, no more diary pages tonight."

It was a stupid game. Or at least that was his first thought. It was quickly followed by a second thought that by plucking, he'd get his hands on Emory. Something he was suddenly itching to do. Plus, he'd win. That dress had at least a thousand feathers on it. No way could he not get three dozen in the next five—

She took off running.

Frowning, Matt stood there for a couple of seconds, until he heard Emory giggle. That giggle sounded like some kind of "nanny nanny boo boo" challenge, and cursing her and himself, Matt took off after her.

The cottage was small so it wouldn't be hard to find her. Or so he thought. But she wasn't standing out in the open in the living room or kitchen. He checked behind the sofa, the chairs and the kitchen island. Not there. And the back door that led to her small porch was locked. Still, he wouldn't put it past her to have sneaked out there so he checked and found no sign of her. Gathering up a couple of feathers as he walked, he headed elsewhere in the house.

Toward her bedroom.

Now, since he wasn't an idiot, he knew that going into Emory's bedroom was risky. Especially since he was trying to play hands-off with her. Well, he was attempting that, anyway. His hands had a totally different notion, and it was those particular parts of his body, and others, that nudged him to continue the search.

The bedroom door was wide open, and Matt flicked on the light to peer in. The decor was a bit of a surprise. He'd expected something bridal-looking with maybe pastels and lace. Or something cottagey. This was more suited to a trendy loft in a big city. Brick-and-wood interior walls, minimal furniture, and the bedding was the color of a glass of merlot. Maybe because she worked with brides all day, she wanted the opposite when it came to her own space.

No Emory in sight, but there were a couple of feathers on the floor. He gathered those, too, while he checked under the bed, though he was pretty sure she wouldn't have fit while wearing that poufy dress. Since his mind was already spinning with a lust haze, he considered that she might have stripped it off.

Failing with his "under the bed" search, he went to the closet. It wasn't much of a walk-in so it didn't take him long to see she wasn't there, either. He glanced around, but there was no piece of furniture wide enough to conceal her.

He caught her scent. Not the feathers. But Emory's scent. And yeah, it did a number on that still spinning lust haze. Of course, just about anything about her right now would fuel that.

With the seconds ticking away, Matt went back in the hall, considering for a moment if she could have managed to squeeze through a window. But then he heard the rustling in the bathroom. He pushed open the door just as he heard Emory say, "Time's up."

She somehow managed to hop out of the claw-foot bathtub. Yes, hop. And laughing like a loon, she launched herself into his arms. Suddenly, he had more than enough winning feathers in his hands, but the realization of that dimmed considerably when her hot clever mouth landed on his. Not for a victory peck. Not this. It was hard, hungry and thorough. It lit even more fires inside him that Matt didn't even know were capable of burning.

Emory hooked her arms around his neck, and Matt anchored himself against the doorjamb to stop them from tumbling out into the hall. Though tumbling could end up being a good thing, for now he just kept on kissing her. Kept on tasting and taking and making the most of what she'd turned into incredibly intimate contact.

She laughed again when she pulled back a fraction and looked into his eyes. "You lose," she reminded him.

"Yeah, I'm all torn up about that." And it was somewhat of a miracle that he could make light of anything connected with the diary.

Emory was responsible for that. She'd pulled him out of that swamp of memories, and while it wasn't a permanent fix, Matt would take it for now.

"So," he drawled, nipping her bottom lip with his teeth. His phone dinged with the reminder for him to call Jack. "I don't like the word I'm about to use, but you and I should have a summer fling."

"Matt, I don't know how to break this to you," Emory said, chuckling again, "but we already are."

CHAPTER TEN

EMORY HAD LOOKED up the definition of *fling* in the dictionary. A short-term sexual relationship. So, not exactly what was going on between Matt and her. It was more of a pre-fling with kisses, skyrocketing lust and interrupted plans.

Multiple interruptions.

It'd been four days since they'd made that fling pact and agreed to do a nightly read of some pages of Candy Lynn's diary, but life and pretty much everything else had gotten in the way. Matt had had to arrest a suspect in a San Antonio robbery who was holed up with his cousin on Old Sawmill Road. That'd involved paperwork and transporting the guy. Then Jack had gotten strep, which meant Matt had been spending a lot of his off-duty time with the boy.

Emory didn't begrudge that one bit since she'd found herself tied up with remaking Madison Dayton's unfeathered wedding dress. Basically, she'd had to start from scratch and was still working evenings to get the one thousand Swarovski beads added to the gown's bodice. If Madison turned out to be allergic to those, then she might end up going naked down the aisle. The woman had plenty of money to cover the costs, but Emory was wearing a little thin working with her.

"You could at least appear to be having fun," Emory heard her mother say.

Emory looked up from her plate and realized she had all

eyes on her. Her father, mother, brothers, their wives and one of her three nephews. The two nephews who weren't there, Ian and Theo, had wormed their way out of this family dinner by claiming to have other plans with friends.

Since a droll *I'm having fun* would just sound snotty, Emory crammed a large forkful of green beans into her mouth and muttered something she was sure they wouldn't understand. That's because it was gibberish. While she chewed, she glanced around, hoping that someone would change the conversation. That didn't happen, though. Happy conversation and accord weren't on the menu for this particular dinner.

Her brothers' wives, Heather and Stacy, were as far apart as they could get at the table since they despised each other, and they often blamed the other for the trouble their sons had a penchant for finding. Her brothers were clearly pissed, maybe at each other, maybe at Emory. Her three-year-old nephew, Greer, was trying to stuff green beans in his ears. A feat he accomplished until his mother, Heather, interceded and yanked them out. And Emory's mom was trying to pretend that they had the picture-perfect life.

Ah, family.

Yet another reason Emory had found herself short of time lately. She figured it was some kind of intervention to try to stop her from seeing Matt, because ever since the drive-in movie kiss, she'd gotten multiple visits, calls and texts from everyone in her immediate gene pool except her nephews.

"You'd better not be mooning over the sheriff," Ryder snarled.

Ah, family, Emory mentally repeated. "Mooning over?" she repeated aloud. Nothing would have melted in her ultracool mouth or the look she gave her thug-head of a brother. "Does that have something to do with astronomy?"

In contrast, everything would have melted in Ryder's mouth where the temp soared to furnace-level heat. "You know what I mean."

"Ryder," their father cautioned before Emory could load up enough mashed potatoes to fling into his lap. She'd gotten good at that over the years, and even though she was in her thirties, she hadn't outgrown the need to match asinine behavior to counter-asinine remarks.

"There's all kinds of talk—" Ryder started, but that was as far as he got because of their dad's scalpel-sharp glare.

"Talk will die down when you quit bringing it up," Emory managed to sneak in for her brother before she got her own dose of their father's glare.

But it was true. Well, maybe it was. She hadn't heard any recent gossip about Matt and her. There was some chatter about the clogged sewer pipe at town hall that had caused two toilets to explode, one of them while Jasper Hennings was sitting on it. It was hard for Matt and her to compete with fodder like bruised balls and damaged johns.

And Emory was thankful for it.

She'd had a lot on her mind, what with the looming fling and the diary. She was looking forward to the first. Dreading, the second. Dreading it so much in fact that she'd nearly broken the pact she'd made with Matt and read some of it on her own. She hadn't done that, but she'd nearly rationalized if she read it ahead of him, she might be able to cushion any blows Matt might get from the other entries.

Of course, that rationalization was BS.

It was just as likely she'd get her own blows if there was anything incriminating in there about her father, and there was that whole deal about not breaking a pact with her fling partner. Hardly a good start to what would no doubt be a brief but incredibly satisfying relationship.

So, Emory had put the disk back in its sleeve and tucked it into the rarely used zippered sections of her organize-all purse that she'd bought off a home shopping channel one night when she'd had insomnia. It felt a little like carrying around a petri dish of Ebola or some other vile stuff, but she hadn't wanted to leave it lying around since she often did fittings and met customers in that room.

When Emory heard the scrape of chairs on the hard-wood floor, she looked up again and realized there were no longer any eyes on her. They'd obviously finished their meal and were getting up from the table. However, Ryder did get in a few mutters that were likely meant for her, and Ruston got in a disapproving glower. She gave him her own glower version—a sappy sweet, glazed-eye look she often gave bridezillas when she was tuning them out and wishing she could fling mashed potatoes at them.

Ryder did some muttering, too, after their parents and the wives started gathering up the dishes. "You should just accept you're bad news when it comes to men," Ryder grumbled to her.

That was possibly true, but it was so not the right thing to say to her. Neither was what Ruston tacked on to that.

"If you want another man in your life, look in a better direction," Ruston advised.

"A better direction?" she repeated and didn't keep it at a murmur. "You mean someone who isn't a self-made man, a decorated cop, amazing father and the owner of a successful ranch? Yes, I can see why you'd want me to steer clear of that."

That tightened Ryder's jaw so taut she could have

bounced quarters off it. Which she wouldn't have minded doing. "Matt's Candy Lynn's son," Ryder reminded her.

"Yes," Emory repeated, "and he didn't have a say in that. Just like I don't have a say in having assholes for brothers." She aimed her index finger at them and would have almost certainly spouted off more, but she felt a hand clamp on her arm.

"Why don't you come help me in the kitchen, Emory?" her mother murmured.

Emory heard something in her mom's tone. One that let her know this wasn't just something to break up yet another sibling argument. Because arguing with Ryder and Ruston would accomplish nothing except upsetting her folks, Emory let her mother lead her into the kitchen.

"Emory and I need to talk," her mom immediately said to her father, Stacy and Heather.

Just like that, they scattered like flies. Possibly so they could get out of kitchen duty, or maybe it was because Nancy rarely made a request like that. It might have been twenty years since the woman had had a mental breakdown because of her husband's affair, but everyone still treated her with kid gloves.

Her mother waited until everyone was out of the room, and she turned Emory to face her. "Did Matt get a chance to ask Bobby Ray if he left that note for me?" she whispered.

Emory had to shake her head. "I don't think so. Matt's been really busy for the last couple of days." But not so busy that he wouldn't have texted or called her if he'd managed to speak to Bobby Ray. "I can mention it to him tonight when I get back to the cottage."

"No, I don't want to put you out like that," her mother insisted.

That was mom-code for "I'd rather you not see the man

who lives only yards away." The man Emory had kissed until her eyelashes had curled. Her mother probably suspected the kisses and equally suspected that more of it would happen if Matt and she got closer than those few yards of distance between their houses.

"And the diary?" her mother pressed. "What became of that?"

Emory didn't want to open this smelly kettle of fish tonight. "Matt and I are still going through it. There's nothing earth-shattering."

"So far," her mother qualified. She sighed loud and long enough to extinguish a small fire. "I don't suppose you'd consider just destroying it? I mean, do you really have to read about what that woman left behind in a diary?"

Again, hoping to tap down a smelly fish kettle, Emory was about to assure her that everything would be okay. But the voice cut off that possible lie.

"What diary?" someone asked.

Ryder.

Emory groaned because she hadn't heard her brother creep up behind them. Emphasis on *creep*.

"Candy Lynn left a diary?" Ryder demanded.

This time, Emory was fast with the lie. "No." And she told that whopper while looking her brother straight in the eyes.

"I heard you say diary," he argued.

"No, you didn't." Again, the lie came easily and was somewhat satisfying since this was Ryder. "Mom and I were talking about...diarrhea."

And Emory wished she'd blurted out something better than that. Still, it stopped Ryder, and she could see him mentally repeating whatever he'd overheard. Thankfully, though, he didn't press it because the doorbell rang.

Ryder didn't budge, but their mother did, and hoping to dodge further conversation with her brother, Emory went with her to answer it. Unfortunately, so did Ryder, and when her mom opened the door, Emory saw Matt on the porch.

Not alone, either.

Her nephews, Ian and Theo, were on each side of him, and behind them stood another boy that she thought might be Cameron Byers. It was hard to tell because all three teenagers were covered with feathers.

"Ryder," Matt said in his flat cop's voice. "Get your brother, because as you can see we've got a problem."

MENTALLY, MATT IMAGINED he was with his SWAT team as they neutralized a hostage-standoff situation. The adrenaline would be pumping. The stakes sky-high. Lives would be on the line.

But he wasn't there.

Instead, he was sitting in a butt-numbing chair at town hall, listening to complaints from the citizens of Last Ride. Stupid complaints in some cases.

The mayor had insisted Matt be present at the monthly meeting, that it was good for morale for folks to know that their sheriff would do whatever it took to resolve their problems and keep them safe. And he would. The badge wasn't just lip service for him. But that didn't mean he couldn't daydream about that rush of doing something more important than listening to Ginger Parkman gripe about ruining her new shoes when she stepped in macaw shit after Dorothy and Toto's most recent adventure.

Before that, the pressing problems had been whether or not to buy new Fourth of July decorations and what kind of roses should be planted in the town square to replace the bushes that'd gotten trampled when several cows had broken the fence.

Apparently, escaped animals was a recurring issue here.

Matt's mind circled around that, circled around the lack of adrenaline and finally the circling stopped when the image of Emory flashed in his mind. Now she was an adrenaline fix of a whole different kind.

It'd been a week since Emory and he had started listening to Candy Lynn's diary. A week since they'd kissed and started their so-called fling. A busy week of work for both of them, capped off with Jack getting sick and Matt having to haul in Ian, Theo and their equally idiotic rival, Cameron, for having another glue-glitter fight. He'd arrested Emory's nephews this time since they hadn't heeded his other warning about stupid pranks, and while the boys hadn't actually stepped foot in a cell, they'd have to go before the judge.

That wouldn't endear Matt to Ryder and Ruston.

But it couldn't be helped. Neither could the time Matt had spent with Jack. He'd wanted to be with his son when he was sick. Now that Jack was better, though, Matt didn't have an excuse not to go to Emory's tonight.

His body buzzed at that thought. Or at least he thought it had, but he realized it was his phone that he'd put on silent. When he checked the screen and saw Bobby Ray's name, he knew it was a call he'd have to take.

Giving the mayor a nod, Matt stepped outside. It was steamy hot with a storm moving in, and despite it being nearly seven o'clock, the temps were still in the nineties.

"I've left more than a dozen messages for you," Matt *greeted* Bobby Ray.

"Yeah, I got them." The man's tone wasn't defensive.

"Sorry, but I was just trying to work out things before I talked to you."

"And by working out, do you mean leaving a note on Nancy Parkman's car?" Matt pressed. His tone wasn't defensive, either, but he was going with the kick-ass attitude. The clown had pissed him off by dodging him, and Matt figured that meant he had something to hide.

"No." This time Bobby Ray sounded surprised. "Did she say I'd done that?"

Matt went with a cop dodge of his own by not answering the man's question. "You overheard Emory's conversation about the diary, and then minutes later a mystery note appears on Mrs. Parkman's car. Hard to believe you weren't behind it."

"I wasn't. I swear I didn't do that."

"But you overheard Emory talking about the diary," Matt snapped, and he walked farther away from the doors when people started to trickle out. Since the meeting was obviously breaking up, Matt tipped the brim of his hat in a farewell gesture to the mayor and headed to his truck so he could finish this conversation in private.

"Yes," Bobby Ray admitted after a very long pause. "I heard Emory, but I also remembered Candy Lynn talking about her diaries. She told me that one of her boyfriends got drunk and trashed her computer. After that, she started putting the diary on a disk."

Of course, his mother would backup something that most folks wouldn't especially want preserved.

"When was this?" Matt asked. Because then he could figure out if they had more "Sweet, Sweet Secrets" disks floating around out there.

"Probably about a year or so before she died," Bobby Ray answered.

So, judging from the dates of the entries on the disk Emory had, maybe this was the one and only. Good. Because even if the other diaries had held the secrets of the universe, Matt wouldn't want to wade through them.

"I didn't treat Candy Lynn right," Bobby Ray went on as Matt got into his truck. He started the engine and cranked up the AC. "Didn't treat you right, either."

"No, you didn't." And Matt had to clamp down on a few memories of the man's fist ramming into his face.

"I'm sorry about that, and I don't want our bygones to play into what's happening now."

Matt took a moment to process that. "You mean you don't want me to use anything incriminating I might learn about you from Candy Lynn's diary."

The man's long silence confirmed that. "Look, you probably know this already, but I'm on a kids' show, and I haven't told the producers about my past. They know I have a record," he quickly added, "but they also know I haven't been in trouble in years. I don't want to ruin the good thing I have going on right now."

Matt totally got that. None of his fellow cops in Amarillo had known about his past. He'd started there with a clean slate where he hadn't been that kid from the wrong side of town who'd had Candy Lynn for a mother.

"Can I have a look at the diary?" Bobby Ray continued. "Just to make sure there's nothing in it that'll embarrass me?"

"No." Matt didn't have to give that any thought. "I'm still going through the entries one by one to look for something that hasn't outlived the statute of limitations."

"That's seven years, right?" the man asked, and there were nerves in his voice. Matt imagined he was sweating, maybe literally and metaphorically.

"For most crimes." And rather than beat around the bush, Matt came out with a direct question. "Did you supply Candy Lynn with the drugs that killed her?"

"No," Bobby Ray practically shouted. "God, no. I had nothing to do with that." He paused again. "But your mama and me did use together. That might be in the diary. And I hit her a couple of times when we got into it. That's probably in the diary." Another pause. "She might have put in there the times I hit you, too."

Bingo, and Matt knew where this was leading. It wouldn't do for it to come out that Squeaky the Clown had punched a kid. Those offenses were well past the seven-year point, but they would taint the hell out of his reputation.

"I just don't want you using anything she wrote about to try to get back at me," Bobby Ray added.

"Trust me, if I find something incriminating about you, I won't be using it for payback. I'll be using it because it's the law."

Matt knew that wouldn't please the man, but Bobby Ray didn't voice that displeasure. He muttered a terse goodbye and hung up. And that left Matt wondering just what the man had done that was making him so nervous. Maybe it was just the reputation thing at stake, but as a cop, this whole conversation made Matt want to dig deep to find the truth. Even if that meant digging through crap that would twist his insides like a puzzle.

Of course, there was a legal problem with actually using the disk or anything on it to go after Bobby Ray or anyone else. There was no verifiable chain of custody to prove that Candy Lynn was the sole person who'd written the diary. Or that she'd written it at all. Matt knew the entries were hers, but knowing and proving it were two different things. Still, the damn thing could ruin a lot of lives.

He started the engine and drove toward Stallion Ridge. It was an hour or more before sunset so there were still people out and about on Main Street. A few of those folks gave him waves and nods. Progress, Matt supposed, when he got a larger than normal number of greetings, and he wondered just how long it'd take him to get rid of most of the stench from his mother. No doubt a lot longer than he wanted, and not for the first time he hoped none of this spilled onto Jack.

Matt pulled into his driveway just as Emory came out of her cottage. As usual, he felt the heat from looking at her, but he also felt his dark mood lift a bit, too. That wasn't good because he didn't need to be relying on Emory for mood enhancement. Still, that beaming smile she gave him caused him to smile back.

"I've got a quick errand to run," she said when he stepped from his truck. "Then, if you're hungry, I made lasagna."

He was hungry, but the lasagna would have to be the precursor to getting through some of the diary. Matt didn't want to put that off any longer, especially after the conversation he'd just had with Bobby Ray.

"I'd like to go through some of the diary entries while you're out," he suggested. "Any problem with that?"

She blinked, pushed her hair from her face. "Uh, you're sure you want to do that alone?"

"I'll just skim and look for anything important."

Emory studied him, probably looking for any signs that it would bother him to do that. It would. But it would bother him even more if he didn't know what his mother had written.

"All right," Emory finally agreed. She unzipped one of the many compartments on her purse, extracted the disk and handed it to him. "I won't be long. I just have to drive out to the cemetery and get a photo of Candy Lynn's head-stone. It's for the research report."

Matt froze with both of their hands still on the disk. He recalled Emory mentioning that a photo would be needed, but with everything else going on, Matt had put it out of his mind. He didn't put it out now, though.

"It'll be dark soon," he pointed out. "Why go tonight?"

"Because it's supposed to rain for the next couple of days, and I have a busy week coming up at the shop."

"But you have two more months left to do the research," he argued after quickly doing the math.

Emory shrugged. "I want to get it done. I won't be long," she added, heading for her car.

Matt followed her. "That cemetery is on Old Sawmill Road. I just made an arrest out there."

"Yes, I heard. Good. That means there won't be any bad guys around."

He scowled at her tongue-in-cheek tone. "I'm going with you," Matt insisted, getting into the passenger's seat when she got behind the wheel. He handed her back the disk.

Emory took it, but she didn't turn on the engine. She tucked the disk back into her purse, sat there and stared at him. "I wanted to do it alone because I figured you didn't want to see her grave."

"I don't, but I don't want you out there alone, either."

She didn't budge. Emory kept staring a few more seconds before she huffed, put on her seat belt and started her car. She waited until Matt had belted in before she drove away.

"Have you been to her grave before?" she asked.

"No. Haven't been there since she died." There was no need to mention that he'd always said hell would freeze over before he did go. Apparently, making sure Emory was safe overruled hell-freezing scenarios. "Grandpa Will went a couple of times, and I know he bought the headstone."

Emory nodded, sighed, drove. "Well, if this bottoms out your mood, we're going to have to play a variation of pluck the feathers again."

That caused some stirrings in his body, but there was little chance that such a session would end with just a kiss. Nope. This fling was moving fast in the direction of the bed. Or the floor. While Matt had to admit that would cause complications, he was beginning to accept that it was inevitable.

In the distance, he saw some lightning vein through the sky, and he would have liked to use the storm as an excuse to try to convince Emory to turn back. But the bad weather was still miles off, and it wouldn't take but a few seconds for her to snap a picture.

Since Old Sawmill Road was only about three miles from Stallion Ridge, it wasn't long before they started passing some very familiar terrain. Definitely not as appealing as most of the other areas in and around Last Ride. There were no sprawling ranches here. No big homes with perfectly manicured lawns. This place had started out in poverty over a hundred years ago and stayed there.

"It's called Burnt Woods Cemetery," Emory murmured. "Any idea how it got that name?"

He was pretty sure the small talk was meant for him. To help him settle his nerves. But it wasn't nerves he was feeling. It was just more of the dread that came with anything related to Candy Lynn.

"According to what I heard, about a hundred years ago, some wood at the sawmill caught on fire, and the wind whipped up the flames into the forest," Matt explained.

"A lot of the acreage burned, and it took a while for the area to recover."

Recover being a relative word. The forest had regrown, the sawmill had continued for another seventy years or so and people had rebuilt the houses they'd lost, but the place had never shaken the name of Burnt Woods.

"I recall going to the cemetery once when I was a teenager. A dare," Emory added when he looked at her. "Because there are legends about the place being haunted."

Yeah, there were, but Matt had never seen a ghost. However, there could be a drunk or two. A couple of times he'd found Candy Lynn there, drunk or high while lying on his father's grave. Or rather by his tombstone since his father had been cremated. Something that apparently Candy Lynn regretted because shortly after his death, she'd had a tombstone made for him.

Matt figured a purportedly haunted graveyard might be a hangout for a new generation who was acting on dares, getting high or both. A few years back, some idiots had even gotten caught setting up a crude moonshine distillery just a few yards away from the graves.

The sky had darkened some by the time they reached the turnoff for the graveyard. Unlike the ones in or closer to town, this one didn't have a nice paved drive. It was dirt and gravel and poxed with potholes, but thankfully they didn't have to go far. After just a couple of seconds, Matt saw the headstones come into view.

He didn't get easily spooked, but he had to admit it was downright creepy with the approaching storm, the occasional lightning on the horizon and the "gray as death" tombstones scattered across the grounds. Emory might have gotten some of that same spooked feeling because after she parked, she just sat still, peering out.

"According to the info I accessed, Candy Lynn is buried there." She pointed to the right side of the cemetery.

Matt made a sound of agreement. "All the way in back by the fence line. She's buried next to my dad's headstone."

"Oh." Her gaze swung to his. "Will that be a bad memory for you?"

"It's all bad memories here," he muttered, getting out of the car.

He hated that he'd put that look of worry on Emory's face. Worry that she'd likely anticipated, which was why she hadn't wanted him to come with her. But he would have been a hell of a lot more troubled had she come here alone.

"This way," he said, leading the way. Not at a slow strolling pace, either. While he kept watch around them for drunks and such, Matt threaded his way through the other graves until they made it to the back.

And there they were.

The double tombstones for his parents. For a father, he'd never known and a mother he wished he hadn't.

"When I was a kid, I'd come here and look at his tombstone even though I knew he wasn't actually buried here," Matt admitted, tipping his head to Johnathon Corbin's headstone. He swatted a mosquito.

"He was eighteen," Emory murmured, doing some mosquito swatting of her own.

His dad had been just a kid. A stupid one to have gotten involved with Candy Lynn. Matt liked to think that had he lived, his father would have outgrown that stupidity. He dragged in a long breath, an audible one, that must have alerted Emory because she whipped out her phone from her purse, aimed it and clicked off a couple of pictures.

"Done," she said. "Let's go." Batting away at the mosquitoes, she caught onto his hand and moved them at an even faster pace to get out of there.

"I'm okay," he assured her.

She made a sound that could have meant anything, but she probably thought he was lying. When they reached her car, she shifted her purse to her shoulder and turned to him.

"Let's make some new memories here," Emory said. "I dare you to kiss me."

Matt frowned. "I don't need a dare for that."

"The dare adds to the ambiance," she insisted.

He doubted that, especially since there was no ambiance, but it was hard to resist a kissing offer, even a bad one, what with Emory standing right there in front of him. Matt ignored the heat, the bloodsucking bugs circling them and the fact that they were in a creepy graveyard. He pulled Emory to him and took the challenge.

Of course, the real challenge was to get out of this without losing a pint of blood, risking heatstroke and not to get carried away. All of that was hard to do, especially the last one, because, simply put, Emory had a mouth that made him want to beg for more. A mouth that sank right into the kiss.

The taste of her gave him a real kick. A hot solid one that caused the heat to skyrocket. Touching didn't help cool that heat, either, but again that didn't cause him to stop. Matt hooked his arm around her, pulling her closer and closer until their bodies were touching nearly as much as their mouths.

Her breasts were soft and warm against his chest, and he got a flash image of her stripping to put on that feather dress. He hoped she was wearing equally skimpy underwear tonight. Hoped, too, that he'd get the chance to discover that for himself.

Slapping at more bugs, he turned her, pressing her back against the car. Anchoring them so he could deepen the kiss, so he could press even harder against her. She didn't protest. Just the opposite. She fisted one hand in his hair and slid her other arm around his waist as if holding him in place. If he hadn't had his tongue in her mouth, Matt could have told her he had no intentions of going anywhere.

Man, this felt good, and it notched up the need in his body. Need that suddenly felt very urgent, very necessary. Very now.

But now wasn't going to happen here. He could already feel the bug bites itching, and it was possible they had indeed reached his pint limit for blood loss.

Easing back, Matt shook his head to clear it. Not too much, though. He wanted the buzz from the heat. However, he didn't want that in the graveyard. It was one thing to make new memories here. Damn good memories. But he didn't want to have sex with Emory on the hood of her car. Well, not the first time anyway.

"Come on," he said, giving the mosquitoes one last swat. "Let's take this back to the ranch."

CHAPTER ELEVEN

THIS WAS THE longest drive in the history of long drives. Emory was sure of it. She wanted Matt's mouth back on hers. She wanted his body to press into her as he'd done against her car just minutes earlier. But for all of that to happen, she had to get back to Stallion Ridge in one piece, and that was the only reason she wasn't groping him and trying to pull him onto the seat with her.

So much for that stupid dare of creating new memories. It had accomplished that all right, but now she felt like a teenager who'd taken a lust bath.

Matt wasn't saying anything from the passenger's side of the car, but the hot glances he kept giving her were enough to give her an orgasm. Nearly. Of course, she wanted the real deal orgasm with him as soon as they got back. Then once the lust was sated…

Well, she didn't know what the next move would be. But flings weren't just a one-time deal. She hoped not, anyway.

"Thank you," she ground out to the powers that be when she pulled into her driveway.

The moment she had the car in Park, she turned to reach for him but Matt beat her to it. He had his arm around her before she could blink. Somehow, he managed to get off her seat belt and haul her into his lap. All in all, it was an amazing place to be.

And speaking of amazing, she got her wish when he

kissed her again. She hadn't thought there could be anything hotter or hungrier than the ones he'd doled out at the cemetery, but she'd obviously been wrong. Hot and hungry were still going strong.

Fumbling and likely giving Matt some bruises, Emory unhooked his seat belt without breaking the kiss. Since she was already on his lap, she did some adjustments. Straddling him, she got a prime jolt of pleasure as the centers of their bodies met. Sweet torture to have the long hard length of him pressing against just the right spot on her panties.

She suddenly hated panties. And jeans. Emory extended that hatred to any fabric that separated her from Matt. Extended even more to include the confined space of her car. Too bad she didn't have a van, which would have given them the room to have a real go at each other.

Of course, that "go" could happen in one of their houses, but even though those structures were only yards away, she wasn't sure either of them were capable of walking. She certainly wasn't with her head spinning, her body on fire and with her hands too busy to do anything like open a car door.

Opening Matt's shirt was much, much more fun.

While she sucked on his bottom lip, she went after his buttons. One by one. It was like a slow torturous reveal, and she made sure she did lots of touching along the way, her palms sliding across all those incredible muscles of his chest.

He had chest hair. She'd already seen that when she'd witnessed his rooster-chasing while only wearing his boxers, but seeing had been a tiny tasty morsel of goodness compared to having her hands on the real deal. The man was built, and Emory was burning from the anticipation of touching other built parts of him.

Matt did his own touching, which of course rocketed

the burning and heat. He shoved up her dress and created his own slow torturous pace with his hands gliding up her thighs and to those panties she hated. Her breath caught. Her heartbeat whiplashed. And she nearly got the orgasm when his fingers caught onto the elastic top of her panties.

And he dipped inside.

Kissing her neck, his fingers went lower, lower, lower. Until he was in exactly the right spot to make sure that orgasm happened.

Then he stopped.

Emory heard herself whimper, and it took her a moment to get her eyes focused so she could see him. And the lights. It took a couple more moments for her to realize those lights weren't from the blinding heat of this kissing, touching fest. Nope. There was a car pulling into the driveway. A very familiar car.

"It's my father," she managed to say after she'd whimpered out a few more sounds.

Her father had the absolute worst timing in the galaxy, and Emory wished she could teleport him somewhere else. Since teleportation wasn't in her particular skillset, and since she didn't want her dad to witness her straddling a man in her car, Emory climbed off Matt's lap. He helped her with that. Then he somehow managed to steady himself enough to pull down her dress and button his shirt.

"How do I look?" Emory asked Matt. Her voice was rushed, and she was breathing like an asthmatic. Still, she could hope a miracle had happened and that she wouldn't look as if she'd just been on the verge of having car sex with the sheriff.

Matt gave her a once-over, frowned. "He'll know what we've been doing."

Crud. The only thing worse than acknowledging parental sex was having those parents witness firsthand that she, too, did such things. Or rather would have done such things if her father had delayed his visit another fifteen minutes.

Emory did a quick check in the vanity mirror and then groaned when she heard her father's car door shut. There was no time to fix herself up, but she was hoping the darkness would conceal the worst of it. One look at her father when she stepped out, however, and she knew the dark had failed her.

Her father seemed to stop in his tracks, eyeing her first before his gaze shifted to Matt, who also got out of the car. Even the night didn't keep her from missing her father's suddenly tight jaw.

"Are you going somewhere?" her dad asked, and yes, there was a boatload or two of concern in that question.

"Just got back," Emory explained. "Matt went with me to take a photo of Candy Lynn's tombstone for the research. He didn't want me going out there alone."

Her father's expression took on a different kind of emotion. Alarm mixed with a smidge of relief. He actually nodded at Matt in a sort of thank-you gesture. Matt nodded back just as his phone rang.

"I have to take this," he said when he looked at the screen, and he headed toward his house.

Emory didn't think his quick exit was because he'd wanted to avoid her father. No. Matt wasn't the kind of man to do a dodge like that.

"We need to talk," her father said, drawing her attention back to him.

That was obvious, and whatever he wanted to say, he'd intended for it to be just between them.

"Does Mom know you're here?" Emory asked.

"No," he answered, glancing off in a weary kind of

way. "I'd appreciate it if you didn't tell her. She's worried enough."

Emory nearly asked if her mom was troubled over the note someone had left on her car, but she wasn't sure her dad knew about that. If so, this was a double-dodge situation, and she hoped she didn't trip up and let the dual cats out of their bags.

She motioned him toward the porch, took a few steps and had to scratch her leg. Darn mosquito bites. The moment she was inside, she went to her kitchen junk drawer and got some anti-itching cream.

Her father came in, shut the door, but he didn't sit. He went on the prowl, walking slowly from the foyer to the fireplace to the window.

"Did you want to talk about Ian and Theo?" she came out and asked.

His look told her that his grandsons and their latest glittered-balls incident had not been high on his mental list. But then she hadn't thought it was. No, if he'd been troubled about Ian and Theo, he probably would have said something to Matt when he arrived.

Emory finished doctoring her bites and washed her hands. "Would you like something to drink?"

Her father shook his head, continued to prowl a couple more seconds before he finally looked at her. "Tell me about Candy Lynn's diary."

Oh, so this wasn't a warning for her to avoid Matt. Or at least it wasn't one yet.

"I heard you and your mom whispering about it at the family dinner, and then I recalled Candy Lynn telling me that she kept a diary."

Even though Emory knew about her father's affair, it nipped away at her to hear him talk about the woman.

Which wasn't very often. Still, the nip was there over the words "telling me." She preferred to believe there'd been no talk between the two, only hot quick sex that had meant nothing to either one of them. But if Candy Lynn had mentioned the diary, then there'd likely been conversation to go along with all that sex that Emory didn't want to think about.

"You have her diary," her father said. Not a question. So the cat had made its exit from the bag, after all.

She nodded. "One of them, anyway. The last one, apparently. Frannie had a box of Candy Lynn's things, and she brought it over after the Last Ride Society drawing. The diary disk was in there."

"I'd like to read it," he insisted.

Emory would have bet the shop, every penny in her bank account and a lifetime supply of Oreos that he was going to say that. Which meant she should have already anticipated giving him an answer that wouldn't keep him pushing to read something that he shouldn't read.

"Not a good idea," she insisted right back. "I'm going through it, and so far I haven't even found a mention of you. Mainly, she talks about going to parties and hitting Matt."

Emory winced a little at that last. That wasn't hers to tell, but she was betting it had not come as news to her father. Or anyone else in Last Ride for that matter. But she hoped her father could breathe easier that, so far, he hadn't made a star appearance in "Candy Lynn's Sweet, Sweet Secrets."

"If there is anything about you," she went on, "it won't come to light." She hoped. It wouldn't come to light from her, anyway. Emory paused, took a risk by adding, "Matt just wants to make sure there's nothing in the diary that's connected to her death."

And she watched her father's face carefully.

If he was alarmed that there would indeed be a connection, especially a connection to him, he wasn't showing it. "I don't want your mother to know about anything that woman wrote," he said several moments later.

Emory couldn't make a sound of agreement fast enough. Her mother wasn't a strong person, and there was no need for her to relive that horrible time in her past with accounts of her husband's affair.

"You never asked about what went on between Candy Lynn and me," he continued. "Thank you for that."

Since Emory had been on the verge of asking just that, she had to shift conversational directions a little. "Candy Lynn was a beautiful woman," she settled for saying. "I figured that played heavily into you seeing her."

He made a sound of agreement, and she thought he might be going back to that time and place. Not a good time and place, considering the way his forehead bunched up. But she didn't need him to fill in the blanks to see how it'd played out. Candy Lynn would have been at least ten years younger than him, and she'd had that whole "forbidden fruit" deal going on.

"Yes, she was beautiful," he admitted, "and she made me feel…well, things I hadn't felt in a while. I'd fallen into being a husband and father, not that I was unhappy with that," he quickly added. "But she made me feel I was missing out on something. Something that only she could give me."

Now they were in the ick zone, and Emory hoped he didn't get into details of Candy Lynn offering sex stuff that Nancy hadn't. That's why Emory didn't prompt him to continue, and she cut him off with, "I've got the picture, Dad."

"Yes," her father said on a heavy sigh. He stayed quiet a long time, but he didn't have an expression of a man taking a trip back through his sexual past but rather one mentally tiptoeing through his sexual embarrassments.

"What will happen to the diary once Matt and you have gone through it?" he asked.

"Matt will probably want it destroyed." Except she could take out the *probably*. No way would he want to hang on to that. "It's technically his since he's her next of kin, and I doubt he'll want to keep it. Like I said, there are some entries about her hitting him." Now she paused and tried not to make her question sound like the accusation that it was. "Why didn't anyone in town put a stop to that?"

Her father's next sigh was even heavier, and he shook his head. "If I'd ever witnessed it or had seen proof of it, I would have reported her. I guess other folks felt the same way. There's a fine line between minding your business and trying to make things right, and the line should have tipped toward doing the right thing."

True, and she hated that Matt had gone through so much bad stuff. "Ryder and Ruston didn't make Matt's life easy, either."

"No," he quietly agreed. "I should have stopped that, too." His groan was soft, barely audible, but it seemed to be bone-deep. "I should have done a lot of things differently."

So much regret, and she figured it wasn't all for Matt. What had happened between Candy Lynn and him was playing into this. Ditto for all the pain and grief this had caused his wife.

"Speaking of Ryder," her father went on, "you'll probably hear it soon enough, but Heather and he are having some problems."

Emory certainly hadn't expected him to say that, but considering the topic, she asked, "Because of an affair?"

"No, I don't think so. Heather says she's not sure she's

still in love with him, that she doesn't think they're on the same page anymore when it comes to their marriage."

Well, heck. That was much worse than an affair. An affair could maybe be forgiven. *Maybe*. Trust could perhaps be regained, *perhaps*, but Emory was a firm believer that love had to be there for things to work out.

"I'll call Ryder and see if he wants to talk," Emory offered. "I'll call Heather, too." Heck, and Ian, once she confirmed that Ryder and Heather had clued their son into what was going on. Greer was too young to understand divorce, but he'd need some extra attention as well.

Her father nodded, stayed put a moment longer and then started for the door. "I'm sorry to have interrupted your evening."

Emory felt a smirk tug at her lips. "No, you're not."

"No, I'm not." He smiled, opened the door but turned back to face her. "Matt and you are getting close?"

She considered shrugging that off, but her dad didn't seem to be on the verge of lecturing her about her love life. "Not as close as I'd like," she admitted.

Still no lecture. He just nodded again.

Maybe it was the lack of verbal response, but she then gushed out something she should have probably just kept to herself. "Matt and I are supposed to be having a fling, but I could end up falling hard for him."

She heard the sound and thought it was her father clearing his throat. But it wasn't.

It was Matt, clearing his throat.

He was on the bottom step of the porch and had no doubt heard every word that she shouldn't have uttered in the first place. *Crap, crap, crappity, crap.*

Thanks to the porch light, she had no trouble seeing Matt's stunned eyes. Her confession was obviously news to him, and that was news of the unwelcome variety. Of course, it was. He hadn't wanted to get involved with her in the first place. Lust had knocked his resolve to stay away from her down some notches, but this might give his resolve a new boost.

"I just wanted to tell you I've been called into work," Matt said, clearly not addressing what he'd heard.

"What happened?" she asked.

"A fender bender on Main Street that caused a fight. The deputies probably have it under control, but I'm going in." However, Matt hadn't said that last part specifically to her but rather to her father. "You're parked in the driveway, and I can't get out."

"Oh, sorry," her father muttered. He kissed Emory on the cheek, issued a "good night" to no one specific, and he went to his car.

"You heard that," Emory said when Matt stayed put.

"I did." He scrubbed his hand over his face and glanced back as her father started his car. "He knows about the diary?"

She nodded. "He's worried."

"So am I." He met her gaze head-on. "I don't think we should read the diary together."

Emory felt the sting, and it had nothing to do with the bug bites that were starting to make themselves known. "Because you don't want me hurt by what might be in there."

"Not just that." He paused, did another check over his shoulder. Her father was pulling out of the driveway. "I just don't want any part of it to play into the research you're doing. So, I'm asking for a favor. I'm asking you to give the disk to me. I can pick up the computer later."

There was certainly no trace of the lust that'd been in

his eyes earlier, and he didn't make a move to touch her. That's because she'd royally messed up things with him. Nothing would send Matt running faster than hearing she might get a broken heart out of this.

"All right," Emory said. She reached into her purse that she'd put on the foyer table, extracted the disk and handed it to him.

Matt didn't blow out a breath of relief. Didn't look at the disk as if it were the miserable chore it would be to read it. He simply took it, muttered a thanks and walked away.

CHAPTER TWELVE

MATT PULLED TO a stop next to his house and stared at Emory's cottage. Since her car was there, she was likely home, and part of him wanted to go knock on her door and check on her. It'd been days since he'd seen her, but Matt had heard she was having a busy week at the shop like she'd mentioned to him.

And she was possibly avoiding him, too.

After that kissing session in her car, he'd thought they were past the avoidance stage, but they'd gone back a couple of steps. Or rather he had anyway, and it had to do with what he'd overheard her say to her father.

Matt and I are supposed to be having a fling, but I could end up falling hard for him.

He'd never been the "love 'em and leave 'em" type so that's why he'd initially resisted the whole notion of a fling. But his body sure as hell hadn't resisted it, and plain and simple, he missed Emory. She'd been able to pull him out of dark places and make him burn to take her to his bed. Probably not a good combination for a man who also wasn't the "break their hearts" type.

Of course, his body, which often had unwise and downright dirty thoughts, wanted him to go for it. To have her and deal with the aftermath. Thankfully, his brain beat that argument, and he got out and nearly knocked into Zella when he went into the house.

"Emory brought that big computer over earlier," she said. She was obviously on her way out because she already had her purse. "I didn't know where to put it so I had her set it in the living room."

"Thanks," Matt muttered. He'd intended on moving the computer himself, but like her, he'd gotten caught up in his own work.

"Remember, Joe and Millie's wedding is coming up," the woman added. "I'm guessing you haven't bought them a gift yet."

No, he hadn't, but it would only take a couple of clicks on the registry site to buy something, have it wrapped and mailed to them.

"Oh, and Zeke wanted to know if he's to get the wood to build a doghouse for the puppy Jack's getting," Zella continued.

Matt had just picked up his mail to go through it, but that caused him to look up. He certainly hadn't forgotten about getting Jack a dog, but there'd been no firm plans. No mention of a puppy, either. Matt had hoped to find a mild-tempered dog from the shelter and not a puppy that would chew the hell out of everything.

"Hold off on the wood," Matt insisted. "I still need to work out the details of getting one with Natalie."

After all, Jack probably wouldn't be content to have his dog live at the ranch where he'd only be able to see him a couple of times a week. Natalie might not be content about having a pet at her place, especially in the grand house that she'd soon share with Vince.

"I'll let Zeke know, but Jack's mighty insistent on a dog-house," Zella mumbled as she headed out.

Yeah, "mighty insistent" were the right words for it. Jack brought it up nearly every time during their nighttime chats and when he visited. He didn't intend to give his son any- and everything he wanted, but having a pet seemed reasonable.

Since Matt had grabbed a burger in town, he didn't have to cook, and for once he was home at a decent hour with no ranch or sheriff paperwork he needed to do. However, he did fire off a quick text to Natalie to ask her to come by his office sometime this week so they could discuss the dog. Then Matt grabbed a beer from the fridge and went to the living room.

Sure enough, the computer was there on the coffee table, and someone had even plugged it in. He'd already gone through the investigation records of Candy Lynn's death that Azzie had gotten from the courthouse. It hadn't been a barrel of monkeys to read it, but in the end it'd turned out to be a relief.

Because there'd been nothing there to indicate her death was anything more than a drug overdose.

He was hoping the same would be true with the diary. Then he could finally once and for all bury Candy Lynn and her sorry legacy of memories.

Without wasting another second, he got the disk from behind a photo on the mantel where he'd tucked it, and he put it into the computer. As soon as it loaded, he went straight to the last page, and he looked for any bombshells. According to the date of the entry, she'd written it the day before her death.

"Damn tired today, and the house is a shithole pigsty," he read. "One thing the kid was good for was keeping the place clean and making sure there was something to eat in the fridge."

Matt had tried to keep it clean, not for her sake, but because he'd hated living in filth. And there'd been food because he'd worked afternoon jobs to buy food. When she'd written this, he had already been living with his Grandpa Will, and Candy Lynn was obviously missing the "contributions" Matt had made to the household.

"I'm tapped out," Candy Lynn had put in the entry, "but I'm sure I can find a party or two. God, I hate this shithole."

And that was it. Her final thoughts that she'd bothered to put in her diary. So, no smoking gun, and it wasn't exactly a memorable legacy to have your last written word be *shithole*.

He scrolled back up to the spot where Emory and he had left off, and he forced himself to read the entries as a cop and not as Candy Lynn's son. Matt was a little surprised that the attitude adjustment helped. The pages continued to be filled with parties, rants and lovers, many of whom she hadn't bothered to name. Small blessings. Matt figured most of her exes wouldn't want their names preserved this way.

The next month of entries were pretty much the same with the exception of Candy Lynn recovering from a broken arm she'd gotten in a fall when she'd been drunk. Of course, she blamed the fall on everyone but herself. Including him.

The woman acted like an irresponsible teenager. One ruled by her sex drive and need for excitement. Since that sounded a little too close to his self-labeled adrenaline junkie and because he felt like a sex-driven teenager when he thought of Emory, he moved on to the next entry.

This one detailed another party with "favors" that he figured were drugs. There were some names here, ones that he recognized, but with the exception of Frannie, Matt didn't know of any of them still living in or around Last Ride.

Continuing through, he stopped when he reached an entry with a nickname. *Doctor Hottie.* "I've got my eye on the yummy doc, and he's got his eye on me. I might ride that gravy train for a while and see where it goes."

Sure enough, Candy Lynn did take that ride because in less than a week, she was gushing about getting the doc in bed. However, she no longer called him hot but rather old. Candy Lynn would have been about thirty-one at the time. Derrick, about forty-eight. An age gap, yes, but the "old" moniker could have been because Candy Lynn seemed to have quickly tired of her conquest. According to the dates, the affair had lasted less than two weeks.

Moving on to the next entry, Candy Lynn hadn't been the least bit upset about Derrick ending things with her, and she'd enjoyed the hell out of the money he'd given her. In the investigation records, Derrick had admitted to paying her five thousand because she'd threatened to tell his wife about the affair. It was possible Candy Lynn had used that to buy the drugs, but if so, she'd made the five grand last for nearly a month. Matt was betting she'd blown through it in under a week since there were entries about purchases of clothes and jewelry.

Matt stopped reading when he saw the flash of a headlight from the window, and he glanced out to see the unfamiliar truck come to a stop next to Emory's cottage. It wasn't unusual for her to get company even in the evenings because some of the brides came here for their fittings and such. But it wasn't a bride who got out of the truck. It was a man.

Verney Parkman.

Frowning, Matt went closer to the window and watched the man as he made his way to Emory's door. Considering that Verney was Frannie's husband and that it was Frannie who'd given Emory the diary, Matt had to wonder what Verney's visit was about.

He continued to watch as Emory opened the door, and Matt saw her go a little stiff. The kind of normal reaction a person might have to an unexpected visitor. She didn't invite the man in, and she didn't have her usual welcoming smile to whatever the man said to her.

Emory might not appreciate his interference, but Matt set aside his beer and went to the back door. The moment he opened it and stepped onto his porch, Emory looked up at him, snagging his gaze. Verney whirled around, his attention zooming to Matt as well. The discomfort was all over the man's face. He muttered something to Emory, something Matt didn't catch, and he started off the porch.

It was more than just tweaked interest that had Matt going down his own porch steps. "Verney," he greeted.

The man stopped. "Sheriff," Verney returned, and he got moving again after sparing Matt one very uncomfortable glance.

Matt went down the steps and into the yard. "Is everything okay, Verney?" he asked, but he was actually aiming the question at Emory. Unlike Verney, she didn't seem distressed.

Verney stopped again and eased back around to face Matt. "Everything's okay." Mercy, the man was a truly bad liar, and that caused Matt to go even closer.

"He asked me about Candy Lynn's diary," Emory provided.

Bingo. Matt had been right about the reason for his visit, and he thought he might know where this was going. "Do you have something you want to tell me about my mother's diary?" he asked the man.

It always felt like a bitter pill to call Candy Lynn his mother, but he thought the reminder might prompt Verney to remember that Matt, too, had a personal stake in this diary mess.

Verney seemed to have a couple dozen debates with himself as to what to say, but the buzzing mosquitoes must have made him realize he couldn't just stand there. Realize, too, that the sheriff wasn't going to let this particular sleeping dog lie.

"Frannie told me about the diary being in the box of things she gave Emory to help with the research," Verney finally said.

Matt looked at Emory to see if she was aware of that. She nodded. "I called Frannie yesterday and asked her if she knew the location of any more diaries. She didn't."

"She didn't know there was a diary in that old box," Verney quickly added. "And now Frannie's all upset about what Candy Lynn might have written." He paused, swallowed hard. "I know my wife had a wild past, but it's just that. The past. Frannie's worried Candy Lynn said something that'll stir up all the old memories for her. For everyone."

Yeah, that was a concern all right. "The diary won't be for public consumption," Matt assured him.

"But someone will read it," Verney argued.

Matt tapped his finger to his chest, saying "I will," just as Emory said, "I've read some of it."

That caused Verney to volley looks at both of them, and Matt figured the man was waiting for them to go into any juicy details they'd found. Or in his case, details that would embarrass his wife. Matt had no intentions of verifying or denying either, but he gave Verney the same spiel he'd given Bobby Ray. That he was looking for any legal ramifications and not gossip.

"That diary should have been destroyed a long time ago," Verney muttered.

"It will be," Matt assured him, "after I've finished reading it."

Then he might have a damn bonfire or something to get rid of it. His adjustment to being the sheriff was enough of a tightrope walk without adding Candy Lynn's shit to the mix. Of course, things likely wouldn't calm down until Emory's research was done and a dozen or so years had passed. He had hoped that by the time Jack made it to high school Candy Lynn was nothing but a very faint, very distant memory.

"All right," Verney finally said, and he gave them each one last look before he got in his truck and drove away.

Matt didn't go anywhere. "Are you okay?" he asked.

She sighed. "Okay enough. Verney didn't upset me or anything. Now that word is getting out about the diary, I suspect a lot of people are nervous about it."

That was true. "FYI, I've been reading it, and I haven't found anything earth-shattering. Including about your father. Candy Lynn wrote about the affair, if you could actually call it that, and she mentioned the money your father gave her. But there weren't any sex details."

He heard the relief in the breath she blew out, saw it on her face. "Good. Do you mind if I let him know that?"

"Hold off until I finish reading it. I don't expect any surprises since I've already checked the last entry and there's nothing about anyone giving her drugs. Or helping her end her life."

The nod she gave had some relief in it, too. "You've been brooding over what you heard me say to my father," Emory threw out there.

Matt scowled. "Not brooding. Thinking." Even though

it wasn't a smart thing to do, he went closer. And as usual, he had to beat back the urge to kiss her. Talk about sending her mixed signals if he did that. "I'm worried about hurting you if things don't work out between us."

"If," she repeated, and her mouth twitched as if fighting off a smile. "Not when. That's progress."

As if she were doing a striptease, she took slow silky steps toward him, and Matt could feel his resolve going straight to hell.

"Besides, we're still in the fling zone, remember?" she continued. "You don't get hurt from flings."

You did if you were falling for your fellow flingee. Still, that didn't stop Matt from slipping his hand around her waist when she reached him. He would have kissed her, too, but another vehicle turned on the road and came toward them. Hell. Had Verney returned to demand the diary be destroyed?

"It's Ryder," Emory said on a groan. She didn't step away from Matt, not even when Ryder got out of his truck. "If you're here to gripe about my personal life that is none of your beeswax, then you can just turn around and go home."

But as soon as she spoke the words, she stiffened. Then she moved away from Matt, turning to her brother.

"Dad came over and talked to me." Her voice was considerably softer and calmer. "Are you all right?"

Matt didn't know what had brought on this change, but it was obvious something was going on with Ryder. Something that made Emory feel sorry for him.

"Are Ian and Theo okay?" Matt asked when Ryder didn't say anything. For once, the man didn't glower, snarl or sneer at Matt. Ryder sighed, but unlike Emory's earlier one, this one wasn't of relief.

"Dad told me about Candy Lynn's diary," Ryder finally said. "You've read it?" he asked Matt.

Matt didn't sigh. He huffed. He was damn tired of talking about this. "Parts of it."

Ryder nodded in a nervous gesture that reminded Matt of Verney's reaction.

"There's nothing bad in it about your dad," Matt assured him. Though *bad* was all relative since the affair had happened.

Another nod from Ryder, then he cursed and scrubbed his hand over his face. "Anything in there about me?"

Even though Matt was paying attention, it still took a second for his mind to shift to the possibilities of why Emory's brother would have been in Candy Lynn's diary. "You used drugs with her?" Matt speculated.

"No." Ryder paused. A very long time. "But I had sex with her."

Emory made a startled gasping sound, a sound that Matt might have made had he not slammed down the shields and forced himself not to react.

"You slept with her?" Emory asked, her voice spiking. "When?"

"I was seventeen, and no, I didn't know she was screwing Dad. Hell, she might have been screwing Ruston, too, for all I know. When you're a teenager, you don't turn down sex."

"I did," Emory snapped. Obviously, this news was not settling well with her.

Matt, on the other hand, was a bit surprised at just how little this affected him. Judging from the entries he'd read, Candy Lynn slept around a lot, so why wouldn't she go after Dr. Hottie's sons? It wouldn't matter to her that at least one of them would have been under legal age.

"You told Dad about this?" Emory asked.

"No." Ryder was fast with that answer. "And I'd rather keep it quiet. That wasn't one of my finer moments," he added with disgust.

"It'll be kept quiet," Matt assured him. It wouldn't do any good to remind Ryder that folks would almost certainly be on his side if something like this came out. Sides wouldn't matter if you still had to weather ugly gossip, and the gossip would definitely run ugly if this got out.

"You got a beer and some time to talk?" Ryder asked Emory. "It's personal," he added to Matt. "Nothing about Candy Lynn. Or you and my sister."

Matt was all for anything that didn't involve his mother or a hands-off lecture about Emory, but he didn't like the troubled look in her eyes. She nodded to her brother and motioned toward her cottage.

"Go on in, get your beer," Emory instructed. "I'll be there in a few minutes. It'll be okay," she added to Matt. "Marital troubles."

Matt hadn't caught even a whiff of gossip about that, but looking back to the way the couple had handled their son's penchant for glittering his balls, they hadn't stood as a unit the way Ruston and his wife had. Since Matt had been through his own marital problems and a divorce, he could feel sorry for Ryder. Almost. But most of his sympathy went to the man's kids.

Emory stayed put and continued to look at him. Maybe because she needed a moment to soothe herself before going inside. Since Matt wasn't moving, either, it was possibly the same for him. Except that was only part of it. God, he'd missed her. Had missed this.

And he pulled her to him for a kiss.

He'd intended to keep it short and sweet. But it was the

opposite of that. It was hard, hungry and trending toward desperate. So desperate that they kept up the kiss until they risked passing out from lack of oxygen.

Emory's breath was gusting when the mouth-to-mouth contact finally broke, and she had a glazed look in her eyes. The kind of look that signaled an end to foreplay and a move to the bed. Which couldn't happen, of course, with Ryder around.

"I'll see you after your brother leaves," Matt said, and he gave her one last kiss before he turned and forced himself to walk away.

EMORY HAD ALWAYS considered herself a good sister, even when her brothers hadn't fallen into the "good sibling" category. Ryder was obviously miserable, and she hated to see him this way, but he also wasn't taking any advice she was giving him.

She'd run through the somewhat limited gambit of possible solutions, starting with counseling. Ryder had nixed that because he didn't want to spill his troubles to somebody outside the family.

Emory had moved on to the suggestion that Heather and he take a trip together, maybe a weekend, and yes, she'd agreed to babysit. Ryder had pooh-poohed that, too, because he was certain that Heather wouldn't agree. Ditto for him and his wife just sitting down together for some long meaningful talks. Or long meaningful letters. Heck, long meaningful anything together.

"I don't know why I came here," Ryder complained. "I mean, it's not as if you're a relationship expert, what with a divorce and an annulment."

Her first response was to bristle at that, but he had a valid point. She could have argued that it wasn't her fault that her first husband cheated on her and then ran off with his lover. Or that her second husband forgot to mention that he'd never gotten a divorce from his wife and therefore wasn't legally married to her. So, yes, she'd made mistakes by hitching her romantic high hopes to the wrong men. Still, she hoped she had an inkling of how to make a relationship work.

Ryder finished his beer, sat stone silent for a couple of very long moments and then he looked at her. "How can you even think about wanting to put yourself through something like that again?"

She knew he was talking about Matt. Or maybe she just had Matt on the brain. The memory of that sweat-lathering kiss he'd given her earlier was still very fresh. "I make wedding dresses," she reminded him. "I'm a hopeless romantic."

Ryder made a sound that could have meant anything, and he stood, getting ready to leave. "Third time's not a charm, sis. It's a bitch. You could end up getting hurt."

That last part was oh, so true. But she thought Matt was a risk worth taking. The trick would be to convince him to take that risk right along with her.

She walked with Ryder to the door, said goodbye and watched him drive away just as the first drizzle from the rain started. Her visit with her brother had definitely put a damper on some of the heat she'd gotten from Matt's kiss, but that heat kicked in again when she saw him sitting on his back porch.

Waiting for her.

She had no doubts about that when she saw him smile, and Emory started the walk toward him. Yeah, a risk all right. A mouthwatering one.

With a beer in his hand, he was in the porch swing beneath the slow lazy whirls of the overhead fans. Talk about making a picture. The hot cowboy at ease. Well, sort of. She figured there was a storm inside him that matched the one that was nearly upon them.

When the rain and wind picked up, Emory raced up his porch steps. Her clothes were a little damp. Clinging. But the cool felt good against her skin.

"Up for some company?" she asked, going to him.

He set aside his beer, pulled her down to him and put his mouth on hers. Definitely up for company. The kisses lingered, slow and easy like the fans. No sense of urgency. No serious demands. Not yet, anyway.

"Is your brother okay?" he asked when he finally broke the kiss.

Emory shrugged. "So-so." And while she was worried about her brother, she didn't especially want to talk about him tonight. However, there were some things she needed to get out of the way before she attempted to kiss Matt's lights out. "Have you called Jack for a good-night?"

"I have," he assured her, "and I've read all the pages of the diary that I'm going to read tonight."

Good. Those were the green lights she'd wanted, so Emory kissed him again. This one had more heat. More urgency, too. And because she wanted him even closer, she shifted positions and eased onto his lap. Her dress was loose enough to slide right up her thighs.

Even if there hadn't been a curtain of rain sheeting down from the tin roof, they still had plenty of privacy since no one else was around. Emory hoped it stayed that way. She'd had enough unexpected visitors for one night.

Once she was on his lap, it was easy for her to wrap her arms around him. Easier for him to do the same to her, but this time he kissed her neck. All those little places that lit very big fires. She'd never made out with Matt when they'd been teenagers, but he seemed to have all the right instincts about kissing the places that made her whimper and want to beg.

And speaking of whimpering and begging, both of those things happened again when he hooked his arm around her backside and brought their middles together. The lust and heat went nuts, sliding and gliding through her body until she was already a puddle of fire.

She went after his shirt again, wanting to get her hands on his chest, but Matt stopped her. Not easily, but he managed to take her hands in his. He groaned, cursed, with a look on his face that had her going *uh-oh*.

"I don't have any condoms," he said, and she somehow managed to hear him over the thudding heartbeat in her ears.

His words had to make it through the heartbeat thuds, the roaring fire in her body and the pounding rain, and when they finally sank in, Emory muttered her own profanity.

"I don't have any," she grumbled, "and even if I did, they would have long since expired." She blamed her hazy mind on why she'd basically just confessed to him that she'd had a long stretch of celibacy.

Emory glanced out at the rain and then cursed and groaned some more. Going to the store was out. Not because of the storm but because the stores were already closed. That left the gas station, and while she was sure they'd have condoms in stock, the gossip would be legion about Matt making a purchase. She didn't mind folks knowing they were together, but she'd rather not add it to the mix of the already existing talk.

Still, she debated it.

What was weeks of gossip compared to having what she was certain would be incredible sex? She was still debating that when Matt surprised her by pulling her back to him. Kissing her. Touching her. And generally making her not care one eyelash about gossip and such.

"For now," he murmured while he tugged up her dress.

Emory probably would have asked him what he meant by that remark, but she lost the ability to speak when he tugged down the cups of her bra and took that incredibly clever mouth to her breasts.

Oh, mercy.

The man was so good at this, and his tongue and teeth would have been more than enough to make the lust soar, but Matt added another heat-searing component to it. He slid his hand inside her panties.

Emory got it then. Not the orgasm, though, that would surely be coming. No, she got what he meant with his *for now*. He was going to give her a hand job, and while she suspected it'd be the best hand job in the history of such sexual pleasures, going solo wasn't what she had in mind.

"I can do that for you, too," she insisted and reached for his zipper.

"No, you can't," he insisted right back. He looked her straight in the eyes. Moved his hand lower into her panties. "One of us has to remember safe sex isn't just a willy-nilly suggestion."

Willy-nilly sounded downright raunchy. Of course, pretty much everything he said right now would because man, oh, man, him slipping his fingers inside her made her want to yell out every raunchy word in her vocabulary.

"For now," he repeated.

She might have still argued with him but he kissed her, and he used enough tongue to make her want to never argue with him again. She had no resistance. None whatsoever to resist any and everything Matt was doing to her. Emory just gave right in to the heat.

Matt touched her. Stroked her in just the right place and until everything inside pinpointed to just him. To just this moment. And in the blinding madness of the orgasm, Emory knew nothing, absolutely nothing about this was willy-nilly.

CHAPTER THIRTEEN

MATT ATE HIS breakfast while he scrolled through page after page of the diary. He wasn't due into work today so he could probably finish the damn thing. Well, he could if he would just focus. But he was having some trouble doing that.

He'd had one hard, restless night after Emory had gone back to her cottage. Emphasis on the *hard*. That's what he got for not being better prepared. For over a month now, Emory and he had been circling around each other, so he should have just accepted he had no willpower around her and bought a jumbo box of condoms.

Something he'd already ordered.

He'd gotten them from an online site and was having them overnighted so they would arrive tomorrow. The next time he got his hands in Emory's panties, it'd be for foreplay and not the grand finale.

It didn't matter that he shouldn't be thinking of future grand finales with her. Nope. Didn't matter if they both could get burned from this. He'd past the point of no return and was going through with this fling.

Cursing because his attention had drifted again, he forced himself to keep reading Candy Lynn's entries. The woman was a whiner and had the morals of an alley cat. Of course, some of those lack of morals had led her to have sex with both Emory's father and brother. Along with a boatload of other people. The woman had been the definition of *love 'em and leave 'em*. Then again, he wasn't sure actual love had ever played into her antics.

A shrink would probably say the constant sleeping around was her way of dealing with the grief of losing her husband. Matt might have bought that if she'd bothered to mention his dad. She rarely did, and when his name did come up, it was to curse him for getting himself killed and leaving her with his *brat*.

Matt made it through nearly fifty uneventful entries and was ready to grab more coffee and continue, but then he heard Emory shout, "Help!"

He wasn't sure where his cup and plate landed. Matt tossed them and ran through the house and out the back door. He was barreling down the steps when he spotted her. She was on the floor, halfway in the house, partly on her porch. At least he thought it was Emory. The only thing he could actually see of her were her legs. The rest of her was buried beneath an enormous garment bag.

"What the hell happened?" he asked, running to her. The storm had moved through, and it was sunny, but the ground was still plenty wet.

"The dress fell on me," she said in such a way that it explained everything. It didn't.

Matt took hold of the garment bag, lifting it. Not as easily as he'd imagined he could. Along with being the size of a grizzly bear, the darn thing was heavy.

"Be careful. Don't crush it," she insisted, her voice muffled since the bag was still partially covering her face. "That's why I didn't just shove it off," she added. Or rather that's what he thought she said.

Trying not to squeeze the bag, Matt wrestled it off her, cradling it as best he could. "What the heck's on the dress that makes it so heavy?"

"Beads, crystals and brass stars," she said, maneuvering to her feet. She was out of breath, frazzled and her hair was messy, and he knew it was a true testament to lust and such that she still managed to look amazing.

"Why would anyone want all that on a wedding dress?" he asked.

"Oh, it's not for the bride. This is for her mother who's really into New Age stuff. She wanted a lot of symbols that she says are good luck."

Well, she'd be lucky if she didn't throw out her back while wearing it. "You want me to help you put this in your car?"

Her smile was a little frazzled, too, but, yeah, it kicked in his lust. "Yes, please. Actually, I have to take in this one and three others to the shop. I've been busy," she added.

Apparently, and he wondered if she'd thrown herself into work those days they'd been dodging each other.

She opened her back car door, and with some gentle nudging, shifting and with brass stars clanging, they got the New Age dress onto the seat. The entire back seat. Worse, it stuck up so high that it nearly blocked the rear window. No way could Emory fit three more dresses in there.

Making a *hmm*-ing sound where she was no doubt assessing the space, Emory opened the trunk and froze. Matt soon saw why. There was a box filled with stuff. Not wedding stuff. These things had been Candy Lynn's, and this was the box Frannie had brought over.

"I'll just take it inside," she muttered.

"No, I'll put it in my kitchen." There was no need for her to have to deal with it. "Unless you think there's something in here for your research."

Emory shook her head and touched his arm. She ran her

fingers elbow to wrist in a soothing gesture. "I don't need anything in it."

Matt didn't look down into the contents of the box. He merely hoisted it up and took it to his place. When he got back, Emory was already bringing out another box, this one containing veils. He positioned it in the trunk while she hauled out another dress. When she repeated that with yet another, it was obvious there wouldn't be enough room in her car to carry all four and the box.

"I'll take the final dress in my truck and follow you to the shop," he suggested.

Her forehead bunched up. "I hate to interrupt whatever you need to do."

Since what he had to do, reading the rest of the diary, was a pain in the ass, he welcomed delivery duty. Plus, on the way back he could stop by the animal shelter and ask them to keep an eye out for a dog for Jack. If Natalie objected, then he'd just keep the dog at Stallion Ridge. Jack would probably be so excited about having a puppy that he'd accept he wouldn't be able to see it all the time.

Matt glanced around to see if there was anyone he should tell he was leaving, but it was Zeke and Zella's day off, and even though it wasn't even eight o'clock, the ranch hands were already out working. Matt knew that because he'd scheduled them to move some of the horses to another pasture.

He used his phone app to lock up his house in case the trip to the shelter turned into something more than just an inquiry. He could possibly even arrange to pick up Jack and they could go together.

He put the dress on the passenger's seat, setting aside the invitation that'd occupied that particular space for the past two weeks when Joe had dropped it off in person at the police station. Seeing it was a reminder that Joe and Millie's wedding was tomorrow. He'd go, of course. So would Emory. And that meant they'd likely show up together. He made a mental note, though, not to do any public kissing that could end up being captured in a picture.

As usual, it didn't take him long to get to the shop, and Matt pulled in right behind Emory in the back parking lot. The place was closed and would be for another hour, so it was just the two of them hauling in stuff. And speaking of stuff, the sewing room had plenty of dresses, too. Every mannequin had been fitted with a garment, all in various stages of the sewing process.

"Wedding season," she murmured when she followed his gaze. She went into the main part of the shop, turning on lights as she walked, and she came back with her arms clutched around another mannequin. "I hire a couple of extra seamstresses this time of year to do beading, hemming, alterations and such, but I handle all the designs. You're sure you don't want to delay castrations and deworming to help?"

"I'm sure. Not enough time, what with shit-shoveling the stalls."

"Ah, yes. No way for sewing clean expensive fabric to compete with shit-shoveling." She glanced at him. "Seriously, have you ever tried to sew?"

"Never. Have you ever tried to castrate anything?"

She paused as if giving that some thought. "My brothers made me mad enough a couple of times that I wished I had that particular skill set. But mostly I just take out my frustrations, and my joy, on the sewing."

There weren't any magical woo-woo vibes coming off the dresses to demonstrate any "mostly lucky" karma, but Matt could see they were in their own way works of art.

Sometimes a weird work of art like the New Age concoction that she took from the garment bag. Emory had mentioned the beads, crystals and stars, but she hadn't said that some of them were much larger than what would likely be considered normal embellishments. The stars were three inches across. So were some of the weird-colored crystals dangling from the mustard fabric.

"Yes, it takes all kinds," she joked as if reading his mind. "Last week, I turned down a woman who came from Houston who wanted me to make her a flesh-colored dress shaped like a penis. Her ex is remarrying, and she wanted to wear it to his wedding."

He shifted, looking at her, just as she shifted and looked at him. Emory was smiling again, and he moved in to brush his mouth over hers. He could practically taste that smile so he delved in a little deeper. Taking hold of her arm, he eased her closer and pushed that "little deeper" to something long, slow and incredibly satisfying. Much more satisfying than wearing a penis dress to an ex's wedding.

Emory melted against him, and she made that sound of pleasure in her throat. A sound that made him want to go past the deeper point. Of course, he couldn't. Even if the condoms had arrived, he couldn't have sex with her in her shop. Well, probably not. Maybe just some heavy fooling around, he amended when she pressed harder against him.

Emory played dirty by nipping his earlobe and making sure she was putting some pressure against his quickly forming erection.

Yeah, he could have "hand job" sex with her. Right here. Right now. Or rather he could have had he not heard the blasted "yoo-hoo" that someone called out. A split second later, somebody opened the back door.

"Emory, I hope I'm not bothering you," the yoo-hooer

added. Natalie. She stepped in. "I saw the lights on—" Natalie froze, blushed and fluttered her hand to nothing and no one in particular. "I'm sorry. I didn't know you were here."

"I'm parked in the back," he said just as Emory said, "Matt helped me bring in some dresses."

Both of them sounded somewhat guilty. As if they'd been caught doing something wrong. They hadn't been. But the truth was if Natalie had walked in five minutes later, she might have gotten an eyeful.

"I can come back," Natalie offered, doing another hand flutter.

She was obviously uncomfortable, and she was dodging his gaze. Matt tried not to read anything into that tightness. Maybe it was just an uncomfortable punch to see an ex kissing someone else. Still, he pushed a little to make sure that's all there was to it.

"You okay? Is Jack okay?" Matt tacked on to that.

"He's fine. I'm fine," she added. Her voice was tight enough to send up a little warning flag that she wasn't telling the whole truth, but he was positive if there was something wrong with Jack, she wouldn't keep that from him.

"I was thinking about picking up Jack and taking him to the animal shelter to look at the dogs," Matt told her while he continued to keep a close eye on her expression.

"Oh." Natalie blinked, checked the time on her phone. "Well, he's spending the morning with Vince's parents, and they've got some things planned. Can you shift the shelter trip to the afternoon?"

"Sure." Matt continued to stand there and watch her until he figured he'd pushed the boundaries between concern and awkward nosiness. After all, since she was here at the shop, it was entirely possible this visit was about her wedding dress.

A dress she might not want to gush and gloat over with her ex around.

What surprised him, though, was her reaction to the shelter visit. No objections, no opinion, no advice. And that gave him an unsettled feeling in his gut because Natalie seemed, well, distracted over something because that normally would have gotten her immediate and full attention.

"I'll see you later," he said to Emory, and he gave her a goodbye kiss. Yeah, there was some awkwardness, too, but he would have felt like an idiot not saying a real goodbye to her after that heated lip-lock they'd just had.

He stopped by his office to check and see if there was any paperwork he could do at home. There was, but there obviously wasn't any field work going on since Buffy Jarvis and Hogan Dayton, two of the three on-duty deputies, were sitting around having their coffees and shooting the breeze.

Both were good cops, definitely not slackers, so he didn't even aim them a raised eyebrow. No need since they practically knocked each other over to get to their desks, no doubt for the pretense of looking busy. Even though he'd only been their boss for over a month now, they'd yet to relax around him.

Buffy sat at her desk that was a kind of shrine to the old TV show responsible for her name. The woman had definitely embraced an image that some might have discarded. Her name tag was rimmed with tiny wooden stakes, and she had a framed, signed picture of the cast of *Buffy the Vampire Slayer*. She looked nothing like her namesake, though, with her black hair and brown eyes, but apparently she worked out enough that she could probably do some vampire slaying if it was ever called for.

In contrast, Hogan's desk was a cluttered mess of files, cup holders jammed with pens and stacks of sticky notes.

No bodybuilding for him. He was short and squat, but since he got all his reports in on time and there wasn't a single complaint on file about him, Matt figured he could rely on the man to keep doing the job—even if Hogan hadn't relaxed around him.

Azzie was at her desk, too, and she was diligently typing away on her computer. She acknowledged him with a grumbled, "It's your day off," without even looking up. She was as relaxed around him as she was with anyone else. Of course, that wasn't saying much.

Matt took the paperwork and headed home, frowning when he spotted Bobby Ray going into the diner. The clown man was certainly around a lot, and Matt made a mental note to question him about that.

The moment Matt pulled into his driveway, he hit the brakes and stared at Emory's cottage. Specifically, at the door that was wide open. He couldn't say for certain that she'd shut it on her way out, but it would have been out of the norm for her to leave it open like that.

It was training that had him undoing the strap over the top of his service weapon. Since he was at Stallion Ridge, he assured himself that it was probably nothing.

But it was.

Keeping watch around him, Matt took slow cautious steps to her porch and peered inside. At the debris scattered over the floor.

Someone had broken in.

"Are you okay?" Emory heard Matt ask. Not for the first time, either. In the past twenty hours or so, he'd aimed multiple variations of that question at her.

She answered him with a variation of *so-so, maybe, not sure* by shrugging and continuing to stare out his kitchen window at her cottage while she drank her coffee. All of those answers were correct and could change from second to second. But along with the so-so/maybe/not sure, she was also pissed off. Someone had gone in her house, tossed around some things, made a royal mess. And the bunghole had even stolen the Mondo Urban Legend chocolate chip cookie with the caramel center that Emory had gotten from the bakery and left on the counter.

In the grand scheme of things, the cookie probably wasn't that big of a deal, but by God she'd wanted to sink her teeth in all that goodness to get to the caramel. She'd dieted for two days just so she could eat the whole saucer-sized triple-chocolate chunk cookie without feeling a morsel of guilt.

"A lot of people are afraid and angry after a break-in," Matt added. He was next to her, having his own coffee while also doing some staring at the cottage.

Yes, anger. Possibly some fear. Some frustration at herself, too, for not having locked her door.

It was the first time since she'd bought the place that she hadn't slept there in her own bed. A first time, too, for someone to have broken in. A first time to have slept in Matt's house—which had turned out to be a hardship of a different kind. Without any condoms, she'd slept in bed with him in what had once been the guest room. They hadn't used his room because it was only a twin size, and they would have been smushed up against each other.

A tempting thought...

But they hadn't been able to risk touching, smushing or kissing because it would have ignited a powder keg of really incredible sex. Since she hadn't wanted to add unplanned pregnancy to her summer fling with him, she'd kept her hands and her mouth to herself.

"We can go back through the place again," Matt offered. "Just to make sure nothing was taken. Other than the cookie, I mean." He'd added that, no doubt because of the fuss she'd made about it.

"Thanks," she muttered, even though this would be the fourth time for that. Since the place wasn't that big, Emory figured she would have noticed anything other than a missing cookie.

Together, they'd already cleaned up the mess the burglar had made while speculating as to who would have done it. And they'd both come up with the same answer.

Someone after Candy Lynn's diary.

Emory didn't think that was a stretch to believe that was the intruder's motive. Word had to have gotten around about it. Word, too, that Emory had the diary. Except she didn't. Matt did, but the cookie thief hadn't broken into his house. Perhaps because the doors had been locked and because of the sheer stupidity of breaking into a cop's home.

Matt would investigate, of course, and he'd personally tried to get fingerprints from the front door and the counter area where the cookie had been. Unfortunately, there'd been a lot of smears. And crumbs. So, he wasn't hopeful they'd get a match. He figured his best shot at finding the culprit was through interviews. He'd already started those by talking to the hands.

They'd seen nothing.

Matt had also talked to his nearest rancher neighbor. They hadn't seen anything either and didn't know a thing about it. That "see no evil, hear no evil" trend had continued when Matt had spoken to Bobby Ray who claimed to have been nowhere near Stallion Ridge.

It was possible that Frannie had had second thoughts about giving Emory that box, so Matt would be talking to her. And to Emory's parents and Ryder. Matt had to interview them simply because they had a connection to the diary, but sneaking into her place wasn't how any of the three would have handled it. Ryder would have just demanded she give them the diary and would have kept demanding until he became a pain in her ass. Her mother would have sobbed, and her dad would have played the "take pity on me" card. So Emory didn't think there'd be a family connection to the break-in.

"I should be able to sleep at my place tonight," she muttered, more to test the waters of how Matt, and she, felt about that.

"You can stay here as long as you want," he automatically said, and she felt the little hitch that came with that.

She turned to him, managed a smile. "Unless you get condoms, I doubt you want to go through another night of sleeping with me." And that didn't even begin to address that he wouldn't want her to become a permanent fixture in his bed. Permanent fixture and fling weren't compatible.

He also managed a smile and kissed the tip of her nose. "There'll be condoms," he promised her. "I'll put some in my wallet, by my bed. Heck, in every room of the house."

Matt hadn't given her a "real" kiss, but she still felt the heat. It was nice. More than nice. Because the heat lessened that pissed off, violated feeling from the break-in.

Her phone beeped with the alarm she'd set, and she frowned when she turned it off. "That's my signal to get ready for Millie and Joe's wedding."

He checked the time. "That's not for five hours."

"The dressmaker has to be there early in case there are any last-minute fixes." Which there usually were. Brides were always snagging something or accidentally ripping hems with heels, and zippers and buttons had a fondness for malfunctions. She'd go armed with her sewing kit, white duct tape and lace.

Emory finished her coffee, rinsed the cup and put it in the dishwasher. She'd already brought over her outfit from the cottage so all she had to do was shower and change. Before that, she had to kiss Matt. Something long and lingering to remind him that eventually they'd get around to actually flinging. At least that'd been her plan, but he spoke before she could pucker up.

"How'd Natalie's visit to the shop go yesterday?" he asked. "I didn't get a chance to ask you because of the break-in."

No way could Emory give him a puzzling look as to why he wanted to know that. Matt had no doubt picked up on the weird vibe Natalie was giving off. Unfortunately, Emory wasn't going to be able to give him a good answer.

"She wanted to look at her dress again and make some small design changes." Emory paused. "Something was bugging her, but she didn't say what. I think she hates the dress and doesn't know how to tell me without hurting my feelings."

She watched Matt process that, and he must have thought that was plausible because he nodded.

"I'll call Natalie on Monday and come out and ask if she wants a totally different design," Emory went on. "If she does, I should have enough time to start from scratch."

Well, she would if the new design wasn't too elaborate. The wedding was about six weeks away, and that wasn't a lot of leeway to come up with a dream dress. While she had Natalie on the phone, though, she'd try to suss out if there was anything else bothering her. Brides often had plenty of nerves to go with their big day.

She was about to attempt the kiss again when she heard

the sound of an engine. Emory's gaze flew to the window, and her first thought was the burglar had returned. But nope, it was Zeke and Zella, and they weren't alone. A familiar truck pulled in behind them.

"Were you expecting Bernie Parkman from the animal shelter?" Emory asked.

Matt shook his head, and they stepped out onto the back porch. "Bernie brought Jack's dog," Zella announced. "Zeke'll get to building that doghouse."

"I didn't know Jack and you had picked out a dog," Emory commented.

"We haven't," Matt answered, going down the steps. "He looked at pictures on the shelter's website and told me about them when I called him last night."

Bernie took something from a carrier and then got out of his truck. A golden lab leaped out with him, and he was carrying a black puppy. "Jack couldn't make up his mind," the man said, grinning. "So, I figured I'd bring both."

Matt opened his mouth, no doubt to object to that, but then Bernie added, "The kid fell in love with both of them. Dr. Vince and his mom are bringing him over in a couple of minutes so he can introduce them to their new home."

Matt only sighed, and Emory chuckled. Apparently, he was going to get two fur-grandbabies instead of one.

"I need to get dressed for the wedding," Emory reminded him. "Don't catch the garter at the reception, and I won't catch the bouquet," she added in a murmur. "No need to spur gossip and speculation like that about us."

Matt made a quick sound of agreement.

She'd already turned to go back inside when Zella brought out something from their truck. At first Emory thought it might be pet supplies, but then she saw the box Zella was bringing their way. Obviously, the company Matt had ordered them from hadn't thought it prudent to conceal what was inside.

"These were in the mailbox," Zella said with somewhat of a smirk.

And the woman handed Matt the jumbo-sized box of condoms.

CHAPTER FOURTEEN

MATT SCOWLED AT the icing-smeared blue-and-white lace garter that he now apparently owned. Stupid traditions.

Really stupid timing.

When Joe had snapped the garter like a slingshot out into the one hundred or so reception attendees, the damn thing had landed right on the piece of cake that Matt had been eating. If all eyes hadn't been on him, he might have flicked it onto the floor and pretended that'd been its landing place all along. But everyone had been looking.

And cheering.

Matt wasn't alone, though, in the new ownership of something he didn't want. He glanced over at Emory who was now holding a bouquet of pale yellow roses. She'd caught the damn thing because it had bounced off several women's heads and smacked her right in the face. It'd likely been a reflex action for her to grab it, and he'd seen her immediate "oh, crap" expression when she realized what'd happened.

Either fate was dicking around with Emory and him, or multiple guests had decided to get in on what would have been a well-timed prank. A prank that the other wedding guests found highly amusing. He actually heard some snickers.

Setting his cake plate aside and stuffing the garter in his pocket, Matt ignored the snickers and the matchmaking goo-goo eyes some people were doling out, and he went to give the bride and groom his congrats. Thankfully, Joe and Millie were too goo-goo eyed over each other to notice what was going on. Matt did the congrats, got a hug from a beaming Millie and he made his way back to Emory.

"I need to stay a little while longer and help put away the dress and veil," she said. "You're heading out?"

Matt nodded and led her away from the other guests so he could tell her what he had to say in private. Of course, folks probably thought he was setting up a rendezvous with her, but it wasn't anything nearly that fun.

"I'm going to your parents' place to talk to them about the break-in at the cottage," he explained.

Emory sighed. "They know you're coming?"

He gave her another nod. "I called your dad before I left the ranch." Matt had done that after he'd watched Jack playing with his new dogs. "I have to interview them. No way around that."

"I know," she assured him, but that didn't ease the troubled look he saw on her face.

Maybe it was that look or the fact that he always had the urge to kiss her, but Matt brushed his mouth over hers. Of course, it would cause talk, but he no longer cared. Well, not for himself anyway. Maybe Emory's family would go easier on her even if they thought he was trailer trash scum.

Since the wedding hadn't been formal, Matt was wearing his jeans, but he ditched the jacket as soon as he got outside. That way, his badge would be visible since it was clipped to his belt. The reminder that he was the sheriff might take a smidge of the sting out of the interview for his parents. Might.

Then again, it just might be more salt to rub in the wounds.

Dreading this probably as much as Emory and her folks were, he drove toward the Parkman house, but when he spotted the For Heaven's Cake sign for the bakery, he pulled into a parking spot and went in. If Emory had had her fill of wedding cake at the reception, she could save the cookie for another day.

The place was more crowded than he'd expected, but the owner, Marla Severs, smiled when she spotted him. "What can I help you with, Sheriff Corbin?"

He drew a blank on the name so he went with the general description of, "I want one of those big chocolate chip cookies."

The woman beamed. "The Mondo Urban Legend. I just made a fresh batch this morning." Slipping on plastic gloves, she took a paper sleeve the size of a hubcap and walked to the display case. "This is for Emory?"

All chatter stopped as if someone had flipped a silent switch. "For me," he lied, though he wasn't sure why. "But add a second one for Emory." Which, of course, only made his lie sound even more half-assed.

Still smiling, Marla got a second sleeve, and using tongs, she took a cookie from the glass-front case. Matt was sure his eyes widened. Yes, it was a cookie in the general sense of the term, but it looked more like a damn cake, one with more chocolate than dough, and as if that weren't enough, it had a quarter-sized circle of caramel in the center. It probably had enough sugar to induce a coma. And now he was the proud owner of two of them.

He paid for the Mondo Urban Legends, heard the already buzzing gossip behind him and went back to his truck. He made the short drive to the Parkmans, only about six blocks off the town square.

Unlike where he'd been raised, their house was in the

right part of town. It'd been built over a hundred years ago, and while it didn't quite reach mansion status, it was big and looked prestigious enough for the home of a prominent doctor with a prominent surname.

Matt parked, and while he wondered just how bad the Mondos would melt in this scorching heat, he made his way up the porch steps, but the door opened before he even reached it. Not the Parkmans but a sturdy-looking woman in a gray cotton dress. Matt estimated she was in her late sixties.

"Sheriff Corbin," she said in a no-nonsense kind of way. "I'm Tellie Tate. Sounds like I've got a lisp when I say that, doesn't it?" She chuckled as if that were a fine joke, though he suspected it was something she said often. "I'm the housekeeper here. How's our sweet Emory?"

That question was more than no-nonsense. He heard the emotion and worry in it. "She's okay."

"Good. I'm a might worried about that girl. Practically raised her, I did, and her knotheaded brothers, too."

Matt liked the woman. And agreed with her about the knotheaded-ness.

"Anyway, I got something for Emory," Tellie went on. She took a bag from the entry table. A familiar bag and scent. "It's a Mondo Urban Legend from the bakery. I heard how that thief ate hers, and that girl loves her Mondos. Might cheer her up when you give it to her."

Matt didn't mention he'd had the same thought. "Thanks," he said, taking the bag.

"Tell her I love her bunches," Tellie added, motioning for him to follow her. "Come this way. The Parkmans are waiting for you."

Matt was still mulling over relaying an *I love you bunches* to a woman who'd already confessed that she was falling for him when Tellie led him into what he supposed was called a parlor. Expensive looking with its muted colors, delicate furniture with lots of dust catchers and paintings. It definitely wasn't a space for kicking back with a beer and watching the game on TV. Tellie made a quick exit, her sturdy shoes thudding against the hardwood floors.

"I hope you can make this visit quick," Mrs. Parkman said from her position at the fireplace. Her voice strained. Her eyes red.

She didn't hope that any more than Matt did. This visit wouldn't have been comfortable under any circumstances, but he had the added guilt of lusting after their daughter. He was pretty sure her parents weren't idiots and therefore had more than an inkling about that.

"You brought a cookie?" Nancy asked, eyeing the bakery bag.

"No. Your housekeeper wanted me to give it to Emory."

Apparently, Nancy disapproved of that. Perhaps because of sugar-intake concerns or perhaps because he'd be the one giving it to Emory.

Along with relaying an *I love you bunches*.

Matt shook off that thought and forced his attention back on the task in front of him. Literally in front of him. Emory's father was already seated and was sipping a glass of amber liquid that Matt was betting was whiskey. He was also betting the man needed it. Bringing up Candy Lynn was like taking a poke at a still-healing wound.

"Dr. Parkman," Matt greeted, "thank you for seeing me." He waited until Nancy sat next to her husband before he took the seat across from them. "I just need to ask, officially, where you were yesterday morning between eight-thirty and ten."

"We were here," Nancy spoke right up. "And we resent

you thinking we had anything to do with burglarizing our daughter's home. Such that is," she added in a disapproving mutter.

Okay. So that's how this was going to be. "I don't believe you had anything to do with it," he assured them, "but I have a job to do. Part of that job is interviewing and ruling out anyone with a motive for breaking into Emory's place." Matt turned his cop's gaze on the doctor. "You had motive if you were looking for Candy Lynn's diary."

Matt saw exactly what he wanted to see in the man's eyes and expression. Anger and outrage. Not guilt. Thank God. Because he really didn't want to endear himself to Emory's family by arresting her father.

"If I'd wanted the diary," Dr. Parkman said, his words somehow making their way through his suddenly tight mouth and jaw, "I would have merely asked Emory for it." He paused. "Did the burglar take it?"

Matt shook his head, looked at Mrs. Parkman and saw the same lack of guilt on her face. Good. One big-assed point down in this interview, one more to go.

"Do either of you know who would have broken into Emory's for the diary or for any other reason?" Matt asked.

The doctor huffed, then sighed. "I suspect there are a lot of people who wouldn't want the content of that diary to come to light."

Bingo. That included Emory's own brother. Heck, her entire family.

"I think it was one of your ranch hands," Nancy interjected.

Her mouth was tight, too, but not in the same way as her husband. She was hoping to put some of the blame for this on Matt. And he did blame himself. Because he sure as hell should have anticipated that somebody would want to take that diary and destroy it. Or worse, use it for some kind of blackmail.

"I've talked to my ranch hands," Matt informed her. "They were nowhere near the cottage at the time of the break-in."

"So they say," she muttered in another grumble. "Did you check their breaths because if you eat one of those Mondo cookies, you're going to have chocolate breath for hours."

Matt gave her a flat look and could honestly say that he hadn't done any breath checks, but the cookie was troubling. If the burglar had been hell-bent on finding the diary, why take time to eat the cookie? And it had been eaten because Matt had found crumbs on the counter and floor. If this had been a "violent crime" kind of situation, there'd likely be some DNA on those crumbs, but there was no way he could justify funding a test like that when there hadn't even been any property damage.

"I suppose any angry bride could have been responsible," Nancy went on. If there'd been a photo next to the expression of "grasping at straws," the woman's picture would have been there. "Some brides aren't very nice and get upset when their big day isn't perfect."

"Are you aware of any specific bride who would have a grudge or grievance against Emory?" Matt pressed.

"No," the couple answered in unison. It was Nancy who continued. "Maybe the grudge or grievance was against you."

That piqued his interest. "Why would you think that?"

Nancy opened her mouth, closed it and repeated that process a couple more times, making her look like a beached guppy. Matt decided to cut the woman a break by stating the obvious.

"If someone had wanted to get back at me, my house is just yards from the cottage," he explained. "No one tampered with the locks. No broken windows. No sign whatsoever that someone attempted to get in."

Though there was a really long-shot theory that whoever had done the break-in would know that it would have pissed Matt off. Still, the way to accomplish that would have been to vandalize something on Stallion Ridge. Something that specifically belonged to him.

"Emory could have been hurt," Nancy went on several moments later. "What if she'd been there when the maniac broke in?"

Yeah, that had given Matt some bad moments, too, but bottom-lining this, he didn't believe the person would have burglarized the place had anyone been there. He suspected the person had waited until he or she was sure the cottage was empty and then gone in.

"I'm keeping an eye on Emory and the cottage," Matt assured them.

That put some fresh anger in Nancy's eyes. "Emory wouldn't come home and stay with us. Is she staying with you?"

This was a "damned if he did, damned if he didn't" kind of scenario. Matt went with the truth. Well, the truth without mentioning that she'd slept in his bed. "She is."

Sometimes outrage and disapproval were silent things. Silent and staring. Which is exactly what Emory's folks did for the entire eight seconds that Matt counted off in his head.

"Emory's always had bad judgment when it comes to men," Nancy declared, and she practically sprang from the sofa and hurried out of the room.

Dr. Parkman stayed put and downed the rest of his whiskey. "She's upset. This has all been rough on her."

"Rough on you, too. And Emory," Matt settled for saying.

The doctor nodded and squeezed his eyes shut a moment. "Saying I'm sorry for what I did will never be enough." He dragged in a long breath. "I'm sorry to you, too. Because heaven knows you've gotten caught up in this mess as well."

He had indeed gotten caught up in it, but it was the first time Matt recalled anyone apologizing for it. It put a twinge in his gut that he hadn't expected. A good twinge that had the faint odor of acceptance. And he hoped that odor didn't have anything to do with it coming from Emory's father. He didn't need any other emotions or input playing into what he was starting to feel for her.

Matt figured a simple nod and a muttered, "Thanks," was the way to go here, and he got up and headed for the door. He hadn't actually learned anything new from the interview. Nothing related to the break-in anyway, but he drove away with a different kind of firestorm that he normally felt for Emory. Oh, the lust was still there. Not even a new ice age could cool that down, but there was something simmering beneath the heat that was starting to bother him.

He drove back down Main Street and had to hit his brakes when he saw the crowd on the road directly in front of the police station. A familiar crowd with a sobbing, yelling Tiffany in the center. She wasn't wearing a bridal gown today or a "skimpy underwear" deal, but she, and the folks around her, were dressed in party clothes. He hadn't spotted any of them at the wedding so they must have come from some other celebration.

Matt mentally put *celebration* in quotes.

Because it was obvious there was no joyous occasion

going on at the moment. Tiffany was yelling, "Keaton is a big smelly dog turd" and other such terms of affection.

Groaning, Matt pulled over, got out and walked to Azzie, who was scowling at the bunch as if she wanted to hose them all down. "Tiffany was at her and Keaton's engagement party when she found out he'd cheated on her again," Azzie explained.

"Engagement party?" he questioned. "They're back together?"

Azzie rolled her eyes. "Were," she emphasized. "She caught him cheating again."

"I want to arrest that lying dog turd," Tiffany insisted through the sobs. "He used the house he bought as a makeup present for me to diddle around with Bambi Grange. That's got to be a crime, right?"

Matt sighed. Apparently, Keaton hadn't learned from his past mistakes and it had cost him a house and, from the looks of it, another big-assed engagement ring that Tiffany was still wearing.

"Is Bambi a minor?" Matt asked Tiffany. "Or a fugitive that Keaton's harbored? Someone that Keaton forced or coerced into diddling around?" And he mentally cringed over having to repeat that particular word.

"No, Bambi's a dental hygienist who hasn't seen the backside of her teenage years in more than a decade, and she wouldn't have had to be coerced into fooling around with Keaton," Azzie provided when Tiffany only gave him a confused stare. "Let me handle this, boss. It's your day off, and you should be getting home. I've heard Jack's there playing with his dogs."

Matt hadn't known about Jack being at the ranch, but it didn't surprise him. The boy was probably chomping at the bit to play with the pets that Matt hoped he didn't regret getting. And keeping.

"Go ahead," Azzie insisted and then stopped. "But hold on a sec." She hurried back into the building and came out with a bakery bag. "It's one of those cookies for Emory she likes. To cheer her up because of the break-in."

Sighing not only at the cookie but at Tiffany's latest round of insults, which involved the size of Keaton's genitalia, Matt didn't argue with Azzie's insistence about handling the "cheated on fiancée" fiasco. He just took cookie number four back to his truck that now smelled like Willy Wonka's Chocolate Factory on steroids, waited for Azzie to clear the street and he headed home.

Matt had just taken the final turn to Stallion Ridge when his phone rang, and he saw Bobby Ray's name pop up on the screen on his dash. He so wasn't in the mood for dealing with the man, but this was all part of the job. Well, maybe it was. Using his hands-free, Matt answered the call.

"We need to talk," Bobby Ray immediately said.

"I believe we're doing that right now," Matt pointed out.

"No, I mean in private. I can't get back to Last Ride today, but I'll come tomorrow so we can have a sit-down."

"And why exactly do we need to do that?" Matt pressed. "Are you confessing to the break-in?"

"Of course not." Bobby Ray sounded plenty offended by Matt's question. "I told you I had nothing to do with that."

He had, but Matt was still deciding if he believed him. Maybe Squeaky the Clown was a changed man from his younger, meaner days, but Matt still considered him a suspect.

"So, why don't you just tell me what you have to say now?" Matt pressed.

"Because I want to go over this in person." Bobby Ray

paused. "I'm pretty sure I know who left that note on Mrs. Parkman's car, and I'm betting my favorite red nose that it's the same person who broke into Emory's cottage."

CHAPTER FIFTEEN

EMORY PULLED INTO the driveway of the ranch and grinned when she saw Jack running around the yard. The boy was giggling like a loon while both the Lab and the puppy chased him. Vince was nearby on Matt's back porch, sipping from a tall glass of ice water.

She stopped her car, got out and glanced around. There was no sign of Matt, but since his truck was parked next to the house, he was no doubt home.

"Matt's inside," Vince volunteered. "He got a call he had to take."

Probably police business and maybe related to the latest Tiffany–Keaton fiasco that had folks buzzing about at the reception. Emory figured she wouldn't have to finish Tiffany's latest dress, after all. If, or rather *when*, she and Keaton got back together, Tiffany would want something entirely different. These breakups and makeups had to be costing Keaton's and Tiffany's parents a fortune.

"I got dogs," Jack blurted out. The boy was certainly happy. Unlike Vince. The man was smiling, but Emory didn't think it was her imagination that the smile didn't reach his eyes.

"Yep, you've got dogs all right," Emory said to Jack. "Did you name them yet?"

"Squeaky and Squawky," Jack answered without hesitation.

Emory looked at Vince for an explanation when Jack continued to run around and giggle. "Jack loves that clown show on TV, and Squawky's the name of Squeaky's mouse sidekick."

Ah. Kid logic. Emory wouldn't point out that ten years from now, Jack, who'd be a teenager by then, might have some namer's regret.

"Squeaky's gonna live here," Jack explained. "Squawky's gonna come with me."

So Natalie had caved about not having a dog at her place. Caved and apparently agreed to the puppy, which would be a heck of a lot more work than the Lab.

"Take a little break and have some water," Vince told the boy. "It's hot, and you'll get dehydrated."

Jack didn't make a fuss about that. He simply scooped up the large plastic cup of water that was sitting on the ground and chugged while the dogs jumped and the puppy nipped at his heels.

"Natalie's at work," Vince added when Emory made her way to the porch. He checked his watch. "She'll be home soon so I'll need to get Jack back. Of course, Jack's not going to like that," he said in a "what ya gonna do" kind of parental, casual tone, but again there seemed to be something off about it.

Vince attempted another smile, and Emory sank down in the chair next to him. "Natalie's dress is nearly ready. I'll have her come over this week for a final fitting, and maybe she can bring Jack and Squawky so they can have a playdate with Squeaky."

Vince made a sound of agreement and drank some more water.

"Is something wrong?" she came out and asked.

He didn't jump to confirm or deny that, but Vince's gaze

drifted toward the back door. "Matt didn't seem upset when he got the call. More like annoyed."

She doubted that Vince had misunderstood her question so he clearly didn't want to talk about whatever was troubling him. The timer on his phone beeped, and he immediately got to his feet.

"Time to go, Jack," he called out to the boy. Now that caused Jack to do some groaning. "Let me see if your dad can come out and give you a quick goodbye."

Vince headed for the back door, but Matt was already on his way out. "I heard the timer," Matt said, muttering a hello to Emory.

Matt slipped his phone into his pocket and went into the yard to give Jack a hug and a kiss. The boy continued to protest until Matt promised he could come back tomorrow. That appeased him enough so that Vince could bundle both him and the puppy into his car. Matt and she stood there and waved goodbye until they were out of sight.

With playtime apparently over and with perhaps exhaustion setting in, the Lab came onto the porch, lapped up water from his bowl and then dropped down beneath the cool whirl of the fans.

"All done at the reception?" Matt gathered the water cup and glass that Vince and Jack had left behind and took them into the kitchen.

"I am. The gown and veil are tucked away, and Joe and Millie have left for their honeymoon," she said, following him into the house. "Is everything okay at work?"

Matt nodded, drank some ice water and handed her the glass. "Just an update from Azzie on the Tiffany drama. Azzie arrested Keaton when he wouldn't get out of the street."

Emory drank, not especially because she was thirsty

but she liked the idea of the somewhat intimate gesture of sharing a glass with Matt.

"The interview went about as I expected with your folks," he continued, causing some of that intimacy rush to fade. "They didn't break in and don't know who did. Your dad apologized to me, though, for all the gossip and such his affair with Candy Lynn caused me."

It took Emory a moment to wrap her mind around that. Her dad was a good man, one who'd made a horrible mistake by having an affair, but she hadn't thought he'd understood just how Matt had gotten caught up in that mistake as well.

"Progress," she concluded, and that brought back a whole bunch of the intimate flutters. So much so that she would have kissed him had Matt not spoken.

"After I left your parents, Bobby Ray called me," he went on. "He thinks he knows who wrote the note that was left on your mother's car, and he believes it's the same person who broke into your cottage."

"Who?" Emory couldn't ask fast enough.

"Bobby Ray wouldn't say, but he's coming in for an interview tomorrow. And yes, I pushed him to give me a name," he added before she could ask.

She thought of all the possible candidates that Bobby Ray could name. "Did he happen to say if he had any proof to back up his claim?"

"No proof whatsoever," Matt said, and he went to the fridge. "Gifts to cheer you up." He took out four bakery bags and set them on the counter next to her. "One from Azzie, one from Tellie and two from me. We were all on the same page about wanting to cheer you up."

Emory felt her eyes widen, and she dragged in a deep breath so she could take in the tasty scent. "Consider myself cheered." Despite the fact she'd consumed way too many calories at the reception, she took one out and bit into it. The sound she made was akin to an orgasm.

"The chocolate chunks melted in my trunk so that's why they were in the fridge," Matt explained.

The chocolate had indeed melted into larger than normal blobs, but that didn't lessen the taste. Or her pleasure in taking a second bite.

"Four of them," she remarked. "It'll take me a while to go through them. Want a bite?"

Emory held it out for him to taste, an intimate gesture akin to her satisfied groan over the cookie. Matt took a bite. Nodded. And made his own sound of pleasure. Man, oh, man, Matt was hot even when reacting to a baked treat.

"A friend of mine had these served at her wedding reception and then wore some of them on her honeymoon," Emory threw out there. "Well, maybe not actually wore them. I guess you could say she used them in a clever way."

That got his attention. A smile tugged at his mouth. Heat lit in his eyes. "Care to show me?"

She smiled back. "That question sounds as if it's coming from a man in possession of condoms."

"Show me," he repeated, and his voice had slipped into a drawl. Matt took a slow step toward her.

Emory didn't drawl, but she did some slipping right into the foreplay arena. She held two of the cookies over her breasts. Then, lowered one of the two to the front of her panty region.

"I think my friend's husband nibbled his way to the gooey caramel center," Emory added.

And with that sexual gauntlet thrown, she waited.

She didn't have to wait long. Nope. Matt went to her, and as if he'd rehearsed it, he swept her cookie-clasping hands aside, snapped her against him and kissed her. Emory had no doubts, none, that he was going to get to that caramel center very, very soon.

IN HINDSIGHT, MATT realized he'd been thinking about doing this all day. Not playing with cookies but kissing Emory with the sole objective of getting her into the bed in the guest room where he'd put the condoms. Well, he'd been thinking about that and also giving her a whole lot of pleasure along the way.

And the pleasure started right away.

Then again, there was always pleasure whenever he kissed Emory. Today, she tasted like naughty little secrets and chocolate. Not a bad combination at all especially combined with the way she kissed him back and the way her arms went around him in a tight "take me now" embrace.

Because Matt didn't want Zella or Zeke walking in on them and that "taking" embrace, he reached behind him and locked the kitchen door. The couple had a key, of course, but unless they'd recently developed severe cases of stupidity, they wouldn't just use that key to waltz in. But since there was still a long-shot possibility of them developing stupidity, Matt got started moving Emory and him in the direction of the bedroom where they'd have a bit more privacy.

It turned out, though, that mere walking wasn't easy, not when he wanted to keep his mouth on some part of her. At the moment, he was going for her neck, but it was hard for him to maneuver with their bodies fused against each other. Not fused as much as he wanted, but there was enough contact that made movement slow. Still, he was kissing and touching Emory so slow was still okay.

Emory sure wasn't holding back on the kissing and touching, either. She slid her hand way down to his butt, and that's when Matt realized she still had hold of the cookies. He didn't mind chocolate and caramel on his jeans, but…

He stopped, rethought any and all cookie objections he'd had. Because he wouldn't mind playing around with those tasty treats on Emory after they'd finished this desperate, needy round of sex that it was turning out to be.

Once they had burned off some of this heat, then they could fool around. With cookies or anything else she wanted to play with. They could do that with a second, third and fourth round of lazy sex that might not have the desperate edge he was feeling right now.

Emory went exploring with her mouth as they continued the groping, stumbling trek to the bedroom. She kissed his neck and then made a breathy sigh as if he'd tasted as good at the Mondo. The sigh and her breath hit against his skin and felt like a notch up in the "let's play dirty" dance they were doing.

Not wanting to wait to feel more of her, Matt caught onto the hem of her dress and pulled it off over her head. He took a moment to ease back and look at her. Another moment to thank his lucky stars. She was built. All those curves. And she hadn't forgotten the skimpy underwear, either. She was practically spilling out of the cups of her lacy white bra.

Matt helped with the spilling.

He pushed down the cups and took her nipple into his mouth. Yeah, this was what he wanted, but it came at sort of a high price. They banged into the wall leading to the hall, tripped and damn near had accidental sex when they caught each other. Emory laughed, an evil little dirty laugh that let him know she considered any and all of this one fine adventure.

The adventure escalated when they made it a couple of

steps inside the bedroom and she went after the buttons on his shirt. She stopped and looked down at the cookies as if she'd forgotten she was holding them. In what had to have been a prime sacrifice, she tossed them on his dresser. The Mondos landed hard, crumbs exploding and igniting the scent of chocolate and cookie dough.

With plenty of that chocolate still on her hands, Emory tried again for his shirt buttons and managed to get a few open while Matt continued to kiss her breasts. Apparently, he hit the right spot and pressure because she threw back her head and moaned. Oh, yeah. It was the right kind of moan, too, and he made it his immediate mission to make her moan even louder.

He unhooked her bra, rid her of it and kept on kissing. Emory didn't give up on the buttons, either, and she finally opened them. Well, mostly. He heard a few pop and ping onto the floor. Casualties of a romping round of foreplay.

Wearing just her panties, she pushed him back so that he landed on the bed. Matt reached for her, but she gave him a sexy little shake of her finger. And eased down her panties. Inch by inch by inch. Until she gave him the hard-on from hell. A hard-on that was demanding to be inside her now.

Matt reached for her again, going for that now, but he got another of those finger wags. A finger she put in her mouth. Sucked. And then she used that temptress's instrument by sliding it down the front of his jeans. Right on his erection, which wasn't hard to find since it was straining against the denim.

He watched her as she flicked open his belt, did more finger play on his zipper. She lowered it with the same excruciating slow pace as she'd stripped off her panties. Slowing even more and smiling like a siren, she shimmied down his jeans.

Then his boxers.

Part of him was eating this up. Mercy, it felt good. But the other part of him was about to explode. It was that part that drove him to take hold of her fingers. Yes, the fingers that were going for his dick. Matt cuffed her wrists in one of his hands and hauled her onto the bed with him.

And the naked kissing began.

He encountered a few crumbs. Also there was a smidge of caramel which he lapped up. He continued the lapping when he trailed those kisses to her stomach. Then lower.

And lower.

Yeah, he heard that moan again. Louder and urgent. She also grabbed onto his hair as if to anchor herself for the on-slaught. Matt onslaughted her a while longer until he figured neither of them could take any more without flying over the edge. Since he wanted to be inside her when that happened, he grabbed one of the condoms and put it on.

Matt managed, somehow, to keep his eyes connected with hers when he pushed into her. When he felt all that wet, tight heat surround him. Even when he thought he'd experienced that "whole metaphorical dying and going to heaven" deal.

Emory didn't look away, either. Her gaze stayed locked with his as she lifted her hips, matching him thrust for thrust. She hooked her legs around him, arched her back and managed to look like a dreamy sex goddess who was savoring every inch of him. Every bit of this.

He savored, too. And took. And took. Until he felt her clamp around him. The orgasm shuddered through her, and the moan she made this time was long, slow and heaped with pleasure and relief.

Matt took just another minute and more strokes to draw out that pleasure. To hold on to this as long as he could. Then he let the relief come and slide right over him.

CHAPTER SIXTEEN

EMORY HAD TO look down to make sure her feet were actually on the floor of her home sewing room. They were. But she certainly felt all floaty as if she could gather up feathers, duct tape them to her arms and fly away.

Yes, that was a whimsical kind of thinking, and feeling, but good orgasms could do that. *Orgasms*, as in plural. Matt had seen to that since they'd spent pretty much the entire late afternoon and evening in bed. The Mondo cookies had come in handy to stop them from starving, but she wasn't sure they would have noticed starvation with them going at each other like rabbits.

Too bad she couldn't have bottled one of those orgasms. Bottled a little bit of Matt, too, because she was missing him like crazy. Work and adult responsibility apparently had to take priority over sex because here she was in the sewing room putting the finishing touches on Natalie's dress, while Matt was in town at the police station. Emory was certain she'd be back over at his place tonight, but with this ache for him spreading in her body, the hours felt way too long.

Forcing herself to focus on something other than Matt, sex and bottled orgasms, Emory stood back and eyed the dress. She did a little adjusting to the lace cuff and followed it up with more eyeing. She loved certain dresses she made, disliked some and was neutral to others. This one she loved, a surprise since the woman who'd be wearing it was Matt's ex.

She wasn't jealous of Natalie, not really, but Emory did worry a little that Matt might make mental comparisons of his ex and her. And that she might not stack up to any comparison made with the stunning Natalie. Still, it was partly because of Natalie that Emory had had that great round of sex with Matt. If Natalie hadn't come back to Last Ride to marry Vince, then Matt wouldn't be here. There would have been no summer fling. No orgasms. No fluttering feeling in her belly that told her what she felt for Matt was well past the fling stage.

It felt cliché to think of falling in love with a man who'd only hours earlier become your full-fledged lover, but Emory couldn't deny that her heart was leaning in the "I love you" direction.

Frowning over that, she felt her feet drift back down to earth, and her heart went well past the leaning stage when she heard the sound. That particular part of her practically jumped out of her chest when she heard the tap at the patio door. For one flicker of a moment, she thought the burglar had returned.

But it was Matt.

He was on the other side of the glass, and he stepped in when he obviously realized that he'd startled her.

"Sorry," he muttered.

He went to her and gave her a soft kiss. The kind of kiss not designed to stir up this instant high level of heat, but it did anyway. Emory was already spinning tales in her head of afternoon nookie until she realized it was way too early for Matt to be off from work. Heck, it was barely lunchtime.

"I can't stay long," he said, sounding disappointed and more than a little heated himself. "I had to pick up some files I forgot to take into the office. But I thought you'd also want to know how the interview went with Bobby Ray."

Emory certainly hadn't forgotten about that. All right, she had, because of the sex and heart thoughts about Matt, but she was remembering it now.

"I do want to know. Did he actually point the finger at anyone for leaving the note and breaking in here?" she asked.

"He did. He believes it was Frannie."

Emory had made a mental list of suspects, but the woman's name hadn't been on it. "Frannie gave me the box with Candy Lynn's things." But the moment she said that, Emory realized something else. "She didn't know there was a diary in it. If she had, I believe she would have pointed it out to me."

"Yeah, that's what Bobby Ray was thinking, too. And FYI, there's no mention of the diary in the investigation reports for Candy Lynn's death. The sheriff had two deputies do a search of her place. It's possible they just didn't see the disk since it was tucked in the book. Also possible that Candy Lynn's landlord or even Frannie moved the box before the cops even arrived. If it was the landlord, I doubt he was trying to hide anything. He just might have wanted her things cleared out of his property. No way to ask him, though, because he passed away a couple of years ago."

Emory took a moment to give that some thought. "Either of those scenarios could have happened. You asked Frannie if she moved the box before the cops went over the place?"

"I did," he confirmed. "She admitted maybe she had. Her uncle told her to get the things out of the apartment, and she can't recall if the deputies had already searched the place or not."

Emory knew Sheriff Lyle, of course, and the man had a

reputation of being a good cop, but it was possible Frannie had gotten to the apartment before the scene was secured. In those hours following the discovery of Candy Lynn's body, the focus would have been on processing the woman's car since that's where she'd died. And the car hadn't been near her apartment but rather in the parking lot behind the Three Sheets to the Wind bar.

"I guess Bobby Ray is assuming that now that Frannie knows a diary exists, she's worried about what her ex-pal wrote in it?" Emory asked.

Matt nodded. "Frannie's worked hard to shake off her roots, her past, and she might not want any of those roots and past being brought to light again."

Well, heck. Maybe Bobby Ray was right about Frannie being the one to break into the cottage. Neither Frannie nor Bobby Ray would have wanted the contents of the diary public since they both knew Candy Lynn would have written about their less than stellar behavior.

Emory hated the idea of anyone leaving that note. It had upset her mother and felt like a threat. She couldn't imagine Frannie doing something like that, but then desperate people sometimes did desperate things.

"What did Frannie have to say about all of this?" Emory pressed.

"Plenty. I dropped by to see her right before I came home. She denies leaving a note and breaking in, but she doesn't have an alibi. She says that's the day she had a migraine and she stayed it bed." Matt lifted his shoulder. "It's possible."

It was. Emory had heard mention of Frannie getting migraines. In a small town, health issues were a favorite with those shooting the bull. Emory was well aware of dozens of folks with hemorrhoids, rashes and other ailments that should have never been offered up in public conversations.

"I need to get this Last Ride Society research over and done," Emory concluded on a sigh. "And I don't really have much to put in the report that won't embarrass or piss off people." Or hurt them as it probably would do to Matt. "I'm hoping there's something I can use in those last one hundred or so pages of the diary." Because that was about all they had left to read. "Something that I can maybe twist or fudge to give her at least one redeeming quality."

Matt didn't jump to say finding such a hidden gem would be impossible so maybe he, too, was holding out hope for such a miracle.

"After one of us has finished the diary, then we can burn or crush the darn thing and let everyone know it's no longer a threat to all their nasty little secrets," Emory concluded.

He made a sound of agreement. "I can get started on that. Or I can just go ahead and destroy the diary today."

She leveled a look at him. "You could do that, without knowing what's in the rest of it?"

Emory could tell from the way his forehead bunched up that doing it would be a problem for him. As a cop, he probably wanted to see for himself that no one else had had a part in Candy Lynn's death. But maybe as the woman's son, he was also looking for something else. That redemption angle. Something that Candy Lynn had done to prove that at least a tiny bit of her heart wasn't stone-cold.

"I'll put out the word that I've destroyed the diary," Matt amended a few seconds later. "That should stop anyone from trying to get it by breaking into your place."

She had no intention of declining that offer, so Emory nodded. While she didn't feel threatened by being alone in her own house, she definitely didn't want anyone poking around for the blasted musings that Candy Lynn had left behind.

"Knock, knock," someone called out from the front porch, and then the person did an actual knock. "Emory, are you in there?"

Emory winced. "It's Tiffany. She's probably here to cancel the order on the dress she wanted me to make for her."

"Then I'll go out this way." Matt tipped his head to the patio doors and then leaned in to give her another of those kisses that made her wish she could haul him off to bed. "I'll catch you later," he added, heading out.

Despite Tiffany giving another knock and calling out a "yoo-hoo," Emory took a moment to let her pulse and breathing level out before she went to answer the door. When she opened it, Tiffany came right in.

Emory had expected the woman to be in tears. Or spitting mad. But Tiffany was neither of those things. In fact, she looked as if she needed to level out her own pulse and breathing because she was practically brimming with giddiness.

"I need a dress," Tiffany gushed with all the enthusiasm Jack had shown when he'd been playing with his dogs. "Keaton and I are eloping." She clapped her hands with that announcement and did little bounces on the toes of her shoes.

Emory had to readjust her mindset. She'd thought she would have to dole out some "there, there" comfort and agree with any name Tiffany chose to call her cheating fiancé, but apparently that wouldn't be needed.

"Keaton and you are back together?" Emory asked.

"Yes, his being with Bambi was all a misunderstanding." The woman pooh-poohed that with the wave of her hand as if she'd been silly to even think that about her beloved. "But I want to avoid future misunderstandings by marrying him ASAP. We have the license, so I want us to get married today."

Emory wanted to point out that speed, or even wedding vows, probably wouldn't help Keaton mend his cheating ways, but it wasn't her place to talk a bride out of making a mistake. Even a mistake that would finally put an end to her run as a "mostly lucky" wedding dressmaker.

"I thought Azzie had arrested Keaton," Emory commented, following Tiffany as she headed to the sewing room.

"Oh, I bailed him out when he explained everything about Bambi." She stopped, glanced around at the mannequins. "Anyway, I need a dress. Any dress will do. As long as you've made it, that'll be fine. I'm sure you've got something lying around here I can use."

Emory did a mental inventory of what she had on hand. All the dresses on the mannequins were spoken for. Ditto for the one she had already in the garment bag, but she went to the walk-in closet that she used for supplies and such, opened it and perused the contents before she plucked out one of the few completed gowns inside.

It was butt ugly.

In fact, it defined *butt ugliness* and was nowhere in the realm of being appropriate for a wedding. Per the bride's insistence, it was made of green-and-orange camouflaged fabric and had silver antlers in places where most brides would have opted for crystals or pearls. Even the accompanying veil had antlers instead of something more traditional like a tiara.

"The bride was marrying an avid hunter," Emory explained, and though she didn't mention who the bride was, the woman's name was embroidered on the tiny tag on the neckline. As Emory did with all the gowns she made.

"She'd planned a hunting theme for the reception. One with cakes shaped like deer and turkeys on each table."

But none of that had happened because the groom-to-be had called off the wedding the night before the big event.

"Uh," Tiffany said, and Emory could see her backpedaling on her earlier comment of *any dress will do*. "This is all you have?"

Emory didn't bother to explain there was a reason for the dresses to be in the closet. They were rejects. Well, all but one, but Tiffany wasn't getting that. No way, no how. So, she took out another gown.

This design had been for a bride who had wanted a fairy wedding. This dress was sparkly rainbow gossamer and had attached matching rainbow wings. It looked like something a five-year-old would have chosen for a Halloween costume. That wedding hadn't happened, either, because the bride had run off with her yoga instructor.

Tiffany's mouth pursed, and she shook her head. "Please tell me you have something else."

She did. Emory took out the third and final option. A dress for a size zero bride who'd gained a couple of pounds and had called off the wedding because she hadn't wanted anyone to see her walking down the aisle like that.

"I'd never fit in that," Tiffany murmured, but then her attention zoomed to the back of the closet.

To the "no way, no how" dress.

"Wow, look at that one. It's amazing," Tiffany gushed.

Before Emory could stop her, the woman took the dress from the hanging rod and started oohing and aahing. It was definitely both ooh and aah-worthy in her opinion.

That's because it was Emory's own fantasy dress.

She'd painstakingly worked on the design, located the right fabric—antique ivory Mulberry silk, which had cost an arm and a leg. And she'd personally stitched on every tiny Waterford pearl bead.

"This would work," Tiffany insisted, her eyes bright as she ran her hands over it.

"It's spoken for," Emory insisted right back, taking the dress from her and putting it back in the closet.

Tiffany's expression was a mix of shock and poutiness. "Whose dress is it? I can maybe talk her into letting me use it."

Thinking fast on her feet, Emory answered, "It's for a client who doesn't want her identity revealed."

Not a lie. Emory didn't want her identity revealed. Definitely didn't want it blathered around that she'd made a wedding dress for herself.

Tiffany stared at her for several long moments and then pointed to the embroidered tag on the back neckline. "It has your name on it. You made the dress for yourself. Is it the one you wore for your weddings?"

This time, Emory didn't manage to think so fast. "No. I, uh, made it as sort of a display product."

"With your name in it," Tiffany pointed out. Her tone and expression had a definite "liar, liar, pants on fire" accusation to it.

Emory would have attempted another explanation, one that wouldn't have Tiffany spreading word that the divorced wedding dressmaker had done something so, well, pathetic as to make her own dream dress. But the movement in the doorway of the closet stopped her cold.

Matt was there.

How long he'd been standing there, Emory didn't have a clue, but it was supremely obvious that he'd heard enough of the conversation to know the dress was hers.

"I just wanted..." he started. Then he stopped. "Uh, I

wanted to let you know I'll be home in a little while and wondered if you'd like to catch some lunch in an hour or so."

She did indeed want that. Wanted more to explain to him that the dress with her name on it was... *Crap.* Emory didn't know how she'd explain it, but she needed for Matt to understand that the dress wasn't about her weaving a fantasy about the two of them getting married.

"Thanks," Emory finally responded. "I'll be over as soon as I've finished helping Tiffany." Which she hoped wouldn't be too long.

Matt nodded, gave the fantasy dress one last questioning glance and left. Emory did no more dress glancing, and she didn't give Tiffany a chance to do that, either. She led the woman away from the closet and pointed to a garment on the dress form. Not a completed bridal gown by any stretch of the imagination. It was just a basic knee-length sheath that Emory had planned on using to make a dress for an informal wedding. Since that particular ceremony was months away and because the sheath was about Tiffany's size, Emory took the garment and laid it on the work table.

"But it's so plain," Tiffany whined. "Can't I use the one in the closet?"

Emory ignored her, grabbed a spool of lace and a roll of white duct tape. She started layering the lace using the tape to keep it in place. She worked fast, because she wanted to get to Matt but also because Tiffany's whining was bothering her. Plus, the odds were this elopement wouldn't happen, not with Keaton's penchant for "misunderstandings."

After about twenty minutes of nonstop taping, Emory had the entire dress ringed with the Chantilly lace, and she held up the dress to show Tiffany. Her whines stopped, and she eyed the dress with enough interest and approval that made Emory thrust it into her hands.

"I'll give you extra tape and lace in case something comes loose when you're getting dressed," Emory said, shoving those items into a bag. She made a show of checking the time. "I'm really sorry, but I have to go."

Emory was a little surprised that Tiffany didn't mention the reason for that "having to go" was because she was meeting Matt. The woman kept her attention on the dress.

"Don't you have to bless it or something?" Tiffany asked.

Emory was sure she frowned. "I'm not a priest."

"No, but you have a good track record, and I want to use any advantage I can get." She paused, clamped her teeth over her bottom lip for a couple of seconds. "Do you think I'm making a mistake by marrying Keaton?"

"Yes," Emory said before she could think it through. She should have just given Tiffany a perky no and assured her that all would be perfect in her Tiffany world. That world didn't include wanting to hear the truth about her fiancé.

Tiffany's bottom lip trembled again. "But I love him."

Ah, there it was. The dilemma of people unfortunate to fall in love with the wrong mate. Emory could have worn a "been there, done that" T-shirt when it came to such a thing.

She took hold of Tiffany's arm and led her toward the door. "I'll bet it'll be a beautiful elopement," Emory settled for saying.

That put some stars back in Tiffany's eyes, and she seemed to steel up a little. "Yes, it will be. Thank you so much for everything, and just send me a bill for this," she added, tipping her head to the dress and the bag.

Emory would, but the materials had cost less than thirty bucks with maybe an hour's worth of labor. Too bad she couldn't add any coating of good luck because Tiffany was for sure going to need it.

She waved goodbye to Tiffany as the woman drove away, and Emory went straight to Matt's. She knocked at the back door, got a "come in," and when she did, she found him in the living room.

At the old computer, reading the diary.

Sighing, she went to him and sank down on the sofa beside him.

"I figured I'd get a few more pages read while I was waiting for you," he said. "Everything go all right with Tiffany?"

Emory nodded. "She wanted an elopement dress, so I made her one with duct tape and lace."

Matt turned to her and his eyebrow slid up. However, Emory didn't think all of that questioning look was for her ability to use such things to create a wearable garment. Nope. This was about what he'd seen in the closet of the sewing room.

"I swear I didn't make that dress with you in mind," Emory volunteered. "I didn't really even make it for me." She paused while he continued to stare at her. That stare was as effective as truth serum. "All right, yes, I did make it for me," she amended. "But I didn't do it with a specific groom in mind. I just wanted to make it while I thought of love that lasts. Of marriages that don't break. Of happily-ever-afters."

She figured there was no way he'd understand that, which was why she was so surprised when he leaned in and brushed his mouth over hers.

"A person who makes wedding dresses shouldn't be a cynic," he said. "That person should have a lot of hope."

Emory was plenty stunned. He got it. Matt got it, after

all. Her breath of relief must have been comically loud because he chuckled.

"So, I don't have time for us to go out to lunch because I have to be back at work in twenty minutes," he went on a moment later, "but since I'm starving and you probably are, too, we could grab sandwiches here. Then I could take you somewhere tonight for dinner."

Two surprises, all in the span of a minute. "You mean something like a date?" she asked.

"I mean exactly like a date. It doesn't feel right to have sex with you and not do other things."

That made her smile. "You know, you've got an old-fashioned streak, Matt Corbin. Not in bed," she corrected when he kissed her with a little more heat. "Your streak in that particular venue is more like down and dirty."

He likely would have kissed her again, and that probably would have led to sex. While Emory was all for that, she heard his stomach growl, and she really didn't want him having to go back to work while he was hungry.

"Ham and cheese or turkey?" he asked, getting to his feet.

"Either is fine. I'll keep going through the diary while you make the sandwiches," she added, and she moved onto the spot he'd just vacated.

She didn't especially want to spoil the mood with Candy Lynn's whining, which was more excessive than even Tiffany's, but the sooner they got through the last one hundred pages, the better.

The whining and bitching started almost immediately with the entry that Emory read. Judging from the date, the woman had written this about three weeks before she'd died, and she was complaining about getting kicked out of a party the night before. There was also a rant about her father not ponying up some money to pay her for giving him the brat he wanted so much.

Emory was actually glad she'd been the one to tackle that entry. No need for Matt to see it, though she suspected there were similar entries that he'd already had to comb through.

She scrolled to the next page. And then came to a complete stop. This wasn't a rant or whine. There were numbers. No, they were dollar amounts, she mentally corrected when she studied them. Dollar amounts with initials and a nickname next to them. She also saw the information for a bank account where at least some of the money had been deposited.

"Matt," Emory called out. "You need to take a look at this."

Carrying a plate with their sandwiches and some chips, he came in, his gaze meeting hers for a split second before he sat down next to her. Emory figured he'd already seen it, but she tapped the screen with the title of this particular entry.

Bleeding the Bastards Dry.

Matt groaned, then cursed as he skirted down the list of initials. Eight of them. And the amounts beside each one made Emory come to one nasty conclusion.

Candy Lynn had been blackmailing a whole bunch of people.

CHAPTER SEVENTEEN

MATT SAT IN his office at the police station and wrote up the report of his latest interview. An interview and a report that wouldn't go into the official records but rather in a file in his desk. A "cover his ass" file in case anything he learned in the interviews actually connected to a crime.

A punishable crime, that is.

Because Candy Lynn was dead, he couldn't charge her with extortion or blackmail, but he allowed himself a couple of moments to savor the image of him cuffing her and hauling her sorry ass to jail. No way he could do that, of course, but he could possibly make restitution to the people she'd blackmailed. Or rather he could if the men would just accept the money by owning up to the fact they'd paid her off.

So far, Matt was batting zero on that.

Over the past week since Emory had uncovered Candy Lynn's blackmail scheme, Matt had located the bank where Candy Lynn had deposited the funds. Not in Last Ride but rather in San Antonio. The nearly twenty grand she'd deposited was now worth close to thirty thousand, what with the accumulated interest for the past twenty years. Technically, the money belonged to Matt because Candy Lynn had left no will and he was her next of kin. But he had no intention of accepting it. He'd donate it to a charity if it came down to it, but first he had to make every attempt to get the money back to the rightful owners.

After he'd located the bank and funds, Matt matched the initials Candy Lynn had used in her diary to possible candidates. D.P. was easy—Derrick Parkman, Emory's father. But Derrick hadn't wanted the money. Ditto for the W.D., Waylon Dayton, who was a real-estate agent, and the E.G., Edgar Granger, who was now a minister. After Matt had pushed, and in Edgar's case, pushed hard, those two men had admitted to affairs with Candy Lynn but didn't want gossip stirred up about it by accepting a penny of the money.

Another of the initials was R.P. That was Ryder, and while he admitted paying Candy Lynn, he didn't want the money back because he'd borrowed it from his mother. Of course, he hadn't told his mom the real reason for needing the cash and had instead made up some BS story about wrecking a friend's car and needing to have it repaired. A story Nancy had apparently bought hook, line and sinker.

Now, despite the passing of those twenty years, Ryder still wanted his mom to keep on buying the story. That's because he hadn't relished the idea of having a conversation with her about Candy Lynn blackmailing him because then he would have had to admit to having sex with the woman. Matt couldn't blame him for wanting to keep the "hook, line and sinker" lie intact. Nancy had already been through enough without adding knowledge of her son's affair with Candy Lynn to the mix.

Two sets of the initials likely belonged to Abel and Kurt Zeller, brothers who had moved from Last Ride years ago. That left only one more victim in Candy Lynn's "Bleeding the Bastards Dry" scheme, and she hadn't used initials this time but rather the nickname, Ace. Matt had asked around, to try to determine if that fit anyone in town, but he'd come up empty. Then again, the "fit" part was plenty vague since

Candy Lynn had spread her sexual favors across generations and any and all economic brackets. "Ace" could be pretty much any male in Last Ride, with the exception of Matt, who was between the ages of thirty-five and one hundred. Hell, the "fit" was complicated even more because it was possible that this particular mark wasn't even from Last Ride. Candy Lynn could have taken her dirty dealings elsewhere.

Of course, all these interviews had meant backpedaling on his own lie to tell everyone that he'd already destroyed the diary. He'd had to admit the diary was still around, but Matt made it clear that Emory didn't have it. He damn sure didn't want anyone trying another break-in to get to it. Instead, Matt had put out the word that Candy Lynn's smut journal was in a secure place. And it was. He considered his own house as secure as it got.

Matt looked up when Azzie stepped into the doorway. Since Azzie had a permanent "I'm pissed and tired of idiots" expression, it was hard to tell if she was more pissed off than usual.

"Tiffany Parkman's mother, Eileen, is on the phone and is demanding to speak to you," Azzie informed him.

He sighed. "Let me guess. She wants me to arrest Keaton for cheating on her daughter?"

"No, she wants to file a missing person's report on Tiffany."

Despite there being no alarm whatsoever on Azzie's face, that got his attention. Matt recalled that Emory had made an elopement dress for the woman so maybe something had gone wrong.

"How long has she been missing?" Matt asked, reaching for his desk phone so he could take the call.

"Twenty minutes." Azzie wasn't an eye-roller, but her

"this is bullshit" expression said it all. "Apparently, Tiffany and Keaton tied the knot without telling their folks and are now on their honeymoon. Tiffany called her mother a little while ago to tell her about being a newlywed, and Eileen... Well, let's just say the woman wasn't happy since she and her husband just spent thirty grand doing reno on a barn for the wedding."

Matt pulled back his hand from the phone. "I can see why Eileen wouldn't be pleased about that. But is Tiffany actually missing?"

"Not in any legal sense of the word." Azzie gathered her breath. "After Eileen demanded Tiffany come home and have a proper wedding, Tiffany hung up. Eileen kept calling, and calling, and calling until Tiffany blocked her."

Matt would have done the same thing, and why Eileen Parkman would want another grand wedding attempt, he just didn't know. Besides, with Keaton's track record, they'd likely soon divorce, and Eileen could be back in the "wedding planning" mode. Heck, Keaton and Tiffany could keep the lawyers, ministers and maybe even Emory busy with their future breakups and re-hitchings.

"Anyway, Eileen's convinced that Keaton has brainwashed Tiffany and is maybe holding her against her will," Azzie added.

Matt figured that was malarkey, but he had to ask, "There's no official report of it, but does Keaton have any kind of history of violence or anything else to indicate he'd do something like that?"

"None whatsoever," Azzie assured him. "He's a weenie with a loose zipper and the itchings of a randy teenager."

Matt nodded. That'd been his assessment of the man, too, but he'd refrained from mentally using the word *weenie*. It was too tame for someone who'd acted like a dick.

"Tell Eileen no on filing a missing person's report," he explained to Azzie. "If she gives you any grief, I'll talk to her."

"Oh, I'm pretty good at giving grief right back," Azzie assured him. She hitched her thumb in the direction of the reception area. "Verney Parkman's out there and wants to see you. I can have him make an appointment for tomorrow since it's the end of your shift."

Matt checked the time, surprised that the day had just flown by. Maybe not flown in an adrenaline rush sort of way, but he'd had a steady stream of things to do, what with the interviews and reports.

"Verney didn't say why he wanted to see you," Azzie added. "Want me to ask him?"

"No, just send him on back."

Matt was pretty sure he knew why the man was here. After all the interviews he'd done today about the blackmail, he'd likely stirred up some gossip about it. Gossip that Verney was probably hoping wouldn't include his wife. There was no proof whatsoever that Frannie had participated in Candy Lynn's blackmail scheme, but some folks might think there was guilt by association.

Holding his Stetson in front of him like a shield, Verney came to the doorway. He was dressed for work in his jeans and denim shirt that had the logo of the hardware store stitched above the pocket. He stepped in and immediately closed the door behind him.

"Thanks for seeing me," Verney said without a trace of enthusiasm or even gratitude.

"Take a seat," Matt offered. "You want some water?"

Verney shook his head, and apparently he was declining both the sitting and a drink. "I'm here about the diary," he said, confirming Matt's theory about the reason for the visit.

Matt could relieve some of the tension that had seemingly stiffened every muscle in the man's body. "I'm nearly done reading the diary, and there's nothing in it about Frannie doing anything illegal. In fact, Candy Lynn doesn't mention her a lot. I think because by the time she wrote the entries, Frannie and she had already parted company."

Verney nodded, but the relief didn't come. "I had sex with Candy Lynn," the man blurted out.

Matt blinked and knew he shouldn't have been surprised by anyone admitting to having sex with the woman. But he was beginning to wonder how Candy Lynn had had time to do anything else since she clearly spent a lot of her time in the company of her steady stream of lovers.

"It was before I started dating Frannie," Verney added, and his grip tightened on the brim of his hat. "I didn't tell Frannie because I didn't figure she'd be happy about it."

Nope, Matt couldn't see Frannie or any other woman for that matter feeling good about having their man dick around with the likes of Candy Lynn. Especially since Frannie and Candy Lynn had been friends.

"Did Candy Lynn ever call you Ace?" Matt asked him.

"No." Verney was quick to answer that. "I wasn't with her but a couple of times, and we didn't have pet names for each other."

Matt believed that. Verney didn't seem like the pet name type, though he also didn't seem like the stupid type, either, to have fallen in with the likes of Candy Lynn. Then again, his mother had been a looker and she must have exhibited at least some kind of charm to coax in the sheer quantity of men.

"I don't want Frannie to know any of this," Verney went on, "but after I broke off things with her, Candy Lynn asked me for hush money." He paused as if that might be a news flash to Matt.

Matt kept his eyes cop flat. "You paid her?" Because if so, Candy Lynn hadn't put that in her "Bleeding the Bastards Dry" list. Unless, of course, she'd thought of the man as "Ace" and Verney hadn't been aware of it.

"Not with cash," Verney explained. "I didn't have the kind of money she wanted. So, I paid her in gift cards."

Matt continued his flat cop look but raised an eyebrow to let Verney know he was going to want the details about that.

"My mom's a hard person to buy gifts for," Verney continued after a short pause and a huff, "and I've got three siblings. So, for years we've all just given her gift cards for things like restaurants, miniature golf, bowling, even horseback riding lessons. She had ones for over three hundred dollars just for the Noodle Barn, that restaurant off I-20. My mom never used the gift cards so I gathered up a bunch and took them to Candy Lynn."

Matt didn't even try to wrap his mind around Candy Lynn playing miniature golf or eating at the Noodle Barn, but she must have been okay enough with the payment to accept it.

"Did you break into Emory's cottage looking for the diary?" Matt came out and asked.

"No." Again, Verney's answer was fast. And believable. "Though I did consider just going to Emory and asking for it."

Yeah, Matt bet he had considered that. Along with countless others, including Ace. Whoever the hell he was.

"Did you ever give Candy Lynn drugs?" Matt pressed.

"Hell, no. She used, I'm sure of it, but she didn't do that mess around me." Verney paused. "But she did talk about hitting you. I'm real sorry I didn't tell anybody about that."

Matt liked to think that Verney belonged to the "welcome to the club" on that particular subject because he was betting Candy Lynn had mentioned the abuse to a lot of her pals.

"You won't tell anybody about me having sex with her, will you?" Verney asked.

"I won't, and once I'm done reading the diary, I'll be destroying it." Matt could have added that Emory wouldn't be using any of it in her research, either, but he didn't want any part of this conversation going back to her.

"Thank you," Verney muttered, and he turned, opened the door and walked out.

Matt went ahead and wrote up the interview to add to his personal files. Then, since he was already past his shift, he gathered his things, checked on the nightshift deputies to make sure all was well. It was, so he headed for his truck.

He hadn't actually committed to memory how many waves and nods of greeting versus the snickers and uppity noses he got as he did his drives to and from work, but he thought the waves and nods were still winning out.

When he pulled up in front of his house, he saw Emory sitting on the porch of her cottage. Not in a chair but rather right on the porch with her back against the wall. She was sipping something from a large Mason jar. Even though she had a couple of fans going, it was probably still too damn hot to be sitting outside, so he figured she was waiting for him.

"How'd the interviews go?" she immediately asked.

Yep. Waiting, indeed. "Good." Matt decided to give her the condensed version of what he'd learned. "Still no ID on Ace, but everyone else fessed up to the blackmail. Verney included."

She shook her head in a little mental double take, and

because he thought she could use a smile, even a dry one, he added, "Verney paid Candy Lynn off in gift cards to the Noodle Barn."

She smiled but not nearly as much as he'd hoped. He made his way to the porch and sank down next to her.

He'd been right about the heat. The fans put it in the "barely tolerable" range. The iced drink was likely helping, though. However, when he had a sip from the jar, he realized it wasn't water but rather a generous serving of white wine. She'd added ice cubes to it, diluting it some but also making it plenty cold.

"Bad day?" he asked.

Emory nodded, sighed, groaned and then had a gulp of wine before she continued. "Really crappy things apparently come not in threes but in fours." She lifted a finger. "Elise Dayton threw up on her wedding dress during the final fitting. Nerves, she said. But the raw silk is ruined, the dress will have to be remade and my sewing room at the shop smells like puke."

Matt frowned. Yeah, that was bad all right. Matt helped her to her feet so he could lead her inside the cottage where he immediately thanked the inventor of air-conditioning.

Emory raised finger number two. "Midge Parkman, who's ninety one, wants a grandmother-of-the-bride gown that turns to fire like the one in *The Hunger Games* movie when she twirls around. To demonstrate this, she brought in some kind of torch and accidentally ignited a basket of sugarplum-scented marabou feathers. That covered some of the puke stench but didn't improve the air quality in any way."

He hadn't heard about the fire, but Matt was sure he would. When Emory lifted a third finger, he led her to the sofa and had her sit.

"Marley Grange brought in her two-year-old daughter

to pick up her flower girl dress, and while I was getting it, Marley let the girl run around," Emory continued. "She knocked down the mannequins, and they fell like dominos, knocking down shelves and bashing into the window display of crystal tiaras."

That would have definitely created a mess, but he doubted that's what had put tears shimmering in her eyes. "What else happened?"

She swallowed hard. "Ryder's wife, Heather, insisted he go ahead and move out. The kids are a wreck. So is he."

And there it was. The core of her pain. All the stench, puke and damage in the shop didn't amount to a hill of beans compared to her brother's family being torn apart. Matt might not care much for Ryder, but because he'd been there, done that with a divorce, he knew some of what he was going through.

"Want some cheese or something to go with that wine?" he asked. "Or maybe some *w-h-i-n-e* and cheese because I can deal with venting if that's what you want to do."

She looked at him, a slight smile tugging at her mouth. "I'll bet you can. You're no doubt getting lots of practice as the sheriff."

"Loads." And because he thought they could both use it, he touched his mouth to hers. "It doesn't hold up to puked-on dresses, toddler disasters and burnt feathers, but I did get a visit from Hank Jenkins who brought in a Tupperware container of cow shit to prove that his neighbor's Holstein had broken the fence again and taken a dump on his roses. The shit was pretty ripe," he added.

Another smile tugging. "You're trying to cheer me up."

"I am," he admitted. "Guess we've both had somewhat of a smelly day." He paused, used his fingers to push a strand of hair away from her face. An amazing face despite the fact it was misted with perspiration. "I'm sorry about Ryder, about the kids, about the whole mess. Anything I can do to help you get your mind off it?"

Now her smile turned a little dreamy. So did the look in her eyes. Then the dreaminess took on some heat. "Matt, I'm sure you're capable of doing all manner of things to divert my attention. I brought home another feather wedding dress. You could put it on, and I could chase you around the house while I try to pluck off the feathers."

The only part of that suggestion that sounded intriguing was all the touching that'd go on with the plucking. Plus, he'd be naked under the dress so that could save them some time if they ended up having sex.

Which they would do.

For them, feather plucking was just a form of weird foreplay. But Matt had a better foreplay in mind right now. One that was a surefire way to occupy both their thoughts for the next half hour or so.

He turned to her, and framing her face with his hands, Matt kissed her. And he made it count. Plenty of pressure. Some fire. A whole bunch of need. He kicked up the need by deepening the kiss and easing her closer to him to add some body contact to that fire.

It worked.

Moaning that sound that had his number, Emory sank right into the kiss, all the while setting her wine aside and maneuvering to her feet. She hooked one of her arms around him, and with her mouth still locked with his, she led him to her bedroom.

EMORY FIGURED HAVING sex wasn't a cure for all that ailed her, but hey, it would be a great temporary fix. Especially since Matt was the participating *fixee*. The man could certainly send her up in flames with just his mouth.

Thankfully, though, he had other flame-creating weapons in his arsenal. His hands and fingers, for instance. While they kissed and fumbled their way through her living room, he put those hands to good use by cupping her breast and flicking his thumb over her nipple. Obviously, her nipple approved of that because it tightened and puckered, making it easy for him to find for the next swipe.

By the time they banged into the doorjamb of her bedroom, other parts of her had tightened. And softened. In fact, she was primed and ready to go. Matt clearly was, too, because she could feel another fire-generating part of him pressing hard and hot against the center of her body.

"Please tell me you have a condom," she muttered.

"In my wallet," he muttered back while his mouth cruised down to her neck. Then to her breasts.

Even though he tongue-kissed her through her clothes, it was still potent enough to have Emory hauling him to the bed. Except she misjudged the distance. Easy to do now that he'd kissed her blind. And they ended up sliding to the floor.

She considered trying to get up, especially since the bed was only a few feet away, but then Matt whipped off her dress, kept mouth-cruising to her stomach, and she forgot all about comfort and high thread count sheets. Heck, she forgot everything except how to kick all of this up to full-blown sex.

Matt was obviously on the same page as she was because he helped her get off his shirt and went after his belt and zipper. She worked with him on that, too, but she did some tongue-cruising of her own. To his chest. To his stomach. And then to his boxers.

After she lowered them.

Emory took him into her mouth and smiled—and blew—when he cursed and called her a dirty name. She would have kept it up, coaxing out more of the smut talk from him, but he turned the tables on her. Or rather did his own version of lowering.

He slid down, taking her mouth out of range of his erection, and he kept sliding until he reached her panties. Which he shimmied off her. Then he gave her a kiss that she was certain she would never forget.

Yes, this magic. Sex magic. And he was making sure she was not only fired up but that she was on the verge of a flash burn. Since she wanted him inside her for that, she did another round of sliding. This time, going up and flipping him onto his back so she could straddle him.

"Condom." He gutted out that reminder while he fished around in the pocket of his now-discarded jeans and pulled out a condom.

He was fast. So was Emory. The moment he had on the condom, she dropped lower, taking him inside her. This was way better than playfully plucking feathers off a dress. Way better than pretty much anything she'd ever felt or experienced.

Leave it to Matt to be able to give her a lustful little miracle.

With his hands clamped on her hips, she rode him hard and fast. No choice in either of those things. The need dictated the pace and produced the pleasure. Oh, so much pleasure that continued to climb, climb, climb. Until she'd reached a very sweet spot of that urgent need for release. Matt helped her with that part, too. Another lustful little miracle when he launched her exactly where she needed to be.

The climax rippled through her, filling every inch of her with pleasure. She could thank his inches for that particular accomplishment. Then again, he could probably thank her climaxing ripples for helping him find his own release.

Matt lifted his hips to push into her one last time, and gathering her close to him, he let go.

Emory collapsed on him, and she felt every muscle in his body go lax. Ditto for her. With her breath gusting and her heart dancing, she smooshed her face into the curve of his neck and stayed there while they both came down from the amazing high of incredibly good sex.

He had certainly managed to do something that the wine hadn't. He'd lifted her dark mood and made her feel as if everything could be right with the world. Of course, that was the musings of a well-satisfied body, but Emory would take it. Take it and dream of the next time she could do this all over again.

"Can you make it to the bed?" he asked, sounding more sated than exhausted.

The tone gave her hope that this might turn into a twofer kind of evening. So maybe it wasn't necessary to just dream of being with him again.

Emory rolled off him and onto her back, a reminder they were on the hardwood floor, emphasis on *hard*. Wincing a little, she did another roll, caught onto the bed and pulled herself up. Apparently, amazing sex could dissolve the bones in a body because she had to flop onto the bed like a landed trout.

Matt got up as well, and he disappeared into the bathroom for a couple of moments before he came back into the room. He did the "landed trout" thing, too, beside her and pulled her into his arms. All in all, it was a tasty dessert to what'd been an incredible tasty entrée.

After a couple of moments for her bones to revive, Emory caught onto the side of the quilted bedspread and tossed it over them. Even though they weren't saying anything, the silence wasn't awkward. However, she had such a wonderful buzz going that it caused her mind to start tossing ideas at her. Ideas that she wished Matt and she could be like this for much longer than a mere fling. That they'd go well beyond the sex to something a whole lot more.

Like love.

He was definitely someone she could fall in love with. Not now, of course. Later, when they had more time together...

Oh, crap.

There was no later or more time together. She was in love with him right here, right now. It didn't seem to matter that the *L* word would complicate the heck out of things because her heart was overriding all her other body parts and was insisting it was true.

"You okay?" he muttered, sounding half-asleep. "You sighed."

Sighing was better than cursing, something she was mentally doing. Great. Now she'd get a broken heart out of this awesome sex deal. Worse, she'd have to keep the whole thing about being in love with him to herself. No way would Matt want to hear something like that.

He rolled toward her, taking hold of her face again. Matt looked her straight in the eyes, and she could tell from his intense expression he had something to say. Maybe something about his feelings for her.

It wasn't impossible for him to be in the same wheelhouse as she was when it came to wanting much more out of this than a summer romance. He opened his mouth. Emory held her breath. Waiting.

Then she did some cursing not of the mental variety when there was a knock at the door.

"That better not be Tiffany wanting another dress," she grumbled. "I'm not answering it."

But the knocking continued, getting louder and more insistent. Also there was no accompanying yoo-hoo as Tiffany had done with her prior visit.

"It might be your mom," Matt said.

That took some of the breath right out of her. Because it absolutely could be. Her mother was devastated over Ryder and Heather's breakup, and she'd probably come here to cry it out. Too bad she hadn't waited until morning to do that, but Emory couldn't just ignore her. Especially since her mom had a key and might let herself in.

Emory leaped up from the bed, pulling on her clothes as fast as she could. Matt did the same at a less frantic pace.

"I'll be right there," Emory called out to her visitor.

"If it is your mom, I can slip out through the patio doors," he offered.

Emory had a quick debate about that. Her family would eventually find out she was sleeping with Matt, but today didn't seem like the right timing for such a revelation. And that's why she nodded and gave Matt a quick kiss.

"Hang around a couple of minutes," she insisted. "This might be just a customer I can get rid of."

She did a quick pit stop in the bathroom so she could wash her hands and face, and then she tried to steel herself up. If her mother was on the other side of the door, then lots and lots of steeling would be needed. But it wasn't her mom.

It was Natalie.

One glimpse at the woman's face, and Emory knew something was seriously wrong. It occurred to her that maybe Natalie had gone to Matt's house looking for him, and when he hadn't answered his door, she'd come here.

"Is Jack okay?" Emory immediately asked. She wanted to rattle off other questions, like had there been an accident or emergency, but Natalie put a quick halt to Emory's panic.

"Jack's fine. He's spending the night with my parents." Natalie blinked back tears. "Has Vince come by to talk to you?"

Emory definitely hadn't expected the woman to ask that. "No, why? Did something happen to him?"

Natalie shook her head and did more blinking back tears. "Can I come in for a minute?"

And that's when it hit Emory. The reason Natalie might be here. She might have figured out that her ex was having sex with her wedding dressmaker. Though Emory didn't know why that would cause this obvious level of distress. Unless, of course, Natalie still had feelings for Matt. If so, that'd likely be a bombshell to both Matt and Vince.

"Of course, you can come in," Emory answered, stepping back so Natalie could enter.

Natalie glanced back over her shoulder at Matt's house. "If he sees my car and asks why I was here, just tell him it was about the wedding dress. Which it is. Sort of. I'll need to talk to Matt, but I can't. Not right now. Not with my nerves all over the place."

Emory had no trouble seeing those nerves, and she considered telling Natalie that Matt might still be here. Might hear this conversation, too, but Natalie spoke before she could say anything.

"I thought Vince had come to see you," Natalie blurted out. "He's so upset, and he thinks this has something to do with Matt and you. It doesn't. This is about me. About this." She tapped her heart.

"All right." Emory kept her tone cautious with more than a tinge of confusion. The confusion was easy because there was plenty of it. "Did Vince and you have an argument or something?"

"Or something." Twin tears spilled down Natalie's cheeks, and her breath hitched. "I told Vince I was having second thoughts about marrying him."

Oh, man. A definite potential bombshell, and that explained why Vince might venture here. He might have assumed Natalie's doubts had to do with her maybe still having feelings for her ex. Which she might.

"A lot of brides-to-be have nerves," Emory said, switching her tone to soothing. This was the talk she had to give at least a couple of times a year. "A wedding generates a lot of excitement and happiness. A lot of stress, too. It's natural to be stressed and worried when you're starting a new life, but if Vince and you love each other, then everything will probably work out just fine."

"No, it won't work out," Natalie insisted, blowing right over Emory's go-to talk. "Because I'm not sure I want it to work. I should be sure," she added.

Yes, but nerves and stress played into that sureness. However, Natalie continued before Emory could say that.

"I feel so guilty about Matt leaving his SWAT job and life in Amarillo. A job and life he loved," Natalie emphasized.

Emory couldn't argue with that. She figured becoming sheriff of Last Ride had been a huge career step down for him. A step down that he'd sucked up so he could be with his son, even though it meant getting daily doses of reminders that he was Candy Lynn's son.

"My house in Amarillo hasn't sold yet," Natalie went on, "and I'm sure I'd have no trouble getting my job back."

Everything inside Emory went still. Natalie wasn't just talking about ending her engagement. She was talking about moving.

And Matt would move with her.

"Uh, what brought all of this on?" Emory managed to say despite the golf ball–sized lump in her throat.

Natalie shook her head, lifted her tear-filled eyes to the ceiling for a moment. Then she groaned softly. "Vince. He's been so distant, and I think he's having second thoughts about marrying me. I want to give him an out. He's a good man, and if I stay, he'll insist on doing what he thinks is the right thing by going through with the wedding."

Again, Emory couldn't argue that. From everything she'd heard about Vince, he definitely fell into the "good guy" category, and he was likely feeling some guilt, too, that Natalie had had to relocate her life, her son and her ex so she could marry him.

"I don't want Vince to make that kind of mistake," Natalie continued. "I don't intend to go through another divorce." She paused, gathered her breath. "Anyway, if Vince comes here, you can tell him that. And don't mention any of this to Matt. I should be steadier in the morning, and I'll come over and talk to him then, before he goes to work."

Natalie muttered a "thanks for seeing me," and she headed out the door. Emory stood there several long moments, wondering what to do. If she went to Matt's, he'd want to know why Natalie had visited her. He'd see on her face that it felt as if someone had grabbed hold of her heart and was squeezing the life right out of it.

Then she heard the bedroom door open.

And she realized Matt wasn't at his place. He was still here. Emory turned, slowly, and saw something else.

That Matt had heard exactly what his ex-wife had just said.

CHAPTER EIGHTEEN

MATT STOOD AT his kitchen window and drank his second cup of coffee. He felt as if he was about to face a firing squad.

This wasn't like the adrenaline rush he got when he'd been a city cop in the middle of a high-stakes case. But he couldn't dispute that there were indeed stakes even if the high was at a different sort of level. Not life and death.

Just life.

Specifically, Natalie's, Jack's and his. And, of course, Emory's. Yeah, she was in this mix now as well.

Emory hadn't pushed him to pour out his heart or talk it over once she had discovered that he'd overheard what Natalie had said. She'd simply given him a "there, there" pat on the arm and suggested he might need some thinking time. There was no "might" to it. He needed the time, and even after sleeping on it, he still couldn't wrap his mind around it.

Natalie and he hadn't exactly spent a lot of time together since he'd moved back to Last Ride, but in the short exchanges they'd had when he picked up and dropped off Jack, Matt hadn't gotten any vibes as to her having second thoughts about marrying Vince. Just the opposite. She'd seemed happy. Settled. So, either his instincts about her sucked—a possibility since they were, after all, divorced—or something bad had gone down in the last couple of days.

If something bad had indeed happened, Jack hadn't picked up on it. When Matt had had his usual conversation with the boy the night before, Jack had gushed about the dogs and had asked if Matt could take him camping. Or rather wanting them to sleep in a tent in the woods so they could find some bears and butterflies. Matt wouldn't look for bears, but he'd definitely take his son camping. The question would be where they'd do that.

In Last Ride or Amarillo?

With that question snaking through his mind and tightening his gut, he heard the approaching vehicle and figured it was Natalie coming to tell him the news about her broken engagement. But it wasn't his ex's car. It was Vince's, and after he'd pulled to a stop, he got out and made a beeline to the back porch.

Gulping down more coffee that he wished he'd laced with a shot of Jamesons, Matt opened the door for the man. Vince didn't issue a greeting, and he sported a very troubled, sour expression when he came right in.

"Natalie will be here soon," Vince informed him. "She plans on telling you that she's breaking off things with me."

Matt nodded. "I overheard her telling Emory last night. Natalie doesn't know I heard," he added when he saw the surprise flicker in Vince's eyes. "I would ask if you're okay, but I can see that you're not. Sit," he ordered, motioning toward the kitchen table.

He poured the man coffee and added some Jamesons that he took from the cabinet. Not a lot of the whiskey since he figured Vince would be driving soon, but Matt thought a single shot might settle him down.

"I don't want to lose Natalie," Vince muttered. His elbows went on the table, and he dropped his face into his hands. "I love both Jack and her."

Well, that answered a couple of Matt's biggie questions. The breakup didn't have to do with the man's feelings for the family he was getting through marriage, and Vince was opposed to ending things.

Sighing, Matt set the doctored coffee next to Vince and took the chair across the table from him. Talking to his ex's now ex-fiancé definitely wasn't something he'd put on a list of fun things to do. Still, this would affect all of them so he needed to hear Vince out.

"Did something specific happen to make Natalie want to break up?" Matt came out and asked. "And FYI, that's not a dig of any kind. I'm just trying to understand what's going on."

"Me, too," Vince snarled, and he drank the whiskey-laced coffee like medicine. "I thought it was because of you. Because you're not happy here. Except now that you're dating Emory, I thought you were happy."

Matt's mood was definitely on the happy scale, and yes, that was in part because of Emory. More in part, though, in a big picture kind of way—Jack, Last Ride, Stallion Ridge and Emory. Added to that, he was feeling more comfortable as the sheriff. That whole nod/greeting to mumbled gossip ratio was definitely landing in his favor.

"I never said anything to Natalie about wanting to move back to Amarillo," Matt volunteered. He paused, considered doing some walking on eggshells for this next part, but it was best just to put it all out there. "Natalie mentioned something about you being distant with her lately, that she thought you were having second thoughts about marrying her. True?"

"No," he jumped to say, but the jumping came to a quick halt. "I'm not having second thoughts about marrying her. Like I said, I love her." He paused. "But I guess I've been distant." His head whipped up, his gaze drilling into Matt's. "God, is that why she's leaving me?"

"It seems to be playing into it," Matt settled for saying, and he waited to see if Vince was going to volunteer the reason for the distance.

He didn't.

Matt might have turned his interrogation skills on the man had he not heard the sound of another approaching car. He got up to glance out the window. "It's Natalie," he relayed to Vince.

Vince looked a little like a jack-in-the-box when he popped up from the chair, and he faced the door with that same kind of "facing a firing squad" look that Matt had had right before Vince's arrival. There was still a strong sense of gloom and doom in the air, but Matt thought it might do Vince and Natalie some good to talk this out. He'd gladly give them the space for that if it's what they wanted.

As he'd done for Vince, Matt opened the back door for Natalie. She didn't rush in. In fact, she hadn't even gotten out of her car. A moment later, Matt's phone rang, and he saw her name on the screen.

Sighing for the one-millionth time this morning, Matt answered the call.

"Vince told you?" she immediately asked.

Matt made a sound that he hoped she would take for an agreement. He really didn't want to tell her that he'd eavesdropped on her conversation with Emory.

"I think he'd like to talk to you," Matt threw out there.

"I can't," Natalie threw out there just as fast. "I just wanted to tell you and then give you some time to think about it."

More time to think about this sounded as much fun as jock itch. "Natalie, you need to see Vince."

"I know. Just not now." Judging from the sniffling sound he heard, she was crying. "I can't go through this again, Matt. I can't deal with having Jack's life turned upside down by marrying the wrong man."

Well, hell. Matt sure didn't want his son messed up over this. "You believe Vince is the wrong man?"

More sniffing. The sound of her blowing her nose. "I don't know, and if I can't be one hundred percent sure, I don't want to risk another mistake. You understand that. I know you do. That's why you're being so cautious with Emory."

There was a whole lot of food for thought in those four sentences she'd just rattled off. Matt had indeed been cautious with Emory. For all the good it'd done him. Caution was a wussy loser when it came to intense sexual attraction. And maybe more. Or at least there could perhaps be more under one huge condition.

If he stayed in Last Ride, that is.

As Matt listened to Natalie's sobs, he had to figure his chances of staying put were growing slimmer by the minute.

EMORY CAREFULLY SLID the needle through the glass bead that she was sewing on the dress. *Carefully* because she'd already stuck her fingers three times, which meant she was sporting three Band-Aids. No way could she risk getting blood drops on the expensive white silk gazar, but the bandaged-up fingers did make her feel as if she was trying to sew with fat sausages.

She'd been at this particular dress for hours, ever since she'd arrived for work at the shop, and during that time, every second of her thoughts kept going back to Matt. They hadn't talked about Natalie wanting to move back to

Amarillo, but that sure as heck hadn't stopped Emory from thinking about it.

And coming up with worst-case scenarios.

Scenarios like Matt would pack up and leave today. That he'd return to his previous life in the city and be so giddily happy that he'd never bother to think about Last Ride or her again.

Of course, Matt wouldn't do something like that. He was the good guy, so there'd be some thinking on his part. Thinking which would almost certainly lead to some regrets over taking the plunge and having a fling with her. That regret would extend to guilt over breaking her heart. If he knew about her broken heart, that is. But Emory had no intentions of letting him know.

Nope.

That was one of those "carry it to the grave" kind of deals. She'd just keep on smiling, keep on having sex with him as long as he was here and still wanted her, and when it was time for her to say goodbye to him, she'd never let him see the cracks inside her that she was afraid would never heal.

Apparently, the third time wasn't a charm, after all.

And these fresh cracks in her heart seemed even deeper and far worse than the ones she'd gotten with her divorce and annulment. Ironic, because she hadn't been with Matt that long, and there hadn't been a commitment like marriage between them. Still, she could make a good argument for her being in love with him since she was thirteen years old. Emory was pretty sure that was only going to make the healing process even longer.

At least she'd yet to hear any gossip about Natalie calling off her engagement. That was something at least. It was hard enough to deal with her problems when co-dealing with questions and unwanted chatter about it. Matt probably felt the same. He'd already been served up as gossip enough that there was no way he wanted more.

Emory looked up when she heard the sharp sound of surprise, and she spotted Susie. Her assistant was in the doorway of the sewing room, and her mouth had dropped open. Not in a "golly gee, wow, amazing" kind of way. This was more like a cartoon mouth dropping that smacked of WTF.

Frowning, Emory followed the woman's gaze to the dress. The very one she'd been working on pretty much all day. Then her own mouth dropped open at the crap show in front of her. The crystal beads, which were supposed to be scattered in a whimsical flow all over the dress, were smooshed together in a large glittering blob on the right breast. Then there was the lace sleeve that was in no way in or near the armpit region. Emory had sewn it onto the waist, and it stuck out like a floppy Chantilly appendage.

"Uh." That was all Susie said for several moments. "I'm guessing you're a mite distracted."

There was no *mite* about it. It was plenty apparent that less than one percent of her brain function had been tuned in on the dress. The rest had been for Matt, Jack, Ryder, Heather and her nephews.

But mostly Matt.

Clearly, thinking about her lover who could soon not be her lover wasn't conducive to creating a beautiful wedding dress. It wasn't conducive to anything except misery and screwing up.

Groaning, Emory dropped her needle onto the sewing table, took hold of her hair in both hands and pulled hard. Maybe this would generate enough blood flow to her brain. Much needed blood flow because it was going to take her hours and hours to fix this crap show she'd just made.

"We don't have any other appointments today so I'll work on the dress," Susie volunteered. "You've got a visitor out front." She hitched her thumb in that direction. "It's Tiffany. She's crying."

That caused Emory to groan again. "I'm not fixing her another dress."

Susie shrugged, nodded. "When you're done talking to her, you should just go home for the day. Might save us some time if you do."

Until Susie had added that last part, Emory had been about to say there was no way she'd just leave this mess to her assistant. But Susie was right. Sewing instruments would be like lethal weapons in her hands right now so it was best to regroup and start fresh tomorrow.

Well, regroup after she'd chatted with Tiffany.

Emory considered just sneaking out the back door, but that would mean leaving Susie with yet something else to handle. Not fair to her assistant who was bailing her out of a seriously botched sewing job. So Emory put on her "big girl" britches and went into the shop.

Tiffany was there, pacing and yes, crying. Judging from the condition of the wadded-up tissues in her hand, she'd been at it for a while.

"Emory," the woman said, going to her. Tiffany shocked the "big girl" britches off Emory when she pulled her into a hard hug. "Thank you for everything."

Tiffany's words and the hug didn't mesh with the crying so Emory was certain she had a confused look on her face when Tiffany finally let go of her. "Thank you?" Emory questioned.

Tiffany smiled, sniffled. Laughed, sending more of those mixed messages. "Keaton and I are so happy, and I just wanted to thank you. You're responsible for the start of our happiness by making me that tape dress."

So these were happy tears. Or possibly ones induced by some kind of brainwashing or heavy drinking. Tiffany didn't have alcohol breath, though, and her eyes were fairly clear despite the crying.

"The elopement worked out?" Emory asked.

Tiffany went through the smiling, sniffling, laughing again. "Yes, it definitely worked. Keaton and I are married, and we couldn't be happier. He's scheduled counseling for his sex addiction problems," she added in a whisper despite there not being anyone else in the room to hear it. "We're going to have the perfect life now, thanks to you."

Emory wouldn't be a spoilsport and mention that a couple of days weren't indicators of that perfect life. Neither was the fact that Tiffany had worn a so-called "good luck" dress. But the counseling was a positive step. Ditto for Tiffany's obvious happiness, so maybe there'd be a miracle and all would work out for the couple. Emory found herself doing some hard wishing that it would. Perhaps because it gave her a glimmer of hope for Matt and her.

Tiffany was still sniffling, crying happy tears and walking on air when she gave Emory another kiss, another thanks and walked out of the shop. Emory stood there, her mind going right back to Matt.

"Go home," Susie insisted. Coming up behind her, the woman practically shoved Emory's purse into her hands.

Emory didn't have the energy left to put up even a token fight. She muttered a thanks and headed outside to her car. Thankfully, she didn't have to put on a fake happy face because there was no one on the sidewalk or parking lot. She did have to smile and wave to some people she passed on the drive home, but at least those were split-second encounters.

When she got home, she wasn't surprised that Matt's truck wasn't in the driveway. He'd likely be at work several more hours. It could be longer than that if he had to talk things out with Natalie. Both were no doubt concerned about Jack's well-being in all of this. The boy clearly enjoyed being with Vince and living in Last Ride, but he'd probably enjoyed Amarillo just as much.

Emory put her purse on the foyer table inside the cottage, stopped and turned around to look at Matt's house. There was possibly one thing that could get her mind off Matt leaving. Well, two. Sex with Matt and reading the final pages of Candy Lynn's diary so she could hopefully then figure out what to write in the research paper. Because the sex option was out, she went with door number two. She could probably dive in to the diary and finish it before Matt even got home.

The back door wasn't locked as she'd known it wouldn't be because Zella was in the kitchen. The woman had obviously been cleaning, cooking and baking because the house smelled like Mr. Clean, pot roast and peanut butter cookies.

"Gonna wait here for Matt?" Zella asked, giving her a knowing wink. Her question seemed to be an invitation for Emory to spill all, but there'd be no such spilling today. Any details about Matt's possible departure would have to come from him.

"I just need to use that old computer. Is it still in the living room?"

"Sure is," Zella verified. "Hard to dust around that thing. When's it gonna be out of there?"

"Soon." Emory would make sure of that.

Zella plucked two still-warm cookies from a cooling

rack, put them on a saucer and handed them to Emory. "Want some milk to go with that?"

"Sounds good. Thanks." Maybe the impending sugar high would improve her mood.

Emory took her snack into the living room and retrieved the disk from the mantel where Matt kept it tucked out of sight. He'd jotted notes on the outside of the paper sleeve to indicate where he'd left off. Judging from his last note, there were only twenty-five pages to go. That told her he'd gone back in and read some more after the blackmail entry.

She sank down onto the sofa and booted up the computer while she bit into the cookie, made a yummy moaning sound and called out to Zella that it was "lethal and delicious." The woman cackled with pleased laughter from the kitchen.

Emory didn't do any scrolling but rather went to the beginning of the last twenty-five pages. It didn't take her long to realize this entry was a near carbon copy of the non-blackmail one. Lots of whining, moaning and bitching.

The next one started out the same, but it morphed into something else. *I'm going to use my money to move from this shithole town. I've just about tapped everything dry, and it's time to move on to greener pastures. One last payment from Ace ought to be enough to round out my account so it's hasta la vista, baby.*

Emory looked at the date of the entry. Just two days before Candy Lynn's death. By then, she'd had the twenty grand tucked away in her San Antonio bank account, and since she was clearly unhappy in Last Ride, it made sense for her to leave. Well, Candy Lynn sense, anyway. Obviously, that would mean leaving her son behind, but she'd apparently washed her hands of the child she'd birthed.

She lingered a moment over the reference to Ace before

Emory went to the next entry. And what she read there had her rereading. Rereading some more. And when the words didn't change and they sank in, she gasped and sprang to her feet.

"Crap, crap, crap." Emory whipped out her phone from her pocket. "I have to call Matt and tell him about this."

But she'd no sooner muttered that when she heard the object of her intended call. Matt was saying something to Zella, and he wasn't alone. There was another male voice. Several moments later, Matt and the other man came into the living room.

Vince.

"Crap," she repeated in a mutter.

Both Vince and Matt glanced at the computer, then shifted their attention to Emory. "I'm in Candy Lynn's diary," Vince said, and it sure as heck wasn't a question.

Emory nodded and studied Matt's face to see if he knew what would be in the entry. Apparently, he did.

"Vince came into the station to confess to having an affair with Candy Lynn when he was twenty years old," Matt said, his voice all cop. However, that wasn't a cop look in his eyes. No. There was plenty of dread. "He's also the one who gave Candy Lynn the drugs."

Emory managed a nod. "Drugs he substituted for the blackmail money Candy Lynn wanted."

Matt nodded as well. Vince just groaned, shook his head and then groaned some more. "I didn't know she was going to overdose. I thought I was clearing the slate with her so I bought them from a friend of a friend of a friend."

Emory believed him, but if this got out, it would be the Armageddon of scandals to hit Last Ride. That friend of a friend of a friend hadn't done Vince or Candy Lynn any favors.

"So, are you the guy Candy Lynn called Ace?" Emory came out and asked.

"I am. I've been torn up about this for weeks, ever since I heard about the diary," Vince went on. "And I couldn't tell Natalie what was wrong. I didn't want anybody to know what I'd done."

She believed that, too. "This is the reason you've been distant," Emory muttered.

Vince made a sound of agreement that he followed with a low rumbling groan. "I was trying to hide it from her so it wouldn't affect our relationship. Wouldn't affect my reputation," he added. "But hiding it has cost me Natalie."

Well, pretty much. There might be other factors playing into why Natalie wanted to end things. Like maybe her feelings for Vince had changed. But the genesis of that change had most likely been with this diary mess eating away at Vince and causing him to act guilt-ridden and withdrawn.

Vince squeezed his eyes shut a moment, and when he opened them again, he looked first at Matt. Then at Emory.

"Please," Vince begged. "You have to help me win back Natalie. You've got to stop her from leaving me."

CHAPTER NINETEEN

MATT FIGURED THIS moment was something that could be prescribed as a serious stress reliever. Emory, naked and warm, was snuggled up next to him. Her body was as slack and spent as his.

They weren't talking but rather just lying there. Perhaps because the long bout of sex had rendered them speechless. Matt wasn't sure he could get his mouth working just yet. Nor was he sure he wanted that particular part of him to work anytime soon. He wanted to hang on to these moments with her for as long as he could.

Outside, a gentle soft rain was falling on the tin roof, and the sound seemed to be coming straight from one of those sleep machines. He'd opened the window next to the bed so the cool breeze was stirring the gauzy white curtains along with bringing in the scent of the rain. Everything felt still, settled and right.

It wasn't, of course.

This moment with Emory was right, but plenty of other stuff was up in the air, including whether or not he'd be staying in Last Ride. That hinged on whether or not Natalie stayed. And that hinged on whether or not she'd get back together with Vince. So far, Matt wasn't sure what the outcome of any of those hinges might be.

Even though Vince had wanted Emory and Matt to go with him to talk to Natalie, Emory and he had bowed out.

Matt had done that because he thought this was a personal deal between Vince and Natalie; and Emory because she'd claimed this really wasn't any of her business. It was since she was naked in his bed. But Matt had appreciated her staying back, and despite Vince's pushing, Matt planned to put the man off as long as possible.

Vince had finally left Stallion Ridge, vowing that he was going to tell Natalie about his decades-old affair with Candy Lynn and about supplying her with drugs. Since that vow was now well over twenty-four hours old, Matt had to figure that Vince had chickened out. Or maybe he'd blabbed and Natalie had chosen to stay quiet about it. If so, then Jack hadn't picked up on any change in vibes from his mom, or his son would have probably said something during Matt's nightly conversations with him.

Emory made a sound similar to the ones that he'd heard her make when she'd eaten one of her favorite cookies, and she lifted her head, located his mouth and French kissed him. And just like that, the slow easy moment was gone. Not gone in a bad way, though. That kiss sent his heart revving and had his dick assuring him that it'd be up for another round.

Or two.

"You're thinking about the talk you're going to have with the DA tomorrow afternoon?" Emory murmured.

"No, that's not what I had on my mind." Matt took her hand, moved it to his dick and had her laughing. But Emory was right-ish. That meeting wasn't far off in his thoughts.

Tomorrow, at the end of his shift, he would have to go into the DA's office and, behind closed doors, tell him about Vince giving Candy Lynn the drugs. The statute of limitations had long passed for any actual drug charges, but the DA could go hard-ass and push that Vince be charged for a drug-induced homicide. The odds were sky-high that wouldn't happen. Vince hadn't been a drug dealer, and there was zero proof that he'd given Candy Lynn the drugs with malice intent or with any kind of knowledge that she would overdose. Still, Matt was duty bound to make this matter official and present it to the DA.

After that, the shit would hit the fan.

If Vince hadn't told her the truth already, Natalie would find out the hard way, through gossip, as to what had gone on between Vince and Candy Lynn. True, it'd gone on twenty years ago, but the gossip could bring it all back to the forefront. The forefront definitely wasn't a good place for bad crap to be, especially when Natalie was already trying to work out her personal feelings and such.

Emory gave his dick a squeeze, pulling his attention back to her. When she rolled on top of him, she got his attention even more. That's because she wiggled herself against him in all the right places.

She laughed again, the easy sound blending with the rain, but he didn't think the easiness was something she actually felt. Yeah, she'd enjoyed the sex and had clearly wanted to be with him, but he didn't believe he was projecting when he saw the ache in her eyes. His leaving Last Ride wouldn't bring her to her knees or anything. It wasn't as if she was in love with him, but that goodbye, if it happened, wouldn't be a fun moment for either of them.

Unlike this moment.

Emory took a condom from the nightstand and put it on him. Or rather attempted it. At first, he thought she just sucked at this particular skill, but when she giggled, he knew the fumbling was on purpose. It was the best kind of foreplay. And she didn't stop there. While she continued to slide and glide her fingers over the hard length of him, she shimmied down his body. Yep, shimmied. Lots of touching. Lots of breath.

Lots of tongue.

With the condom on only over the tip of his erection, that left her plenty of room to play around and up the torture she was doling out to him. Matt groaned, ground his teeth and took that torture for as long as he could. Then, with her giggling all the way, he flipped Emory onto her back, scooted down with her and moved on top of her.

Much kissing followed.

The right kind of kissing. Deep and needy. Of course, they were both already fired up enough, and his body was already begging for him to take her, but Matt still took the time to savor those fiery kisses. To savor her. Mercy, if he had to leave, he was going to miss this. He would miss *her*.

Since that thought didn't play well with everything else going on—the woman had a clever tongue!—he finished getting the condom in place. In the same motion, he pushed inside her. He went still, letting every inch of the pleasure she was giving him slide through him. Yeah, he'd miss her all right.

Surprisingly, his dick cooperated with long slow strokes. The long slow kisses, too. This wasn't the heated rush of their usual sex, even though the need was stronger than ever. And had some teeth. He smiled when she nipped his bottom lip.

Matt shifted his weight to his forearms and used his hands to frame her face. He just watched her while he kept up those strokes. While he watched her eyes glaze from the heat. She was probably having trouble focusing now, he sure as hell was, but Emory watched him, too. Even when the need made him up the pace, he didn't take his eyes off her.

He saw the heat rise. Felt it. Felt the tremors of her body before they turned into a full-blown climax.

Still, Matt held on.

He kept moving, kept drawing out the pleasure as long as he could. And it was Emory's name he muttered when he finally let the heat, and her tongue, win.

STILL MENTALLY SCRATCHING her head over this appointment, Emory stepped into the Three Sheets. AKA, Three Sheets to the Wind saloon. And she glanced around. The place wasn't packed, not yet anyway, but it soon would be since it was a little past 5:00 p.m., and it was one of the few places in Last Ride to get a drink.

Or rather to get the adult equivalent of mother's milk— a beer.

Most men steered clear of the bookstore, First Draft, that served wine and local craft beers with names like Butterscotch Biography, Fluid Pulp Fiction and Blood Orange Mystery. Plenty of casual drinkers, like her, steered clear of Three Sheets whose menu included deep-fried anything and everything. As usual, the place smelled of musky peanut shells on the floor, clashing scents of beer and the grease used to fry up all those brown-colored blobs of whatever.

Emory stepped in, letting the old-style double doors swing shut behind her, and without the outside light, the visibility in the large room dimmed considerably. On purpose, no doubt, since Three Sheets was the poster child for a seedy joint.

She took a moment to let her eyes adjust and then did another glance around. Once she spotted Azzie in one of the booths, Emory headed her way. When Azzie had called earlier, she hadn't said why she wanted to have this meeting, but the deputy had insisted it was important—and private.

Emory didn't think of Three Sheets as especially private, not with all the customers already milling around, but the volume on the George Strait song on the jukebox was cranked up, and the chatter and the slap of the pool balls was probably enough so that no one would listen in on them. Then again, Azzie tended to make people want to give her a wide berth.

"Thanks for coming," Azzie said, and she slid a Lone Star beer, a Coke and a bottle of water across the table to Emory. "I went ahead and ordered for you so we wouldn't be interrupted by the waitress. I didn't know what you'd want so I got a variety."

Azzie had gone the variety route, too, for snacks. There were small bowls of pretzels, peanuts and a platter with chips and salsa.

Emory muttered her own thanks and took the Coke. Azzie had opted for a pitcher of draft beer, and judging from the suds/scum on the side of the glass, she was sipping what appeared to be her second or third mug. That made Emory wonder just how long the woman had been here.

"I've got two problems," Azzie said in that no-nonsense sort of way of hers. "I need a dress, and the sheriff is lower than a fat penguin's pecker."

Emory had to assume that was pretty low since she'd never seen that particular part of a penguin's anatomy, but she couldn't quite figure out what that had to do with needing a dress. Or this appointment.

"By sheriff, you mean Matt?" Emory clarified.

"Yes. He's low, and I can see it's bothering the piss out of him."

Emory was going to make another assumption that the *piss* remark was a metaphor. "What does Matt have to do with you needing a dress?"

For the first time, Emory saw Azzie's usual no-nonsense slip a significant notch. Her mouth tightened, and she drank more beer at the rate a camel would. "I have a date."

"Oh," Emory remarked. That answer definitely hadn't been on her radar.

"With Sheriff Lyle," Azzie added in a murmur.

Emory bit off another, "Oh," but she thought she knew where this was going. Everyone in Last Ride knew that the former sheriff had had a thing for Azzie for years, and the only reason he hadn't asked her out was because she'd worked for him. But now that Sheriff Lyle had retired, apparently dating had gone onto the proverbial table.

"He wants to take me to his niece's wedding," Azzie went on. "I know you usually make bridal stuff, but I need a dress, and I don't want to have to fuss with going in a shop." She extracted a piece of paper from her pocket and slid it toward Emory. "Those are my measurements. If you could just make me something, I could drop by the shop and pick it up."

Azzie was right. She normally did *bridal stuff*, but Emory didn't have the heart to turn her down. It was obvious this wasn't an easy thing for Azzie to discuss.

"Did you have a type of dress in mind?" Emory asked. "Or a particular color?"

"No. I don't own any dresses, so whatever you come up with will be fine."

Even though it was hard to tell in the dim light, Emory knew the deputy's eyes were blue. She could make something in that color family and maybe keep the shape slim enough to show off Azzie's well-toned body. The woman might be in her seventies, but she was still ripped.

"Anyway, the wedding is in two months," Azzie added. "Think you can have something ready by then?"

"Of course. I'll get it done so you have time to pick out shoes and accessories to go with it."

Azzie's eyes widened as if horrified by the idea of shopping, so Emory made a mental note to buy her some costume jewelry and footwear other than the boots the woman normally wore.

"Just jot down your shoe size," Emory said, passing the paper with the measurements back to her. "I'll take care of everything. And who knows, this date might be the start of something really good for you."

Azzie pooh-poohed that with a huff. "I'm too old to start shit like that."

Emory got a flash of being naked in Matt's bed, and she smiled. "Trust me, you're never too old for that."

Azzie smiled. Well, sort of. Her mouth quivered a little while she wrote down her shoe size and passed the paper back to Emory. Then the deputy leaned in closer.

"Now, to Sheriff Corbin and that penguin's pecker," Azzie said, dropping her voice somewhat lower than usual, but it still didn't hit the whisper mark. "I know you're probably wondering why I'm sticking my nose in it, but I'm worried about him. Whatever's going on is affecting his work."

That caused Emory's shoulders to go stiff. "How?"

"Well, for one thing he stepped right in a big pile of bird shit when me and him went up to Jenny Barlow's hair salon where those damn macaws had flown in and made a right mess of things."

Emory relaxed a little. In the grand scheme of things, that didn't seem like a big deal. A smelly one, yes, that would require some cleaning, but not the disaster that she'd braced herself to hear from the deputy.

"Then he stepped in cow shit when we were looking into the mess that an escaped Angus made of Hank Jenkins's roses—again," Azzie went on. "When a man has to scrape off his boots twice in the same day because of something he's stepped in, his head's not in the game. For a cop, that's a bad thing."

Emory quit relaxing and tightened up again, but it could very well be a bad thing. The sheriff of Last Ride rarely had to deal with "life and death" situations, but if one came up, Matt needed his A game. No more stepping in shit, literally or metaphorically.

"So, what's going on with him?" Azzie pressed.

Emory figured the deputy knew at least some of what had happened. Azzie might even know that at this very minute Matt was in a meeting with the DA to ask about possible drug charges against Vince. But what the deputy probably wasn't privy to was that Natalie had called off her wedding. Emory hadn't caught any whiff of gossip about it, which meant Vince and Natalie were still keeping it to themselves.

"Did you ask Matt about this?" Emory said, clearly dodging Azzie's question.

Azzie gave her a textbook "flat cop" look. "I did, and he told me he had some things to work out. Since he didn't get into what those things were, I'm figuring it has something to do with Candy Lynn. Or you."

Emory didn't answer that, not with words, but apparently Azzie was watching closely enough to gauge her reaction.

"So, not Candy Lynn or you," Azzie concluded, and then she paused to top off her beer. "That leaves his family."

Emory decided it was a good time to shove a loaded salsa chip into her mouth. A good time to glance away, too, so that Azzie couldn't read her.

"Shit, you're in love with him," Azzie concluded. She shook her head, drank a generous gulp of beer. "Yeah, that would make him miserable all right because he's not a dick and wouldn't want you hurt."

Good grief. Either the deputy had ESP, or Emory had the absolute worst evasion tactics. "Look, I'm not comfortable talking about this—"

Emory stopped, took the Lone Star beer and chugged down some. For a couple of moments, she just focused on scraping off the label with her thumb. She could feel Azzie's intense stare, could feel her impatience over not getting to the bottom of the big reason she'd wanted this meeting. A reason that didn't really have to do with Emory's feelings for Matt but more like the effect those feelings were having on him.

"All right, I am in love with Matt," Emory finally blurted out.

Emory looked up when she heard the gasp. She hadn't expected Azzie to have that kind of reaction.

And she hadn't.

The gasp hadn't come from Azzie but rather from the woman who was only a couple of feet away from their booth. The woman whose glare was drilling holes into Emory.

Natalie.

"You're—" Natalie started, but she stopped, glanced around and then came even closer. "You're in love with Matt?" she asked in an angry whisper.

Emory had no clue how to respond to that, other than digging a hole in the floor or knocking through the wall to escape. "Uh, Natalie, what are you doing here?" she managed.

Natalie took her time answering. Probably because she had to get her jaw unclamped first. "I'm having a drink with my dad. This is his favorite place, and it's his birthday." She slashed out those words as if they were part of an angry whispered argument, and she stayed right by the booth but folded her arms over her chest. "When I saw you, I thought I'd come over and say hello. I didn't know I'd overhear why you're stabbing me in the back."

Emory just stared at her because, hello—she didn't have a clue what the woman was talking, or rather whispering about. "What do my feelings for Matt have to do with back-stabbing you?"

"Everything!" Natalie threw her hands up in the air, and even though she still didn't raise her voice, the anger was there in spades. "Matt is torn about going back to Amarillo. I can see he feels that way because of you. What did you do? Convince him to stay because you're in love with him?"

Emory shook her head. "No. He doesn't even know—".

But Natalie's anger and words rolled right over her. "Just remember that you're not lucky in love and your family hates him. Where will Matt be if he stays and things don't work out with you?" Natalie didn't wait for an answer. "He'd be giving up a life with his son because of you." She turned and delivered the rest of what she had to say from over her shoulder. "Matt will be a lot better off without you."

"Well, if that isn't a pissant kind of reaction," Azzie grumbled, already moving to get out of the booth. "I'll get her back over here so you two can talk it out."

Emory caught onto Azzie's arm to stop her. "No, don't do that. No talking is necessary." Because Emory knew one very big, very important thing.

That Natalie was right.

CHAPTER TWENTY

MATT STUDIED THE dozen or so Sherlock Holmes wannabes in full costume who were carrying on like sleep-deprived toddlers on one side of the squad room. They were armed with books, pipes and bad insults aimed at the group on the other side—the Tributes, who were decked out like characters from *The Hunger Games.*

"Take your wussy meeting to District Thirteen," one of the Sherlocks called out. "The library should be for real fans of real literature."

That was like pouring gasoline on the fire of the Tributes, and one of them, the ninety-something-year-old Midge Parkman verbally fired back, "All y'all can shove those pointy deerstalker hats up your derrieres."

"'Tis up to you to make us," a Sherlock sneered, putting on an English accent that sounded as fake as it was.

Matt heard the sound of bows being raised and arrows being pulled from quivers. Sighing, he turned to the Tributes. "If you aim one of those arrows at anybody, I'm arresting the whole lot of you," Matt warned the crowd. "I don't care if they have sponge tips on them or not."

That brought on some snorts and sounds of "nanny nanny boo boo's" from the Sherlocks, so Matt turned to them next. "Say another word and I'll arrest you, too. Since we only have one cell, that means you'll all be crammed into a very small space with clearly rabid readers who have a mindset of fighting to the death. Is that what you want?"

That shut up the Sherlocks. A hard stare from Matt shut up the Tributes in mid-growl and mid-snickers.

"All of you stay quiet," Matt reminded them.

Matt was flanked by the two day deputies, Buffy Jarvis and Hogan Dayton. Since Matt wanted to cut through this by getting the shortest and most concise answer, he turned to Buffy who was standing on his left. She'd actually been in the squad room with the groups when Matt had heard the commotion and come out of his office to check it out. Hogan had been in the breakroom and hadn't made an appearance until Matt had already yelled out a couple of "pipe down now" demands to the dueling readers' groups.

"Do you have any idea what's going on here?" Matt asked Buffy.

"I do," she answered. "There was a screwup at the library, and they scheduled both groups for the meeting room. The librarian tried to reschedule." She tipped her head to the sole visitor not in costume, Sheila Merryweather, who gave Matt a nervous little wave with fluttering fingers.

"We got a new appointment system, and I made a mistake, a triple booking," Sheila explained. "I worked it out with the *Twilight* and Harry Potter groups before they arrived so that's why they're not here."

Well, that was something at least. No need to add wizards and sparkly vampires to this lot. The vampires probably thought the same thing, considering Buffy's penchant for displaying objects on her desk meant to eliminate their kind. Still, Matt was somewhat impressed that a small town like Last Ride had so many avid readers.

"I take it the Sherlocks and Tributes didn't get notified in time before their meetings?" Matt pressed.

Shelia shook her head, sighed and let Buffy continue with the explanation. "The double booking apparently spurred tempers and resulted in some name calling and pushy-shovey. They then decided to bring their dispute here."

Matt saw a few mouths open from both groups, no doubt to defend their actions or to add something else that he in no way wanted added. He silenced them with a lift of his hand and a glare that he knew was darn effective.

"Was anyone hurt?" Matt pressed, aiming that question at Buffy.

"No," Buffy said, and then she repeated her "no" in a "don't test me" snarl when one of the Sherlocks lifted a hat that appeared to be scuffed up, and a Tribute pointed to the missing tip of an arrow. "But they did knock into some bookcases so there's a mess at the library."

"They downed the Dickens and the *Little Women*," the librarian provided.

Matt was going to assume she was talking about books and not actual short-statured females. "Any damage?"

The librarian shook her head. "No, but the books will all have to be re-shelved. In the correct order," she emphasized. "I won't have them put back all willy-nilly."

Matt turned back to the groups. "The Tributes will shelve the *Little Women* this morning. The Sherlocks will shelve the Dickens this afternoon. If you balk, if Mrs. Merryweather isn't pleased with the shelving results or if you go willy-nilly with the books, I'll be making arrests."

"Thank you, Sheriff," the librarian said on a relieved breath.

However, there was nothing relieved about the groups. Muttering, griping and doing a whole lot of headshaking and sulking, the groups turned toward the door.

Just as Emory came in.

She froze, her eyes widening at the sea of people who were moving toward her. She quickly stepped out of the way to let them pass, but she locked eyes with Matt.

Even though Matt hadn't been expecting her, he was glad to see her. He'd texted her yesterday afternoon to tell her that the DA wouldn't be filing charges against Vince and to see if they could grab some dinner together, but she'd responded with a Sorry, but I'm swamped.

Matt had felt plenty of disappointment over that. More than "lack of sex" disappointment. He'd wanted to just be with her. And that was a reminder that being with her probably wasn't a good idea. If he was going to end up moving, then more sex was definitely out. He couldn't lead Emory on like that.

"Uh, I'm guessing you've had an interesting morning," Emory muttered, dodging a quiver as one of the Tributes filed out a little too closely to her.

He managed a smile. "Keeps me on my toes." And it did. It was a totally different kind of adrenaline high.

"I, uh, dropped by to see Azzie and you," Emory said, the uncertainty coating her voice. She eyed him as if looking for his reaction to that.

He was damn happy about the *you* but confused about the *Azzie*.

"She's not on shift today. Anything I can help you with?" Matt asked.

Emory paused, kept staring at him a couple more seconds before she shook her head. "No. I had something for her." She lifted a sketch pad, one of the two things she had with her. She also had a thick envelope tucked under her arm. "I'll just give her a call."

Matt nodded, and since it was obvious Emory had something on her mind, he motioned for her to follow him into his office. She did, hesitantly, and that caused him to frown. He didn't want this distance between them. Hell, he wanted to ask her what was wrong.

And kiss her.

He mentally shook his head over that. Obviously, the lecture he'd just given himself about not leading her on was failing big-time.

"I'm making Azzie a dress," she explained when she stepped into the doorway of his office. Then, with no pause or transition, she added, "Thanks for letting me know the DA wouldn't be filing charges against Vince."

Matt nodded and motioned for her to come all the way in, but the chatter coming from the squad room stopped her. They both turned and saw former Sheriff Waldo Lyle making his way toward them.

Waldo had *good ol' boy* written all over him. Literally. It was on his T-shirt and sewn onto the band of his battered cowboy hat. He wasn't a big man, barely five-five and was seriously bowlegged. With his narrow face, he reminded Matt of a cartoon rooster.

"Sheriff Corbin," the man greeted, and as usual Matt was surprised that such a big voice could come from such a small man. He gave high fives to Buffy and Hogan, both of whom had been his deputies, and he made his way to Matt's office. "Emory," he added, tipping his hat in greeting.

She muttered a greeting back and stepped into the squad room. "I have an errand to run," Emory told Matt. "I'll be back."

He nearly stopped her, especially since it was obvious she had something to talk to him about, but she was gone before Matt could say anything.

"She sure is good-looking," Waldo commented. "Too bad she's got shit luck with men."

Yeah, too bad, and Matt was afraid that shit luck now extended to him. Not her fault, though. No. This was on Natalie's and his shoulders.

Speaking of shoulders, Waldo gave Matt a friendly slap on one of his, and he came into the office, his gaze sweeping around. "You did some redecorating," he said, frowning.

"Some," Matt agreed, following the man's gaze to the walls that had far less stuff than they had when he'd taken over this office.

Waldo took off his hat, scratched his head. "You mighta taken down the horseshoes, but I can still see them. Memories." He chuckled as if recalling something from those memories. "Every time I closed an investigation, I'd nail up a horseshoe. Didn't matter if it was a big case or a little one. Though in Last Ride, most of them were little."

Matt hadn't known about that at all, and since none of the deputies had mentioned it, he wondered if that was a sentimental gesture Waldo had kept to himself.

Waldo went to a spot on the wall behind the desk. "That one was a biggie. Manslaughter of old Mr. Peterson about thirty years ago. His wife objected to him cattin' around and clocked him with her Lodge cast-iron skillet when he came home smelling of Chanel Number something. She did eighteen years up in Waco, got paroled and now runs an artist commune over in Kerrville."

Hearing the story had Matt studying the small nail holes where the horseshoe had been. He was a little sorry he'd taken it down.

"That one there was another biggie. For your mama," Waldo went on, pointing out another spot, this one directly in front of the desk. "I closed that case as an accidental overdose." He eased the door shut. "Was it accidental? Did I get it wrong?"

Obviously, the former sheriff had heard some gossip. "No, you were right."

"But Candy Lynn was blackmailing some folks. I missed picking up on that."

Matt could hear the worry in the man's voice. Worry that he thought he could put to rest. "The men didn't come forward, so you couldn't have known. I found out about it because of a computer diary she left."

"And none of those men killed her, did they?" Waldo pressed.

Matt shook his head. "No. She took the drugs and died from an overdose. I've gone through the investigation with a fine-tooth comb, and you and the deputies didn't miss anything."

Not completely true. One of them could have maybe found the diary if they'd looked harder. Maybe, if it hadn't already been removed from the house by the time they'd searched it. But there was no reason to point a finger. Plus, there was nothing in the diary that would change the conclusion that she died of an accidental drug overdose.

"Good," Waldo said, and he let out a big breath. The relief came, but it faded when his attention landed on Matt. "I didn't do right by you. Like everybody else, I heard about the shit your mama put you through, and I didn't do anything. I could pawn it off on that being different times, but hell, time ain't got nothing to do with it. I just figured if you weren't showing up in the ER, then I should stay out of it."

"It's okay." It took digging down damn deep for Matt to say that.

And mean it.

Yeah, Candy Lynn had put him through plenty of shit, but he'd come out the other side and was nothing like her. He was a good parent. A good person. She wasn't, never had been, and now she was dead.

"You're a big man to forgive all the ills that folks did to you. Me, included," Waldo went on. "I'd worried about retiring, but now I can see you're the right pick as my replacement."

Matt didn't respond. Couldn't. The compliment reached him in a place he hadn't known he wanted to be reached. An acceptance. All coming at a time when he might be turning in his resignation.

Waldo scratched his head again. "Say, how do you go about gettin' a woman to fall for you?"

The question threw him, and Matt just stood there for a couple of dumbfounded moments. He wondered if Waldo had picked up on the sizzling vibe between Emory and him.

Waldo chuckled. "I guess I didn't say that right. How do you think I should go about getting Azzie to fall for me?"

Well, that sure as hell wasn't an easier question, and it caused Matt to take the dumbfounded route a little longer before he managed to say, "You have a thing for Azzie?"

The man laughed, a real belly laugh, complete with enough volume that anyone in the building would have heard it. "Hell, yeah, I do. Always have, but I've kept my hands off because, well, she worked for me and all. I don't hold to taking a crap where I work. Anyway, she agreed to go with me to my niece's wedding, but I don't know how to make the rest of it happen."

Matt certainly hadn't been expecting to give relationship advice, especially to a man forty years his senior. He especially hadn't expected to be giving advice like this when it was connected to Azzie.

"Just keep asking her out on more dates. Maybe to a movie at the drive-in or O'Riley's for dinner. That sort of thing," Matt added when it appeared that Waldo was taking mental notes.

Waldo nodded, smiled, blew out another of those breaths. "Thanks. I want this to work with her. Of course, you're probably thinking since I'm seventy-three that I've missed the boat for any romance stuff."

Matt shook his head. "I'm betting that boat can still sail." And he winced because that sure as hell sounded like a dick metaphor.

Waldo laughed and repeated his "thanks." He reached for the doorknob, but then he stopped and glanced around the room. "I sure do miss those horseshoes, though."

Suddenly, so did Matt. "I kept them. They're over there if you want them." He tipped his head to the box on the floor next to the filing cabinet.

"Naw, they're best suited for here. If I take them home, they're just a bunch of horseshoes in a box."

That sounded like some kind of deep life metaphor, one that Matt didn't get, and while he rolled that around in his mind, he walked Waldo out. He didn't make it far, though, outside his office when he saw the woman in the waiting area. Not Emory. But rather Natalie, and Jack was with her. One look at her face and he knew something was wrong.

Matt said a quick goodbye to Waldo and went to Natalie while he looked Jack over from hair to shoes. He didn't see any signs of an injury, thank God.

"What happened?" Matt asked Natalie, just as Jack gushed, "Squawky founded a green snake and taked it to Emory. She screamed real loud."

Squawky was still the name Jace was calling the puppy,

and using his dad translator, Matt deciphered that Emory had *squealed* when the puppy had brought her the critter.

"We stopped by the ranch earlier this morning so Jack could see Squeaky, and we took Squawky with us so the dogs could play," Natalie explained. Her jaw was tight, and it looked as if she'd been crying. Maybe Emory and Natalie had had words.

Rather than speculate, Matt took Jack's hand and led him to the office where they could have some privacy and so Natalie could tell him the reason for this visit. Of course, they weren't likely to have a whole lot of privacy with Jack around.

"What happened?" Matt repeated to Natalie once they were in his office.

As Waldo had done, she closed the door, and she nailed her weary gaze to his. Jack didn't do any gaze-nailing or standing still. With all the energy of a three-year-old hyped up on Mondo cookies, he ran to every corner of the room and settled his attention on the box of horseshoes. That would entertain him for a couple of minutes, Matt guessed, and he doubted whatever was bothering Natalie would be dealt with in that short period of time.

"Vince told me about Candy Lynn," Natalie whispered.

Yep, this would take more than a couple of minutes, and Matt realized he should have expected this visit and this conversation. He had to applaud Vince for biting the bullet and fessing up, but Natalie might not be buying into the old adage of confession being good for the soul. Her soul, anyway. She looked miserable.

"That all happened with Candy Lynn a long time ago," he said, hoping it would soothe some of that misery.

"But he gave her *d-r-u-g-s*, and they had *s-e-x*. *S-e-x* with your mother," Natalie snapped.

"Yes, I got that." Matt definitely didn't relish the idea of thinking about Candy Lynn having sex with anyone, but he'd had a lot of that shoved in his face with practically every page of her diary.

Matt glanced at Jack to make sure he was otherwise occupied. He wasn't. Jack was looking at them. "*A-B-C-D-E…* I can spell-y, too," his son said.

Matt had to smile at that. "You sure can. Why don't you take out the horseshoes and count them?"

Jack clearly thought that would be fun so he started right away. Again, it would be a short activity since Jack could only count to ten.

Matt turned back to Natalie, and he chose his words carefully. "Vince was distant with you because all of this was eating away at him. I believe he loves you."

That did not have the intended soothing effect that Matt had hoped. Some anger flared in Natalie's eyes. "Are you saying that because of *E-m-o-r-y*? Because you want to stay here and have *s-e-x* with her?"

Matt was sure some shock and some anger lit in his eyes, too. "I'm saying it because it's the truth. You and Vince had nothing to do with Emory and me having *s-e-x*."

Judging from the look Natalie gave him, she wasn't buying that one little bit. "I want you to stay out of it, to keep your personal feelings for *E-m-o-r-y* out of it." She'd kept her voice at a whisper, but there was still a lot of anger in it.

He wanted to whisper back, *I am keeping Emory out of this*, but he wasn't sure that was true. Maybe he was trying to rekindle Natalie and Vince's engagement so he could stay here in Last Ride with Emory.

Maybe.

Matt didn't want to think he was capable of something like that, but his feelings for Emory ran deep. And he didn't want her getting hurt with the decisions he was going to have to make. Still, he couldn't put her hurt at the top of his worry list. That was a spot that Jack occupied, and his son's happiness was tied to Natalie's, which meant he had to put her high on the rungs of the ladder.

He finally nodded. "All right. I'll stay out of what's going on between Vince and you."

Matt didn't add any more about how he believed Vince deserved a second chance. Didn't remind Natalie that she might want to stand by Vince because of the shitstorm he was about to face from the gossip. He just waited for Natalie to deliver a verdict. To tell him if she was staying in Last Ride or moving back to Amarillo. But if she'd had any intentions of doing that, the knock at the door stopped her.

"Boss, we've got some trouble," Buffy announced. "We need you out here."

Matt groaned. Talk about bad timing. But Natalie seemed relieved that the pause button had just been put on this discussion.

"Come on, Jack. It's time for lunch," Natalie insisted. Jack mimicked Matt's groan until Natalie added, "We can get nachos at O'Riley's."

That had the boy springing off the floor, and he gave Matt's legs a quick hug before he hurried out the door, pulling his mother along with him while he bubbled out a "Bye, Daddy."

"Goodbye," Matt said, but every ounce of fatherly love and affection drained from his body when he looked at the two boys waiting to see him. The *trouble* that obviously needed his attention.

Ian and Theo.

"Did you glitter your balls again?" Matt snarled.

"No," Buffy provided when neither boy said anything.

"But they squirted four cans of string cheese on Ethan Darnell's car."

Well, at least it didn't involve genitalia, but in this heat, cheese or any dairy product for that matter would do a real number on a vehicle.

"Their folks will be here soon," Buffy provided. "Want me to go ahead and book them?"

Matt sighed, shook his head and motioned for the boys to follow him into his office. They did, moping every inch along the way, and they sank down into the chairs across from his desk. He didn't bother to shut the door because he figured it wouldn't be long before Ryder, Ruston and their spouses arrived. Which meant there was a high probability of a shitshow showdown between him and Emory's brothers.

"Any reason you two can't stop dicking around and screwing up?" Matt asked. Unlike their other dicking-arounds and screwups, Ian and Theo didn't jump to volunteer some half-assed excuse.

"Well?" Matt prompted, staring down at them.

"Mr. Darnell asked out my mom," Ian finally grumbled, not in his usual challenging, snotty way. The tone was more of a kid instead of a defiant teenager. "I don't want her to go out with him. I want her to stay married to my dad."

Matt sighed again. He was certainly getting the variety pack of issues today. "And you decided to help Ian with this deterrent?" Matt asked Theo.

The grunt the boy made had a *yes* ring to it. "I figured if Uncle Ryder and Aunt Heather got a divorce, then my folks might, too."

"Then we wouldn't get to see them," Ian piped in. "Because they might move or something. They might get married again, have a whole new family and forget all about us."

So, fear of abandonment was at the core. Well, this particular core, anyway. Like an onion, Ian and Theo had lots of layers that often got their butts into trouble.

"The way I see this playing out is that you'll pay for any damages to Ethan Darnell's car," Matt started. "Then, as punishment, you'll get lots and lots of hours of community service. Maybe cleaning out the public toilets at the fairground and the town park."

A look of sheer horror crossed the boys' faces.

"I'll see to it that you'll be so busy cleaning up after people that you won't have time for any more pranks," Matt added, and then he paused. "I'll also advise your parents to get you into counseling to help you better deal with a divorce in the family."

"You don't know nothing about it," Ian snarled.

"I don't know anything about it," Matt said.

"What I said," Ian fired back and seemed unaware that Matt had given him a grammar correction and wasn't merely agreeing with him. Perhaps he should suggest some tutoring as well.

Matt huffed and fixed his attention on Ian. "I moved here to Last Ride to be with my son. Even when good parents aren't married to each other, they usually find a way to be with their children. Your dad will do that. Any good father would."

He sensed more than heard the movement in the doorway and turned, expecting to see the parents. But no. Emory was there.

Shit.

She'd heard enough of that to assume he was talking not just about her brother but also himself. Which he was.

"Sorry," she muttered. She glanced down at the boys. "I just heard about the string cheese."

Matt nodded. "I'm sorry about the dog bringing you the snake." And he was equally sorry about what she'd overheard, but he kept that to himself. Now wasn't the time for a heart-to-heart chat about their future. Or the possibility of them having no future together at all.

She waved that off, literally, and smiled. A smile that would have seemed real to someone who didn't know her. Matt knew her. "The snake surprise was better than caffeine for getting me awake." She took the large envelope that she had tucked under her arm. "I won't keep you. Besides, you're about to get very busy."

Matt knew why she'd said that. He could hear Ryder talking to Buffy out in the reception area.

"That's a draft of the research report for the Last Ride Society," Emory continued, handing him the envelope. "Read it and make any changes you want."

Emory turned, walked away and muttered the rest of what she had to say with her back to him. "Goodbye, Matt."

Not a *see you later*. Not a *good luck*. Not even an *I'm sorry you'll have to wade through the crap about your mother or whatever my brothers are about to sling at you*.

Just her goodbye.

And, to Matt, it sounded like the real deal.

CHAPTER TWENTY-ONE

EMORY SAT IN her car, staring at the drive-in movie screen. Well, staring through the rain sheeting down her windshield, anyway.

Sandy and Danny from *Grease* looked sort of like squiggly aliens, but Emory didn't bother turning on the wipers so she could actually see them play out their own scene at the drive-in. She hadn't come here for the movie but rather to have some alone time. And to eat her way through a sampling of all the food she'd bought at the concession stand. Food that had taken her two trips to get back to her car.

Now her car smelled of fresh popcorn, the warm mustardy pretzel, a corn dog equally mustarded, greasy onion rings, nachos and chocolate-covered peanuts. Not a bad clash of scents, but Emory was well aware if she ate even a fraction of everything that she'd bought, she'd be puking her way back home. Still, it was better than actually being home where she'd be so close to Matt. Home, where it somehow made the memory of what Matt had said to Ian even louder in her head.

Even when good parents aren't married to each other, they usually find a way to be with their children.

Emory knew that wasn't just lip service from Matt, that he hadn't said that just to reassure Ian all would be well. Also, there'd be no *usually* when it came to Jack. Matt would be with his son. It was the reason he'd moved to

Last Ride. It was the reason he'd move back to Amarillo if that's where Jack was. And she was just going to have to learn to accept it.

She ate more of the popcorn that she'd over buttered and washed it down with some of the mega-barrel of Coke. The rain came down even harder, kicking up the wind so it was hard to hear the audio coming from the FM station on her car radio. No biggie. She'd seen this movie so many times she could fill in the blanks.

And continue her own personal pity party.

Emory didn't bother rationalizing that this pigging out whine-fest was something else. Nope. She was hurt, felt sorry for herself and just wanted to wallow in the misery of a broken heart.

Alone.

Without interruptions.

And with no one to mention that she was making herself sick or that she could probably find a more constructive and less caloric way to deal with what she was feeling.

To make sure that alone/without interruptions happened, she'd turned off the ringer on her phone and tucked it out of sight in her purse. Later, there'd be tears. Later, there'd be a goodbye, a final one, that she'd have to give Matt. But later could screw itself six ways to Sunday. For now, she would aim for a full belly of junk food and these rainy moments of losing herself in, well, the solo rainy moments.

The solo part of her fest came to a fast end, though, when her passenger's-side door flew open. Emory shrieked and went into the fight mode by whopping her tub of popcorn at the intruder's head.

"Shit," the intruder snarled. "It's me."

Me in this case was her brother Ruston. He was dripping wet, scowling, and in his haste to get out of the rain, he dropped right down onto the seat where she'd stashed her corn dog. His scowled deepened considerably when he yanked out the corn dog, the mustard drippings smeared all over his fingers, and he tossed the now-smashed treat onto her dashboard with the other goodies.

"You had food on your seat," he snapped.

"So? I wasn't expecting visitors." In hindsight, she should have locked the doors along with those other precautions she'd taken so there'd be no interruptions like this one. "What are you doing here?"

"Finding you. Mom's worried about you, and since you're not answering your blasted phone and you weren't at your house or the shop, I drew the short straw in the hunt for a sister who sure as hell shouldn't be worrying her mother."

He raked his hand over his face to sling off some rainwater, scowled when he no doubt felt more than water, and cursing, he flicked on the lighted mirror on the sun visor. Since Emory was annoyed at him, she was pleased to see the slathering of mustard now on his left cheek.

"I wanted to watch this movie in peace," she snapped back. "And I didn't want or need siblings drawing a short straw to check on me."

Ruston, whose middle name was *snark*, made a show of looking at the rain-flooded windshield and the radio that was merely a stream of whispery static.

"You wanted to sulk about Matt," he corrected, "and you didn't care if you worried Mom when you did that."

Emory rolled her eyes and wanted to insult him by calling him a Mama's boy, which he was, but obviously their mother was worried enough to prod Ruston into tracking her down.

"I'm fine," Emory insisted, and she took out her phone

and fired off a text, repeating those two words to her mother. She added that she was at the drive-in and would be home soon.

With that daughterly duty finished, she put away her phone without turning the ringer on, and she looked at her brother. "You can leave now." But the words died on her lips when it hit her what he'd said. "Why do you think I'm here sulking about Matt?" Mercy, had word gotten around about the move back to Amarillo?

"I think that because you are," Ruston answered without a shred of hesitation and in his know-it-all tone. "Theo told me you looked upset when he saw you earlier today at the police station."

Oh, that. She probably had looked upset, but she sure as heck hadn't expected a teenage boy to pick up on it. Especially a boy who'd just gotten in trouble over his liberal use of canned cheese.

"I was worried about Ian and Theo," she argued.

That was true-ish. But, yeah, most of the upset face she'd had at the police station was because of what she'd heard Matt say to Ian. Still, there was no way on God's green earth she would admit that to the blabbermouth Ruston who'd take that info straight back to their mother and anybody else he grumbled to along the way.

"You should be worried about Ian and Theo," Emory went on, turning the tables on her brother. "In fact, you should be home right now, dealing with your son and not pestering your sister who wants to watch Olivia Newton-John sing 'You're the One that I Want.'"

It had been a challenge to stop herself from shouting, and her voice had gone up some with each word, but she hadn't yelled. Better yet, she'd made her point. Made it even clearer by adding, "Go home, Ruston. I'm fine."

But Ruston didn't budge. He sat there with his mustard-smeared face and stared at her. And stared. Until he finally sighed. Even in the dim light, she saw his expression soften a bit, and then he helped himself to some of the nachos from the dashboard buffet. Helped himself to some of her Coke, too.

"I know I didn't give Matt a fair shake when you two were in middle school," her brother said after he'd finished his mini chow down. "And I didn't go out of my way to be friendly to him when he came back to town. I'm sorry for that. He's given Theo and Ian more than a fair shake. He could have put them in jail, but he didn't." He paused. "Matt seems like a decent guy."

Oh, how times had changed, and Ruston hadn't even choked on the words.

"He is," she muttered. Decent "doing the right thing" kind of guy. Which meant he couldn't stay in Last Ride with her. Since that reminder caused her eyes to water, she shook it off. "Go home, Ruston," she repeated, and then she added a lie to get him moving. "I'm not here sulking about Matt."

Ruston kept staring at her as if he might challenge that, but he finally nodded. "I'll report back to Mom and then go home. But FYI, I'm the father of a teenager so I know sulk when I see it," he added, with some snark included.

He threw open the door and dashed out into the rainy night but not before Emory murmured a "Thanks," and caught a glimpse of the mustard streak on the butt of his jeans. He'd curse her for that later.

Using the wad of napkins she'd gotten from the concession stand, she mopped up the corn dog mess from the seat as best she could, turned up the volume on the radio and dived back into the popcorn.

By God, she was going to finish this pity party. However, she was having to do that now while making mental notes. She'd need to check in with her mother tomorrow. She would also need to make sure Ian and Theo were okay. Ryder, too. And while she was at it, she needed to buy some upholstery cleaner for the car seat.

Emory gave the wipers a quick flip so they'd slash a single time over the windshield. Just enough for her to catch a glimpse of the movie and reorient herself. Of course, she was so familiar with every scene and every line that it was more like white noise than a reorientation, but she needed to settle her thoughts. She'd gotten a good start on that when the passenger's-side door flew open again.

"Oh, for Pete's sake," she snapped as the man ducked inside. "I'm fine. I'm not here sulking about Matt."

This time, she hadn't quite managed to keep that at the level below a shout. It was a full-fledge snarling, yelling protest aimed at her brother. Except it wasn't Ruston.

It was Matt.

Groaning and wishing she could dissolve right into the seat, she looked over at him. Like Ruston, he was rain-soaked, though, his cowboy hat had kept the wet off his face.

"Good to know," Matt drawled. "I mean about being fine and not sulking about me." His gaze glided over her pity-party food stash. "Expecting someone?"

"No." Her voice was the opposite of his easy "drown in me" drawl. It was tight and whiny-sounding. "I was hungry."

The corner of his mouth lifted in that damnable smile that made her want to lick his lips. Then kiss him.

"Your mom's worried about you," he said. "She called me to ask if I'd look for you."

That brought on another eye roll, and Emory rattled off

the pertinent info to bring him up-to-date. "Ruston was just here to check on me. I texted my mom to let her know I'm okay. And you're sitting in mustard and some squished bits of corn dog."

"Good to know," he repeated, not doing the obvious thing of feeling around on the back of his jeans to see what damage had been done. He kept staring at her. "Are you really okay? You seemed pretty upset when you were at my office."

"So I've been told," she grumbled under her breath.

Hearing the whine in her voice go up another notch was what caused her to rein in her nasty mood. Even if her heart felt bruised and heavy, it didn't mean she had to take it out on Matt. After all, he wouldn't be making an exodus from town because of her.

"Sorry," Emory said. "And I'm sorry about dumping that research project on you and then just leaving like that. You shouldn't have had to read that alone."

"I didn't," he answered. He paused, blew out a long breath. "In fact, I don't think I'll read it at all."

Boy, could she understand that. It wasn't a situation of him burying his head in the sand, either. He knew what Candy Lynn was, knew the mess she'd made of her own life and so many others. Knew the mess she was still making with Vince's life. There was no need for Matt to put salt on those particular old wounds. Still, she'd wanted his insight as to whether or not to remove, or add, something to the info she'd collected.

"It's probably best if you just turn in whatever you think is right," he continued a moment later. "I trust you to make it as right as it can be."

That was a lofty amount of trust. One that Emory didn't especially want, but it was better for the final product to be in her hands rather than someone else's. Someone who might have delighted in spilling every ugly, mean detail about an ugly, mean woman.

"Maybe we can burn the diary and the rest of Candy Lynn's things tomorrow," Matt added. "There's no rain in the forecast. Then I can spread my father's ashes somewhere."

"Colts Creek," Emory suggested when it flashed into her head. "Not the ranch but the actual creek. Candy Lynn mentioned in her diary that your dad liked to go there. It was one of the few entries she wrote about him when she wasn't ranting and such."

Matt nodded. "All right. Colts Creek. I can maybe do that tomorrow, too."

He was tying up loose ends. It was hard for that not to send her back down pity-party lane, but the sound of his phone ringing stopped her from turning the trip from a stroll to a spring. Matt scowled when he pulled it from his pocket and looked at the screen.

Emory groaned again. "If it's my mother—"

"It's not," he assured her. "It's my old boss at Amarillo PD. I'll keep this short, but let me just see what he wants."

After clearing his throat, Matt answered it when she made a sound of agreement, and even though he didn't put the call on Speaker, he was only inches away, and Emory caught the friendly greeting from the booming voice on the other end of the line.

"Yeah, I'm staying out of trouble," Matt answered in response to whatever the other man had said. "Hey, can I call you back tomorrow?"

She caught a *sure*, but the man just kept on talking, and even in the dim light from the movie screen, she saw a muscle flicker in Matt's jaw. Again, she tried not to eavesdrop, but it seemed as if the weather itself cooperated to help her do just that, and Emory heard some very crucial words and a full sentence that sent her popcorn-filled stomach to her knees.

Your old job. I'd be damn glad to have you back.

"Thanks," Matt said, and he wasn't gushing like the caller. "I appreciate that offer."

More weather cooperation allowed her to hear his old boss say, "Good. We'll talk about it tomorrow."

Matt ended the call and stared at the screen a moment longer before he put his phone back in his pocket. So, another loose end. One that Matt wasn't tying up himself, but it would make things so much easier for him if he could walk back into his job in Amarillo. His adrenaline-packed job where he didn't have to deal with rabid Sherlock Holmes and *Hunger Games* fans and would still get to see his son every day.

She didn't ask him if he intended to take the job or what he might say during that conversation he'd have tomorrow with his former boss. Nope. That would take her to something well beyond the pity-party path, and if she only had a few days left with Matt, she wasn't going to spend it boohooing and sulking.

There'd be plenty of time for that after he left.

Emory reached out, hooked her arm around the back of his neck and pulled him to her so she could lick his lips. And kiss him. She probably should have set the tub of popcorn aside first because she felt it slip from her arms and spill on their laps. She didn't care. Apparently, neither did Matt because he did some hand hooking of his own—around her waist—and he dragged her across the seat closer to him.

The kiss was hard, deep and plenty hungry. Not at all like the start of a make-out session but rather the tail end of one where both of them had been worked up to the point of needy desperation. Emory forgot all about her dinged heart, all about tomorrow's conversations, all about the popcorn that was crunched between them. She just kissed Matt as if her life depended on it.

Because in an odd sort of way, it did.

She needed to hang on to all of this. To make these kinds of memories with the man she loved.

The taste of him was so much better than any movie snack she had in the car. So much better than anything, period. Matt could kiss. No doubts about that. He could make her body zing. And ache. And need.

He shifted her, pulling her onto his lap so the center of her body pressed against his already-forming erection. She had to amend her "better than anything" thought because sex with him would top it all. Emory let him know that by grinding herself against him.

Matt moaned, cupped her butt and pressed her even harder against him, and he didn't forfeit any kissing while he did that. He claimed her neck with his tongue and then dipped his head lower to her breasts.

The sound had him stopping. And had her groaning because of the stopping. A sudden gust of wind rocked the car, and she heard the squeal of surprise from another vehicle. A reminder that there were other people nearby. It must have been a reminder for Matt, too, because he took his mouth from her breast, lifted his head and stared at her.

"Let's both drive back to the ranch," he said on a rush of breath. "If we try to have sex in this small car, we're going to end up pulling a muscle or two. Plus, I really don't want your dad or brothers to come walking up on us."

Until Matt had said that last part, Emory had been about to tell him that a pulled muscle be damned, that they should go for it right here, right now. But after a couple of seconds of thought, she wouldn't put it past her father or Ryder to come here looking for her. Heck, even her mom, since Ruston had probably already let her know he'd found his "sulking sister" at the drive-in.

"Okay," she agreed. She glanced around and spotted his truck parked in the spot directly behind her. "I don't have an umbrella. You're going to get even wetter than you already are."

"Then you can just strip me down when we get home," he drawled.

He kissed her. A dirty little maneuver with a flick of his tongue that had her wanting to latch on to him and develop amnesia about the idea of someone catching them fooling around.

Chuckling, Matt eased her back behind the wheel. "Drive safe," he cautioned her, and he hurried out and to his truck.

Since *safe* was indeed a key word, Emory took a moment to steady her nerves and to pluck some popcorn off her palms so she could drive. With the rain pounding her car, she pulled out behind Matt and onto the road.

She cursed the turtle speed they were having to go. This was the second time she'd had to endure a ride back to the ranch when every inch of her was burning for a taste of Matt Corbin. That other time, her father had interrupted them, but there sure as heck better not be any interruptions tonight.

The sky kept dumping gallons on them through the entire fifteen-minute drive, and Mother Nature also decided to up the wind gusts. By the time Emory took the turn to Stallion Ridge, her hands were cramping from the white-knuckle grip she'd had on the steering wheel.

Thankfully, there were no other vehicles parked by the cottage or the house. She'd worried that her mother might be here, waiting for her, but maybe the rain had staved off a visit. Hopefully, the staving would continue until she'd gotten an orgasm or two from Matt.

His truck came to a stop just ahead of her, the flash of his red taillights cutting through the rain. Matt got out and looking like a wild man in search of his mate, he stalked toward her car, threw open the door and pulled her out. His mouth was on hers before both of her feet even landed on the ground.

He didn't rush to take her inside. Matt just pinned her against her car door and kept on kissing her. Kept on touching her, too. He slid his hand down her soaked top, shoved it up and went after her breasts again.

Emory started to unravel right there, and she might have slid bonelessly to the ground if she hadn't caught the motion out of the corner of her eye. Matt must have seen it, too, because in a blink he went from wild man/mate searcher to all cop. Catching onto her arm, he shoved her behind him, and even over the slap of the rain, she had no trouble hearing what he said.

"Someone's in your cottage."

That knocked the heat, and her breath, right out of her, but it wasn't fear she was feeling. It was anger when she saw the door wide open and someone standing in the shadows of the open doorway. How dare some moron do this to her again, and Emory would have marched straight inside to confront the intruder.

She stopped, though, when she saw exactly who the "intruder" was. Not one of the possibilities that Matt and she had discussed. Nope.

This was someone in her own blasted gene pool.

CHAPTER TWENTY-TWO

MATT SAT IN Emory's living room, and he kept his attention nailed to their intruder. The intruder who was now slumped on the sofa across from him. Emory's nephew.

Ian.

The boy just seemed to have a penchant for getting into trouble, but this time even he seemed to realize that he'd screwed up big-time. He wasn't spouting excuses or trying to put the blame on someone else. Instead, he was sitting mostly closemouthed, except for the "I'm sorry" mantra while they waited for his parents to arrive.

Emory was waiting, too, but in a whole different kind of way. She was pacing, all the while mumbling and shooting occasional glares at her nephew. Matt couldn't blame her. That first break-in had caused some sleepless nights, had made her afraid to be in her own home, and Emory obviously believed Ian was the culprit for not only this break-in but that one, too.

Matt was sure of the boy's guilt as well, but so far Ian hadn't fessed up. That might have had something to do with Matt reading Ian his rights shortly after they'd spotted him in the cottage. Rights that included him not having to say anything without a lawyer present. Even in the rainy dark, Matt had seen that being Mirandized had put the fear of God in Ian's eyes.

Or maybe that was the fear of his parents and Aunt Emory.

Of course, Matt had done the rights reading before, but Ian had had his partner in crime, Theo, with him then. Maybe because he was now the solo recipient of the Miranda, he wasn't bothering to put on a defiant, sneering front.

"Why would you do this? Why?" Emory muttered, something she'd repeated more than a couple of times.

Ian went with his "I'm sorry" response, which caused Emory to huff and throw her hands up in the air. Her hair was still wet, clinging to the sides of her face, and neither of them had changed their rain-soaked clothes from their kissing session by her car. Ian was right there with them with the wetness, causing Matt to believe he'd likely ridden his bike over.

Matt had suggested that Emory find something dry to put on, especially since her bedroom closet was only steps away, but she hadn't budged out of the living room for even a second. He would stay wet right along with her because he didn't want to leave her alone with Ian while he went to his house. Not because he believed Ian would try to leave or do something to hurt Emory.

No.

But Matt thought there was a possibility that Ian might do something to harm himself. He knew the look of rock-bottom despair when he saw it, and he was looking at it square in the face.

"You're the one who ate my Mondo cookie," Emory snarled when she paced by her nephew.

Then she stopped and took a long look at Ian. Matt could see the slow change in her expression, and he could practically feel the anger drain from her. Probably because Emory was finally noticing the bone-deep sadness all over every ounce of his expression and body language.

Sighing and muttering a few PG-13 curse words, she sank down on the sofa beside Ian. "If you needed something from me, all you had to do was ask. You didn't have to break in." She stopped again. Cursed again. "I'll see if I have some dry clothes that'll fit you."

"No," Ian said, catching onto her hand when she started to move away from him. "Don't go."

Since this seemed to be the start of the boy's explanation as to why the hell he'd done this, Matt leaned in. Even though he'd already guessed the motive, he wanted to hear it without any prodding questions.

"I'm sorry," Ian repeated, and he'd already opened his mouth to say something else when there was the sound of not one engine but rather two outside the cottage. That caused the boy to groan because he knew this was no doubt his parents.

It was.

Anticipating her brother and sister-in-law's arrival, Emory had left the front door slightly open, and it didn't take long before both Ryder and Heather rushed in. Apparently, neither of them had bothered with umbrellas, either, which Matt considered a good sign that maybe they'd been so focused on getting to their son, they hadn't bothered with their own comfort.

Ryder and Heather weren't alone. Dressed in dinosaur pj's, their three-year-old son, Greer, was with them. He was also wet but didn't look the least bit worried or annoyed. Clearly, he was happy about being up past his bedtime and on this "adventure."

"Can I have a snack?" the boy immediately asked Emory. Matt wasn't even sure she noticed when the boy plucked a piece of popcorn off her jeans and ate it. That's when Matt also noticed she had bits of popcorn in her hair and on her shirt, a reminder that he probably had mustard and corn-dog crumbs on the butt of his jeans. As upset as Ryder and Heather were, though, they probably wouldn't even notice.

Keeping all her attention on Ian, Emory absently pointed to the fridge in some "help yourself" gesture to Greer. The kid took off running while he whooped in delight. Matt figured it was a good thing he'd be occupied for at least part of this conversation.

"What happened?" Ryder snapped, aiming the question at no one in particular. His second question, however, was obviously meant for his son. "What the hell are you doing here? You should be home."

"He broke in," Emory provided when Ian went back into the silent "hunched shoulders" mode.

That caused Heather to gasp, and she hurried across the room, sitting beside Ian so she could pull him into her arms for a hug. Another good sign and a contrast to the anger coming off Ryder in hot thick waves.

"How did you even get here? And why would you break in?" Heather repeated in a concerned mother's voice.

Time and talk stopped. Well, except for Greer who'd managed to get the fridge door open and was rummaging around inside.

"I rode my bike," Ian muttered. "I was looking for the diary."

That response clearly stunned the boy's folks and Emory. But not Matt. He'd mentally already gone through all the possible reasons the boy would break in to his aunt's house, and the diary was the only thing that made sense. Or rather it made sense to a teenager who'd clearly heard just enough talk to make him do something like this.

"Candy Lynn's diary?" Ryder said, looking at Matt, and Matt nodded.

Obviously, Heather had heard talk about it because she didn't ask what it was. Or why her son would have ridden his bike through the pouring rain to come here to look for it.

"The diary's the reason my mom and dad broke up," Ian muttered, volleying a glance first at Emory and then Matt.

After several moments of surprised silence, the denials started. A flat loud "No" from Heather.

Emory voiced a "No" as well and added, "The diary had nothing to do with that."

Ryder growled, "No, hell, no, it didn't. What the hell were you thinking?"

"He was thinking if the diary disappeared, that you two would get back together," Matt provided.

Ian grunted an agreement. "I heard Mom and you arguing, and she said she didn't want to deal with the gossip about you messing around with the sheriff's trashy mother. Sorry," he added in a mutter to Matt.

Matt could have told him that *trashy* was a kind word when it came to Candy Lynn. She took trashy to a whole different level.

Greer came running back into the room with a bottle of wine, thankfully unopened, in one hand. In his other hand, he appeared to be eating a squeezed blob of chocolate cake.

"Greer," Heather snapped, getting to her feet.

She yanked the wine bottle from his hand, and in the same motion, she scooped him up to take him to the kitchen sink where Matt heard her turn on the water. And scold the boy for his choices of snacks.

"Anyway," Ian went on after his mother had returned with a now clean-handed Greer in tow, "I figured if the diary was gone, then there'd be no gossip and Dad could move back home." The boy folded his arms over his chest, aimed a glare at Ryder. "Then that a-hole Ethan Darnell wouldn't be asking out my mom."

And there it was in a nutshell—the logic of a teenager. Logic that caused a whole lot of sighing and headshaking in the room.

"The diary isn't even here," Emory said.

"And it's not the reason your mom and I broke up," Ryder added.

"Why would you even think the diary was the cause?" From Heather.

"I wanta drink." That from Greer. "And some Jell-O."

Heather managed to scold Greer with a glance and turn back to scold her older son while she obviously waited for an answer to her question.

Ian first went with a shrug for his response, followed by a long pause. "I just wanted to read it for myself and see if I could use it to help fix things."

Now it was time for Matt to get verbally involved. "Trust me, there's nothing in that diary that'll fix anything." Dragging in a weary breath, he looked at Ryder and Heather. "Emory won't want to file charges against Ian," he said with absolute certainty. A certainty that Emory quickly confirmed with a nod. "But I'm going to suggest counseling."

"I don't want to talk to some doctor," Ian grumbled. "I just want my mom and dad back together."

"That's not going to happen," Ryder said, his voice cutting through the silence that had stilled over the room.

Ryder gave another breathy sigh and sank down on the coffee table across from his son. He opened his mouth and then appeared to change his mind about what he'd been about to say when Greer asked if he could have the popcorn stuck on Emory's shirt. Obviously, the man needed to watch his language, so that would cut down on the possible cussing.

"You should see the counselor," Ryder said, his voice strained but lake-calm. "I'll go with you if you'd like."

"I want Mom and you back together," Ian argued.

"That's not going to happen." Again, Ryder stayed calm and didn't get distracted when Greer asked Emory why she had food on her clothes. "People should be in love when they're married, and if they're not happy, they should try to look for that happiness. That's what your mom and I are going to do. We're going to try to be happy while still loving and raising you and your brother."

Since Matt knew that Ryder hadn't wanted this breakup, saying that had likely cost him. But that's what Dads and Moms did. Good ones, anyway.

Ian shifted his gaze to Matt. "Divorce sucks."

"Yes, it does," Matt agreed. "But your dad is right about everything he just said."

Ian didn't look totally convinced of that, but he nodded anyway, stood and turned to Emory. "I'm sorry about breaking in. Sorry about eating your Mondo cookie, too. I'll buy you another one."

"No worries," Emory assured him and gave him a kiss on the cheek. "I got a lot of replacements. But next time you want something from my house, just ask."

Ian nodded and didn't resist the hug she gave him. "Thanks for not throwing me in jail," the boy said to Matt as he headed out with his mom and brother.

Ryder stayed put, looked at Matt. "Thanks for not throwing my son in jail." He held out his hand for Matt to shake.

Matt accepted the handshake. Considering the source, he figured that was as close to a truce as he was going to get with one of Emory's brothers.

Emory went to the door to watch her family get in their vehicles and drive away. Matt went to her, and they just stood there, staring out at the rain. It was a lousy night, weather-wise, but the "closure" he'd gotten with Ryder made him want to move on to something else.

"I'm thinking about burning Candy Lynn's things in my fireplace," Matt said. "I'll toss what I can't burn. You want in on that?"

She didn't even hesitate. "Absolutely." Emory took hold of his hand as they ran out into the rain.

WHEN EMORY HAD started her pity party at the drive-in, she'd had no idea the night would take the turns it had. No idea, either, that it would continue to turn.

She stood back and watched as Matt lit the oak logs that were already stacked in his fireplace. The flames flickered up, automatically kicking out the smoky, fragrant scent of the wood. Emory welcomed it. Welcomed the heat, too, because she felt a little chilly with her wet clothes.

Matt got up, hauled the box of Candy Lynn's things to the fireplace and set them down on the stone hearth. "You want to do the honors?" he asked, holding out "Candy Lynn's Sweet, Sweet Secrets" diary disk.

She almost said no, that he should do it, but she realized they'd been in this together with the diary. So she went closer, and with both their hands on the disk, they tossed it into the fire.

It felt amazing.

Emory hadn't expected the giddy thrill of seeing it burn, baby, burn. The flames gobbled up all the woman's ugly thoughts, words, secrets and deeds. Of course, the memories of her nasty doings were still there, but time was Mother Nature's fire for that sort of thing.

Matt tossed the art pencils next, then the paperbacks, the coasters, then the cock ring—that he handled by not actually handling it. He used a pen to scoop it out of the box, and he flicked it into the fire. While it burned, and melted, he put the doggy-sex figurine in a plastic bag that he first stomped and then dumped into the trash in his kitchen. Judging from the smug smile he had when he returned from that task, he was in the "this feels amazing" zone, too.

That left the container with his father's ashes, the photo of Candy Lynn and his father and the sketchbook. When he looked down at them, the amazing vanished. Since the sketchbook had a metal cover, it wouldn't burn, and it was rather large to shove in the trash.

"I'll get rid of the sketchbook," she offered.

Emory was a little surprised when he nodded and tucked the photo inside the sketchbook. "She tried her damnedest to break me," Matt muttered.

"And she failed," Emory assured him. "The only person Candy Lynn broke was herself." It was Emory's wish that one day soon Matt would know to the marrow that it was true.

She took hold of his arm, turning him to face her, and she kissed him. It was time to finish what they'd started in her car at the drive-in. Time to shove aside the Candy Lynn memories and burn up some of this need she had for him. Not just lust, though it was there in spades.

But she had this need to comfort him, too. Good sex could do that. Of course, it was possible this would be the last time they could go the "good sex" route. Emory doubted that Natalie would want to linger around Last Ride, and now that Matt knew he could get his old job back, it eliminated any obstacle to his leaving.

She didn't want to think about that now, though. Emory

only wanted to focus on the sex. Thankfully, Matt made that easy for her since his kisses put her back in the needy stratosphere. It was as if they picked up exactly at the point against her car when they'd been about to drag each other to the rain-soaked ground.

They kept kissing as they fought with their clothes. Darn jeans. She should have worn a dress because it meant Matt was tugging at her zipper while she was tugging at his. They did that all the while backing and maneuvering their way to the sofa.

Matt still had on his shoulder holster, so the moment he had her unzipped, he ditched that onto the coffee table. In the same motion, he went after her top. His nimble fingers didn't fail him because he got it off her, shimmied down her jeans and panties, and then he used his foot to push them to the floor. He managed all of that before she could take off even a stitch of his clothes.

He laughed when she cursed him and toppled her onto the sofa. It was a race now, and apparently speed counted. She figured that's because his body wasn't giving him a choice about this particular battle they were waging. It wasn't the time for slow and easy. This was going to be fast, hard and perfect.

With Matt, it was always perfect.

It took some doing, mainly because he was driving her crazy with the kisses on her neck and because he now had his hand in her bra and was pinching her nipples, but she finally got off his shirt. Finally got him unzipped, too, before they stumbled and fell onto the sofa with him landing on top of her.

In the back of her mind, it occurred to her there wasn't much space to move around, but that thought didn't last long. Not when Matt lowered his teasing, pinching fingers to the center of her body. Oh, man. Talk about a way to make her melt into a puddle of goo. He touched, kissed and added the right amount of pressure in the right spots.

"Condom," she managed to say.

Since he still had on his unzipped jeans, he took one from his wallet and freed himself from his boxers. The moment he had the condom on, Emory took hold of him and pushed his erection inside her.

She lost her breath a moment, and her heart possibly stopped. All usual sensations when having unusually amazing sex with a man who knew exactly what he was doing. And what he was doing was making every part of her beg for more, more, more. Matt had no trouble whatsoever with that more, and he kept up the "speed matters here" pace of their fierce battle. Kept it up until the orgasm wracked through her. Until her heart and breath stopped some more.

Until Emory surrendered every last inch of herself to Matt.

CHAPTER TWENTY-THREE

MATT WOKE UP to Emory's scent. And he smiled. Because that scent was right next to him, just as she was. She was warm and naked in his bed. Soon, he wanted her to be warm and naked beneath him, but for now he took a few waking moments to, well, savor the moments.

Somehow, after their diary-burning, followed by a frantic round of sex, they'd eventually made it to his bedroom, and he'd been pleasantly surprised when Emory fell into bed with him, literally, instead of going back to her cottage. But even though the sex had been great as usual, he'd felt her pulling away.

No, it'd been worse than that.

He'd felt as if she were saying goodbye.

A farewell orgasm of sorts. But instead she'd stayed the night, cuddled up next to him as if she didn't have a care in the world. Of course, he knew all about the cares she had, and he was no doubt at the top of the list for things bothering her. Then again, she was at the top of the list for things bothering him.

When they'd started this fling, he'd thought the heat and what they felt for each other would just fizzle out. And after the fizzling, Matt had figured there'd be some hurt, probably some seriously awkward moments since they lived practically on top of each other. The worst-case scenario was that he'd considered Emory might get a broken heart out of the deal. But his own heart wasn't feeling in the best of shape right now, and he felt torn.

Being torn wasn't a first for him. He'd had it in spades when Natalie had told him she was moving to Last Ride. The tearing had continued when Matt quit his SWAT job and moved back here to be with his son. More tearing had occurred when Emory drew Candy Lynn's name, and the shitty memories of her and his childhood were all dragged out in the open. But leaving Emory suddenly seemed like it would top all of that shittyness combined.

And yet, it was something he might have to do.

That reminder wiped the smile off his face, and the guilt came. Man, did it. There was no way he should be thinking about having sex with Emory again. But even guilt didn't cause the heat to evaporate when she stirred, moaned and then kissed his neck. That would have almost certainly given the guilt a kick in the ass if he hadn't heard someone knocking at his door.

Frowning, Matt checked the time. It was nearly seven-thirty, and he was usually up well before this, but it was his day off. Zella and Zeke knew that and wouldn't bother him. Unless it was an emergency. And that had him cursing and getting out of bed.

"Stay put," he told Emory, kissing her before he dragged on his jeans.

Matt grabbed his shirt and phone, and he headed for the door, hoping that this was a problem he could solve in a very short amount of time. He rammed his arms through the sleeves of his T-shirt and was still pulling it down when he opened the door. Not Zella or Zeke.

Vince.

The man looked as if he'd been through hell and back. His hair was a mess, the stubble on his face was well past the fashionable stage and there wasn't an inch of his clothes that weren't wrinkled.

"Can I come in?" Vince asked at the same moment Matt blurted out, "Is everything okay with Jack and Natalie?"

"Jack's fine," Vince assured him. "He's with my folks, but I don't know where Natalie is. She's not answering her phone, and I've been out looking for her all night."

Well, shit. Cursing, Matt immediately tried to call Natalie. It went to voice mail, but before he could leave a message, he got a text. From Natalie.

I'm okay, she messaged. Will tell you about it later.

Puzzled over that response, he showed it to Vince, who did some puzzling of his own. His forehead bunched up, and he shook his head, but there was also some relief on the man's haggard face.

"She doesn't want to talk to me," Vince murmured.

The emotion in Vince's voice plucked plenty of emotion for Matt. He didn't totally give up on the notion of finishing up this conversation and getting back to Emory, but he knew that it would have to wait.

"Come in," Matt said, standing back so Vince could enter. He motioned for the man to follow him into the kitchen. He'd no doubt need some caffeine for this so he got the coffee started. "Tell me what happened. Did Natalie and you have a big blowup?"

"No." Still shaking his head, Vince sank down at the kitchen table and put his face in his hands. "I messed up and gave Natalie an ultimatum. I told her if she was moving back to Amarillo, then I'd move there, too."

That didn't sound like an ultimatum to Matt. It was more like grasping at straws if Natalie did indeed want to call off the wedding. Still, it was pretty unselfish of Vince to give up his practice here in Last Ride to follow a woman who might or might not give him the time of day.

"What'd Natalie say about that?" Matt pressed.

"She started crying, and then she said I was confusing her, that she couldn't think straight. She told me she was scared because she'd messed up by marrying you and didn't want to mess up like that again. Sorry," Vince added in a mumble.

Matt waved it off. Natalie and he were on similar pages there. He didn't believe he'd messed up by marrying her, but he sure as hell didn't want to go through that kind of pain again. He understood Natalie's fear of taking that huge step again. He certainly wasn't anywhere ready to do that.

And then Emory walked into the kitchen.

Like Vince, she was rumpled, but she managed to make it look amazing. Like a welcoming, warm unmade bed that you wanted to climb right back into. Matt found himself wanting to do exactly that.

"I, uh, need to get home," she murmured, her voice nowhere near as amazing as her looks. There was caution with a generous helping of nerves, and she already had Candy Lynn's sketchbook tucked under her arm. Obviously, she was ready to go. "Sorry, Vince," she added. "I didn't mean to overhear what you said."

"It's okay." He scrubbed his hand over his face, glanced at her. "This is your business, too, since it affects you."

Yeah, it did affect her, and that reminder put Matt right back on guilt road. Soon, very soon, he would need to have a heart to heart with her and learn just how much damage he'd done by pushing this fling into something a whole lot more. And it was more. Matt had no doubts whatsoever about that.

"I'll be tied up with work today," Emory told him. "Lots and lots of sewing to do."

Matt heard the subtext of that. *Give me some space. Don't try to soothe me just yet.* He was trying to wrap his mind around that and figure out if it was something he could actually do when there was a knock at the back door.

"It's me," Natalie said.

Vince practically leaped to his feet, steeling himself up and looking "puppy dog" hopeful. Matt unlocked the back door, opened it and Natalie marched right in, her attention nailed right on Matt.

"I've made a decision," Natalie announced. "And we need to talk." She opened her mouth but then froze when she saw Emory. "Uh, I didn't know you were here."

"I was just leaving," Emory assured her. "I need to get home," she repeated.

She murmured a quick goodbye to Natalie, an equally quick goodbye to Vince and him, and she hurried out the door.

EMORY TRIED TO shut out the world and focus on the wedding dress she was making. A corseted-back ball-gown style in peacock green.

The unusual color choice was obviously the bride's doing, but Emory had to admit it was coming together nicely with some cobalt seed pearls spattered on the bodice. Adding those pearls was tedious and time-consuming, but it wasn't anywhere effective in keeping the thoughts out of her thought-filled head.

Thoughts of Matt, of course.

After she'd come back to her cottage, she had immediately gotten into the shower, and by the time she'd finished and dressed, Vince's and Natalie's vehicles were gone. So was Matt's truck.

Since she knew this was his day off, Emory figured his absence had to do with Natalie's "I've made a decision" announcement. Maybe Matt had gone to talk to Jack about the move they'd soon be making.

Eventually, though, Matt would want to have that talk with her.

Emory was dreading that enough that she'd nearly chickened out and taken the dress to the shop to work on it there. But since a face-to-face with Matt was inevitable, she'd decided it was better for it to happen in the cottage rather than at the shop where someone might overhear.

So, instead of taking the chicken route, Emory had stayed put at Stallion Ridge. First, working on the final research report for Candy Lynn and then shifting to the dress. Neither project was particularly pressing time-wise. The peacock wedding wasn't for another four months, and she still had a few weeks before she'd have to turn in the research. However, there'd been an urgency to finish anything and everything connected to Candy Lynn. The drawing had hung over her head long enough, and it was time to put it aside.

Of course, the moment she'd finished it, it had felt like a goodbye not just to Candy Lynn but to Matt. This research was what had spurred them spending time together. Which had, in turn, spurred the attraction. Though there was a reasonable argument that the attraction had been there long before the drawing of the Last Ride Society. Emory had the sickening feeling that it'd be there long, long after she'd turned in the report.

Maybe forever.

With that dismal thought, she reached across the table

for the container holding the seed pearls, fumbled it and dropped the darn thing onto the floor. Seed pearls scattered like tiny rolling stones. Cursing and snatching the dustpan and brush that she kept nearby, she stooped down to sweep them up and just sort of froze there.

She felt on the verge of giving into the gloom and just crying. And she might have done exactly that if there hadn't been a knock at the patio doors. Emory barely had time to turn in that direction when they opened.

And Matt was there.

Oh, her heart did that little jig that it always did whenever her gaze landed on him, and as usual, she forgot how to breathe. Apparently, forgot how to stand up, too, because Emory just continued to crouch.

Matt eyed her and then eyed the seed pearls. He didn't have to look far and wide for those because some had rolled right toward his boots.

"Need some help?" he asked as if absolutely nothing was wrong with the world.

Emory shook her head, forced herself to start sweeping. She considered several things to ask him or say to him, but she decided any and all questions and comments would contain a sad whine so she just waited him out.

"I went to Colts Creek," he said. He didn't come closer. He seemed to be frozen, too, in the doorway. "I scattered my father's ashes."

That brought her upright, and Emory studied his face to see if that'd been tough for him. It had been. Part of her wished she'd gone with him, but obviously this was something Matt had needed to do himself.

Tying up yet another loose end.

"I'm sorry," she murmured.

She took a deep breath, set the dustpan aside and went to

get one more loose end. One that he likely didn't want, but Emory wanted him to have the chance to see it. She went into the living room and came back with Candy Lynn's sketchbook.

"This is what I'm turning in for the Last Ride Society research," she explained, holding out the book for him.

Matt took it with all the caution a person would use while handling something both dangerous and fragile. Which in a way, it was. He probably used the next couple of seconds to steel himself up, and he finally opened it.

His gaze skirted over what was there on that first page. That didn't take long because it was only one sentence.

"Candy Lynn Donnelly Corbin was a troubled local artist who led a complicated life," Emory repeated from memory.

Beneath it, she'd put the required photo of the woman's tombstone, along with Candy Lynn's dates of birth and death. Emory had also included a copy of the picture of his dad and a very young Candy Lynn by the motorcycle.

Matt turned the page to the drawings, and he kept turning, glancing at the sketches. "You're not doing a research report?" he asked.

Emory shook her head. "Some of the butt drawings are risqué enough that they should satisfy the folks who like to pour over these things." She'd rather the gossip be about artful asses than anything she'd written that would spur talk about Matt's poor, pitiful childhood.

"Some legacies just need to be squashed like bugs," Emory concluded. "This is one of them."

The corner of his mouth lifted into that panty-melting smile, and setting the book aside, Matt went to her. He didn't pull her into his arms. Didn't kiss her. But he kept smiling.

"If I asked you, would you consider moving to Amarillo?" he said.

Her mind had been racing, going at breakneck speed, but that caused her to mentally trip and face-plant on the floor with all those seed pearls. "Huh?" she managed.

Still no kissing or touching. No repeating the question, either. He stood there, obviously giving her some time for it to sink in.

"You're asking me to move with you?" she clarified.

"I'm asking if you'd consider it," he *clarified* right back.

Clearly, this was huge and something she should give a ton of thought to. She didn't. "I'd move," she blurted out.

That deepened his smile, and he finally touched her. Sort of. He took hold of her hand in a chaste kind of way. Well, chaste except that his fingers did some dallying on her palm.

"You'd leave all of this behind?" His gaze skirted around the room.

It was "big girl panty" time. She could go on about how she'd miss her family. And she would. About how she'd miss Last Ride. And she would. About how tough it might be to start a new business elsewhere. And it would be. But all of that paled in comparison to one thing.

Matt.

"I'd make compromises to be with you," she admitted. "Because I'm in love with you."

That would have sent some gun-shy, once-burned men running for the proverbial hills, but Matt kept up the finger-dallying and moved in to brush his mouth over hers.

"Good," he murmured against her lips.

Then he really kissed her. Tongue and all. With the kind of heat that Matt and only Matt could generate. It was hot, long and deep enough to nearly make her forget what he'd just said.

Nearly.

"Good?" she repeated. "That's it?"

He eased back, looked in her eyes. "No, that's the beginning. I just wanted to make sure we were moving in the same direction."

With his next scalding kiss, he proved to her they were not only moving in the same direction, but they were also on the exact same road, traveling at the exact same pace.

The pace got even better when he said, "Because I'm in love with you, too."

After a few moments of stunned, delighted, dumbfounded silence, rockets went off in her head, and she launched herself at him. Probably not the wisest move since he was already standing so close, but Matt was right there to catch her. Right there to kiss her lights out. It didn't take long for Emory to be ready to haul him off to bed.

But Matt stopped the hauling.

"Natalie and Vince are going through with the wedding," he said. "They're not moving to Amarillo and neither am I. Are you okay with that?"

Emory did a mental blink and an actual one. "But you asked me to move with you?"

"I asked if you'd be *willing* to move. Just wanted to see where your head was at."

"My head is with you," she murmured. Which, of course, sounded stupid, but it made him laugh and kiss her again, so Emory didn't care about stupidity.

The joy flooded the thoughts that started racing through her head again. "I'll be able to have my cake and eat it, too," Emory added. "That's the bottom-line definition of a really good deal."

"For me, too," he assured her. "There's just one thing." He took her by the hand and led her to the closet.

Her body tingled, anticipating closet sex with the man she loved. But the man she loved didn't go "the closet sex" route. Instead, he lifted out her dream dress, the one she'd made for herself.

"See this?" he said. "If and when we do the whole 'I do, till death do us part' thing, you won't be wearing this."

There was a lot to absorb in that one little sentence. *A lot.* Her future. Her happiness. Her life with Matt.

Oh, mercy. A life with Matt.

That skyrocketed the tingling and the happiness to the extreme giddiness level. She very much wanted the whole "I do, till death" package with Matt, but she hadn't expected him to be considering that, too.

"I won't be wearing this?" she managed to ask.

"Nope." He shook his head. "I say we dodge the whole deal about your *mostly lucky* wedding dresses by having you wear something you haven't actually sewn. But don't worry. You'd still get this dress."

The giddiness was obviously affecting her brain. "How?"

Matt grinned. "I'd be the wedding dressmaker. I'd put aside castrations and such and personally take this one apart so I can put it back together myself."

Now Emory grinned right along with him. "But you don't know how to do that."

"For you, Emory," he drawled. "I'll take sewing lessons."

And with that, Matt pulled her to him and kissed her.

* * * * *

Turn the page for
USA TODAY *bestselling author*
Delores Fossen's bonus story,
Corralled in Texas*!*

CORRALLED IN TEXAS

CHAPTER ONE

CALLIE PEARCE DIDN'T see the pie in time to dodge it. The lemon meringue dropped right on her, the aluminum serving dish thudding onto her head. The sugary goo oozed down her face and toward her mouth. With just one lick—a practically involuntary one—she consumed her entire daily calorie count.

"Oh, no," someone blurted out.

Even though the lemon filling had temporarily blinded her and awakened her starving taste buds, Callie knew that voice. It belonged to Aunt Mildred, and it was filled with distress. Footsteps followed. Mildred was obviously scurrying toward her, coming to the rescue.

"The pie was on the baker's rack," Mildred blurted out. "You must have bumped into it."

Probably. Callie had on a black puffy parka that added several inches of width to her torso. Along with making her look like a stumpy stack of radial tires, the coat made it hard for her to judge how much room she needed to maneuver.

And she'd needed maneuvering room, all right.

She'd come through the back door with a large rolling suitcase, a large purse and a stuffed-to-the-zipper gym bag looped over her shoulder. All while carrying a smoothie in a to-go cup. Added to that, the driveway had been scabbed with ice patches, which had now slicked the bottom of her boots. Callie had no doubt bumped into a lot of things as she'd made her way up the porch steps and once she stepped into the kitchen.

As for the baker's rack, it hadn't been there the last time she'd come back to her hometown of Lone Star Ridge about two months ago, but Mildred was always making changes to the kitchen along with the rest of the house that she called the Old Belview Estate Inn.

It was a lofty name for a place that was missing some of the *loft*.

The yellow Victorian house was indeed old, but not in a restored-to-historic-perfection, "wow, look at that place!" kind of way. It was also big enough that some might consider it an estate. *Loosely* consider it, that is. But the ambience and overall general appearance were more along the lines of what you'd get in the "before" picture on one of the home improvement shows.

Despite its shortcomings, the inn was her home, and Callie was sure she would have gotten that all warm and welcoming feeling if it hadn't been for the pie. And she'd still get it, eventually.

Because this wasn't an ordinary trip home.

Nope.

In thirty-six hours or so, her aunt would be marrying the love of her life, Birch Carson. Callie's only complaint about the marriage was that it'd taken Birch way too many years to ask Mildred to be his bride. The couple had "courted" for thirty-five years, longer than Callie had been alive.

"Oh, no," Mildred repeated. She began to wipe the lemon meringue off Callie's face.

Callie dropped her purse and gym bag on the floor and let go of the suitcase handle so she could help clean up. It took a minute or two, because the pie filling had temporarily adhered her eyelashes shut, but she was finally able to see. What she saw made her want to shut her eyes again. And curse.

"Ace Brandon," Callie ground out like the profanity she barely managed to hold back.

The man who'd crushed her heart and given her emotional baggage for life was standing right next to her aunt. He was wearing a Kiss the Cook apron and sporting a concerned look. Well, cocky concern, anyway, because no matter which expression Ace wore, it always had a cocky edge to it. That was possibly because he was the hottest cowboy in Texas.

And he knew it.

Of course, it would have been impossible for him not to know such a thing, since there were mirrors and other reflective surfaces in Lone Star Ridge. He could see for himself that he had the face of a Greek god, fallen angel and rock star all rolled into one. Naturally rumpled black hair, bedroom-blue eyes and a smoking body earned not in a gym but in the hours working with the livestock on the nearby Jameson ranch. If she hadn't despised him down to the soles of her icy-soled boots, Callie would have melted into a puddle of lust.

"There," Mildred concluded after a few more wipes to clear the pie filling from her head. "All better now." Her aunt stepped back, studied Callie and smiled.

Callie felt like a puddle of a different sort then. Love. The unconditional kind. Aunt Mildred was her family. Her only family, because the woman had raised her after Callie's worthless parents had dumped her at the inn when Callie had been eight, and they'd never come back. Mildred had not only taken her in, she'd also doled out plenty of love and mothering. Callie would have endured a hundred falling pies, radial tire coats and icy roads to be here for her.

Even Ace's presence couldn't dim that enthusiasm, but he had put a damper on her homecoming.

"What are you doing here?" Callie asked him.

"Cooking," he said, as if that explained everything. It didn't.

Yes, she knew that Ace enjoyed cooking, and yes, she'd known he'd be at the wedding. After all, Birch was his uncle on his mother's side, and the man had had a hand in raising Ace. But Callie hadn't expected him to be here *today*. She'd needed those extra hours to steel herself for seeing him. She definitely hadn't wanted this face-to-face to happen while she was covered with lemon meringue.

"That pie was for the wedding, wasn't it?" Callie asked her aunt. She glanced up at the baker's rack and saw the other pies, cakes and cookies on the wire shelves.

Mildred gave her a dismissive wave and did some more wiping of Callie's face. "Not to worry. We have plenty. Ace has been baking since five this morning."

So, the pie had been his creation. And she supposed it shouldn't have surprised her that he'd be cooking for the wedding. It wasn't a formal to-do, and in fact would take place in the living room at the inn. Callie suspected that some guests would even bring side dishes to give it a potluck feel. Lone Star Ridge and Aunt Mildred weren't exactly high society. Another plus in her favor, as far as Callie was concerned.

"Don't worry," Mildred added. "Ace knows that you'll want to cook some reception food, too, and he'll make room for you in the kitchen."

At the mention of Ace's name, Callie's eyes went back to him. She was certain she scowled. He didn't. He smiled as if sharing the kitchen with her would be the most amazing experience they could have since the last orgasm he'd given her a decade and a half ago.

Something Callie wished she hadn't remembered.

Parts of her, the wrong parts, went tingly and warm when thinking of that said last orgasm. And the ones that'd come before it.

"I'll need to do some cooking," Callie verified. "Not just for the reception. But also for the diet," she added in a grumbled whisper.

"Oh, yes." Mildred bobbed her head, causing locks of her silver curls to dangle and bounce around her face. "I told Ace about that, too. He knows you're still doing that whole blog thing."

The *blog thing* was Callie's job and had been for twelve years since she'd moved away from Lone Star Ridge. She wrote the blog and did other PR for Upscale Fitness, a chain of elite gyms and spas in Houston. However, she now needed a dose of her own medicine and fitness advice, because she had to drop the fifteen pounds she'd put on after her breakup with Chad Devers, the owner of Upscale Fitness. If she didn't shed the weight, Chad probably wouldn't fire her.

Probably wouldn't.

But Chad had made it clear that he didn't want her making any public appearances on behalf of Upscale Fitness until she was back in shape.

She hated that she couldn't argue with him about that. After all, it wasn't good advertising to have a health and fitness guru with a highly visible muffin top. And she'd been the one to put on the weight—after Chad had dumped her for the size-two yogini that he'd added to their fitness team.

Callie had never been a size two, nor had she wanted to be. She just wished that Chad hadn't made such a big deal about the extra pounds. Wished, too, that Upscale Fitness put as much emphasis on fitness as it did the scale.

"You look good to me," Ace drawled. "Really good." And, yeah, there was cockiness there. His voice was like foreplay, but it was still BS.

She looked out of shape and jiggly, sort of like the pie filling that was now oozing its way down the front of her coat. But she'd drop the pounds, and with her monthlong hiatus from work, just a handful of people would see her the way she was now. Only the bride, groom and several of their senior, hopefully poorly sighted guests.

And of course Ace.

But she could just ignore him.

"I obviously need a shower," Callie said when a blob of crust dropped from her head and onto her collar. She'd also have to use the washer and dryer.

"When you're done, come back down and join us for breakfast," Mildred invited.

It was late for breakfast, nearly eleven, but whatever was warming on the stove smelled great. Callie's stomach began to growl, and the idea of finishing her kale smoothie suddenly sounded revolting.

"We're sort of Ace's guinea pigs since he's trying out the recipe on us," Mildred went on. "It's chocolate crème–filled crepes…"

Callie tried to tune her out. Unfortunately, even with her stomach making a horrible racket, she could still hear her aunt, and she could smell the evidence of Ace's morning labors.

"…crisp smoked bacon…" Mildred went on.

Callie started to salivate. Worse, she knew this wasn't just boastful talk on Mildred's part. Ace was a master with food products, particularly those of a high-fat nature. He had no doubt created that and more. But Callie didn't intend to let it get to her. She'd hurry up to her room, shower and drink the rest of the miserable smoothie in solitude.

"If this breakfast is any indication," Mildred added a moment later, "I guess we should thank our lucky stars that we'll get to sample a lot more of Ace's cooking after we're back from the honeymoon."

Callie had already reached to pick up her bags, but that stopped her. "What do you mean?"

"Oh, didn't I tell you?" Mildred said as she went to the stove. "Must have slipped my mind." Her eyes rolled back in her head when she sampled a crepe that was on a warming dish next to the stove. "Mmm. It's heaven, Ace. Pure heaven."

Callie didn't plan to be distracted by her aunt's *mmm*ings. "What slipped your mind?"

Mildred *mmm*ed a few more times. "Well, I told Ace he could stay here next week while Birch and I are away on our honeymoon. We won't have any guests, but it'll be nice to have him here to keep an eye on the place. He's promised that he'll freeze lots of goodies for us to sample once we're back."

"What?" Callie managed to say in protest. "But you knew I'd be here for a while."

"Yes, but I didn't know it when I told Ace he could stay here," Mildred chided. "Ace just needs a quiet place to whip up some recipes, that's all. It's for a big competition, and he can't do it in that little kitchen at his place. Besides, this is sort of Ace's home, too, now that Birch and I are making things official."

"Recipes? Competition?" Callie grumbled after she'd mentally replayed her aunt's comments.

Mildred nodded. "If he wins, he gets a lot of money."

"Please tell me this is for some liver and onions cook-off," Callie said.

"Nope." Ace shook his head. "It's for the Valentine's Day Smothered in Chocolate competition."

Of course it was.

Callie's heart dropped to the vicinity of her kneecaps. That meant Ace would be trying out those irresistible, high-fat recipes right under her dieting nose.

"Don't worry," Ace added with a wink. "You'll never know I'm here."

Right. And premium chocolate was a proven weight-loss product.

Callie closed her eyes so she wouldn't have to gaze at the sinful-smelling breakfast any longer. She fumbled around to pick up her bags again, but she felt a hand close over hers. Ace's hand.

"I'll carry up your bags for you," he offered.

"I can manage," Callie fired back.

But she was talking to the air, because Ace already had her rolling suitcase and her gym bag, and he was hauling them across the foyer/reception area. Callie shucked off her coat, rolled it into a bundle so that she wouldn't leave pie droppings all over the floor and hurried after him. She caught up with him when he was already on the stairs. Because the inn was over a hundred years old, the staircase creaked with each step she took to the second floor.

"I know you don't want me here," Ace said, taking the words right out of her mouth. "But I really do need the kitchen, because I have to film myself making some of the recipes. My place just isn't big enough."

Yes, she remembered that. It was a small two-bedroom house that'd belonged to his grandfather, and Ace had moved in with him in high school. Things hadn't been that great for Ace at home, and he'd inherited the place after his grandfather passed. It had what Ace had called a "one-ass" kitchen. Not even room for two people in there unless you wanted a lot of body-to-body contact.

Which had happened on occasion when Ace and she had been together.

Of course, the body-to-body contact hadn't lasted long, because Ace had stomped on her heart when he'd broken up with her just days before she'd left for college. That might have been fifteen years ago, but Callie could still feel the pain of it. And worse—he hadn't even been able to give her a reason.

Well, not a good one, anyway.

He'd fallen back on the old pathetic excuses that she needed to focus on school, that she was too young for a serious relationship and that she shouldn't try to deal with a long-distance relationship. She'd been going to college in Dallas, for Pete's sake, and yes, it was a four-hour drive from Lone Star Ridge, but love should have been able to overcome a few tanks of gas and some time.

And Callie hated that she was still stewing about it.

"The competition's big for me, and I need to submit the recipe within the next two days to be considered for the finals," Ace went on. He opened her bedroom door, set her bags inside and turned to face her. "I want to use the money to buy some livestock. One day I'd like to own my own ranch rather than just work at one."

Well, heck. His sincerity made her feel a little ashamed that she was doing all the wallowing in her mental pity party. "So, you don't have plans to run off and have your own show on the cooking channel?" she joked.

The corner of his mouth lifted into one of those smiles that only Ace could manage. It was a mix of cocky, heat and something that dissolved willpower. But Callie resisted by looking away.

Ace put his fingers beneath her chin, barely a touch, but she felt the tingling again. He turned her head ever so gently until they were eye to eye. "I can stay out of your way," he said in that damnable tempting voice of his. As tempting as the pie filling that she could still smell. Could still taste. "If you want me to stay out of your way, that is."

That last bit might have only been a handful of words, but it was like throwing down a challenge. A proverbial line in the sand.

Of course she wanted him to stay out of her way.

Of course she didn't want him looking at her as if she were the yummy pie filling that he'd like to lick.

Of course she didn't want him to make parts of her tingle and heat up.

But Callie didn't move. Worse, she didn't balk when Ace continued to stare at her. No objections when his gaze slid down her body. Nor when he leaned in much too close to her.

And she sure as heck didn't balk when he kissed her. Callie just stood there and let him take her mouth for a slow, wild ride.

CHAPTER TWO

"I'M AN IDIOT," Ace mumbled under his breath as he eased back from Callie.

He saw the dazed, aroused look in her eyes. A look that didn't last. Nope. As if pulling herself out of a trance, the daze faded. The aroused part, too. And in their place was a very pissed-off woman.

Crap. Why had he pushed this by kissing her? Ace knew the answer to that. Because he was an idiot, that's why.

"Sorry," he managed to say a split second before she slammed the door in his face.

If he hadn't moved back, fast, the door would have landed *on* his face, so he considered himself lucky. Callie wouldn't have intentionally harmed him—probably not, anyway—but she'd had a right to be pissed off at him. And now that he'd kissed her, her right to that particular pissed off–ness had gone up a notch.

Ace wanted to think that it meant he'd keep his mouth and hands off her, but this was where the idiot part played into things. One look at her—yeah, a look even with her head and face covered with pie—and he'd wanted her more than he wanted to win the cooking competition.

More than his next breath.

Idiocy had caved to that kind of need, but it was a need he was going to have to keep in check. He didn't want to spoil Birch and Mildred's wedding, and that might happen if he continued to go after Callie. He could keep his jeans zipped, his mouth unkissed and his hands to himself. Then he could go back to his own house with its little kitchen and make do and get those recipes recorded.

When he made it back into the inn's sprawling kitchen, Ace saw that the pie mess was all cleaned up from the floor. Birch had joined Mildred at the breakfast table, and they were chowing down on the crepes he'd made for them. They definitely seemed to be enjoying them. However, they both looked up at him, and Birch studied him with more interest than he should have, considering they'd just seen each other minutes earlier.

"You have some pie filling on your lips," Birch pointed out, and he added a wink. Since his uncle wasn't an idiot, he likely knew what'd just happened upstairs. Plus, Birch was well aware of Callie and Ace's history.

Well aware, too, of why Ace had broken her heart.

Mildred was probably in the know on that particular subject, too, but the woman had thankfully never held it against Ace. Nor did she mention the dab of lemon meringue that Ace wiped from his mouth. It wasn't just the pie he could taste now, though. It was Callie.

Yeah, he was an idiot, all right.

"Hope this snow doesn't put a damper on the wedding," Mildred commented. She took her now-empty plate to the dishwasher and peered out the massive bay window over the sink.

"It won't," Birch assured her. "It's just a few flakes."

Ace looked outside, too, and while it was indeed just some flakes, he made a mental note to check the weather. Something he hadn't done already because he'd been so busy with the baking.

Since Mildred was letting him use the kitchen, Ace

thought it was only fair that he do the bulk of the cooking for the reception. Plus, he did enjoy it. Not nearly as much as he enjoyed working with the horses at the Jameson ranch, but it was a nice break. If the cooking and baking led to that prize money for the competition, then it was even better.

Ace was still gazing out the window when he felt Mildred's hand on his arm. "Birch and I want to talk to you a minute," she said.

Oh, hell. This was about that kiss, and it'd turn into a lecture for him to be mindful of dealing with Callie. "I won't kiss her again like I just did upstairs," Ace blurted out.

Judging from Birch's head shake and Mildred's surprised expression, they definitely hadn't expected him to make that confession.

"Oh, okay," Mildred murmured. Then she paused, cleared her throat. "Callie didn't object to you kissing her?"

No way did Ace want to get into that, so he gave a so-so motion with his hand and hoped he got a fast subject change. He got it.

"Birch and I want you to consider starting your own ranch here," Mildred said, smiling.

Ace was certain he wore the same surprised expression that Mildred had just seconds earlier. "What?"

Birch got up to join them at the sink. "The inn has nearly a hundred acres of land," he explained. "It hasn't been used for pasturing livestock in decades, but it could be made right for that. Plus, there's the creek at the back of the property, so water wouldn't be an issue."

Ace heard every word, but it took a while for those words to process. "You're offering me the land?" he clarified.

Mildred beamed. "We are. I just wish we'd thought of it sooner, but I didn't realize just how much you wanted your own place until you said how you'd use the money if you won the cooking competition."

"You could still use the money for buying livestock," Birch piped in before Ace could say anything. "And if you could stand to part with it, you could sell your granddad's place and buy even more."

Mildred took up the explanation. "You could live here at the inn in the attic apartment."

Ace just stood there and stared at them. His first instinct was to say no. Not because he was attached to his grandfather's place. He wasn't. But... "The inn and the land should go to Callie."

"Callie won't use the land." Mildred answered so fast that it made Ace think she'd already considered any argument he might have. She put her hand on his arm again. "Just sleep on it while we're on our honeymoon. If you want the land, I'll start the paperwork when we get back."

"You'd be helping us out," Birch added. "It'd be nice to have family living here with us."

Ace opened his mouth, closed it and decided that sleeping on it was exactly what he needed to do. And talk to Callie about it. He'd already given her enough grief in life without horning in on something she might want for herself.

"Thanks," Ace told them. "I'll let you know what I decide."

Birch smiled as if he knew what the answer would be, and he slipped his arm around Mildred's waist. "Now, I need to give my fiancée her surprise for the day. Then I'll come back and help you with the dishes."

The surprise likely wouldn't be sexual, Ace knew that, but it would almost certainly be weird. Birch had a good heart, but he didn't always have good judgment about such things. Glow-in-the-dark toilet paper, a coffee cup in the shape of a nose and that risqué leg lamp from the Christmas movie. Despite Birch's bad taste, though, Mildred always proudly displayed his gifts.

That had to be true love.

Something that many had once thought Ace had with Callie. And he had. Ace had loved her enough that he hadn't wanted her stuck here in Lone Star Ridge with him. Yes, this was her home, but she'd wanted to try out her wings. She would have stayed had he asked her. But Ace also knew she would have come to resent it.

Would have resented *him*.

He'd thought it would be easier just to hurt her with a breakup so she could get on with her life. And she had clearly done that. Man, had she. Callie had left and hadn't given him a look other than a scowl. Heck, she'd intensified the scowling expression after that idiotic kiss just minutes earlier.

The kitchen landline rang, the sound slicing through his thoughts. He waited a couple of rings, but when Mildred or Birch didn't answer it, Ace did.

"This is Chad Devers," the caller said before Ace could even get out a hello. "I need to speak to Callie."

Ace had heard the name plenty enough. This was Callie's boss. Along with being her ex-boyfriend. According to Mildred, this guy had hurt Callie bad. Since Ace had done the same thing to her, he probably didn't have a right to mentally snarl and sneer at the man, but that's exactly what he did.

"Callie's in her room," Ace informed him, and yeah, he wasn't about to completely contain the snarl. "Try her cell."

"I did, and she's not answering."

"She's probably in the shower." He wouldn't mention

the pie crash. "I can tell her you called, or you can try her again in a few minutes."

"Tell her I called." No snarl, just plenty of impatience in his voice. "I'm leaving on a trip and won't be answering my phone for the next day or two. Oh, and tell her I expect her to lose that weight while she's there on vacation."

Ace felt every rile-able part of his body stiffen. "Excuse me." And he darn sure didn't say it like an apology.

"That weight she packed on," Chad *clarified*. "Remind Callie of what I expect of her." And with that, the moron ended the call.

Considering the grip he had on the phone, Ace was surprised it didn't crack in his hand. He practically rammed it back into the holder mounted on the wall, and without bothering to cool down his temper, he hurried out of the kitchen and up the stairs to Callie's room.

He knocked, waited and was ready to knock again when Callie threw open the door. She had a towel coiled around her dark blond hair and was wearing an old white terry-cloth robe. Her face was still damp, so obviously, he'd been right about her having been in the shower.

"Why are you working for an asshole?" Ace snarled.

Callie blinked. "Chad?"

"Yeah, Chad." He made sure the name sounded like toenail fungus. "The moron just called on the landline because he couldn't reach you on your cell."

That sent her hurrying to the bed, where she scooped up her phone, then muttered some profanity. "He didn't leave a message," she said, looking at the screen.

"No, he left it with me. He's an asshole," Ace repeated.

Callie pulled back her shoulders and probably didn't realize the motion caused the front of her robe to gape, giving him a really nice peek at the curve of her right breast.

Ace didn't let it distract him—not much, anyway—because he wanted to get to the bottom of why her a-hole boss had said what he did.

"Chad wanted me to remind you to lose weight," Ace snarled. "Should I remind him that he's got a face that my fist can punch? Because he had no right to say that."

Callie sighed, her shoulders dipping back down, and dang it all to hell, that gave him a peek of her left breast.

"He has the right," Callie argued. "He can't have me working at Upscale Fitness while I look like this." She fanned her hand over her body.

Ace frowned and skimmed his gaze over the parts of her that she'd just pointed out with the hand fanning. Not only didn't he see anything wrong, he also saw plenty that was right. Right in a groin-tightening kind of way. Yeah, she had curves, but they were in all the best places.

"You look great," he said, and no, it wasn't his erection talking.

"I don't." Her voice wasn't a snap, and he thought it was doused with hurt. "I gained fifteen pounds."

He had no idea if that was a lot, but again—it was in all the best places. And even if it hadn't been, there was no way in hell he wanted Callie to beat herself up about this.

Ace went to her, took hold of her arms and turned her to face him. *Crap.* Her dark green eyes were watering. That only made him want to punch the Chad dick even more.

"I have to look fit when I do workshops at Upscale Fitness," she added, her voice trembling a little. "I have to get these pounds off."

"Do you want to lose them?" he asked. "*You*," Ace emphasized. "Not your a-hole boss."

She opened her mouth, closed it and moved out of his grip. "Yes."

Ace frowned again. Her answer wasn't exactly said with a lot of conviction and enthusiasm. So, Ace tried a different angle. "What's your dream?"

She blinked, clearly not expecting the question. "What do you mean?"

"I mean, is it your dream to work for an asshole?"

Now, she blinked again as if not expecting that, either. "I want an interesting job, something I enjoy."

"And you enjoy working for an asshole?" he pressed.

Her chin came up, and he saw the argument forming. An argument he wouldn't win. Not with the way his temper was raging. So, he spoke before she could say anything.

"Don't sell yourself short, Callie," Ace said while he headed for the door. "You need a better dream."

CHAPTER THREE

"A BETTER DREAM," Callie muttered, and she said it with plenty of snark as she made her way down the stairs. What the heck did Ace know about her dreams?

Plenty, she reluctantly admitted.

She'd poured out her heart to him so many times when they'd been teenagers. All those young hopes for a bright and rosy future.

A future with Ace.

She couldn't count how many times she'd planned their wedding. Their lives. Lives that she thought would begin as soon as she'd gotten her degree in public relations and started her own business.

Of course, she'd never been able to figure out how she'd run that business in a small town like Lone Star Ridge, but Callie had been certain that Ace and she would have worked that out in the white-picket-fence life she'd envisioned for them. But the envisioning had come to an abrupt end when he'd broken things off with her.

Callie pushed that last thought aside. Pushed aside, too, that whole better-dream comment Ace had made right before he'd left her room. She wished she could completely push Ace aside, too, which was why she didn't head for the kitchen—where he was likely to be. That turned out to be a good move on her part, because she found Mildred in the front living room. Her aunt was at the window, peering out at the fat snowflakes that were whirling around on the breeze.

"Isn't it cute?" Mildred said.

For a moment Callie thought she was talking about the snow. However, when her aunt held out her hands, Callie saw…whatever the heck that was. It appeared to be a blob of twisted and matted holly.

"It's a gift from Birch," Mildred explained. "Isn't it just adorable?"

Callie looked for something cute or adorable but just didn't see it. It was a ball of slime-green plastic. Then Mildred squeezed the sides of it, and a reindeer popped up from the center. It, too, was plastic with disturbingly large eyes. Again, nothing cute or adorable.

"Birch always gives you interesting gifts," Callie remarked, knowing she had to say something.

"Doesn't he?" Mildred agreed as if Callie had just given the man a huge compliment. It wasn't. "He knows how much I love Christmas things."

Yes, the gifts were interesting, but Birch had some seriously bad taste. Many examples of which were knickknacks now scattered around the inn for guests to enjoy. Such as the fossilized dung in amber. And the taxidermy possum with a Santa tie. There were also dozens of signed photos and other memorabilia from local country music singer Marty Jameson, her aunt's favorite. Mildred even had a pair of Marty's boxer shorts—autographed—in a glass display case. Marty was also the father of Ace's boss, Shaw, who owned the Jameson Ranch.

"Marty will be here for the wedding, you know," Mildred remarked when she followed Callie's gaze.

Callie knew the singer had been invited and had RSVP'd that he'd come. But Marty wasn't very reliable at keeping his promises, not just for wedding invitations but to his family. Still, Callie hoped he'd be there to make the day even more special for her aunt.

"Ace told me about the message your boss left for you," Mildred threw out there, causing Callie to groan. "Are you okay?"

"I'm fine." It was a lie, of course, and Mildred knew it. Callie was pissed. "Chad shouldn't have called here and told Ace that."

And that's why Callie had tried to call Chad back, to tell him to back off. Along with giving him reassurance that she'd lose the weight. But Chad hadn't answered, probably because he had indeed left on a business trip.

Mildred set aside the plastic holly and patted Callie's hand. "Well, I'm sure you'll work it all out, since you love your job so much."

Callie frowned. Once, she had indeed loved her job. That was before Chad had dumped her and started giving her grief over, well, everything. Suddenly, her work wasn't good enough. *She* wasn't good enough. And Callie was having a hard time finding any one aspect of her job that fell into the *love* category.

"I just want you to be happy," Mildred went on. Then she paused. "You are happy, right?"

Not at the moment, she wasn't, but since she didn't want her aunt to worry, Callie just smiled and nodded. Maybe that would stave off a discussion about her being in her thirties and still single. It was a topic that Mildred brought up occasionally, and it was often layered with a cautionary warning for Callie not to be an old maid like her. Well, Mildred was about to be a married woman, so maybe that would put an end to the lectures.

Or not.

"You still want kids, don't you?" Mildred pressed.

"Look at that snow," Callie said, pointing out the window. Nothing had changed weatherwise in the last five minutes, but she thought maybe that would cue Mildred in that it wasn't something she wanted to discuss. Yes, she still wanted a family and kids, but she first had to get her life together.

"Suit yourself," Mildred murmured, and then she snapped her fingers as if remembering something. "You need to talk to Ace. Birch and I have made him an offer that might affect you."

That got Callie's attention. "What offer?"

Mildred patted her arm. "It should come from Ace. He's in the kitchen if you want to talk to him now."

Callie didn't want to talk to him. Nor did she want to go into the kitchen, where he was no doubt whipping up something delicious. But she was pretty sure Mildred would dig in her heels about this, so Callie went to the kitchen, aka the lion's den, where she found Ace decorating a cake with what appeared to be chocolate buttercream frosting.

Her stomach started to beg.

So did other parts of her. Specifically, her mouth. But it wanted more than just to lick the buttercream spoon. Why did Ace always give her a gut punch of attraction? Better yet, when would it stop?

He looked up and grinned as if there was actually something to grin about, then he put aside his frosting knife to come to her.

"You don't look so upset now," he said, confusing her.

Callie was certain a picture of her current expression would be the very definition of upset. But that didn't last, because Ace leaned in and kissed her. It happened so fast that she didn't have time to dodge it, not that the gut punch wanted her to do any dodging. Still, she backed away from him.

"There, I just wanted to get that out of the way," he said, wiping his hands on a dishcloth. "And I need to confess that I saw your breasts."

Now, her current expression was the definition of confusion. "Of course you've seen my breasts. We were lovers." Correction—he'd been her first lover. Ace had seen every inch of her stark naked. And vice versa.

"No, I mean I saw them more recently," he explained in his discussing-the-weather tone. "Upstairs. Your bathrobe gapes when you move around."

Callie was reasonably sure that she now just looked stunned. He'd gawked at her breasts when they'd been having that intense, humiliating conversation about Chad's message? Apparently so. Callie didn't know whether to be flattered that Ace was still interested in seeing her breasts or if he was just pointing out that she needed to buy a better fitting robe. She decided neither mattered and moved on to the reason she'd come in here.

"Aunt Mildred said that Birch and she made you some kind of offer," Callie threw out there.

That rid him of any trace of cockiness, and while he didn't exactly dodge her gaze, he did glance away for a second. "Yeah, they want to give me the land around the inn so I can start my own ranch."

That wasn't as much of a surprise as Ace probably thought it was. Years ago when Ace and she had still been a couple, Mildred had suggested it. Along with Callie running the inn, but that hadn't felt right to Callie.

It hadn't been a *better dream*.

She'd wanted adventure. With Ace. She'd wanted that business of her own. With Ace. An exciting life. Again, with Ace. After Ace had exited the picture, all the rest had faded, too.

"I'll understand if you'd rather keep the land for yourself," Ace said.

She didn't want the land, and it was probably best for it to go to someone who would put it to good use. But Callie thought of something else. Something sneaky that could be going on.

"Does my aunt also want you to live here?" Callie asked.

Ace sighed, nodded. "In the attic apartment. Yeah," he added a moment later as if he knew exactly what she was thinking.

Callie thought of the conversation she'd just had with her aunt. The question about marriage and babies. And Callie suddenly knew what this was all about.

"Mildred's matchmaking," Callie grumbled.

Well, it wasn't going to work. No way. Ace was firmly in the *been there, done that* column, and she wasn't going there, doing that again.

"Does this mean you'll be keeping your distance from me?" Ace asked.

"You bet." And that made her next decision so much easier. As soon as the wedding was over, she'd be leaving Ace and his high-calorie concoctions behind. She was going back to Houston.

CHAPTER FOUR

ACE FORCED HIMSELF to concentrate on the mini-sermon that the heavily jowled Reverend Sanderson was giving the wedding party and their three dozen or so guests. However, those words of reverence and wisdom didn't lessen the feeling of total idiocy that was coursing through Ace.

Nope.

Of course, that likely had something to do with the fact that Callie—the primary cause of his idiocy reminder— was standing directly across from him. Mere inches away. Too bad she somehow managed to look darn good even in that god-awful tangerine-colored chiffon ball gown that Mildred had chosen for her niece and maid of honor.

Other than Callie herself, there were other contributing factors that helped Ace identify his stupidity status. And it didn't have much to do with the fact he was practically drooling over a woman in a tacky dress that resembled a runny gelatin mold.

For one thing, he'd thought he was well past being over Callie. Wrong. Dead wrong. He couldn't have been more wrong if he'd set out to do it. And yet, he'd actually flirted with her and kissed her. Kissing and other carnal things couldn't happen again, of course. Callie already thought he was slimier than a slug trail for dumping her. No sense contributing to that notion, especially since Callie and he wouldn't be on the same path for long. After her vacation, she'd be going back to Houston, and he'd be staying here in Lone Star Ridge.

And that led Ace to yet another reason for his verified lunacy: his planned stay at the Belview. He'd agreed to that when he'd been thinking about all the advantages of using the inn's huge kitchen. But at least for the rest of her vacation, Callie would very much be around, and *around* in this case wasn't a good thing. With all the other complications he was facing, he needed that kind of distraction about as much as he needed a taste bud–altering sinus infection. So, that meant one of them had to leave.

He'd head out right after the reception.

Yes, he'd told Birch and Mildred that he would keep an eye on the inn, but he'd have to do that while staying at his own place. Ditto for perfecting and filming the recipes in his small kitchen. Somehow, he'd make it work.

"And now Birch has a surprise for Mildred," Reverend Sanderson announced, the minister's words garnering Ace's attention. "It's his wedding gift to her, and it commemorates her favorite song."

Hell. Not a *surprise*. Just that one word created a huge knot in Ace's stomach.

Birch clapped his hands, and Wilburn Starling, the handyman at the inn, jumped from his folding chair and opened the door to the storage closet. One by one, Wilburn hauled out a fake tree and several covered cages, which he promptly uncovered.

"Good grief," Callie muttered.

Even though it wasn't a very manly reaction, Ace nearly gasped. Before Ace could stop him, Wilburn opened every cage and set the menagerie free. One partridge. Two turtledoves. Three French hens. And four calling birds.

Feathers and fowl flew in every direction.

Ace and the minister both ducked as the partridge ignored the artificial pear tree and zipped past their heads. It dive-bombed some of the guests, causing a few shrieks, before it joined a turtledove, who'd perched on a rustic pine beam of the massive gathering room.

"This wasn't a good idea," Ace told his uncle.

Even though he shouted it, Ace wasn't sure Birch heard him because of the commotion caused by four canaries, otherwise known as calling birds. Their *calling* was on the loud side, and blended with the squawks of the three French hens, it was practically deafening.

Ace wasn't alone in his thinking that his uncle probably should have come up with a better way to surprise his bride. The guests were certainly none too pleased and were making as much noise as the critters. Thank heaven it appeared that Birch had stopped at the five golden rings part, or they would have had a wedding disaster on their hands. Heaven only knew how much racket all those pipers piping, lords a-leaping and drummers drumming could have created.

Callie shooed at one of the hens as it pecked at the seed pearls on her gown. The other turtledove made a beeline for Eddie—the short order cook at the inn. The bird landed on Eddie's head and proceeded to rummage through his heavily waxed, crude oil–colored hair. Eddie batted and otherwise squawked, adding some creative profanity that insulted both the fowl and Birch's knack for really awful gift selections.

"It's probably a good idea if y'all just do the *I do* part so we can get out of here," the minister called out above the noise.

"We do," Birch and Mildred yelled in unison.

"Then I pronounce you husband and wife." Reverend Sanderson dodged a lunging canary just in time.

While Birch put the five golden rings on each finger and thumb of Mildred's left hand, Ace did what he could to help Callie with the pearl-pecking hen.

"Please tell me you didn't know about this," Callie snapped.

"Didn't have a clue." Ace shoved the hen away with the toe of his boot, but it just squawked and came back for another go at those pearls. "I don't know where Uncle Birch has been hiding all this stuff."

But that wasn't what worried Ace most. He was more concerned with secondary surprises and gifts. Hopefully, this wasn't just the start but the fowl finale.

Callie whirled around and batted at the bird with her bouquet, showering them with fragrant orangey petals. With all the batting and whirling, she tangled her feet in the wads of fabric and netting and would have fallen if Ace hadn't caught her.

And catch her he did.

Well, in a manner of speaking.

For a second or two, his arms were filled with a chiffon-slicked woman—the operative word being *slicked*. Callie went one way. Ace's hands went the other when he tried to hold on to her. Inadvertently, he groped her in places best reserved for highly intimate situations. Inadvertently, she kneed him in a place best reserved for criminal apprehension.

"Ohh," Callie squealed.

Ace didn't exactly squeal. It was more like a not-so-muffled howl, and he saw stars the size of Texas.

Callie caught onto him when he doubled over. "Sorry. My knee slipped."

The apology would have gone over much better, however, if they'd had their balance. Her feet went out from beneath her, and since Callie had hold of him, Ace went down as well. They both ended up in a heap at the foot of the fake tree. The hen went right after the seed pearls again and didn't seem to care that a few of its pecks poked Ace's leg.

Miraculously, Birch and Mildred were able to shut out everything else and seal their vows with a kiss. A rather lengthy kiss. One that went on for several long moments. Long enough for the guests to stop ducking the fowl and focus on the newlyweds.

Trying to ignore his aching backside, and front side, Ace somehow got to his feet and helped Callie to hers. But like the others, he couldn't get his attention off Birch and Mildred's kiss. It wasn't necessarily a pretty sight, but that nuptial lip-lock brought back memories of his encounter with Callie. Bad memories. And good ones. Really good ones. One glance at Callie, and he thought maybe she was thinking the same thing.

The scowl she gave him confirmed it.

"Birch," the minister prompted. "You might want to hurry this kiss along a little. The bird droppings are starting to collect on the floor."

That seemed to do it. Thankfully, Birch and Mildred tore themselves away from each other, and despite the fact that most of the guests were senior citizens, they practically sprinted in the direction of the dining room. That included their star guest, Marty Jameson, the town's celebrity.

Ace and Callie got everyone inside and slammed the double doors, shutting out all but one very persistent French hen and a partridge that made a fly-through at the last second.

There was a moment of silence, when everyone looked around as if trying to figure out if they'd survived with all their clothing and hair intact. Then the accusing eyes slowly turned in Birch's direction. Since the mood in the place suddenly seemed a little ornery, Ace decided to try to stave off another disaster.

"There's plenty of food and drink," Ace announced. "Help yourselves."

Ace had already arranged the buffet on the right side of the room. The heated serving dishes were filled to the brim with some of his best recipes that had taken him hours to prepare. Not to be outdone, Callie had taken over the kitchen that morning to do her cooking and had now placed her lower-calorie, healthier wares on the left side of the room.

Right where the French hen and the partridge took roost.

Callie groaned. Since the critters immediately started to peck away at her wrapped fig leaves, she simply shook her head and sank down into a chair. "This day couldn't possibly get any worse."

Ace hoped she was right, but that knot in his stomach wasn't easing.

He took the chair next to her so he could catch his breath. "The stuffed mushrooms I fixed aren't too high in calories," he let her know. "And if you're going for a low-fat kind of thing, there's champagne."

When she snapped her gaze toward him, her eyes were narrowed. "Do you know what I've had to eat in the past twenty-four hours? Fruity fresh antacids and cherry cough drops," she answered before he could guess. "And I had to pick disgusting lint off the cough drops."

He wrinkled up his forehead. "That doesn't sound like much of a diet, if you ask me."

She groaned. "I'm not intentionally eating like that," Callie snapped. "I'm doing it to avoid you."

Oh.

Well, talk about a hard slap upside the head. Ace had

known that Callie had ill feelings toward him, of course, but he hadn't understood the depths of it until now. For her to have submitted herself to a semimedicinal, linty diet just so she wouldn't have to see him meant that he was a couple of steps below slug slime.

And it stung like crazy.

"Don't worry," Ace assured her. "I'll be leaving in a couple of hours. Then you can eat your linty cough drops in solitude. Well, as much solitude as you can get in this crowd."

She shoved a thumb against her chest. "No. *I'll* be leaving in a couple of hours. I've already packed."

Ace shook his head. "Nope. I insist. This is your home—"

"Looks like neither one of you'll be going anywhere," he heard Eddie say. He hitched a shoulder to the windows at the far end of the room.

"No!" Callie mumbled, her gaze following Eddie's hitched shoulder. "This can't be happening."

Eddie's grin widened. "Oh, but it is. Know what else? The weather station says we're in for some heavy snow, and the state troopers have already closed the highway leading into town. Who knows—we might get stuck here for days. Good thing we'll have you here to do some fancy-schmancy cooking."

He ignored Eddie's remark. As if approaching a deadly rattler, Ace walked to the windows with Callie following right behind him.

It was indeed a sickening sight.

Crystalline white snow was everywhere. Sparkling on the cars. Glistening on the treetops. And especially gleaming on the road. It wasn't a thin layer, either. It was thick, gloppy and would no doubt prove formidable to his speedy exit, especially since there probably wasn't anything resembling snow removal equipment within the tricounty area.

Ace looked at Callie. She looked at him. And he saw the horror that was no doubt mirrored in his own face as the next few days flashed before their eyes.

Him, cooking. Her, dieting. Him, lusting after her. Her, pretending not to lust after him.

Callie didn't curse, didn't whine, didn't even groan. She made a beeline for the champagne. Ace bypassed the bubbly and went to the bar for something with a little more punch to it. He tossed back a double shot of whiskey, poured himself another one and prayed like crazy that it'd stop snowing. If not, he was in a heap of trouble.

It was the cliché of clichés, but the colossal ten-bedroom inn just wasn't big enough for the both of them.

CHAPTER FIVE

THE SNOW WAS coming down in buckets. At least Callie was pretty sure it was. The champagne had hit her harder than a two-by-four, and her vision was now a little spotty. That was as good a reason as any for her to be in her room and away from the guests.

Away from Ace.

When she'd left the reception an hour earlier, the guests were still trying to catch the loose fowl, while Mildred and Birch were singing rather colorful Irish ditties and Christmas carols. Callie had finally gotten away from the mayor, who had insisted that she dance the fandango with him, and made a mad dash for the stairs. With luck, she could hide out until the snow cleared.

Or until starvation set in.

Or until she could no longer tolerate the dress.

Try as she might, she hadn't been able to get out of it. The zipper had gotten stuck on the satin and wouldn't budge. Nor would the strong-as-steel fabric tear. After she gave her arms a rest, she'd have to try again.

Her hiding out came to an abrupt halt when there was a knock at the door. Callie had every intention of ignoring it and pretending she wasn't there, but then the man spoke.

"Callie, it's me, Marty Jameson," he said. "Can we talk?"

She frowned but got up and opened the door. Marty

knew her, of course. Everyone knew everyone in Lone Star Ridge, but this was the first time Marty had sought her out.

"I want to offer you a job," Marty went on without hesitating. He was tall, lanky and still had his looks. "The person who does my web page, fan club and stuff quit, and I need somebody right away. I've heard you do that kind of work, and you'd be able to do this job from home."

Callie's frown deepened. "Did my aunt put you up to this?"

"Yeah." Again, no hesitation. He flashed her an easy grin. "But I really do need somebody, and Mildred showed me the stuff you've been doing for the gym where you work." He took a card from his pocket. "That's the name and number of my manager. Just give him a call, and he can get you started. He'll also work out salary, benefits and junk like that with you."

Now she huffed. "I don't want a pity job."

"Wasn't offering pity," he assured her. Another grin, followed by a shrug. "It's a job. If you want it, it's yours." With his grin still in place, Marty made a glance over his shoulder. "Maybe you could think of it as a better dream."

Callie came up on her tiptoes to see what Marty had glanced at. Ace. He was just up the hall and was sitting on the floor outside the room where Callie knew he was supposed to be staying.

"Call my manager if you're interested in the job," Marty repeated to her, and he strolled away, whistling and easing his hands into the pockets of his jeans.

Once Marty was gone, Callie shot Ace a frown. He had ditched his tie, and several buttons on his shirt were undone. He still had on the jeans he'd worn for the ceremony, but there appeared to be buttercream icing stains on his right leg.

"What are you doing up here?" she asked.

He had a long pull on the beer he was drinking. "There are several dozen drunk senior citizens in the dining room. They're singing very confusing songs while clamoring for more booze. Eva May Rachett—who's a couple of years past eighty—keeps pinching my butt. And there's a French hen with a serious attitude problem who's taken up residence in my room and won't leave."

So, she wasn't the only one having a bad day, and despite that, Callie had to give a weary smile. "I drank too much, I'm stuck in this dress and I'm starving."

Ace combed his gaze over her dress, reached down and picked up a plate that held a huge piece of chocolate wedding cake. "Help yourself."

Callie considered the humongous calorie count for a second or two, and then, on a heavy sigh, she sank down next to him and took the plate. "Did you have anything to do with Marty offering me a job?" She took a bite of the cake and moaned in pleasure. Mercy, it was good, like biting into a creamy chocolate cloud.

"No. But he did run the idea past me when he saw me sitting here. And yeah, I mentioned the better-dream thing." Ace snorted. "Marty said he was going to use those words in a song he's writing."

Great. Now, her life would be crooned out in country music lyrics. Probably bad ones.

"Here's a recap of our situation," Ace went on after another sip of his beer. "I just phoned the sheriff, and he told me the roads are all blocked. It's going to be at least until late tomorrow before they can clear them."

Callie figured she would have groaned a lot louder had her mouth not been filled with cake. Talk about a better dream. Yeah, this cake qualified as that. Besides, the road clearing wasn't a surprise, since Lone Star Ridge would have to rely on tractors with makeshift plows.

"That means we have to occupy the same general area for about twenty-four hours," Ace continued. "That can't happen with this old baggage between us. You'll continue to starve to death just to avoid seeing me. And you could be stuck in that dress the whole time."

He had a point. "You could be stuck in the hall if you don't want to fight the bird," she reminded him.

Ace shrugged and made a sound of agreement that was laced with weariness and frustration. "I say we call a truce, and then once the roads are clear, I'll go back to my place. That way, you can have some peace and quiet here alone."

Well, crud. That made her feel petty and guilty. She wasn't completely over what'd happened between Ace and her, but it wasn't right to have that old baggage get in the way. They were adults now, after all.

And there was still that lust simmering between them.

"No. You stay and work on the baking competition stuff," Callie told him. "You could win with this cake."

"You think so?" he asked, his tone changing. He seemed to perk right up at the compliment.

"I *know* so. It's better than…" She'd nearly said "sex."

"Sex?" Ace obviously had no trouble filling in the blank. No trouble adding a grin to it as well. Yes, he'd definitely perked up.

Maybe it was because of the sugar rush she was getting, but Callie found herself smiling, too. She intended to say yes, but that wasn't what came out of her mouth. Instead, she muttered, "Almost."

Of course, that sounded like some kind of come-on. As in sex with him was still better than the best cake she'd ever eaten in her entire life.

And maybe it had been.

Even though she didn't say that last part aloud, the moment seemed to freeze, and she could practically see her deepest thoughts whirling over her head like a cartoon thought bubble.

Thoughts like Ace was still hot. Thoughts like he still made her tingle and go warm at the worst possible times. Like now, for instance. That darn lust did indeed rear its head. And worse. There were all these feelings that went with it. It was impossible for her to forget that once she'd been crazy in love with this guy.

Now, she was just crazy.

"Think about this," he went on, his voice all low and slathered with testosterone.

She expected him to say something about their past. Maybe about this truce. Heck, perhaps even about the recipe for that sinful cake. But he just leaned in, millimeter by millimeter, moving so slow that Callie could have easily stopped him when she realized his intention.

She didn't.

In fact, Callie found herself leaning in, too, until their mouths met. It wasn't exactly a flavorful combination, what with the taste of his beer and the cake. Still, it worked. But who was she kidding? Kisses always worked between Ace and her.

One touch of his lips to hers, and it was as if the past, flavor clashes and common sense evaporated. The lust took over, and it apparently had something to prove. She moved in, fast now, and she took his mouth as if it were a second helping of that cake.

Ace sped things up, too, and even though he was taking her for a ride with a kiss, she felt him fumble around between them. At first, Callie thought he might be trying to touch her—something she would have welcomed now that the insane heat had consumed her—but he was merely setting her plate and his beer aside. The moment he'd done that, his fingers dived into her hair, and he hauled her to him.

Burning, burning, burning. That was what kept repeating through Callie's mind. She was on fire, something she should have expected, because it'd always been that way between them. She wanted to curse him for that. Wanted to curse herself, too, but it wasn't enough to stop her.

He pulled her onto his lap so that she was straddling him. Not the best position, considering they were in the hallway of the inn and someone could come up the stairs at any second. However, the position did have its advantages, because it put the suddenly very needy center of her body against his clearly needy erection. Ace made full use of that, too, by hooking his arm around her butt and pulling her forward to grind against him.

Callie lost her breath. Saw stars. Did some cursing, too. At least in her head, she did, but it would have been impossible for her to actually speak, what with the French-kissing going on.

Ace maneuvered to do some more grinding. This time with her breasts against his muscled chest. Like everything else he was doing, it was effective, but it wasn't necessary. Callie knew she was already past the point of no return.

"My room," she managed to say.

He didn't argue with her, but he also didn't stop kissing her. It wasn't easy, but they sort of crawled and dragged each other toward her room. They'd likely have rug burns, but she was sure it'd be worth it. At the moment, no price seemed too high to pay.

When they bumped into her doorjamb, they fell back

on the floor, still kissing, still dragging until they were far enough away from the door so he could kick it shut. The privacy gave her another shot of heat and urgency.

Suddenly, speed mattered. Maybe it was because her body wasn't giving her a chance to change her mind. So many parts of her wanted to get lucky. To feel release from this pressure-cooker heat. And Ace, she knew, was a pro at releasing pressure-cooker stuff.

"Clothes off now," she grumbled, already fighting to remove his shirt.

Of course, things would have gone a lot smoother had they actually paused the kissing and touching, but that didn't seem optional. She needed the heat from his mouth, and she had to get her hands on him. She finally did when she shoved apart the sides of his shirt and went after his chest. As always, it was groping at its finest. Ace had an amazing body.

He did some groping, too, and in what had to be a miracle move, he unjammed the zipper on her dress and shoved it down. The slick fabric worked in their favor, because it practically sloshed down her body. Ace followed the trail, tongue kissing her body as he bared it inch by inch. By the time he made it to her panties, she was ready to beg.

Begging wasn't an option, though, because he rid her of the capacity to speak when he kissed her through the flimsy fabric of her panties. Then the panties were gone, too, shimmied down like the dress, and he rid Callie of her breath with a very well-placed tongue kiss in the center of her hottest heat.

Oh, man. He was good at this. So good that it took her a moment to fight through the hot haze in her mind and remember that she wanted him to be on the receiving end of this lust, too.

She caught onto him, dragging him back up to her, and immediately started work on his zipper. He helped with that. Probably because she was practically giving him a hand job with her impatient, needy fingers. Ace not only got his jeans off, he managed to extract a foil-wrapped condom from his wallet and put it on.

He kissed her again. And again. Until the only emotion she could feel was raw, hot passion. Ace lifted her, wrapped her legs around his waist and pressed her back to the bed. He entered her slowly. Too slowly. Callie wanted hard and fast, but he actually stopped and looked at her.

"Think about this for the next couple of minutes," he said.

And he kissed her one more time. Not hungry and hot, but slow and burning. The kind of kiss meant for a welcome home rather than sex. It stopped her for a moment, but then thoughts vanished when he slipped inside her and started to move. It was deep. It was perfect. But then he slowed just when he had her so close to the brink she could taste it.

"Think about this," he repeated, giving her another of those confusing welcome-home kisses.

But he didn't give her much thinking time, thank goodness. Ace sent her spinning out of control to a place where words weren't even possible. She clung to him. He latched on to her, and they went to la-la land together. It was better than she'd ever hoped. Even better than that cake. And that's when Callie realized something.

She'd just made a huge mistake.

CHAPTER SIX

ACE FIGURED THIS had been the best thing that could have happened. Sex with Callie. Something he'd thought he would never experience again.

Yet here she was, still shuddering from the orgasm and looking, well, not as if it'd been the best thing that could have happened to her.

Well, hell.

He'd expected her to have some regrets, but he hadn't figured they'd set in so soon—while he was still inside her.

Since she definitely looked as if she had something to say to him, Ace rolled off her and headed into the bathroom for a pit stop. He didn't dawdle, but in the less than two minutes that he was gone, Callie had already gotten up and had put on that gaping robe. Great. Now he was going to get another peep show while he was trying to convince his body to cool down.

"I'm sorry," she said.

Yep, she was having regrets, all right. "I'm not sorry," he insisted. But he did sigh, located his boxers and pulled them on. "I wanted to be with you."

Of course, that didn't mean he *should* have been with her, but Ace hadn't been able to resist. When she'd kissed him with her chocolate-scented breath, he'd been a goner.

Still was.

He knew that some men didn't hang on to their first loves, but he sure had. His first and only. That was Callie.

"You dumped me," Callie quickly fired back. "You broke my heart."

So, she had jumped right back into that personal time machine and aimed right at the core. He had indeed broken her heart, something he would never forgive himself for doing. It wasn't hard for him to remember what he'd been thinking, why he'd done the only thing he'd believed he could do. But he doubted there was anything he could ever say to Callie to make it right.

"I just thought you deserved something better," Ace explained while he tugged on his jeans.

Clearly, that wasn't the answer she'd wanted to hear. Callie stared at him, not with regret-filled eyes but with more than a smidge of anger. "I had better. *We* had better. And you threw it away."

The raw emotion in her voice stopped him. This wasn't just anger. He could see and feel the hurt. Hurt that he was responsible for. It didn't matter that it had happened so long ago, because it was still fresh. Still there. Maybe it always would be.

"I needed to do that so you could decide if *we* was what you really wanted," Ace said. "I didn't want you to look back and regret…anything."

What Ace really meant was *him*.

He hadn't wanted Callie to regret loving him and settling for a life that wasn't all she deserved. But he'd been young and stupid, too, and he'd thought that once she'd finished college and spread her wings a little, she would have come back home.

To him.

She hadn't.

Callie had continued the wing-spreading by graduating from college and then moving to Houston to create a life there. One obviously filled with resentment for him.

"I'm not sorry for what just happened," Ace said. "But I am sorry that I hurt you."

Knowing that it was a dumb thing to do and figuring it was yet something else Callie would regret, he leaned in and kissed her.

And then he walked out.

CALLIE STOOD AT the dining room window and watched as some of the wedding guests drove away from the inn. Seeing them go was a relief, because it meant the roads were clear and that Birch and her aunt could soon leave on their honeymoon.

She could leave, too.

If that's what she wanted to do, that is.

And that was the debate Callie had been having with herself throughout the night and now into the morning. Yes, she could leave, but she wasn't sure that's what she wanted to do.

She silently cursed Ace but then cursed herself more for landing in bed with him for some incredible sex. But if it'd just been sex and only sex, she would have already said goodbye and been on her way back to Houston. But it wasn't. It was more, and it was the *more* that had her anchored at the window, sipping her coffee and wondering what the heck she was going to do.

Callie turned when she heard the slight tapping. Not footsteps. It was one of the birds pecking at something on the floor. Apparently, Birch and Ace hadn't managed to round up all the fowl, and she wondered if Ace had gotten the French hen out of his room. She hadn't asked. In fact, she hadn't seen him since he'd left her room the day before.

His truck was in the parking lot, so he was still likely somewhere at the inn. Probably in the kitchen working on a recipe. That was the reason she'd asked Eddie to bring her a cup of coffee.

She heard the front door open again, heard her aunt thanking and saying goodbye to another guest. Minutes later, a car drove off, and Mildred walked into the dining room.

"There you are," her aunt said. She went to Callie, kissed her cheek and then handed her something. It was the amber with the dung. "I want you to have this."

Callie couldn't stop herself from making a face. Yes, it was encased in amber, but it was still fossilized poop. "Aunt Mildred, you should keep this." *Really*, she should keep it. "It was a gift from Birch."

Mildred practically shoved the amber into Callie's hand and pulled something from her pocket. "He found a bigger piece for me and gave it to me as a wedding gift."

Again, Callie made a face, but she bit off the *ew* she was itching to verbalize. It was indeed a larger chunk of amber that contained disembodied parts of various insects. It looked like a creepy-crawly crime scene.

"I want you to have it," her aunt repeated when Callie tried to hand her back the dung.

Resigned that she was now the owner of a piece of old crap, Callie shoved it into the pocket of her jeans. "Thank you." And while she wasn't happy about the actual object, she was grateful for her aunt's generous heart. Callie kissed her cheek.

Mildred kept her gaze on Callie. "You'll be leaving this morning?"

Callie wasn't prepared for the question and attempted to shrug and nod at the same time. It probably looked like some kind of muscle spasm.

"Well, no need to make up your mind just yet," Mildred assured her, as if she'd had no trouble interpreting Callie's conflicted response. "But I do hope you'll have it out with Ace before you go."

Callie stared at her, a little confused with her aunt's choice of words.

"You have a right to have it out with him," Mildred went on. "After all, he hurt you. It doesn't matter that he thinks he had a good reason for doing that. He still hurt you."

Since Callie had told him exactly that the day before, she simply nodded. "That happened a long time ago," she felt the need to say. Though sometimes it felt as if it'd only been a few hours since that breakup.

"Yes," Mildred agreed. "But it hurts because you still love him."

Callie nearly got choked on the breath she sucked in too fast. She wanted to blurt out a "no way" denial, but then she remembered Ace's mouth on hers. Remembered his hands. Heck, she remembered everything about him. That was the problem. The man was unforgettable, and she'd been carrying around the hurt—and the love—for a very long time. That was the real reason she'd landed in bed with him.

Though that cake had helped.

Mildred patted her arm. "Ace is in the kitchen if you want to talk to him." Leaving it at that, her aunt turned and walked out.

And the mental debate started again. Good grief. Her

thoughts felt like a tennis match with the feelings volleying back and forth. However, that got interrupted when her phone rang, and she felt herself making another face when she saw Chad's name on the screen.

"I'm glad I caught you," Chad said the moment she answered. "I don't have much time, but I wanted to check in with you and see if you got my message."

In the background, Callie heard her replacement, the size-two yogini, purr for Chad to hurry up so they could go for their couple's massage. It surprised Callie that it didn't set her teeth on edge, but that was possibly because her teeth were already on edge at the mention of the message that Chad had left with Ace.

"I got it," Callie informed him.

"Good," Chad said, obviously not picking up on Callie's icy tone. "I know weight loss isn't easy and that you're probably trying your hardest. You're well aware of what's at stake."

Yes, she was. Maybe it was all that volleying introspection she'd been doing, but things were suddenly a whole lot clearer. Well, clearer when it came to Chad. She wanted him to have that couple's massage—wanted him to have an allergic reaction to the goop the masseuse would smear on his body.

But most important, Callie realized that Chad was a putz.

Maybe he always had been, but she had no doubts about that now. No doubts, either, that he'd made the job that she'd once enjoyed a miserable experience.

"I'm not dieting," Callie told him. "In fact, I'm planning on having leftover wedding cake for breakfast."

Silence for a long time. Well, silence from Chad. The

yogini was still purring reminders for him to hurry. "You're not going to lose those fifteen pounds," Chad finally said.

"Maybe," Callie answered. "But if I do lose them, it won't be because of you. It'll be because it's what I want."

She hit the end-call button and blocked his number. That last part was probably childish, but it felt so darn good. Later, she'd call the office and give her official notice. She'd also call Marty Jameson's manager and discuss the job that Marty had offered her. But for now, she had to see a man.

Callie walked into the kitchen and nearly lost her breath when she saw Ace at the window. She felt that punch of heat. The punch of irritation, too, that he could cause such a punch, and then she felt the relief. There was heat. Yes. Always had been. Always would be. And maybe it was time for her to stop fighting that heat and see where it could take them.

Well, other than the bed.

She was pretty sure it could lead there, but there was another layer to this. Again, always had been.

Ace was wearing his usual jeans, but he seemed a little spiffed up in a crisp pale blue shirt. She spotted the camera nearby, and judging from the way it was aimed, he'd filmed something going on at the stove.

"I submitted the recipe for the competition," he said. "I went with the cake."

"Great choice. What'd you name it?"

"Foreplay." The corner of his mouth hitched, causing a dimple to flash, but his grin was short-lived. In fact, his expression got serious. "Are you okay?"

There was genuine concern in his voice. Concern that was yet another layer to this odd relationship. Who knew that Ace and she were like an onion?

"I quit my job," she said, and Callie immediately waved off any words of comfort or support he might have given her. "It's okay. It turned out to be a lousy job with an equally lousy boss."

He set his coffee aside, went to her and studied her face. "Are you okay?" he repeated.

Much to her delight, Callie could answer that truthfully. "Yes."

Of course, quitting her job didn't fix everything. The PR for Marty might turn out to be a bust, too. And then there was the question of where she was going to live now that she could no longer afford her place in Houston.

Actually, the question was—what was she going to do, period.

Callie got a huge clue about that when she looked at Ace again. There were plenty of answers there in his face.

She wanted to kiss him, but she held off, put her coffee cup next to his and took out what her aunt had just given her. This was a very short turnaround for a regift. However, it felt right.

"This is for you," she said, handing him the amber.

Ace glanced at it. Then at her. "You're giving me crap?" He looked as if he didn't know whether to laugh or scowl.

"Prehistoric crap," Callie verified. "And I'm not really giving it to you. It's more of a symbolic gift. Think of it like a key."

Now, he didn't scowl, but there was sort of a smile tugging at his mouth. "What kind of key?"

"One that unlocks what you want most. You should accept the land. This place," she amended. "If you win the competition, great." Though she didn't see how he could lose with foreplay cake. "But even if you don't, you shouldn't have to wait to get your ranch and the life you've always wanted."

As if testing the waters, he leaned in closer. "And what about you?" His warm breath hit her mouth.

"I don't want to wait, either. I can start my business here in Lone Star Ridge, and if all works out, Marty Jameson will be my first client."

The logical part of her wanted to start working out the details like office space, a website, etc. But there was more than logic here.

There was Ace.

"If you move into the attic apartment," she went on, "and if I stay in my room, we'd be able to see each other more often."

Now, he smiled, and she felt that on her mouth, too. He moved in. Kissed her. It was long, deep and perfect.

"We'd get to see each other more often if we shared the attic apartment," he suggested.

Callie would have said that was a good point indeed if he hadn't kissed her again. This one robbed her of her breath and possibly of her sanity. But it also made things crystal clear.

"I love you," she told him.

He made a sound that seemed to be a mixture of relief and pleasure. A sound that she quickly cut off by kissing him. If this continued, they'd need to take this upstairs.

Callie intended very much for it to continue.

"Good," Ace said with his mouth against hers. His body was against hers, too, and the hand he put on her backside aligned them in the best possible way. "Because I love you, too."

There it was. Just a handful of words that Callie realized

were the only words she wanted to hear. Well, that and perhaps some dirty talk once they were in bed. She intended to kiss Ace the whole way there.

"Come on," she whispered. "Let's get started on that better dream."

* * * * *

Chapter One

Cora Brooks stopped washing the few dinner dishes she'd dirtied while making her meal, dried her hands and picked up her binoculars. Through her kitchen window, she'd caught movement across the ravine at the old Colt place. As she watched, a pickup pulled in through the pines and stopped next to the burned-out trailer. She hoped it wasn't "them druggies" who'd been renting the place from Jimmy D's girlfriend—before their homemade meth-making lab blew it up.

The pickup door swung open. All she saw at first was the driver's Stetson as he climbed out and limped over to the burned shell of the double-wide. It wasn't until he took off his hat to rake a hand through his too-long dark hair that she recognized him. One of the Colt brothers, the second oldest, she thought. James Dean Colt, or Jimmy D as everyone called him.

She watched him through the binoculars as he hobbled around the trailer's remains, stooping at one point to pick up something before angrily hurling it back into the heap of charred debris.

"Must have gotten hurt with that rodeoin' of his agin," she said, pursing her lips in disapproval as she took in his limp. "Them boys." They'd been wild youngins who'd grown into wilder young men set on killing themselves by riding anything put in front of them. The things she'd seen over the years!

She watched him stand there for a moment as if not knowing what to do now, before he ambled back to his pickup and drove off. Putting down her binoculars, she chuckled to herself. "If he's upset about his trailer, wait until he catches up to his girlfriend."

Cora smiled and went back to washing her dishes. At her age, with all her aches and pains, the only pleasure she got anymore was from other people's misfortunes. She'd watched the Colt clan for years over there on their land. Hadn't she said no good would ever come of that family? So far her predictions had been exceeded.

Too bad about the trailer blowing up though. In recent years, the brothers had only used the double-wide as a place to drop their gear until the next rodeo. It wasn't like any of them stayed more than a few weeks before they were off again.

So where was James Dean Colt headed now? Probably into town to find his girlfriend since she'd been staying in his trailer when he'd left for the rodeo circuit. At least she had been—until she'd rented the place out, pocketed the cash and moved back in with her mother. More than likely he was headed to Melody's mother's right now.

What Cora wouldn't have given to see that reunion, she thought with a hearty cackle.

Just to see his face when Melody gave him the news after him being gone on the road all these months.

Welcome home, Jimmy D.

Get 4 FREE REWARDS!

We'll send you 2 FREE Books plus 2 FREE Mystery Gifts.

Both the **Romance** and **Suspense** collections feature compelling novels written by many of today's bestselling authors.